I0760784

Maud's Inn

Jan Blissit

MI-5F
ISBN: 9781945190582

Published by: Intellect Publishing, LLC
www.IntellectPublishing.com

Foreword

Every person needs a special place - a temporary place - to find solitude and peace. It should be a place of reverence, not in a religious sense, but a place that becomes a refuge or a sanctuary. It should not be a place to escape from one's life, but a place to be open to imagination and inspiration that feeds one's soul. It is a place to listen to the silence one hears only in near-holy places. But when you find this special place, you will understand you cannot live there, for it is only temporary. Long after your visit you will remember the smell of old paint among the art, and the indirect lighting from a high window floating onto a painting of a dense forest. You will be able to envisage the crepe myrtles in bloom, the walking path through the dense woods, smell the caustic odor of the river, listen to the trickling of the little stream, count the bricks on the old cistern, or remember the wild beans growing on the garden wall. You will reflect on the flowers you failed to identify and hear the voice of the cardinal and the robin, or perhaps shut your eyes and be thankful for being there.

In moving around through the years, I searched for such a place in every city I lived, but I was not always successful. In one city my place of refuge was an art gallery. Occasionally during my lunch break, or after an intense business meeting, I would escape to a small art gallery and spend time studying the paintings and the artists: Who are you? What or who inspired you? How could you have parted from this great piece of art? Who taught you to paint? One odd painting showed the relief of great pain or perhaps the expression of wild passion: Random black and orange streaks blasting against a blue sky. I thought about buying it, but decided visiting it was best for me. The gallery owner welcomed my visits, and if someone recognized me, she would remind them that I was there to relax. Even today I often wake before dawn with the thought of how much joy those painting brought me.

In another city my refuge was a cemetery. One cool spring morning a mother, whose son was killed in an accident when he was a teenager, invited me to go with her to the city cemetery to visit his grave. In the large plot she had chosen for her son, she was able to create a beautiful garden. We walked across the small arched bridge that spanned a steady stream of water wiggling over implanted river rocks. The azaleas, buttercups, and the dogwood trees were in full bloom. She snapped a blossom from one of the trees and tossed it in the water, and I felt free to do the same. Without words we watched the blossoms trickle away. Finally, she said to me, "Not many people are aware of this little garden, perhaps only the man who keeps it up, but I invite you to use my son's garden as a sanctuary."

It is difficult for me to put into words what that small garden meant to me, nor do I remember how often I went, but I will always be grateful for it and will never stop wondering why a seventeen-year-old boy had to die so soon while driving his car on a Sunday afternoon. I accepted the gift that was offered me in his honor, and allowed the rippling sounds of the water flowing over the rocks, to refresh my soul.

A year ago, I created a place of refuge in a story, *Maud's Inn,* after finding the original owner's diary. In my mind Maud's Inn has become a place I go when I am in a fit of pondering. I enter my car in North Atlanta and drive along south for over an hour, until I am driving through a forest of trees. Finally, an arrow on a simple sign points to Maud's Inn. There is no post with a light atop, and one doesn't often drive over gravel roads. I make a quick stop to soak in the scene before me - an Inn almost woven into the forest. After making the owner aware of my presence, I follow a path toward the river. It always seems further than it is, but worth the extra steps. I sit on the bank of the river and listen to the birds chirping their songs. I bless the wind blowing in the trees on a hot summer day, and wonder who tied a hammock between two old oak trees. I marvel how the Chattahoochee River can begin as a small stream in north Georgia and become a large waterway carrying water to the many towns bordering the states of Georgia and Alabama. Of course, it is not as wide as the great Mississippi River, on which I have traveled. I wonder if one could travel this river to its end. On occasions I climb the steps to my private room with a lover or by myself and examine the covers of books left by the owner.

Oh, the Inn is a beautiful place for people like me – far away from expectations, business, crises, hurts, or anger. I send my characters there to experience the solitude and to relax from the busy city. It is the perfect place to lie in the shadow of a huge maple tree near the head stones of Maud and her husband, the couple who built this refuge.

I develop the six main characters of this story slowly: Writer, Joan Randolph; Attorney, Randy Phillips Walker; Attorney, Bob Barnett; Attorney Fredrick Winchester; Minister, Leonard Childs, and Mr. Roger Waddell.

You will meet their families, be present at a few weddings, chill when clients experience tragedy, hate the man who entices young girls, delight in Randy Walker's secretary, Ms. Bee. When cancer consumes a beautiful woman you will cry aloud, as I did, when I wrote about her. You will watch characters mature as they find a cause that benefits a whole community of people. There are several intimate scenes that may remind you of your own lover or imagined lover, and you will blush.

Actually, this book is indeed a love story.

Maud's Inn

CHAPTER 1
Joan and Randy

The Party

Believing everyone had departed from her Celebration of My New Home party, Joan closed the front door and turned to the large mirror in the foyer she had purchased from an antique gallery in Savannah. The dealer had assured her the frame was gold plated, but her decorator did not care for it, saying it was quite garish, so Joan had someone else hang it. Somehow mirrors seemed to beckon her though they could be a curse or a blessing. As she stared at herself, she challenged the mirror, "I may be middle aged but my red hair does not have a visible white hair, and there are not too many wrinkles on my face. Mom, this is your daughter whose spirit you crushed when you made me believe I was unattractive and wondered why you could not have a beautiful blond-headed girl." Then he came up behind her. He winked that wink she had seen across the room before. What room? A restaurant? A party? The wink turned into a smile as he stood behind her. He placed his hands on her shoulders, "Don't move," he said. "I want to see the back and front of the most beautiful woman I have ever known." Then slowly and carefully he turned her around, put his finger under her chin, and pressed his mouth to her lips: one short kiss, then another. His kisses were a reminder of a thrill that had not happened to her for years. Then he said, "Joan, you are as lovely as ever. I curse the day I didn't call John Randolph and tell him I was in love with you."

"Randy, were you really thinking about doing that?"

"No, I was a coward. I wished him to die, and he did, but not soon enough. I'm sorry that I said that, but it is the truth. Is it too early for me to tell you that I want you to be a part of my life? All these years being so near you, yet so far away, have been torture for me. It's been a *long* time, Joan. I married two women I didn't love because I couldn't be with you. I've endured parties, like tonight, just to be in the same room with you. I don't want to get too old before I can be a part of your life."

"Oh, Randy, I wish I had known. No, perhaps I did know or suspect. I remember sitting on the bench with you at school. It was outside the library, wasn't it? You were so easy to talk to. I suppose the timing was always wrong. Is now the time?"

"I certainly hope it is. Joan, I have always loved you since the day I saw you walk across the campus of William and Mary. I swear that is the truth. Now that it is possible for us to be together I can hardly wait, so I'm leaving before I do something both of us might regret. I will call you." He blew her a kiss and left before she could respond. He cursed himself as he walked out into the night, and had to control the urge to turn around, but he knew she should have time to think about what he said.

Joan tossed all night. She could not stop thinking about the long, miserable years with John and how he controlled her and bullied her in subtle but hurtful ways. *Were those wasted years? Did I have opportunities, but ignored them? No, I have two beautiful children who love me. Am I too old to find romance that I never experienced?* Morning could not come fast enough, and the evening felt like a dream.

CHAPTER 2

Joan
Isn't there always –
The Morning After

For the first time since John's death, Joan felt isolated and unsure about her future. The pleasure she enjoyed sitting at her little marble table and sipping a morning cup of coffee with no sounds or noises in the house, had brought peace to her existence. Now a strange and heavy silence filled room, but a storm was raging inside her head. She opened the door to retrieve the morning newspaper. Flipping through the headlines and the news section, she realized she wasn't reading. Touching her lips and imagining they still tingled from the soft pressure of his lips, she said out loud to no one, "*I have always loved you*, should be the headlines today." She remembered the moment when her body wanted to melt into his embrace. She trembled at the thought, but couldn't suppress that tiny seed of guilt. "Why, in heaven's name should I have guilt?" She said to the kitchen sink as she poured out her coffee, and was surprised there was no answer. Slamming the paper on the table, she said, "I will not allow guilt to destroy my feelings this morning. I want to wallow in the excitement from the time I looked into the mirror to the moment of his first touch. I want to play the event over and over like rewinding an old cassette, and have soft music playing in the background. Did I write that in a book? If not, I should."

She felt young again, remembering what it was like to be captured by the few moments and forgetting everything else. How did the kiss happen? Did she say something during the evening that was improper? Was she overly excited about having guests for the first time? She remembered laughing a lot for the first time in months, and she felt alive as if she was nineteen again. It was a good feeling. She was no longer the person who feared change. She was reborn - something akin to a spiritual experience like the words of an old hymn she sang when she was a child, *I Was Lost, But Now I'm Found.*

Then she remembered the slight brush at the kitchen sink when Randy brought in some empty glasses to be washed, and how quiet he was all evening as if he were studying the room and the people in it. He stood beside her at the piano with his hand on her shoulder while Judy played the piano and everyone sang some old Neil Diamond songs, like "Song Sung Blue" and "Sweet Caroline." There was a lot of laughter. She remembered the people standing around her new Steinway piano, but there was no one she wanted to talk to, except him.

"Why am I so excited?" She said to the tiny mirror over the sink. "It was only a kiss, well maybe two, but I will never forget his words." She turned toward the phone, "Ring, dammit. I want to hear his voice." If not his voice the magic that filled the room would snap like the egg she dropped on the floor. She thought about his farewell, "I have always loved you." Confusion, hesitation, longing, sadness, and expectation - all words she felt, but could not say out loud. Suddenly she was lonely in her new home. She had not expected that. She was not the same person she was yesterday; she had been kissed.

Randy
The Morning After

It was Sunday morning, but Randy wanted it to be Saturday night again when the room became free of intruders. He wanted to be sitting on her new sofa, waiting to hear her sigh after the last guest left. He had no expectations, but knew he had to linger. He was not going to pass the opportunity of being alone with her. He wanted to kiss her and smell her skin. He remembered how fast his heart was beating as he waited for all the *good byes* and *I had a great time* voices.

His coffee tasted like mud and he had burned the toast. So what; he was not hungry. He kept trying to re-live the kiss and his words, but it was impossible to recreate those moments. He walked to the window. "God! I hate to think what happened is in the past tense, but it *happened!* It was real - every minute and every second." He realized he was sweating. "What gave me the courage I had not taken in years? What is wrong with me? It was just a kiss. Why did I need courage?" He was angry because he could not hold her and remove her blouse to kiss her shoulder and…it was the magic of the moment, and he took it, and she responded. "Yes," he said, nodding his head, "I know she responded but maybe she was lonely. Maybe she was starved for real affection. No! She understood me. I know she did. I felt her response. What in heaven's name am I supposed to do now?"

He envisioned every inch of her condo. She had done a great job decorating it, and the aroma was exotic, but best of all there not a hint of John. The vases of fresh flowers and the brilliant colors she had chosen for the room were like new life, but she was the only flower and the only color. He remembered empty faces even though he had known most of them for years, but he wanted them to get out and leave him alone with her. He had worked all day and was dead tired, but it was the people who were tiring. How did he ever get involved in that pretend game of having fun? He hated parties with everyone walking around the room, holding a glass of wine or sipping a bottle of beer, laughing for no reason at all. He watched her as she floated across the floor asking if anyone needed his or her glass refilled. He took his glass of wine and dropped himself into one of her new matching chairs. The plaid of the chair was sprinkled with the color of her hair. Of course, only he would have noticed that. He was nurturing his wine, looking off into yonder, when someone passed their hand across his face, "Randy, where are you? Wake up." Everyone laughed. He didn't remember who it was or what he was thinking at that moment. Maybe he was trying to get drunk so he wouldn't have to think.

Since *the kiss* he couldn't plan - not even the next week of his life. Now that she was available, he wanted her here in this room with him. He wanted to feel her body and smell her breath. He wanted to talk to her, to look into her face and say the many words he had been holding back for years. He needed to call her just to hear her voice, but what if someone else was there and answered the phone. Then he remembered, "Hell, I am her estate lawyer; I can call her any time." He had to try or go mad.

CHAPTER 3

Joan

Nine months, almost to the day John died, Joan sold the house his parents bought for them and moved into a condo. At least thirty years old, the building was an old brick apartment complex that had been remodeled by a group of investors and turned into an attractive place for buyers. Her old neighborhood was in a proper neighborhood for successful people: lawyers, doctors, engineers, and bankers. All the neighbors were nice to her after John's death, but she sensed it was because they felt sorry for her. They acted like she needed tending to by bringing her food and inviting her to be the odd person at dinners and parties. She began to believe she was *poor Joan*. She didn't want pity; she wanted space. She wanted that house and everything in it to be in her past.

New condos and apartments were springing up all around Atlanta, but she wanted one with some age on it - a solid brick with a hint of *built when they were made to last*, and with beautiful grounds surrounding it. She wanted a doorman to welcome her every time she entered and who made her feel safe. She wasn't thinking Hollywood; she wanted New York. She used to pass this one and admire it. It was perfect. Last night was a celebration: Decorator finished, estate settled, children successful. She had been counting the months.

At first saying *my condo* sounded strange and even wrong, but it *was* hers, and not at all like the huge house she and John shared. She got rid of almost all of *their* furniture. She gave some pieces to the Center for Abused Women. Her children were not settled to take any, but her brother's children wanted a few pieces. She livened up the condo with loud colors that make her want to sing every morning. She was not afraid to be alone. She had met a few tenants who were also living alone. Some of the women had made an effort to include her. She heard one of them say, "I don't think she's ready, yet." She wanted to say, "Ready for what? Lunching with a group of single women, or being the odd one at another party? All so irritating."

Those long months John was so sick were painful. First came the diagnosis, then the treatments, followed by bad weeks and good days. Finally he rose late and went to bed early. He spent more time in bed than sitting in his vibrating chair. The progression was visible. His muscular body turned to putty, and he couldn't straighten his shoulders because of the constant pain. She and John never spent a lot of time with each other, so it was strange being together all day and all night. Surely he knew that he was dying, but still he had no sweet words to say to her, nor regrets for practically abandoning her and the children. She finally ran out of things to say and do. The kids started visiting, allowing her to get out more, but she had no privacy. She began to realize she was also taking care of them. Looking back to those long days, their visits were good for her, for it took him a long time to die.

With all the resentment she had against him, she still harbored doubts. *Did I do enough? Did I give my best? Had I let him be a man instead of an invalid? Did I say the right words? Had I kept the promise of our marriage to be beside him in life and death?* But her doubts were slowly fading away. She could answer "yes" to all those intruding questions. She blamed the devil for making her wonder why she played the role of the good wife, for she and John had not been lovers for a long time.

She had dreamed of having her freedom. Friends kept saying to her, "Keep busy, so you won't get bored." Bored? Not even a little bit! She took a leave of absence from the country club and the women's club, and told the kids they did not need to come home so often, which was good for them and for her.

———

In August Joan and her brother, Thomas flew to Chicago to check on their mother. They found her in bad condition. Obviously, she had not been eating and was not keeping her body clean. Though she was dangerously thin and could hardly move, she ordered them to leave, but they refused. Against her threats they were able to get her into a decent nursing facility. She was a bitter old woman, swearing that she had been cheated all her life. Her whole life had been spent regretting what she missed and the person she married. Saying goodbye in the parking lot, Thomas said to Joan, "Joan, I am certain our mother had not wanted children, especially by the man she married. I can't remember any special feeling or words of love or praise from her, so every day I tell my kids I love them."

"I'm grateful that you and I were close; at least we had each other. Mom should have kept her teaching job. I believe she loved those third graders more than us," Joan said. "They were the evidence to her that she had made *some* accomplishments."

Two weeks later the nursing facility called to tell Joan that her mom was dying. She and Thomas flew up again. She did not recognize them or pretended not to. Her doctor told them she could not live much longer because she was refusing to eat. She died while they were there. They buried her beside their father. As they stood by the graves, Thomas said, "She may come back to haunt us for doing this."

Joan and Thomas started the long process of clearing her house, getting death certificates, and all the other procedures required by the state. Wow, were they surprised! She had not touched the money their father set up for her when he walked out. She had vowed not to touch that "dirty money," and she didn't. Neither Joan nor Thomas needed or wanted the money, so they gave it to their kids. They practically gave the house away to get rid of it.

Joan's *Welcome to My New Home Party* had been a good idea. It was a tough invitation list. She was certain someone was left out, but she decided not to worry about it; she had been on the *got no invitation list* before. She invited the usual persons she had known since college and a few others she had met through the years. Frederick kept them laughing with his jokes. No one knew where he got all those stories. He should be on stage, for he knew more jokes than any person she had ever known. His friends said he could cheer up the dead and make his pastor faint. He and Elizabeth called Joan several times inviting her out, but she wasn't ready to be entertained, and they understood. Randy was helpful getting her through all the legal procedures necessary, and their friend Bob Barnett was also helpful.

CHAPTER 4
Randy

Louise Wallace and Randy met when they were in their late thirties. She claimed she loved him the first time she saw him. Of course, he found that a tad unlikely. She owned a publishing company in Atlanta, and definitely had the ability to get interesting stories out of people. She had not been married before, but Randy had. One day they decided they were seeing each other so often, and sex was good, so they might as well get married. Randy couldn't think of any reason why they shouldn't. Later his mother chastised him, "You should have realized good sex was not a reason to marry." How right she was.

Both of them realized it was a mistake shortly after the "I do," but their counselor, they should not have hired, kept saying, "Randy, you haven't tried long enough. It's Louise's first marriage. She needs to get used to living with a partner, and besides do you want another failed marriage? Do you? Try again."

He looked at Louise, and she was actually shaking her head, *no. Why didn't she say, no way, it's over; I'm sorry we called you? Better yet, why didn't I say it?*

Like stupid teenagers they believed their counselor, but both were still miserable. They dragged it out six months, which was a long time. When the divorce was final they each took what was brought into the marriage. That's how much they wanted the divorce. Randy went on a two-week trip to Las Vegas to clear his head. Louise went to Europe with some friends. Two weeks alone, without hearing her nag, was a relief. There are not enough words to say how contented he was and how pleasant it was. One of the women who went to Europe with Louise became her partner, and they moved in together. Randy didn't see that coming.

Upon his return from his self-exile he visited Joan and John. It appeared that John was dying and wouldn't last much longer. He and John had known each other win law school. He was a couple of years ahead of Randy. Randy detested arrogant people, and John was one of them. After John's graduation he and Joan married, and Randy married some gal who was also in law school. That marriage didn't even survive law school. John became a trial lawyer and Randy went into estate law. He thought that would be less tedious. Wrong! He fell in love with Joan in college when she was already engaged to John. Perhaps he was one of those people who never gets the girl they want, and when they do that doesn't last either.

Quite often he beat himself up: why didn't I push my way into Joan's life? Well the timing was off, and why was she always telling me what a good friend I was? Friend, hell! I wanted to hold her, and kiss her, play with her hair, and...well it didn't happen, but maybe the hair. I remember smoothing her wind-blown hair outside the library. She was beautiful. I used to watch her walk across campus with her friends. She wasn't hard to spot, being a head taller than all of them. I'd deliberately place myself on a bench outside the library with my buddy Roger Waddell and wait for her to come out so I could wave to her. Sometimes she excused herself and come over. At first, I had to give Roger the shove-off punch in the ribs, but he finally got the message. I didn't want to talk; I wanted to kiss her, but that never happened.

CHAPTER 5
Joan

One lazy summer morning, about a year ago, an incident happened that could not be discarded as a mere coincidence. John and Joan had gone over to see Randy's new motorcycle. Joan always had a fear of riding any vehicle without metal covering her head to toe, but John insisted she get on the back of the seat behind Randy and ride around the block with him. It was such and innocent thing to do. Her arms were wrapped tightly around Randy's waist to keep from falling off. Down the street and around the corner he made a sudden stop, turned around, looked at her and said, "This is the way we were meant to be. I have always loved you." For days she was in shock. From that moment on she knew what Randy meant, but she couldn't dwell on it for John was already ill. But the years they had spent in college flashed into her mind: w*hy was I so blind?*

———

Early on in their marriage it was apparent to Joan that John was a miserable match. Unknown to John, Joan visited a therapist. Near the end of one session, the therapist said something to her she never forgot, "When love and trust is gone in a relationship there is nothing left." Joan didn't know whether she meant theoretically or *really*. She had been miserable for long time, but she couldn't desert John and disappoint her children. They had enough to think about with their own lives. Cassie had decided she wanted to be a lawyer and an artist on the side, and Rick thought he wanted to be an architect. He was always drawing houses and buildings.

———

Both John and Joan had off and on affairs in college: his with some gal in Atlanta, and hers with some guy she would rather forget he ever existed. John was from a wealthy Atlanta family. Joan's background was far below their standard. The Randolph's lived in one of Atlanta's exclusive sections of grand mansions. Becoming a part of the Randolph family seemed to be the best thing for her to do. The truth is she fell in love with his parents. She had never met people so loving and so generous with their time and their money. Anyway, that's how it looked being from the outside.

After John finished law school he and Joan were married in Atlanta - a fabulous wedding planned and furnished by the Randolph family. Joan's total contribution was showing up. Her mother and brother were her only relatives to attend. It appeared some people felt sorry for them and voluntarily moved over the aisle to sit on their side, or perhaps someone directed them to move. Her mom fussed about what it was costing her to be there losing time at work. Her only comment about the wedding was, "I do not enjoy being with uppity people with all their snobbery and finery."

———

Joan and John began marriage with a new car, new house, new furniture, and money put aside for their existence until John's law practice started producing, all from the generosity of John's parents. Joan became a part of a society she had only read about. All the young adults in their social circle seemed to have an endless amount of money, so perhaps their parents were funding them also. She thought they were exceeding their means, but who cared - parties, socials, luncheons, clothes, and then the first baby, Cassie arrived. She never imagined John would refuse to be a part of that exciting experience. He came by the hospital when she was in labor, but left after less than ten minutes, and he was also not present when their second child, Rick was born. He hired a limousine to take her home and a nanny to help her.

Finally, she realized he did not want a relationship; he wanted a business partner. When she questioned his interest, he said to her, "My job is to make a decent living, and your job is to keep the house tidy for me, and take care of *my* children." She was shocked that he was so blunt. He set up a separate bank account for her and never inquired about her expenditures. If she needed more money she was to let him know. She accepted the agreement. Sex was always on his terms and that was rare. Being so naïve about the way of Southerners and those who were well-to-do, she believed she was doing what was expected of women.

After the two children were born their marriage and relationship continued to fall apart, but John seemed to be satisfied that everything was working fine. He was the responsible one, and she was the caretaker of their properties, including *his* children.

Looking back it is amazing how fast the years passed. Soon their children were out of high school and off to college, and she and John were alone. That's when she began to write. She published two books, one of poetry and the other a novel about a dysfunctional family. They both sold very well, and she started on a third. John had little to say about her writing, only that he was glad she had something to do with her spare time. He stayed late at work, and Joan volunteered two evenings a week at a women's shelter. Occasionally they entertained by meeting other couples for dinner. She was not at all sure they were happy, but she had been doing what was expected of her for so long everything seemed quite natural. She had money when she needed it and could travel with or without him. As the saying goes she was *a kept woman*. Yet a lot of women envied her, and they were pleased to have an author in their crowd, but she doubted any of them ever read her books.

One day Joan decided to confront John, "Don't you think we need to work on our relationship? We never have time just for the two of us." His response was shocking, "I have all the relationship I need. You'll have to find some of your own. I should think your women friends would provide some of that. Don't talk to me again about a relationship."

"Women friends are not the kind of relationship I am talking about." She said

"I'm sorry, Joan. I have nothing else to give. If you want out of this marriage you are free to leave."

She didn't know whether his words were bomb or bait. Later Joan realized that he must have thought she was stupid for staying.

CHAPTER 6
Randy

John Randolph's Will

Randy felt a tad guilty helping John and Joan, but it was the only way to be with her, and besides he was John's executor. After John died he handled everything like a lawyer should, but being so close to Joan was complicated. He put on his business face and didn't cross any unethical lines. Another lawyer would have charged Joan at least $10,000, but he never sent a bill and she never asked for one. His secretary, Ms. Bee asked him if he wanted her to prepare an invoice and he said, "No, these are friends."

"You can't make a living on friends," she chided him. Her blunt honesty had a way of irritating him. He was glad his father wasn't alive. He was an old pro at infidelity and he would have seen right through him.

John Randolph was fairly wealthy, but his will was not complicated. Everything was spelled out in detail. Joan was left their home, savings, his office building, stocks, cars, and everything else, except the kids were left $40,000 each in stocks. At John's insistence the will carried an unusual clause:

No person/s shall have the right to make any personal claims, nor offer further interpretation, or demand rights against this Last Will and Testament, and signed his name after that sentence.

When John told Randy to insert the statement he wanted to inquire, but it is not his job to tell a person what they could or could not put in their will. Later he realized leaving Joan and the children everything must have been a confession or an apology.

Randy was not sure how he survived those next few weeks. He called Joan often to see how she was. He would do anything to be near her. Joan's house sold quickly since it was the right location, condition, and price as realtors say. Randy worked harder than ever to keep busy, and for once he made Ms. Bee happy. He thought about going to a therapist and blabbing his insides out, but he would never trust the friends he knew in Atlanta, not that they weren't good, but most likely they needed counseling as much as he did. He should have gone to an old college buddy in Nashville who was smart to get out of Atlanta, far enough from his own parents.

When Joan called to invite him to her party. He wanted to say to her, *why would I want to be in a crowd of people with you; I've been doing that for years*? He expected it would be torture, but he accepted her invitation. Anyway he supposed all their old friends were invited. After the call, he was mad at himself that he had never invited her out, but he had no idea how much time a man should wait to ask a woman out after her husband died. *How stupid I am; this is not the 1920s.* John wasn't much of a husband, and he guessed Joan knew that. There were always rumors circling around him. Word was he would disappear from his business for days, but somehow he managed to make a small fortune.

So, he went to the party, and was as miserable as he predicted.

CHAPTER 7

Trip to Maud's Inn

The morning after the party Randy made the call, "Joan, would you like to go for a ride?"

"Yes, I would like that." She thought to herself, maybe I answered too quickly, and he said, "I'll pick you up in thirty minutes."

"Thirty minutes. A lady needs more time than that."

"Okay, forty-five minutes." She waited for him in front of the condo, like she was trying to hitch a ride. Was she supposed to wait for him to come up to get her? Standing outside might seem she was eager. She was.

Being in the car with him was awkward at first, and she sensed some tension from him. For a few minutes they didn't talk other than words of greeting. There they were sitting side by side with no one between them to interrupt or criticize. She wondered if he was thinking about the *encounter* after the party. He moved his hand over and squeezed her hand. It sent shock waves throughout her body, and for some reason they both laughed. That broke the silence. She never thought to ask any questions about their destination. Finally, as if he was reading her mind he said, "We are going to a little country inn on the Chattahoochee River called Maud's Inn. Is that all right with you? It's out in the woods, peaceful and private. I think you'll like it."

"Maud's Inn?" She asked. "What a name for an Inn." She was glad he was driving because her heart was racing so fast she was certain she could not speak, but she kept thinking – *what next?* He glanced sideways at her and started singing,

'Merrily we roll along, roll along, roll along.
Merrily we roll along o'er the deep blue sea."

She couldn't believe it. *Merrily we roll along* had never been a funny song but it was then. She couldn't remember when she had laughed so hard. "You are an idiot," she said, "but a delightful one, and you sing with such enthusiasm. Maybe you should be on

Broadway." Suddenly he jerked the steering wheel to the right and pulled off on the side of the road almost throwing them into a ditch. Joan thought they were having car trouble. He opened his door, walked around to her side of the car, and practically lifted her out of the car into his arms and kissed her. He kissed her again and again. There they stood in the knee-high grass holding hands and gazing at each other, "You are so beautiful," he said. "You almost make my heart stop, but I don't want that to happen for I would miss you. Are you all right?"

"Well, I can hardly breathe," she said, "Plus you scared the hell out of me. Give me a little notice next time."

Randy said, "I didn't mean to scare you. I have loved you for so many years. Being so close is the car, didn't seem close enough. Now that I have the opportunity to be with you, I am afraid something might happen to keep us apart. I would as soon be dead."

"Randy, surely you don't mean that."

"Yes, I do."

"Well, since you kissed me in front of the mirror I have not been myself, or perhaps my true self has been exposed. These past years have been so empty for me. Your kiss in the foyer was a wake-up call. It stirred something inside of me that I knew existed, but I had smothered. I wanted to stand there forever. Yes, I can say that my life changed the moment you created a story without an ending. What does the future holds for us?"

"Let me answer that question. Perhaps what I am about to say is far too early, but I have to say it. I want you to be my lover and my wife. I want to take you places we have never been and see things we have never seen. I want to wake up every morning watching you beside me. I want to know Cassie and Rick because they are a part of you, and I want them to be a part of me, in time of course. I have waited a long time to say those words."

"Wow! Are you a poet? I know this is quick, yet I don't have to think about it. I have been unable to get you off my mind, and one day I will be proud to wake up beside you in the morning. I can't believe I just said that. This sort of incident only happens in the movies." And they laughed when they realized drivers were lowering their windows and giving them a thumb's up.

Back in the car, Randy was unable to focus. He wasn't even clear he was headed in the right direction. Their pause in the grass created tension in the car because they were so close. He had never been so reckless and silly. He felt like a teenager sitting so close to his sweetheart – so close that he could actually smell her. He wanted to stop the car again, but instead he threw her a kiss.

"What are you thinking," Joan Asked.

"Well, had we been somewhere else, instead of knee deep in the grass, I would have…I'll not finish that sentence, Madam." She touched his face with her hand, and leaned onto his shoulder.

They had not missed the Inn after all. *Why in the hell are we going to lunch*? *I'm not even hungry*, he thought. Then he remembered that he was the one who had suggested it. He said to Joan, "Well here we are. The Innkeeper has promised us a simple lunch." He looked around for cars, but they seemed to be the only guests.

The Inn was crafted to look old and partially worn out. There was no pavement, only river rocks covered the ground, and they could feel and hear the rocks rolling under the tires, and when they opened the car doors the birds were chirping about their arrival. Once upon a time he knew the Fowlers who owned the place; they were lovely people. If he remembered correctly they had one child, Charlie who had inherited all their assets along with this property.

Though it was midday outside, the dim lighting inside the Inn brought eerie shadows on the wall, and suddenly the Inn Keeper stood up from behind the bar and said, "Hello, you must be Randy," and motioned for them to sit at the bar. "Yes, and this is my friend, Joan. Well not exactly a friend; hopefully more than that one day."

"I understand that sort of hope. Your meal is almost ready." Randy had not been hungry, but the smell of food cooking on the grill and holding Joan's hand awakened all his senses. He felt as if he was on the top of the winding stairway watching the scene take place.

He couldn't decide what to say while they ate, but something finally came out of his mouth, "Joan, after so many troubled years, I finally feel comfortable. All that nasty tension I carried around, for what seemed forever, seems to be drifting away. I have the urge to stand up, beat my chest, and roar like a lion, *I'm alive! I'm alive!*

Joan, I can't take my eyes off you. I feel wonderful." She looked at him and laughed.

After lunch the Inn Keeper suggested they walk around the property on the trails that had been created for visitors who have the desire to experience something other than city sidewalks.

Outside, they held hands and laughed at everything. They sat on a log and he counted her fingers. Coming to the ring finger there was a small emerald ring. "It was my mother's," she said. *Thank goodness it wasn't a gift from John.* He kissed her hands, her forehead, her cheeks, and down to her lips. They moved to a canvas tied between two trees, but the movement made him so dizzy he almost fell to the ground. It reminded him of the vertigo episode he had a few years ago. He knew what he wanted, a place, any place, to lay beside her. But yet he did not want their relationship to be built on sex. Still he wanted her more than ever. Then, as if she were reading his mind, she asked, "Do you suppose the owner might have an available room where we could relax?" *Relax! That's what I need, to relax beside her, and a place to talk. Why didn't I think of that?* When they returned to the Inn, Randy asked the innkeeper, "Are you Charlie Fowler, the person I spoke to on the phone *and* the son of parents whose will I wrote?" Charlie answered, "Indeed, Charlie Fowler speaking."

"So glad to meet you, Charlie." Randy said, "Your parents were lovely people. You must have been a good son. She spoke of you as tenderly as Mary must have spoken about Jesus." Charlie laughed. "I'm serious. Anyway, we have decided to stay a while, and we might even spend the night if you have a room available." Charlie seemed delighted to have guests and inquired, "Do you have luggage?"

"No luggage; we were just sort of riding around." Mr. Fowler nodded his head. Then Randy said, "That is not exactly true; I talked her into coming here because I knew she would enjoy it." That must have sounded like a stupid teenager. He tried again, "You have such a beautiful place we decided to stay over and relax."

"I get it, man. Don't try to explain it again. Let me know if you will be here for breakfast. I cook a mean omelet." Randy looked toward Joan and she nodded. Turning to Charlie he said, "We have decided to stay, and an omelet for breakfast sounds great. Yes, we'll have breakfast."

Joan asked, "Mr. Fowler, Maud's Inn is such an unusual name. Wasn't that your mother's name?"

"Yes, Maud was my mother's name." He paused, "She was a most usual woman. My father named this inn after her and it was their home after they retired. They built it large enough for their friends to visit. I hope you enjoy it. Here is the key for Margaret's room, named for my grandmother. It is on the right after you go up the stairs. Hope you enjoy your stay: breakfast will be at nine o'clock."

CHAPTER 8.
Margaret's Room

They climbed the stairs, paused for a few minutes in the room, and opened the door onto the balcony. They were facing the sunset that could barely be seen as it dipped over the treetops. It was so quiet they could hear the trickle of the creek that wiggled through the property. The fresh country air was cool and they were high enough to watch the afternoon melt away as twilight began. It was a sight they would remember forever, but there was a lonesome feeling that the view was temporary. When they went back inside they seemed to carry the country aroma with them. After Randy turned on the lights, Joan was amazed at the bright colors in the room and the beautiful art on the walls. Later she learned that the owners had been avid art collectors. She said to Randy, "No motel would have such a beautiful room."

"Well the most beautiful scene in this room is the woman standing in front of me. Joan, I don't want our relationship to be about sex, but right now I'm holding back as much as I can. I want to search every part of your body, and I know it will be the most wonderful moment for me. When you feel the time is right just say the word."

"Oh, Randy, after a fun trip we have discovered nature again, something the city doesn't allow us to do very often. Here we are in a beautiful place together - free and happy. We are not strangers for we have known each other for years. I believe sex will always be a part of our relationship. Yes, now is the time."

"May I undress you?"

"Yes."

Slowly he unveiled her as if he was unwrapping a beautiful gift, and she was patient. He wanted to see and kiss every inch of her body - the body he had dreamed about for so many years.

"It's only fair that you allow me the same pleasure," she said. She was a little clumsy, first the tie, then the jacket, the shirt, the undershirt. He had to help her with the shoes and pants. Finally they sat on the foot of the bed together.

"First, I want to say something," he began. "What I want more than anything in this world is your love. You are the one person I admire more than anyone I have ever known. You are worth every second I waited, through college and two marriages that I detested, and of course watching you live your own life while John lived his. A few times I had sincere thoughts of killing him, but I knew that would permanently separate us. Thank God I had nothing to do with his dying; someone else had that responsibility. All this talk may seem sudden to you, but I want to share the rest of my life with you."

"Randy, I am reminded of a time and a place - the day you came to our house to see John's new motorcycle. You and John insisted that I get on the buddy seat while you drove around the street. Somehow I felt you might be my destiny."

"Oh my God, you remember the motorcycle ride!"

"Of course I remember. I even remember your words, 'This is the way we were meant to be.' My heart almost burst. I must have been blind in college, but maybe I was trying to be faithful to a promise. I don't want to think about those long years right now. We are here where we should be. I'm trembling sitting on this bed beside you, and I am cold."

"Never before have I wanted to be with someone as I have longed for you," Randy said. "Your voice and the way you laugh, raise your eyebrow, and straighten your wind-blown hair have stayed with me throughout the years."

They fell into an embrace and the outside world ceased to be. The fears, the years, and the longing were fading into a past that need not to be mentioned again. He wanted to search the body he had craved for many years, so it was a long time before he entered her. He wanted it to last forever. She held his face in her hands that brought him to her breasts. Then she did something for him no other woman had ever done, and nor she for any man. She played with his breast, something she had always wanted to do to see if it felt the same for a man. The sensation was so intense he thought he would go mad.

Though they were lying in an Inn on the Chattahoochee River, it was home because both of them were together. She studied the walls, the ceiling, and the aroma. She did not want to forget any feature. Both of them were thinking, *what do we do now? How do we choreograph this union?* They looked at each other and laughed, and Randy said, "We will be together, for I can no longer live without you." And she knew it was true. No matter what, she wanted his love. They both fell into a deep sleep and nothing else in the world mattered to them.

———

The chirping of birds woke them early in the morning, dozens of them swirling around the Inn singing sweet, happy music. She reached over, put her hand on his face, and he kissed it. Breakfast would have to wait. She was content to fold up in his arms and relax. They had found the end of frustration and loneliness. Their first night together would be the beginning of many.

As they descended the steps, the aroma of coffee floated in the air. The Innkeeper welcomed them with a glass of mixed fruit juices. "Well, good morning, Mr. Walker, I didn't want to mention it last night, since you were having a difficult time finding words. Yes, you also helped my mother with her estate, after my father died. I believe I was in your office with her. She had dreams of making the cottage into a weekend get-away for others, but my dad did not live long enough to accomplish it."

"Oh I remember your mother. She could have run any business in Atlanta, but I also remember your father. He was known as a man of honor and would help anyone. Well Charlie, both you and I have gotten a bit older, haven't we? You have a lovely place here. When did you decide to fulfill her dream and become an Inn Keeper?"

"A little trip to Germany sealed my plans."

"That's all?"

"No, but it was a beginning."

"Charlie, I would like for you to know I brought the most wonderful person in the world to your Inn. This is Joan Randolph, soon to be my wife."

"I recognized you. I've seen your pictures in the paper, ma'am, something about a women's center, *and* I have read one of your books, "The Wilting Willow Tree." It is about a woman who returned to her birthplace in Mississippi. See I am not lying.

"You are not! Thank you. It's always nice to hear from a reader. I give all my friends a book, but they never tell me they have read it."

"I knew your husband, but can't say I liked what I saw or heard. But you've got a good man here."

"I know. Nice to meet you, and I ditto this place is beautiful."

"I don't have menus, just tell me what you want."

"I thought you promised omelets."

"I did indeed, two omelets coming up. Everything on it?"

"Yes, don't spare a thing," Joan said.

The three of them lingered over breakfast until it was time to go. They thanked Charlie, settled the bill, and they started back to Atlanta.

"Randy, our visit went too fast," Joan said.

"I know. I'll drop you off and get some work done, then I'll be back this evening. Can you wait that long?" he said laughing.

"It won't feel right without you, but I can wait."

The trip back home seemed much shorter than when they traveled the other direction, a fair description of anticipation and apprehension.

Back in town, he kissed her and said, "I don't like being in separate places, give me a few hours to get my work done."

"I'll be here waiting and waiting."

"Before I leave, for some reason, I want to tell you about my mother, Ana Marie, and you will meet her soon. She lives in a condo at Lenox Square where she has access to all the shopping. She and her sister, my Aunt Pearl, live together. Pearl, who is three years younger, is a great artist. I want you to have one of her paintings. Pearl bought that particular condo because the light in one of the rooms was perfect for a studio. Maybe you will have a chance to see her paintings in many homes and businesses around town. She signs them *Pearl*, and paints a pearl on every painting. Did you notice the two large paintings on the wall in the lobby of Maud's Inn? One of the paintings was the work of my Aunt Pearl. I meant to ask about the other painting. Well, another time."

"Yes, I noticed, but I had no idea the painting was by someone in your family."

"Ana and Pearl were so close all their lives their brother and sister called them A&P. Pearl never married. I suppose she saw the mess my mother made, so she vowed to stay single. You might say she rescued my mother. My dad was such a Romeo. Pearl talked my mother into staying with her, and she has been there ever since. That was after I left home. Mom and Dad never divorced. I believe he loved her, but he had moral issues he was unable to conquer: women and booze. Well, I don't think he tried to be a husband or a father. The only time I remember him being a father was when he gave me a dog for my birthday. I named him Robert. Robert was like a brother. Isn't that funny? He loved me. He slept in my room at night, and waited at the door for me when I came home from school. When I went off the college he died. Mom said he grieved himself to death. I cried when she called and told me he died. That house was never the same anymore, and I never even thought about having another dog."

"My Dad never talked about his childhood, but I have reasons to believe it was not a good one. I do know that my grandfather, his father, stayed gone most of the times. It was rumored he had another family in Birmingham. My dad must have learned a lot from him. Now back to Mom. She would come back home for holidays and special events, but then return to Pearl's. For some reason, I believe there was never much intimacy between my Mom and Dad. Maybe that's why I am her only and darling child."

"I'm impressed by your description of them, *Darling*. I do want to meet them soon."

"You will, and one of her paintings will hang in our home."

Joan was revived by the weekend. After Randy left, the first thing she did was listen to her phone messages, to see if the kids had called. There was one from Cassie, and a few calls from friends. She called Cassie, hoping nothing was wrong.

"Mom, I haven't heard from you for awhile; are you okay? I know I should call more often but these classes are tough."

"Never felt better. I'll tell you about it when I see you. When will that be?"

"At least a couple of weeks. Mom, you are almost singing. Have you been on a trip or dating someone?"

"Why would you ask that?"

"Well, you haven't sounded like this for a long time."

"I do have someone, and I am in love. I am *really* in love"

"Mom, no kidding. That's great. Tell me, tell me, tell me; who is it?"

"It's too soon. I will tell you later. You won't be surprised."

Joan decided she would return the other calls the following day. She needed to take a shower, wash her hair, and read her mail. After awhile she couldn't wait any longer. She called Randy, "It's lonesome here," she said.

"Lonesome: A word that makes my heart beat faster. I'll be there in about two hours. I have one more appointment. Till then."

"Till then."

CHAPTER 9.

Wanda Wallace (WW)

Wanda Wallace was the reason for Randy's delay. First, he went through a lot of paperwork Ms. Bee had piled on his desk. Some of it she could have handled herself. She came to his door, "I don't like running this office alone," she said. "Mrs. Wallace is here an hour before her appointment. Remember George and Wanda Wallace? You did their wills."

"I remember. Her husband called her WW. She is one good-looking, feisty woman. I also remember dealing with her kids when her husband died last year. Put on your nice face and bring her in."

"I need to go to law school to work here."

"You know more than many lawyers, so knockers up."

"Behave yourself."

Without even saying good morning, Wanda Wallace walked in. "I have a problem, Randy - the same old problem, children! I want to sell some of my property but they are trying to stop me. Can they do that? I thought I was in control of my life, now they think *they* are. You have to get me out of this mess. I am as mad as hell."

"Calm down, WW, I am an estate lawyer. You need a trial lawyer, then you and the lawyer could try to work things out."

"You are my lawyer. Why do I have to get another one?"

"Well, your case might go into litigation, and I would be able to testify for you concerning your husband's wishes. I recorded his wishes. *You* are the one who has control over *all* your assets, *not* your children! There is a lawyer I trust, and his office is in this building. I am going to send you to him right now."

"Kids," she said, "I wish I'd never had any. What's his or her name? I wish your daddy were still alive. He had a mean streak, but I liked him. You know he flirted with me a couple of times."

"I would imagine so, but surely you must know there were many others besides you."

"I guessed as much, but if I had been looking, whoopee!"

“Let’s get back to business. The lawyer’s name is Frederick Winchester, and he is a very successful lawyer, else I would not recommend him.”

“Tell me about him.”

“He’s smart, a good friend, and an old classmate of mine. He is a mixed Black and White American and happily married to a lady named Elizabeth, who is white, but if that bothers you, I’ll find your another lawyer.”

“I’ve been in this town all my life, don’t you know. I don’t care if he is Black or White as long as he knows how to fight for me. I’ve heard of him, plus I like his name. You know a name says a lot about a man. Your daddy called you Randall. I like that name. Randy is a name for a boy, not a grown man.”

“Well, I don’t sign my name Randy, but it’s what my mommy calls me, and I *love* my mommy. Let me see if Frederick Winchester has a few minutes right now.”

“Don’t patronize me with your mommy talk. Tell Mr. Winchester I need more than a few of his minutes.”

“WW, Mr. Winchester can’t hear through walls, so this has to be an introduction meeting.”

“I like that you called me WW. I never hear that any more since… Oh hell, never mind. Okay, let’s have an introduction meeting.”

“Well WW, Frederick Winchester isn’t in. I’m going to try Bob Barnett.”

“The Wallace kids?” Bob asked Randy. “They’ve been sucking on her since they were born. The oldest one has never kept a job. She should have drowned him at birth, and the two girls are no better. Susie has been married four or five times, and Joy spends all her time and money with psychologists. I’m going to love this, Randy. Send her over. I don’t believe those rotten kids will want to go to court, not after I get through with them.”

“Boy, you’re getting specific. How do you know so much about the family?”

“It’s a long story buddy, and I don’t have the time to tell it.”

“By the way, Bob watch her. She’s known to be quite affectionate to men.”

“Thanks for the heads-up, buddy. Come on up.”

WW said, "Shame on you Randy Walker. Quit telling all my secrets." Randy asked Ms. Bee to take her up to his office. She made a face at him as she left the room.

Randy dealt with a couple of other clients, then went by his house, grabbed a few things, and headed over to Joan's. In his mind he was going through procedures – that's what lawyers do. *How do we proceed? Is tomorrow too soon to get a marriage license? Shall we buy another place or live in the one she has? She certainly wouldn't like the decor in my house. When is she going to tell Cassie and Rick? Patience. After all these years I should have developed some.*

He had to go inside to ask the night clerk where to park his car. Then the clerk had to call for permission for him to go up. He felt like a teenager.

I'm in love with a wonderful gal
So in love for a long, long time.

Oh, if I could take back those missed years. Well, I don't have a key, so I'll have to knock like a visitor. She opened the door and pulled him inside. "Are you afraid someone will see me," he asked.

"No, I want you to smell that great aroma coming from the oven."

"Hum, what is it?"

"Two delicious frozen dinners."

"Oh, my God, you must be a good cook. Lover and cook in one package. How lucky can a fellow get?"

"Oh, I have many talents."

It had been a long day for each of them. So they ate, sat on the couch, and talked about the day. Suddenly Randy jumped off the couch and knelt before her. "I've always wanted to do this: Alicia Joan Bonaville Randolph, I am a good man, with enough income and savings to support us, and I don't snore, drink too much, or run around, but my best of all characteristic is, I love you, only you, all my adult life. Will you marry me?"

"Let's see, after all these years, you finally ask?" She got down on the floor and said, "Yes I will marry you, Randall Phillips Walker," and kissed him on the cheek. "Isn't it amazing we don't have to inform our parents? But remember, I have two children we need to inform."

"Why don't we just surprise them?"

"Oh no! No surprises. I'll call them tomorrow."

"My house, your condo, or new condo?" Randy asked.

"I've been thinking about that all morning. Two bedrooms are definitely not enough, so a new condo, saving some things, and buying new. This is going to be fun. Buying a new place will be good for both of us. I hope your taste in furniture is good."

"I do have talents you know, and I am *not* a slob." And they both laugh.

In between kisses the evening was spent planning. They laughed like twenty-year old lovers planning a grand wedding.

"Where are we going to be married? Have you thought about that?" Joan asked.

"There is a small chapel at a local Presbyterian Church where our old friend Leonard Childs is the pastor. I hope you don't mind, but I have already talked to him, and he has agreed to marry us. It's the perfect place," Randy said.

"Leonard Childs! Good Lord! So you've already made the arrangements?"

"Yes, and since we haven't had much contact through the years, Leonard wants to see us before he marries us."

"So it is the perfect place. In what way?"

"You'll love it."

They lay on a bed where no other man had slept, and they held each other, not wasting a moment.

Randy woke in the morning to hear dishes rattling in the kitchen. He put on his pants, slipped into the kitchen, propped on the door facing, and watched her. She was in her pajamas, her hair uncombed, and no makeup. He stood silently, watching the only woman he had ever loved cook his breakfast. He was a lucky man. "Good morning."

"Go back to bed." Joan said. "This is supposed to be eaten on a tray, and I need to comb my hair."

"Why? You remember I've seen you naked, Miss Alicia Joan. I want to see everything I'm getting, even uncombed hair."

"Well, you don't look so good either, so sit and let's eat."

"Eggs and bacon; my favorite."

Joan said, "I suspected."

"Joan, if you have time today, go to a couple of places, and see if there is any place you might like. I'll look for condos on the Internet in between clients, as long as Ms. Bee doesn't catch me. But now I've got to go to work. I'm far too young to retire. Don't want to be late, Ms. Bee will give me that special 'you are late again' look. Sometimes I dream she is my real mother. Joan, I can't wait for you to meet her. She is one of the funniest persons I have ever known, but I wouldn't tell her that. I don't think she tries to be funny; she's a natural. Back to our business, I can take Friday off so we can search together."

"Perfect for me."

CHAPTER 10

Judy Barnett: Lost lover

After Randy left for work Joan decided to answer some of her calls. One call was from Judy Barnett, the wife of Bob Barnett. Joan said, "She never calls except about an upcoming party, and if so, my answer will be, no!" But she called her, "Judy this is Joan."

Judy answered, "Are you free for lunch today?"

"Sure. Where would you like to meet?"

"I'll pick you up at twelve o'clock. Okay?"

"Make it an hour later; I have some shopping to do. I'll be waiting outside."

"That's odd," Joan said out loud after she replaced the phone. "I don't believe we've ever had lunch together. She and Bob were at all the parties we attended, and John and I ate dinner with them several times, well more than several. Humm."

Judy arrived on time, and they drove toward Roswell, north of Atlanta. "Do you think you have time to go out to the Villa Roma?"

"I have about three hours, so the Villa would be fine."

During lunch, Judy felt a bit uneasy for there was not much conversation. After the meal was served Judy chastised the waiter because her food wasn't to her liking, so they had to wait for another order. Her reprimand to the waiter was embarrassing and made Joan uncomfortable. After they finished eating Judy suggested they find a seat in the corner of the bar. After Joan looked at her watch, she agreed. The bar was quiet since it was too early for the after work drop-ins. "I have something to tell you, but it has to be between the two of us," Judy said. "Can you agree to that?"

"I am not sure I can agree without knowing what I am agreeing to, and I don't make promises when I don't know what I'm promising. Have you murdered or poisoned someone."

"No, certainly not. It's about my daughter, Julia."

"Yes, John and I went to the hospital when she was born."

"It's time you know this, she is *not* Bob's child."

"Really? That is none of my business."

"In a way it is, Julia is Jonathan's child."

"You want me to be surprised? If you think I care, forget it. If what you are saying is true then John was even more despicable that I thought. I'm not at all surprised. I suspected that John was unfaithful, but I believed in marriage and stayed with him." She rose from her seat. "I'm leaving. I hope you don't ruin Bob and Julia's lives by telling them what you just told me."

"No, don't go yet; I have something to ask you. Jonathan promised he would leave money for Julia's education, so I have been waiting to hear from you. There has certainly been enough time for the will to be probated. Has it?" Joan did not answer. "Well then, there is one other thing I must tell you, if Julia is ever sick and needs some treatment her half brother and sister can give her, I will ask for it."

"Is something wrong with Julia?"

"Not that I know of now, but something could come up."

"So all those years John and I were with the two of you, attending the same parties, and when he couldn't come home because of business, he was screwing you *and* going to the hospital to see *his* daughter was planned by both of you. And you call him Jonathan when nobody else does. Wow. What was his pet name for you?"

"Don't get angry, Joan; it was what it was. We loved each other in high school long before he met you. We were going to get married, but I had a fling with another person, and Jonathan got mad and dumped me. Then I married *the fling,* Bob Barnett, and Jonathan got engaged to you to spite me, but we have always been in love."

"I need to go home," Joan said, "I've heard enough. I don't really care about all this, but there was absolutely no provision in the will for you or Judy."

"Then I'll sue for it. Wait, there is more, then I'll take you back."

"Not on your life! I know someone who will pick me up." She rose, told their waiter that Mrs. Barnett would be paying, and called Randy, "Can you pick me up at the Villa on Roswell Road as quickly as possible?" Joan turned her back when Judy walked past her. "You'll be hearing from me," she said.

It seemed forever until Randy arrived. When Joan got in the car she couldn't speak for a while, and Randy didn't ask her to. Almost home, she told him everything. Randy said, "There were always rumors about them, so I am not at all surprised."

"I'm sort of in shock, but looking back I can remember a lot of odd situations. How could I have been so stupid? They used me for cover, Randy. Hadn't they ever heard of divorce?"

"Don't blame yourself, Joan, you had no control over their actions. I still don't understand that clause at the end of his will. If he loved her so much, why didn't he leave her something, or at least something for Julia? Actually I'm glad he didn't love you, just sorry you had to take care of him."

"Would you really have told me, if you knew?"

"I knew a lot, but you remember the saying, *the messenger always gets shot*?"

After a long pause, she asked, "Should I tell Cassie and Rick?"

"That is a decision you have to make, but they have to know sometimes. You don't want Judy Barnett telling them, do you?"

"Of course not," Joan said. "I'll ask them to come home, but first I want them to come home for our good news that you and I are getting married."

"Joan, don't allow Judy Barnett to ruin your life, nothing would make her happier. We are going to make a new life together, but we cannot begin our lives by looking back. Let's put our focus on starting over."

"Randy, you are so right, but I want you present when I tell the children we are getting married. I know they will grow to love you."

"Joan, let's not talk about bad marriages any more. We can't erase our memories, so let's admit that and move on. Growing up, when I did something wrong, my mom would correct me and say, "Now that's enough said about this; put it in your forget pocket." That was always a good thought to me. So let's clear the slate and start over. We have a wonderful life ahead of us. You have no idea how much I love you."

That evening she called Cassie and Rick, and asked them come for the weekend, even if they have to change their plans. "It's important," she said to them.

The following day Randy took the afternoon off to go with Joan to look at condos. Afterward they had dinner at the Ritz Carlton. A couple of their old friends waved at them, but before they had time to invite them over, Randy asked the waiter, "May we have a table that is private?" He said, "I have just the place." The location and dinner was perfect.

"Randy," Joan said, "I didn't like any of the condos I looked at today. They were too new, and they have all the amenities young people want which I don't care about, and two of the managers said they had a few renters. I want to ask you a serious question, "Do you like where I live?"

"I do," he said. "Your condo is perfect, but it has only two bedrooms. We have two children, remember?"

"Why don't we ask the manager if there is a larger one coming up for sale in my building, then have a decorator help us decide what to keep and what to give away?"

"That is a wonderful idea. You won't believe it, but I got so tired looking today I thought of the same thing."

"You are joking, right?"

"No. I'm serious. Is it settled then?"

"You wonderful guy. Ask me again to marry you."

"Joan, do you really love me, and will you still marry me?"

"Yes to both questions; with all my heart, yes. When?"

"Tomorrow would not be soon enough. Let's call the kids."

On the way back to her condo they decided to stop by Randy's house. It had been a long time since she had been inside. It was a beautiful French Tutor and the landscaping was finely chiseled to feature the style of the house, but inside was a lot of leather furniture, what Joan would describe as *leather, leather everywhere*.

"Don't hurt my feelings now. Some of this was my father's stuff. My mom didn't like it either. Can I at least take one chair with me when I move?"

"I think that one red chair over there is pretty. I like red. Did your mom buy it?'

"She did, and she has impeccable taste."

"Impeccable? Then it goes with us."

"Goody, I can take my chair. Mom always liked you. She used to run into you at the country club, and she told me the two of you talked a few times."

"We did. She always asked about the children. She told me she would have liked two or three more. Then she would tell me how proud she was of you."

"Thanks for telling me that. I'm sure you wouldn't hear those words from my Father. He was a nasty bastard. I'm sorry, but he was. He called me a mama's boy and a tit sucker more than once. When I was young the only way we would have had a conversation of any length was if I had confided to him I was screwing a lot of girls, which I wasn't. God, I don't know how Mom put up with him."

They went into the bedroom. It was decorated in cool blues, and had indirect lighting. "I love this room, can we do something like this?" she asked.

"You mean like this," he said, pulling her on to the bed. He sat beside her, leaned her onto the pillow, and kissed her. "Have I told you in the last hour that I love you? I want to live inside of you, or as close as I can."

In a few minutes, the blue room became their world. He kissed every part of her body, even between her legs. It was a new experience for her, and she could hardly breathe. Her reaction invited him to linger. Then he held her sides with his arms, and gradually lifted himself into her. She journeyed into another region of ecstasy – a valley she did not know existed - a place where there are no words to explain the experience. She thought, *I can live now; I've had the best.* Afterward, they lay side-by-side holding hands. She thought he was asleep so she lay still, too happy to move.

His voice startled her, "What are you thinking about?"

Slowly she tried to express her feelings, "What just happened to me was new, and something too sweet to try to explain. Now I am thinking about us. About our future… About our expectations… About *our* home… It's going to be lovely with the two of us in it, isn't it?"

"Joan, as long as you are in my life our home could be a dump."

"You don't mean that. You have *never* lived in a dump. I went though plenty of dumps helping battered women get out of hell. Yet, that was a good part of my life. I'm ashamed I didn't help them more. Most of us donated our out-of-style outfits from our closets for the women to wear for job interviews. I'm ashamed we didn't give them our best. A group of us raised money for the shelter, but it was never enough."

"We can give money, and you can work there again, after all you know how it feels to be double crossed by a man."

"Wow, you know how to end a conversation, but you are right."

CHAPTER 11

Cassie and Rick

Joan called Cassie and Rick to make sure they were still coming for the weekend. Because she was so insistent, they had an idea of what was going on. It had been a long week. Joan had been too busy to prepare food for the weekend, so she had the meals catered.

Saturday afternoon the house was filled with laughter. Cassie was so unlike her mother. She didn't mind giving her opinion, and refused to tolerate negative people. She was tall, like her mom, and was vivacious and never still. She had ideas that couldn't come out fast enough, and she was excited about the up-coming occasion.

Rick was not as tall as Cassie, and he was extremely thin and pale. If he interrupted a conversation, which was rare, everyone stopped to listen. He seemed to enjoy the interaction between his mother and Cassie, and his eyes scanned every inch of the room. He commented, "I like the combination of colors in this room, they are vibrant, and they give the room life: an artist's dream." Before anyone could respond the doorbell rang. It was Randy. He entered, and after being introduced he shook hands with both of them, hugged Joan, and stood aside, like an intruder.

Joan said, "Cassie and Rick, Randy is no stranger to you. I have known him since our college days. Well, we have fallen in love. That is a brief description of a long story. Randy will tell you he loved me even back in college, but I was too blind to see it, besides I was engaged to your father. Oh well, it's a long story and a lot of years."

"Mom, you're rambling."

"Okay. Anyway the two of you would not have been born, and I am most happy to have you. Randy, maybe you'd better finish for me."

Randy began, "The truth is we *have* known each other a long time, but there was never any sexual contact between us all the years your father was alive. Now, having explained that, can we move on?

Cassie and Rick, We don't want your permission to marry; we want your blessings. These past few days have been the most exciting time in my life, and I believe your mom feels the same. I have asked her to marry me, and she has said, yes. Forgive me for saying this, but lately I feel as young as the two of you."

Cassie applauded and said, "Yea! Enough conversation. Mom you are still young. I want you to be happy."

"Ditto," Rick said. "Cassie and I will support you all the way. Actually we did have an idea of this and we talked about it. Randy was the only possibility we could think of, besides I used to watch the way he looked at you, Mom. Randy, you've got to admit you didn't hide it well."

"Well, Mom," Cassie said, "A couple of times when we talked you mentioned you were going out to dinner with Randy, so I called Rick, and we put two and two together. Hey, give us a little credit."

"Thanks, kids. You are so sweet and thanks for supporting me. I'll return the favor whatever you want."

Rick asked, "Whatever?"

"Whatever."

It was an exciting weekend. Randy was beginning to understand what having children meant. He was already dreaming about adopting them, though that thought was a little too early. As the evening began to end Randy offered to take Rick home with him since Joan had only two bedrooms. Rick quickly agreed, which surprised everyone.

"Mom, before we leave; when is the wedding?" Rick asked.

"Can the two of you be back in two weeks? I wish it could be tomorrow."

"Wouldn't miss it," both of them said.

"Invite a friend to come with you if you wish," Joan said. "There is plenty room in the Chapel.

Joan and Cassie spent most of the night talking mother and daughter things such as what are you wearing for the wedding? Are you going on a honeymoon? "Mom, I knew Daddy had another life, didn't you know?" No response. "Mom, Rick actually saw Dad and Mrs. Barnett together."

"Did he now?"

"When Rick saw them Dad was already sick, and it wasn't a good time for you to know what was going on."

"I found out for certain this past week. You know, Cassie I really don't care right now. Randy and I have a lot of background to bury, and we are doing that."

Across town Randy and Rick stayed up until midnight, and the conversation eventually landed on how he was doing in his classes, and about getting a position afterward. Rick said, "Randy, I am not sure what I want to do the rest of my life, but right now I would appreciate any advise you might have."

"Wait just a minute. You are about to finish a degree that may not be your life's calling? What is?"

He paused, trying to find the right words. "I am an artist. I love every minute standing in front of an easel staring down at a canvas whether I draw, paint, or make splashes with the brush. In my mind I dream of painting flowers and people and towers, but I am driven to insanity for I cannot make a living painting."

"Most artists are poor at first, but I know you have money. Remember, I was your dad's estate attorney. Plus you can always depend on me now that I'm going to be family. Here is my advice, Rick, never, *never* give up your dream."

"Yes sir. Thank you, sir!" Then there was the topic Rick had been holding inside, "Randy, I caught my dad and Mrs. Barnett together one night, but I couldn't say anything to Mom. He and I had an agreement."

"An agreement with your dad?"

"Yes. I was with another person that night, my friend, Colin. I saw Dad and Mrs. Barnett just as he spotted us. Immediately he came over and said something nasty, and I gave it back to him. He pulled me aside, and said, "You are despicable."

And I said, "And so are you. I'm not forgetting this. Does Mom know?"

"No, and if you tell anybody, I will tell them you are a fag and a liar."

"Oh, Dad," I said, "You have always been an adulterer and a liar as long as I have known you. I wish you weren't my father. I should hit you right now just for Mom. Colin and I turned and walked off."

He yelled out to me, "You're a bastard! Forget you are my son."

Randy said, "Wow! That must have hurt. How could any father be so vulgar to his son? Rick, tell your mother about your friend this weekend. It will not make any difference to her. That is one of the reasons I love her so much."

"Randy, I gave my dad no indication that Colin and I were lovers. I could have been having dinner with a friend. He made the assumption without asking me."

"I'm sorry Rick. Put that in your forget pocket, as my mom used to say. Do you have one of those?"

"Yes Sir. Mom always called it a trash button."

Sunday morning the four of them were together.

"Mom," said Rick, "I need to tell you something. The person I want to bring to your wedding is my friend, Colin. Well he could be a bit more than a friend."

"How long has this been going on, and why haven't I been told?"

"Several months, and I chose not to tell anyone."

"Dear, you bring Colin. I want to meet the person who knows my son."

"Wait a minute," Cassie said. "Don't you want to know who I will be bringing?"

"Is this going to be another twist?" Joan asked. They all laughed.

"No, I will be bringing a man I might be able to love. We aren't living together, but that could come later. His name is Arthur Thompson, but everyone calls him Art. Mom, he's nice, maybe too nice, but he wants to meet you. Your wedding will be the perfect time for him to meet both of you."

"Randy, my children have been keeping secrets lately. What do you think I should do to them?"

"After you paddle them, kiss them, and tell them how much you love them, then send them to bed. Can I watch the paddling and the kissing?" They all laughed.

Sunday lunch went fine. There was a lot of laughter and planning. After the kids left, Randy said, "I am in love with them. Rick revealed to me something you need to know, and then throw it out with the trash. He ran into John at an out of town restaurant. John was with Judy, and Rick was with Colin. John had a few nasty words, but Rick held his ground and let him know he was a scoundrel, a liar, and everything else. Don't be upset that Rick didn't tell you. John might have disinherited him."

"Poor Rick. John always picked on him, what little time he had with him. Okay, I've just clicked the trash button and sent it away. Happy?"

"Rick trusted me with that information. That must mean he feels comfortable with me, don't you think? I've never been a father. This is going to be interesting."

"Who wouldn't be comfortable with you?" she asked. "You are my hero, and I know the kids will love you." It was two good days. Randy already felt the responsibility for Cassie and Rick as if he was being trusted with their lives.

———

Monday morning Randy worked hard at the office to plan for some time off. Ms. Bee came through his door with a pile of papers, as was her usual trick, and after dropping them on his desk, she said, "I'm tired of taking so many orders, 'get this, and get that.' I'm an old woman, don't you know? And all those telephone calls and emails. We need another person in this office. Well?"

"Well what?"

"You are inviting me to the wedding, aren't you? I haven't seen or heard an invitation. If you don't, I quit. "

"No, you won't quit; you love me. And you are not an old woman, so drop the shit. Sure you'll be there. You're family. So doll yourself up. By the way, we may have a new person in our law firm. My new daughter, Cassie is about to finish law school."

"I'm getting tired, you know. If we bring another lawyer in this office, I'll be hiring my own secretary."

"Don't be pulling that *I'm tired* and other junk on me. You know I wouldn't know how to run this office if you weren't around to beat me up every now and then."

As she walked away she said, "Sometimes I believe he thinks I'm his nanny."

"I heard that," Randy yelled.

CHAPTER 12

Judy Barnett

The next two weeks Judy called Joan several times a day, leaving threatening messages. "I know about your son. That's not going to go over very well around here." Another message, "You didn't promise me that you wouldn't tell. If you tell Bob, I will deny it." Then another, "I want that money; I deserve it. Do you understand?" The last call came shortly afterward, "If I don't hear from you, I will assume you are not going to answer. You will wish you had."

With the insinuated violence in Judy's calls, it was plain she was preparing to take some sort of revenge. Joan wanted to delete the messages, but she knew Randy should hear them. When he came in after work he listened to the messages, "We can't ignore these. I have to think. Maybe we should have a lawyer contact Bob, though he might already know. No, wait a minute; I have a better idea. Let me call Frederick." He rang, "Frederick, so glad you are in. We have a crisis here. Would you do us a favor by coming to Joan's condo as soon as possible - like right away - to listen to some threating recordings from Judy Barnett." Frederick sensed the urgency and said he would be over as soon as he could. Joan called the night security to notify him that Mr. Frederick Winchester would be there shortly, and to allow him to enter, but only him and no one else.

In about an hour Frederick walked in, "So let's play the recordings." Everyone was quiet while he listened. "I agree with you, Randy. Judy is angry and possibly vindictive. About that time the phone rang. Randy put the phone on speaker, "This is not going well is it, Joan? You're going to tell Bob, aren't you? I'm at a service station around the corner from your Condo. Watch for me, and when I get there you'd better come out and have a good answer for me, or you will regret it. It will be good gossip when all your friends know your husband had a child by another woman."

"Whoa! What kind of car does Judy drive?" Frederick asked.

Joan said, "I rode in it last week. It is a fairly new Mercedes, sort of a light tan color, but she can't get in the gate. She has no entry pass and she knows that. It's just a threat."

Randy called the security, "I'm calling from Joan Walker's residence. She has had some threating calls. Would you go outside, walk around casually, and see if a tan Mercedes is sitting near the entrance?" After a few minutes the security called and said, "Yes Sir, there is."

Randy said to him, "She has been making threatening call to Joan Randolph.
Call the police and ask them to stop and ask her if she needs any help, nothing else."

"Will do. I'll watch out."

In about fifteen minutes he called back, "The police came, talked to her, and she drove away."

Frederick said, "Thanks. If she comes back call us."

"Yes sir, I will."

Fredrick put his hand on Joan's shoulder, "I'm afraid we have to do something. From what I've heard on your phone, and knowing she was parked outside your building, the whole situation is about to explode. Poor Bob is going to be one upset person."

Joan said, "You know something. I have a feeling Bob already knows. Randy, how can we find out?"

"You may be right. Frederick, I have a plan," Randy said, "Will you meet me at my office in the morning?"

"Is ten okay?" Frederick asked. "It will give both of us time to get ready. Joan, if at all possible, stay inside tomorrow. I need to take this phone and recordings with me. Use your cell phone today."

"Shouldn't I go with you."

"Sorry Joan. You need to stay by the phone."

Frederick went to Randy's office a little after ten the following day. Randy said to Ms. Bee, "Hold all calls and interruptions."

"And if you have an emergency?"

"Take care of it yourself. Just do your sweet talk."

"Oh goody."

They devised a plan. Randy said to Frederick, “I hope this works, if it doesn’t, I don’t know what we do next.” He called Bob Barnett, “Bob, are you busy? Okay. Can Frederick and I come up when you are through? Fifteen minutes? Okay, we’ll give you time to finish, and Bob, we need at least thirty minutes of your time.”

They took the phone and recordings with them. After greetings and small talk Randy spoke, “Bob, we want you to listen to some recordings.” Bob appeared restless. He leaned back in his chair, folded his arms across his chest, and began rocking. As they listened he became tense and emotional. During the last message he put his elbows on the desk and hands over his face and waited. Then finally, “This is painful and embarrassing. I’m a fool, a damn idiot. For years I had a suspicion about Judy and John. I knew she married me on the rebound, but I thought after Julia was born their affair would be over, and certainly I thought she would get over him after he died. I stayed with her because of Julia. I’ve always wondered if Julia is John’s child. He came to the hospital when Julia was born and at least once after she came home. Coming home for lunch one day, I saw John going into the house with flowers, so I pulled into a neighbor’s driveway and sat until he left.” He paused. “I asked Judy, who brought the flowers, and she said Joan brought them. Julia is my life; I will do anything to keep her from being hurt. Judy has never loved me.” He paused. “She has always loved John Randolph. Now she is lost. These recordings seem to indicate she wants revenge. She must feel double-crossed that John left her nothing. She has lost her pride, and could be dangerous, even to herself. My fear is, she will tell Julia that I am not her father. I’ve got to stop her.”

“Bob, don’t do anything until we think this out,” Frederick said.

“This is not your problem,” Bob said.

“Not true, Bob. Joan and I are getting married, and right now she is scared to step outside her condo.”

“Randy, you have always loved her. I’ve known that since college. Frederick, how did you get involved with this?”

“Randy called me. Joan may need a lawyer.”

“My God, you really think this will go that far?”

"Listening to Judy's threats to Joan, don't you believe there is a problem? She is angry that John didn't recognize her in his will. We have to take her threats seriously."

"First of all," Randy said to Bob, "We need to get her out of the house, away from Julia, and get her some help."

"Let's go," said Bob.

———

They arrived at Bob's house, just as Julia was running down the sidewalk. "Daddy, Daddy, Mama has gone crazy. She's saying all sorts of things. I'm afraid. And Daddy, she has a gun!"

"All of you wait out here. I'll go in and see what I can do." They heard a gunshot. Randy stayed with Julia, and Frederick ran inside. He saw Bob on the floor, and Judy was standing in the corner sobbing. She had the gun in her hand, "I shot him. I shot him. Is he going to be okay?"

Frederick said, "Give me the gun, Judy." She hesitated. "Put the gun on the floor, Judy! *Now*! I need to check Bob and I don't want you shooting me."

She put the gun on the floor and Frederick picked it up. He went over to Bob, who had pulled himself in a sitting position against the wall. "I was trying to get the gun away from her. She shot me in the leg, damn it. Frederick, call an ambulance."

Frederick went to the door and shouted, "Randy, call an ambulance. Bob's been shot! Keep Julia outside! It was only minutes until the ambulance came, and a patrol car was right behind. The emergency medical team stopped the bleeding and loaded Bob into the ambulance. He held Julia's hand and said, "I love you Sweetheart. Frederick and Randy will take care of you."

The police questioned Judy, "Why did you shoot your husband."

"He was hollering at me and tried to get the gun."

"What did he say?"

"He yelled at me to put the gun down."

The policeman said, "Is there anybody here to go with her to the Jail?"

Judy was crying and talking, "I have nobody now. John left me without a word and nothing. Nothing! *Why*, after all those years?

She got everything, and I got nothing. He didn't love her. He loved me. Just let me die."

"Officer, I am attorney Frederick Winchester, a long time friend of her husband, Bob Barnett. Mrs. Barnett has been threating my client, Joan Randolph, but I don't believe jail is the best place for her tonight. The psychiatric ward at the hospital might be better. She could harm herself."

"I'm Lt. Roberts. I've seen you in court a few times. You're a criminal lawyer, aren't you? You think she's a criminal?"

"Mr. Roberts, I cannot answer that question, but I do believe she will harm herself."

"I'll post what you said. You can follow us."

"Frederick, where are they taking Bob?" Randy asked.

"Piedmont Hospital, I believe. Let me check. Yes, that's right. Randy, take Julia to my house. Right now that seems the best place for her."

"Okay, will do. She's going to need some clothes and other things. We'll get her things and then lock up." Julia was silent most of the trip. She had to be in shock to have witnessed a scene no teenager should ever have to experience. Finally she spoke as if talking to no one, "My mom hasn't been herself lately. She has been rambling on about a lot of things. She kept looking at me, and saying, 'who are you? I don't know who you are any more.' I'm scared."

"Julia," Randy said, "Whatever your mom said these last few days might not be true. She is sick and needs help to get well. You and Mrs. Winchester get along well, don't you?"

"Yes sir, and Molly is one of my friends."

"You might be staying there for a few days until your dad gets out of the hospital. Can you manage that for awhile?"

"I'll be all right. Will she take me to see my daddy sometimes?"

"You ask her, and if she can't, have her call me or Miss Joan."

"Thanks, Mr. Walker. I'm a little scared right now, but I'm very mad at my mom. I just remembered something. I need to let my grandparents know."

"Call them as soon as you get there."

Randy called Joan from Elizabeth's, "I'm on my way. Sorry I haven't called, but we had a crisis. Judy shot Bob in the leg. They have taken him to the hospital, and I'm leaving Julia with Elizabeth. I'm out the door, on my way home."

Joan was rather upset she had not heard from him. He understood her anger, since she might have been the victim. "I don't blame you for being angry. It does appear Judy was prepared to harm someone, and indeed you could have been her target. I doubt if she was considering suicide. She acted confused, and kept talking about John not leaving her anything. At some time in the past John must have promised to leave her an insurance policy or money, but she doesn't have it. Judy may believe you are hiding it from her."

"I've been through all of John papers. How could I have missed it? I even went through his desk and the cabinets in his office."

Randy said, "Well, we need to look again. What company had his office and practice insured?"

"Coleman and Coleman. I'll call them tomorrow. I feel so sorry for Julia. I'm glad she is with Elizabeth. It would not have been a good idea to bring her here."

The next morning Joan called Phyllis Coleman to ask them about the policy. "Of course we know you, Mrs. Randolph, but you must come to the office for identification. Now is a good time."

"I'll be there within the hour."

In the office Ms. Coleman tried to explain the policy to Joan, "Mr. Randolph set up a trust for Julia Barnett to be given to her when she is twenty-six. He put in writing that the child was not to be informed. We contacted Mr. Randolph's office and instructed his secretary, a Mrs. Johnson to contact Miss Cassie Randolph for us, but we did not tell her why. That is the person Mr. Randolph listed as the Executor for Julia Barnett. Mrs. Johnson has not responded. We knew Mr. Randolph had died but there was nothing we could do. Somehow Cassie Randolph did not ring a bell with any of us here."

"You didn't recognize the Randolph name? It's been almost a year. Couldn't you have called me?"

"Mr. Randolph made it plain that we were to call Cassie Randolph."

Joan said, "I can't imagine why you waited all this time. You should have contacted Mr. Randolph's lawyer. I'm sure you have that information. It appears you weren't interested in solving the issue, so I have to wonder how many other people you were prepared to cheat. Cassie Randolph is my daughter and the daughter of John Randolph. There should be some penalty levied on your company for not settling this. I will inquire about that. Here is Cassie's address and phone number."

When Joan left, she called Cassie and informed her of the crisis. "Well, I'll be damned," she said. "Rick told me he saw him at a restaurant with Judy, so I am not surprised. That was an ugly scene. I guess Rick has told you that by now."

"Randy told me about it. Rick told him."

"Mom, this is a tricky situation. Am I supposed to tell this child that we are half-sisters? I have a problem with that."

"That is not our worry right now. It's a long time until Julia is twenty-six. We will work these things out later. I'm sorry he did this to you."

"Better me than you, Mom."

"You've got that right. Your father was a strange man. I should have left him years ago, but I can't say I stayed for your and Rick's good. I just rocked along doing my own thing. We were estranged long ago, rarely had sex, lived our separate lives, and never had a decent conversation. As fragile as his relationship was with Judy he never got over her. He probably married me to spite her."

"Mom, he married you because you were a beautiful trophy, and he didn't want Randy to have you. That's the truth."

"How do you know that?"

"He wanted both of you, and since there is a law against plural marriages, he kept both of you."

"When did you figure all that out?"

"It wasn't hard, I can tell you that."

Joan called the firm that was John's accountant for many years, "This is Joan Randolph, the widow of John Randolph. Do you still have Mr. Randolph's information on file?" She answered, "Yes, certainly we do."

Then Joan said "We are wondering why Mrs. Johnson, who worked for Mr. Randolph for years, refuses to respond when we call her. We have reason to believe she may have been dishonest. Would you check his records at least two years before his death? This is crucial. Can you get those records for me?"

"Sure, Mrs. Randolph, give us a few minutes." Joan waited. "Mrs. Randolph, it appears Mrs. Johnson wrote several checks to herself. The only checks signed by Mr. Randolph were her salary checks. We are talking about a lot of money Mrs. Walker, not only to her, but also to family members. You need to turn this over to an attorney."

Joan called Frederick and gave him the information. He said he would have someone in his office get right on it. "No wonder Judy is ill," she said to him. "She must have planned to tell Bob about Julia when she got the insurance money, *but* she had no way of knowing John was leaving a trust to Julia and not to her. After all those years they were involved, that surprises me. John must have been trying to make it right with Julia and everyone, except Judy. Perhaps he had a conscience after all. That trust will seem strange to Julia; she will want to know why, and Cassie will have to deal with that."

"It's a mess," Frederick said, "I believe John finally trapped himself. If I had known what was going on, I would have suggested he divorce you. Living two lives all those years, wow! Maybe he was trying to figure out a way to make restitution. That's enough talking, Joan. Let it go for now. I will have to involve Bob in all this; he needs to know. I hope you understand that, and I will have to contact Cassie."

"Yes, I know."

CHAPTER 13

The Wedding

Taking the advice of Frederick, Randy and Joan choose to delay moving until after their wedding. They wanted to put aside all that had happened in the last few weeks and have fun with the kids and their friends. Frederick would take care of any legal issues while they were on their honeymoon. Expected to attend the wedding were the kids and their two friends, Randy's mother, Ana Marie and his Aunt Pearl, Joan's brother, Thomas and his wife, Catherine and their children, Ms. Bee, Frederick and his wife, Elizabeth and their children, Bob Barnett and Julia, and a few other acquaintances.

The wedding took place in the Garden Chapel at the Southside Presbyterian Church. Leonard's final words were perfect, especially his benediction, "My friends of years past, 'tis sweet I am the one to bind the two of you in marriage. May God be with you as you live the adventures for which you have long awaited. Amen."

The wedding party gathered at Anthony's for dinner afterward. As a surprise Cassie and Rick offered a little entertainment. First they sang a duet, "Let There Be Love" without music and accompaniment. Then Cassie read a poem written for the occasion. "A poet I am not, but on this occasion, every one will be interested how you the two of you met. So here is the story.

Above the shaded college quad
on a bright and sunny day
an Angel spotted two students
and flapped her wings
to the rhythm of love.
She spoke words not heard on earth,
not today, nor tomorrow
not until, at my will,
I pass over twice times ten
to sing my song of love again.

Twice times ten, indeed
the Angel appeared once more
and beheld the two lovers
on the bank of a creek
watching the sun descend.

"My task is done said she,"
and blessed the two
she choose to woo
and pointed her wings into yonder
to sing again her song of wonder.

After great applause, Randy and Joan expressed wonder at her lovely creation. Randy introduced Rick to his aunt Pearl. "Rick, here is someone you need to get to know, my Aunt Pearl. She is a damn good artist. I want you to see her work. She may have some advice for you."

"Randy tells me you are interested in art, Rick. If that is true, then everything else you have planned to do is useless. You and I will get together while your parents are away. Okay?"

"Sure. Can I call you Aunt Pearl?"

"Yes, you may. Give me your phone number and I will telephone you tomorrow."

Joan's brother, Thomas took Randy and Joan to the airport. Their destination was Bar Harbor, Maine to The Cottage Inn Bed and Breakfast. Unknown to Joan the Inn belonged to their college classmate, Roger Waddell, whom they had not seen in years. Randy said, "I am not going to carry you across the threshold, until we get our own place."

"As far as I am concerned you can put me in a wheelbarrow."

"Goody, I can dump you inside."

CHAPTER 14
Maine

Their suite was perfect, near to cafes, galleries, historical places, and not far from the ocean. Both were so tired they collapsed on the bed until they saw the champagne Randy had ordered for their celebration. “After all those long years my dream has finally come true. I believe we should stay awake long enough to celebrate.”

“Yes, Randy Walker this dream is real. I love you.”

The evening was quiet. They lay together on the bed holding hands, talking about snippets in their lives, silly little things like, “Sometimes my mom would dress me like a girl,” Randy said. “I’m embarrassed to say that.”

“Did you have long curly hair?”

“No, but my dad said she was screwing me up. I would allow her to do almost anything. She was all I had.”

Joan said, “My mom ignored me and my brother most of the time, so we had fun doing whatever we wanted to do. I was a little wild.”

“I don’t believe that. What, or who, tamed you?”

“Guess I just grew up, or maybe it was boys.”

“I should have known.” It was fun just lying there.

The next morning Randy was the first to rise. He called the desk to arrange for their breakfast to be sent to the room. Joan was in the shower when Roger burst in with their breakfast trays. “Good morning, Randy. Wow! Look at you. You are an old man? Give your old buddy a hug.”

“I believe you are not too far behind, my friend. Roger, you know I couldn’t resist bringing the prize of my life to our old college buddy’s dream cottage. How are you doing?”

“Well, when you called I wanted to ask, what took you so long? I remember your drooling over Joan when we were in college.

She was so beautiful. Sometimes this week you will have to tell me how you pulled this off."

"Joan, hurry up; we have company."

"You must be kidding," she said as she peeped from behind the bathroom door. "Say hello to Roger!"

"Roger? Oh *that* Roger. I'm not dressed; go away. Randy, you're a bad person for not telling me."

"Get your robe on, honey, and put a comb through your hair. This breakfast is for three. You will see how much I love both of you, Roger said."

"Close your eyes when I come in; this body is for Randy only."

"You selfish girl. Do not bother to put your face on. Roberta will want to see the most beautiful graduate from William and Mary without makeup."

"You and Roberta? Is that the girl you mentioned once or twice when we were in school? After so long? What? How?" Randy stuttered.

"It is a long story with a beautiful ending, perhaps like your story."

While they ate, Roger talked, "After all those long years, I ran into Roberta in New York. I was there for a meeting with Bill Vickery, a guy I met who owned a bed and breakfast in Albany, and guess who I saw? Roberta. I had to look twice, or three times, for it was not possible. She was with another man. I discovered later he was the detective she hired to find me. I embraced her, and let me tell you, I bawled. Those few days with her healed the years that separated us and helped me believe in fate. When I mentioned buying a bed and breakfast with some of the money from my inheritance, she said, 'I have always wanted to do that.' So that is when it happened. I told her she could be a freeloader. Short story: We married, and here we are having the time of our lives. You cannot understand how excited I was to know you were coming. I have spent hours planning your visit, but Roberta reminded me, 'They are not coming *just* to see you, Dude,' so I canned it all."

"Hey, hey, maybe we ought to look at some of that planning," Randy said.

"No, you do not. He is planning to be your guide," Roberta said as she entered.

"Well, Roger thanks anyhow. The lady of your house says, no." Roger and Joan almost gasped when they saw Roberta. She had dark olive skin, dazzling black hair that hung in curls, and a figure carved out of dark marble. Her eyes were decorated with long back eyelashes, and her mouth was full and sensuous. She was straight out of a photographer's dream. Joan noticed that Randy was photo gaping.

After breakfast they brought each other up to date on what had happened through the years.

Joan said, "What a surprise. I had no idea Randy got in touch with you, Roger. Randy, any other surprises I don't know about?"

"No this is it, Joan. I knew you would love seeing him. I think he lusted after you as much as I did."

"Well, whatever. Roberta, how do you stand him? He used to play tricks on me. Does he do that to you?" Joan asked.

"All the time, Honey, all the time. But he is a damn good lover, and everybody likes his hospitality. We have a great time every moment of our lives."

"Okay, enough small talk. What's good around here that we must see?" Randy asked.

"I have all the pamphlets that you need," Roger said. "There are a lot of restaurants, and to tell the truth, there are no bad places to eat. The coast is beautiful, and there are several companies that will take you out on the water or into the Acadia National Park. Just have fun. Roberta and I will see you later."

———

After breakfast Randy and Joan walked about to see where they were. Following the map Roger gave them, they decided to walk along the Shore Path and sit on the benches and wonder about the depth and vast distance of the great Atlantic Ocean. Joan said, "The Ocean is marvelous. We land lovers in Atlanta are missing this grand view."

"Speaking of grand, Joan. I imagine the people who live here travel to see the Grand Canyon and other marvels in our country."

"Oh you are right. There is so much of the world to see; we need to travel more often." At midafternoon, on recommendation, they walked into a small café for afternoon tea and popovers. At the table next to them sat a couple of tourists from Birmingham, Alabama. Their Southern accent was a give-away, and they were full of information about places to see. After a while Joan began to tire, so they decided to return to the room and relax.

Randy said, "Joan, this place is better than I dreamed of. I have the urge to pinch myself to see if this is real.

"Randy, what a perfect place to spend every minute with you. I need a nap."

"How about a nap after…? She removed her clothes as Randy watched. Then he removed his. They lay together for a while under the covers. "What are you thinking Joan?"

"It's strange, but I'm thinking of that little poem Cassie and Rick wrote. Randy, do you suppose there was an angel?"

"Why not? It made sense to me."

He began kissing her from the top of her head down to her neck and hands. He became overpowered with emotion, bringing tears to his eyes. It had been years since he had cried, and that was at his grandmother's funeral. It disturbed him. "I'm sorry," he said to her. "Maybe these are tears of relief. Who wouldn't cry with the woman of my dreams finally in my company for the rest of my life? It has been too long since I've had tears in my eyes."

She was speechless. She wanted to feel, not talk. There were times for words, but she wanted to experience the joy of being loved, and his hands roaming over her body searching for exotic places, and knowing there would be many other times.

He found her breasts. He played with them until her nipples became hard and inviting. He couldn't wait; there would be other times to wait, but he needed to enter her. The explosion was powerful for both of them. She felt a deep sensation that flowed from her breasts to her vagina. She had heard about women screaming during sex, and she was not certain whether she had. No, it was Randy who called out. "Are you all right?" Joan asked.

"Yes. Though that wasn't our first time of intimacy it was different from all other times - strange, exciting, and inviting, but not disturbing. Maybe it was the marriage license." Neither of them could speak. They held hands and fell asleep. The most delicious and sound sleep ever. Everything was right. Everything was complete.

This is what a union of two people should be about: no flowery speeches, no apologies, celebrating for a love that was meant to be.

In another part of the inn Roger said to Roberta, "It is fun to see old friends. You and I know exactly what they are doing at this moment. The thought excites me. Got a minute for another renewal of our love for each other?"

"A minute! No, I do not have time for just a minute; thirty maybe."

She led him into their bedroom, beautifully decorated with Waddell money, and a touch of fresh mint stirring in the air to awake their senses. This time was special. He said to her, "Every time I enter this room I remember what a lucky man I am. What can I do for you that will emphasize that I mean what I say?"

"My dear Roger, you are my life. We live it together entertaining others. This afternoon let me entertain you."

They fell into the bed. Telephone, visitors, and other duties passed into another world. They embraced like two hungry persons, who smiled for others all day long. But together they had another name for love. She lay on top of him, stroking every part of him, then helped him reach a climax, for she could not offer herself – a body almost destroyed by cancer. Afterward he kissed her, and pressed his head where there were no breasts, and said, "I love every part of your body, even the missing parts." And they laughed and cried together.

It was almost evening before Randy and Joan arose and dressed. They decided to walk about and roam the area like lost people. They might eat, or might not. Bar Harbor was so beautiful it brought out the poet in Randy. Holding her hand, he sat down on a rock, pulled out a piece of paper and read,

Joan my love, my beautiful wife
You have given me new life.
"Oh, that's sweet," She said.
"Hush, I'm not through yet."
Your love gives me a new start
You will always have my heart.

They both laughed at his attempt at poetry. Finally they walked into a bar and ordered a glass of wine. It went to straight to Joan's head, because she had not eaten. So they ordered a lobster salad and fresh chips. Food had never tasted better. Outside again, they could smell the salt in the air, and the brisk breeze gave them the urge to walk backward. They kept saying, "Amazing." Though many places looked old, everything was fresh for them - new lives, new places, new adventures.

They enjoyed every minute with Roger and Roberta. When Roberta looked puzzled at their reminiscing they had to bring her up to date, explaining places and people. She laughed along with them, not because she understood, but because they took the sadness out of Roger's eyes. Joan whispered to Roberta, "They are reliving college and law school."

"Roberta, guess who suddenly appeared out of nowhere our junior year at William and Mary," Randy asked. "Yep, poor ole Roger Waddell. He must have worn the same pants for a week. If I remember correctly, he had only two pair. We felt sorry for him, thinking how poor he was. Joan, Frederick, Leonard, Bob and I sort of made a circle around him, and he became part of our small group. We even bought him some clothes, and the rascal was glad to get them. Occasionally a package would arrive from his parents, more of the same sort of clothes. Some of them looked like they came from the Salvation Army Store."

"You are kidding me, of course," said Roberta.

"No, he is not. My parents thought most of the students would be tight for money, so they decided I should be like them. Occasionally I received some money in the mail, but it was never enough. Thank goodness my meals were paid with the tuition. I did not get to know many of the people in our classes, especially those who flaunted their money. To tell you the truth I could not complain; I just thought my parents did not have the money to send. They were more into hopping from one country to another, and did not pay much attention to the wealthy things of life. To them education, the arts, and customs of different countries were the important things to teach me."

"Roger what happened to you and the law?" Randy asked.

"Too confining, Buddy. I went with a law firm in Nashville that made me, the new guy, take all the left over cases. I asked the senior partners to stop doing that or I was out of there. I worked eighteen hours a day for half their pay. They said they were teaching me because they thought I had *potential*. Dude, I kept my word and left. Well, there was another reason for my departure. My dad's lawyer called and said both of my parents were ill, so I flew to New York to help take care of them. I did not tell them about leaving behind the career that made them so proud. One day I began to realize they must have money, or they would not be living where they were. Randy is right, I had only two pair of jeans, and there they were living in a lavish hotel. My Mother died of heart failure, and my Dad wished for only one thing: To be with my mother. He refused to eat or take his medicine and got his wish. Our lawyer had known them for years, and he said he was not at all surprised of my dad's decision. Goodness, they were much older that I thought.

"They were so dad-burn tight, we stayed in small inns across Europe and the States. I loved that part. Each place we stayed I was tutored by both of them and some of their friends. After Dad's death I got to be friends with their lawyer. When he informed me of my inheritance I almost fell over – ten million dollars, and part of that hotel! I said where? When? How did they accumulate that much? The lawyer handed me a portfolio to read in my spare time. I did not know what I was going to do, but I sure was not about to blow that money. I called up Bill Vickery. You remember him in law school?"

Randy said, "Vaguely."

"I knew he had an inn in upstate New York, and he convinced me of the joys of being an innkeeper. I lived with his family for three months to learn the business. Actually, I was their slave, but more fun than being a law firm slave. I learned quickly. Then I found Roberta, or she found me. It was love all over again. Right, Honey?"

"You better believe it, and in just two months we were married."

Roger said, "Bill Vickery found this inn for us. The couple had been operating it for years, but they were getting old. I had my lawyer research it for debts, etc., and he came back with squeaky-clean information. And here we are!"

Roger and John went out on the porch and sat in the rockers. "Roger, this place is beautiful. You found your Roberta, and I finally have Joan. Everything is good, and we are two lucky blokes."

Roger spoke, "All that is true, Randy, but the deal on selling this paradise is about to be finalized. No, please do not interrupt. Roberta is ill. The doctors have removed almost all of her, except her beautiful body and face. She is dying. I cannot imagine life without her." He paused. "Of one thing I am certain, I will not stay in this place where her memory is in every inch of it. I have sold the place with the stipulation we can stay until the end comes for Roberta. I can tell you right now, her death is not far away. One day, when you get home, you will get a call from me, so make room for me until I find something – maybe a couple of weeks. All I will have with me is my clothes, Roberta's jewelry, and a few other things I can ship. That is about it, buddy."

Randy didn't know what to say, so he was quiet a while. Finally, "Roger, I am so sorry. Your life here seems so perfect. What are you going to do? I cannot imagine what you are going through. If I knew Joan was dying…well you know. Old friend, we will do anything for you. Can I come back and help you pack?"

"That is a nice offer, but I can do it. I have already been grieving, so maybe by the time I get to Atlanta I can rest."

"Do you want to go back into law?"

"Hell no! I would suffocate. I want more freedom than that. Sorry, I know you must love it, but it was my parent's wish, not mine. I will find something. I have all that money in the bank that ought to work for me somehow."

"Roger, you and I being the only child, our parents seemed to have given us plenty to make the rest of our lives easy as far as money and education is concerned. I know some people throw their inheritance away, but we haven't. You've told me how much you loved your parents, but I feared my dad. He was not loveable. I guess he saved his love for all those other women he screwed."

"Wow! I am truly sorry for that. Both my parents were my heroes. Do not worry about it, Randy. You have everything now."

"You can say that again and again. I am a lucky person."

"Roger, what did you mean when you said you ran into Roberta *again* in New York?"

"We met years ago in Israel when we were both very young. It is a long story, and I may share it with you, but not at this time. Joan and Roberta came out to check on them. Roberta and Joan knew what they were talking about, for Roberta had shared everything with her.

Leaving Roger and Roberta was going to be painful. Joan took Roberta by the shoulders and said, "Stand very still, and allow me to look at you. I want to remember your silky black hair and your beautiful face. Looking into your dark eyes, I am mesmerized, and to beat it all, I am angry we may never meet again. If I were an artist, you would be my perfect model. Who knows, you may have more time left than you know to tempt this guy of yours and make other men drool."

"Oh, my dear, you do have a way with words. Are you a poet?"

"Definitely not. Poetry is Randy's talent, and he's pretty good."

"He and Roger must have loved English literature, for Roger is also rather good with words. I thought law made people forget all about romance."

"Oh, we saved our thoughts of romance for one of our professors," Roger said.

"You got that! She made all the girls jealous and gave us boys a hard."

"Boys grow up to be boys, wouldn't you say, Roberta?"

"Hey, girls you mean there was no professor you coveted?"

"We are not telling," Roberta said.

Roger interrupted, "Knock, knock, who is there?"

"Who?" They answered, as one.

"The plane you are going to miss, if you do not get going."

They didn't speak on the way to the airport. With one hand they held each other, and with the other hand wiped away the tears. As they sat waiting to board, Randy said to Joan, "Let's remember the good part of this trip and cherish the sad."

CHAPTER 15
Frederick Winchester

Back in Atlanta, Randy said to Joan, "I want this move to be perfect, and we need to let go of all the troubles we left behind, and begin our lives with good thoughts, that is after you talk to Frederick. I regret having to interject that last statement. But we must take care of that situation." There was a message on the recorder that Joan's condo had sold for more than she was asking, because of a bidding war among three prospects, and she needed to sign the papers right away. The board of directors had approved the couple that submitted the highest bid.

"Randy, those days in Maine literally flew by. I wish it had been a month."

"That's because we were relaxed for the first time in years," Randy said.

"We'd better get back to work. Have you called Ms. Bee?"

"Not yet. I don't want to be fussed at. I'm sure she took care of everything:
Making a few people happy, and annoying a few."

"Oh, you love her, just admit it."

"I love only you. I tolerate Ms. Bee."

"Buying furniture is going to take time. I need to get in touch with my decorator, to see what she did to the place while we were gone."

"Good idea, go for it."

When Randy left for the office, she called Frederick. "Frederick, this is Joan. How are things going?"

"Hi, Joan, did you and Randy have a good time?"

"Of course. Remember Roger Waddell? We stayed at the inn he and his wife, Roberta own."

"Good God, Roger Waddell the rich kid we thought was poor?"

"That's almost right. When we get together, we will bring you up to date on him and our trip."

"No pictures. I hate looking at photos of someone wonderful trip."

"You don't have to worry about that, we didn't even take a camera. The only pictures we have are those made by Roger's caretaker of the four of us standing in front of their beautiful little Cottage Inn B and B."

"Okay, good. Down to business. Everything is working out. John's former secretary, Mrs. Johnson and her family have agreed to pay back most of the money she stole from your company, *if* we do not bring charges against her. I gave them two years to pay. Hope that's okay. Cassie came down and took care of the trust business. You know she is one good looking gal, just like her mom. She took it better than I would. That can turn out to be a big responsibility.

"Judy remains in the hospital, and is receiving counseling. They have allowed Bob and Julia to visit her twice. Bob's leg is doing well, but he probably needs counseling himself. He turned his cases over to his partner, and is taking some time off. He has a lot of things to deal with. But there is no doubt he doesn't love Judy, but you can tell he adores Julia. I suggested they have a blood test to make certain she is his child. Don't know how he convinced Julia to have blood drawn, I didn't ask. And guess what, Julia *is* definitely Bob's daughter."

"Frederick, that's wonderful. Was he surprised?"

"Joan, he cried like a baby. Maybe he and Judy can work things out for Julia's sake. It was decided that Julia is to be told a wealthy friend left the trust for her. Does all that sound too good?"

"Yes it does. Do I hear reservations? Joan asked."

"None of us were asked to see the results of the tests, but that is none of my business or any one else. It's better that way. I didn't ask him how he was going to tell Judy, but that is none of my business either. I am certain Judy would ask for another test. She may or may not divorce Bob, but you can bet your life, Bob will fight for Julia. I did pretty good while you partied don't you think?"

"You are a miracle worker. Maybe we can all have peace now, Joan said."

"Just a minute, I have a call waiting from Bob. After he ended the conversation he said, "Don't count on peace, Joan. Bob just informed me Judy has contacted a lawyer."

"Damn! Back to Julia, how did she and Elizabeth get along?"

"Perfect. Elizabeth could mother anybody, even me."

"You don't need a mommy, dummy. Thanks, Frederick. Send us our bill."

"I've already been paid. Mrs. Johnson came up with $3000. I kept that, and gave her a receipt. Hey, you couldn't pay me enough, while you partied in Bar Harbor."

———

Joan picked up a key and went down to see the condo. She thought her own condo was large, but this one was definitely bigger. She liked it. Some men were working in the kitchen area updating the appliances, and they were about through.

One of them said, "You can move in tomorrow. We'll be all through here in less than an hour. It's a beautiful location. Look out that window at the view."

Her new condo faced the opposite direction, and the view surprised her. Below was a lovely park she had not noticed when walking, and there were so many trees it was hard to see the streets *or* the houses. "You are right," she said to the men. "The view is lovely and private."

"Bet you're paying for it," one of them said.

She gave him a silly answer, "Inherited the money; have to spend it somewhere."

"Lucky lady."

She had already tagged the furniture she wanted moved, so had Randy. Red tags go to the new condo, green left for the kids. The decorator, Margaret Tillman said, "Leave everything to me. Just tell me how much money you want to spend on the new items. I'll call a mover to pick up the red-tagged pieces, and fill in with the new stuff. I called the new owners of your condo and see if they want to buy any of your pieces. They will be up tonight. Later I will call a realtor to look at Randy's house. It should sell fast being in that neighborhood. Am I Done for now?"

"You've left me quite breathless, but done! Sounds like you spent a lot of time, but I still have a lot to do. The kids will be here this weekend with a truck."

"I'm looking forward to meeting them."

"I bet you are. If Cassie moves to Atlanta, you'll have to create your magic for her home.

The weekend came fast. Joan and Randy were anxious to see the kids again.

Randy had always wondered how it would feel to be a father, and he was about the find out. They were going to be his family now.

He found Cassie and Rick intelligent and interesting. He and Joan took them out for a fish dinner, and he couldn't remember when they had laughed so much. Joan thanked Cassie for taking the responsibility of the trust.

Cassie said, "Mom, I guess it means I am all grown up now and doing big time stuff. I would like to get to know Julia better."

"I think we can do that, but let it lie for now. I'll tell you more about it later."

The night was perfect with all four of them on the floor, shoes off, and propped on one arm. Joan explained that blood tests showed that Julia is actually Bob's daughter. "No one has seen the test records, but we'll leave it at that. If Judy has anything to do with it, the money might be a family challenge when Julia turns twenty. Cassie, you and Bob can work that out."

Randy said, "Tomorrow is moving day for the two of you. I hope your truck is large enough. Want to take a look at the condo?" Going down the elevator Randy said, "Each of you will have a room and a bath, but it's not like you're going to move in with us; they are for your *visits*."

Entering the front room, Randy was the most excited. "Isn't this the greatest place? Everything is so handy. I'm not even sorry to move from my house to get into this. Good job, Joan. Sorry to say there'll be no babies to roam around, but I got a bargain, two grown babies: a lawyer, and an artist. So I am a happy daddy. Not everybody is this lucky - no diapers or night duty."

"Cassie said, "Oh Randy we are so happy to have you in our family. We will finally have a true family, where the father loves his kids. You think we could call you Dad?"

"If it is all right with your mom, I'm for it."

"Let it begin," said Joan.

Randy took Rick home with him, because the men he hired would start loading early in the morning. Both of them were so tired they didn't talk much during the drive. When they entered the door, Randy said, "Oh hell, I'm spending the last night in what was an old bachelor's house. Shall we go to the bar and toast the occasion."

"By all means," Rick said.

"Rick, did you visit Pearl?"

"Yes I did. What a woman! What an artist! She put me in my place right away. She took me by the arm, looked right into my face and said, 'Now Listen to me. Forget whatever you planned. I have big plans for you.' "

"I understand she has always been a take charge person. Are you going to listen to her?"

"Well, it appears she likes me and my work. Yes, I'm going to listen to her. I will allow myself to be clay in her hands."

"Good for you, Rick. I can't wait to see what you do."

The next morning was work, but fun. The moving crew couldn't understand all the singing and laughing. Randy's house was beginning to lose its flavor, if it ever had any, but it wasn't empty yet. He still had to take some things to their new condo. There were a few things he had not thought about, like towels sheets, and dishes. He said to Rick, "Take whatever you want of all that. Some of them even have an **R** on them. You can have the **W** towels too, if you want them."

"I'm poor, I'll take anything you give me," Rick said.

"Don't forget, I did your father's will, so don't try to pull your poor talk on me. Did we find the items Cassie wanted?"

"You mean all four of them."

"Don't get sassy now. I don't think she liked my stuff."

It was much easier at Joan's condo. They loaded the furniture on the freight elevator and crammed it into the truck. Cassie and Rick sat in the truck looking like they had just robbed a bank.

Rick said, "Neither of you have much left. Mom your condo looks poorer than Dad's house."

There was a long silence, 'till all four of them burst out laughing. Randy patted Rick on the back, gave him a big hug, and said, "Thank you, son."

Pulling away Cassie yelled, "Goodbye you lovers. Goodbye Mom and Dad."

"Wow! That was nice. I'm going to love being a dad."

"You lucky duck, quit bragging. Being a dad is hard work."

"I'm up to the challenge. What can I buy them for Christmas."

"Already? After all that loading, I don't think they will need much."

"Yep, but they didn't get my red recliner. I won that battle."

They went back up to the condo, fixed some popcorn, filled their glasses with Pinot Noir, and sat on the floor enjoying every quiet minute. Then the doorbell broke the spell. Randy went to answer it, and there stood Margaret.

Randy said, "Go away; we're having a love-in party."

"So? I'm inviting myself. I have some pictures to show you. I've been busy. You are going to owe me a *lot* of money, and I am going to enjoy taking every bit of it."

"Sit down and have some popcorn, and forget business talk for a while," Joan said. "We have changed the world, so don't spoil it. Randy just inherited two children, and we lost some of our possessions."

Randy said, "Margaret, do you see me smiling? Just wait till the grandchildren come. I'm going to spoil every one of them."

"Margaret, when will you finish?" Joan asked.

"For everything? Give me a month. I found a chair that needs recovering, and had to order a few things. Can I eat popcorn out of your bowl?"

"Sure, why not," they both said.

"Margaret, are you a caterer?" Randy asked.

"No, but I can get one."

"Good. When all this is ready I'm planning a party to celebrate being with the woman I have loved for many years."

"Here's to both of you," She said lifting her glass. You two are the luckiest people in the world, or at least in Atlanta. Well, in this room. Maybe I'll find a dashing hero sometime. Oh, that was a downer. I'm sorry. Congratulations to both of you."

"I'm hearing you, Margaret. I waited many years for this woman sitting here between us. I'll whip anyone who comes between us."

"Ah, romance. Isn't it wonderful." she said.

"Just wait, Margaret, you'll find someone, but I really didn't know you were looking," Joan said.

"I've had plenty of offers, but they were all married."

"Jesus, Margaret I don't like hearing that," Randy said.

"Jesus has nothing to do with it. There just aren't a lot of single men out there. Let's change the subject. Here's to your everlasting happiness."

CHAPTER 16

Professor David McKinney

The month flew past. Randy got his work done at the office under the critical eyes of Ms. Bee. She even ordered out for lunch to keep him busy. Five appointments were scheduled with him for the day, and he had to return a call to Bob Barnett. One of the appointments would be creating a will for a local college professor, Dr. David McKinney, who was sitting in the reception room. Ms. Bee brought him into the office. He could have popped out of a fashion catalogue for men: Tall and handsome, distinguished thick white hair and a slight British accent. He told Randy he had lived in England for several years when he was a young man. He was having trouble walking, even thought he was using a cane, and he could hardly stand straight. Ms. Bee helped place him in the chair. After light conversation they began their business.

"Let's talk about the money, Professor McKinney. Do you have a financial advisor?" Randy asked.

"No. I do not know any Financial Advisors. I have not been this route before. I always managed my own accounts."

"Are you presently working?"

"I am a recently retired college professor."

"Do you have a wife, children, siblings?

"No wife; Divorced years ago by mutual agreement. No children. One sibling."

"Do you want to include your sibling in the will?"

"No, I want to leave some of my assets to her child, Julia."

"Judy Barnett's child?"

"Yes. You know her?"

"Bob is a good friend of mine. Have you talked to him lately?

"No, but when I die, Judy might try to get into my assets, and I do not want that to happen."

"Are you ill?"

"Yes. I am one of the unlucky men to have breast cancer, and it has spread. I waited too long to have an examination. As intelligent as I am, I did not realize men could have breast cancer. I am leaving the house, furniture, and my car to The Reverend Sarah Marshall, a cousin of mine, who is an associate pastor of a Presbyterian church here in town, but I am not a member of her congregation or any congregation. Sarah and I live near each other, but at present she is renting a space in one of the Church member's homes. She has assisted me with buying groceries, transportation to the doctor, and comes at night when I am too sick to rise. Since I have no one else, she has been with me through many dark times. It does not matter to her that I am gay. She is like an angel and seems to know when I need support. She drove me here today. Presently, she is sitting in your waiting room. It will require money to maintain my house, but Sarah will have the right to sell it should she desire. And because of her, I would like to designate a gift to her church."

"Do you know the amount of your liquid assets?"

"At this time, well over a million, not counting the house, furniture, art and present bank account."

"Let's go back over this: What you want to do with the house, etc."

"The house, all its contents, and the automobile will be Sarah's, plus $200,000. I wish to designate to her Church, $200,000 and to Julia Barnett $100,000 plus the interest. At what age do you suggest for Julia?"

"Anywhere in the twenties, would be fine. I would suggest twenty-two."

"All the royalties from my books will go to the university, even the one that is unfinished. I have asked the President of the college to find a proper ending and have it published."

"Can you be back here in the morning with a list of your assets?"

"Here is that list and other information, in case I do return tomorrow. Inside is a letter you and I will sign now, saying I have retained you as my lawyer to do as I have requested."

After they signed the papers Randy said, "Take care until 9:00 in the morning."

"Yes sir. Thank you for taking care of my business."

"Whoa, can I meet your cousin, Reverend Marshall?"

"Certainly, call her in."

"Ms. Bee, please ask Reverend Marshall to come to my office."

"Sarah, this is my lawyer, Mr. Randy Walker."

Randy said, "I wanted to meet this cousin, The Reverent Sarah Marshall, who has been so kind to Professor David McKinney. I understand you are the person who encouraged him to settle the appointments for his estate."

"He is a brilliant man, but he is stubborn."

"Well, I will see both of you in the morning at 9:00."

"If I have to pull him out of bed, he will be here."

After they left Randy said to Ms. Bee, "There is something tragic about being an estate lawyer: There is joy, but there is also sadness. He brought both into my office. What a nice person."

"I'd take him home with me anytime," She said.

"Make copies of all of these papers, and don't drool over them. This is going to be a sad one."

"I never drool, Mr. Randolph. I may be nosy, but I am not a drooler."

"I'm sorry if I offended you."

"No you're not. Remember you need me."

"Yes ma'am, I do."

———

Joan was waiting at home with a to-do list, which made it good for him to put his mind elsewhere.

They went down to the condo to see Margaret and her results. Everything was coming together smoothly. Margaret was a whiz at her job, but she was not happy about combining his furniture.

He said, "Do what you have to do, but don't get rid of my red chair."

"Is there money hidden in it?" Margaret said.

"If you find any you can have it."

Joan and Randy realized they were exhausted, so they retired early. When they arose in the morning both felt revitalized. Randy said, "It's hard to believe I went to bed so tired that I didn't even pretend that I wanted to make love to you. I never thought that day would come. The work yesterday was exhausting, and part of it was sad. I can't get my mind straight this morning thinking about it."

"Can we both agree there are many ways to be intimate? Intimacy is what we share everyday, and it doesn't have to be sex. When the time is right maybe you can tell me why you are so sad."

"I will do that later.

———

At nine, the next morning, Rev. Marshall brought David McKinney back to Randy's office to finish his paper work. He was so weak she had trouble getting him out of the car and into the office, and he looked worse than the day before. It took over an hour to finish their work and to get the papers signed. By that time he was exhausted. He handed Randy a list of his stocks, money in the bank, the key to his safety deposit box, the deed to his house, and other papers necessary for the transfers.

As David was leaving he said, "Sarah will have me cremated. I have asked her to prepare a farewell party at my home, now her home. I would appreciate it if you will come and bring whomever you wish. You might even ask Ms. Birkenstein to be there. I do not feel well at this moment. Goodbye Mr. Walker, I am glad to get this over with. I feel my requests are in good hands."

As they were leaving, David said to Ms. Birkenstein, "I hope you will attend my party in a few days. Mr. Walker will let you know."

"Why sure, Mr. McKinney, I would be happy to."

The next morning when Randy arrived at his office Ms. Bee said, "You received a call from Rev. Sarah Marshall. The news is not good. Is that party for Mr. McKinney's *passing*?"

"Yes, it is." He called Sarah to get the particulars.

"David died last night, and I called the funeral home to pick him up. He gave me the money to make the arrangements for his cremation. May I call you later?"

"Definitely, we need to have that party. Call as soon as you can."

———

Four day later there was a gathering in David's home. Sarah had called the people on the short list David gave her. Randy and Ms. Bee were also there. The house was exquisite, exhibiting items he had collected from all over the world, and there were books and more books on the shelves. Sarah said, "He read all of these and many others that he gave away to students."

After Sarah recited a few passages from Scripture, she told stories about how David had influenced many people during his life, especially students. Then she read a poem he wrote especially for the occasion:

MY EULOGY, by David McKinney
We have no decisions of our birth
Nor can we choose our final hour.
Fate puts us in a mother's womb
And lets us grow- weed or flower.
"Go," said my mother, when I was young,
"Discover life's meaning:
Your gifts, whether heart or hands,
So these words might oft be heard,
Your life had meaning because you were."

After a long pause, close to a meditation, three of David's students spoke about how important he was to their peers. Michael, the first student said, "I learned more about the meaning of life from Dr. McKinney than I learned from any books. He was brilliant and exciting. He taught philosophy the way he lived it, and encouraged us to think and make good decisions. He didn't make appointments for students, yet he was always available."

Clark, the other male student, said, "I have all three of his books. He was not like a father to his students; he was sort of a guru. You could drop by his office or home any time for discussions, and he always had a pot of tea ready. He said to me, 'You can share a lot over a cup of tea,' and we did."

JoAnn, the female student, said, "Michael and Clark have given many compliments about Professor McKinney. I can add a few thoughts. He was the same with female students as he was with male students. I enjoyed conversing with him because he was open to new concepts. If you had an idea, he was the one person on campus who would listen as you tried to figure it out."

Last to speak was the President of the college, Dr. Robert Wells. "Professor McKinney was responsible for many students enrolling at our college. His invitation to speak at schools and functions helped put our small institution on the map in many ways. He encouraged students to think and not believe everything they read or were told. He discouraged them from finding all their answers in books. 'Use the world' he used to say. He also listened to members of the faculty and learned from them. I was proud to be his associate."

They drank the bottles of champagne he saved for the occasion, and shared other stories. It was a splendid party.

Three weeks later Randy called a meeting of the principles to start the process of the will. Present were Rev. Sarah Marshall, Bob Barnett, Rev. Leonard Childs, and Dr. Robert Wells. Randy gave out copies of the grants Dr. David McKinney had bequeathed: There words were at the top of the first page: *My estate is limited and I have no splendid words to stir one's imagination. There is no way I am able to carry out the many wishes I had hoped.*

To The Rev. Sarah Marshall: my home, the furniture, car, $200,000, the contents of my bank accounts and deposit box, and any fees she is required to pay.

To The Southside Presbyterian Church: $200,000, to use as they wish.

To Julia Barnett, my niece: $100,000, with accumulated interest, at age 22.

To Attorney, Randy Walker: $4,000, for his legal advice and assistance.

To the college, that has been gracious to me for years, the royalties of my books and the remainder of my estate to be endowed to the college, for students in the studies of Philosophy and/or Ethics.

Randy asked for comments. There was a long silence. With tears rolling down her checks, Rev. Marshall spoke first, "I am truly unable to express how I feel, but I am beyond grateful for his gifts."

Bob Barnett said, "I express thanks for my daughter, and please inform Cassie Randolph, her executor."

Rev. Leonard Childs said, "Our members will be most grateful by his special gift. Sarah, your deeds went far beyond what anyone would do in this situation, and because of your compassion, much good can be accomplish."

Dr. Wells accepted the royalties from the books and the other grant, and said, "I will instruct the trustees to name a scholarship for professor McKinney."

Randy spoke, "David's will is clear and legal. Sarah, here is the deed to your property, and the car is signed over to you. If you wish you may go ahead and move into the house. After the will goes though probate the stock can be sold, and everyone will receive the designated allowance. Sarah, David put your name on his checking account. Here is the letter detailing that. You may use what is in the account. The bank has been given the notice. It is a simple will, and I'm sure all of you are worthy. Bob can you stay afterward?"

After a few pleasantries everyone left, except Bob. He said to Randy, "Looks like my little girl is going to have to hire a broker one day."

"Bob, I got a phone call from you yesterday. How are things going?"

"Could be better. Judy has obtained a lawyer and is suing for divorce and custody of Julia. That is not going to happen! In the state of Georgia, Julia is old enough to choose the parent she wants to live with. Right now she is afraid of Judy. Frederick said he would help me out, so we will have to wait and see. Judy will not be told about this event today, it will only make her angry. I believe she had no idea David lived in town. As far as I know they had not seen or contacted each other for years. She will eventually be told that Julia is my child, not John's, as she believes."

Randy said, "Bob, do what is best for your and Julia's welfare."

Sunday morning, Randy said to Joan, "Let's go to church this morning to hear our old friend, Leonard preach, and I'd like you to meet someone."

"That is not a reason for me to go to church," Joan said.

"It's the only reason I have right now," he said.

"Sure, I would be glad to go. I was raised in the Presbyterian Church."

"You never told me that!"

"You never asked."

"Good Lord, I'm married to a Calvinist and not aware of it."

"That's not so bad, you know."

The church was packed. They were a little embarrassed when an usher led them to the second pew up front, where few people rarely sit. The sanctuary was rather ornate with lots of stained glass depicting biblical stories, which gave the reason for its being. They settled down to listen to the organist play the prelude on the pipe organ. Rev. Sarah Marshall opened with a prayer. Afterward, she gave a short meaning of the celebration of Advent and assisted a family of four with the lighting of the Advent candle.

Randy whispered, "I don't think I've ever seen this ceremony before."

"Hush. Don't admit your ignorance; just watch and listen."

Sarah was the liturgist of the day. She gave the announcements, smiled at Randy and Joan, and welcomed everyone. Her voice was magical and commanding.

"She would make a good lawyer," Randy whispered.

"You realize that may be sacrilegious," and grinned at him.

Leonard rose to the pulpit, "This sermon's title is The Last Days of Our lives." Without looking up at the congregation, as if he were re-arranging his notes on the pulpit, he said, "I learned a lot this week from a man I had never met or even heard of. From him, I was reminded that the day we are born we begin a journey, and one day we will die. Yes, death is the reality of being human." Then he faced his people. "Birth and death are so important that we celebrate those events by christening our babies and by having a fine proclamation given at the time of our death. But! It is most important how we live all those *other* days in *between* birth and death. Of course we live forever in the mind of God, but we can also live in the mind of others, after we die, by what we have accomplished with our love, gifts, works, hospitality, and our generosity.

"A man, not many of us knew, left our church a large sum of money this past week because of the love and care of *one* person. Just one! During his short career he changed the lives of many college students and friends by teaching them more than the fundamentals of education. He taught them how to apply their lives - living within the realm of their careers and relationships." (Pause) "You know? Many of us read the Bible and worry about the end times on earth. We say to ourselves, 'we had better be ready the Lord might come at any time.' My friends, that is not what living is about. That is not the life the Lord wants us to have – spending our time worrying about the end, or the Second Coming, for who knows when or where that will happen? Who knows if it will be soon or whether it is eons away? We are in the midst of those centuries behind us, and the centuries before us. We are *here*! We cannot change what went before us. We are here at this time in history, to change *our* times, to choose to give *our* best, to help others, and to *share* what we have been given – our lives, our talents, our love, and our inheritance." He abruptly closed his notes, turned and sat on his velvet chair. It was a short sermon, but powerful. It did not promise answers but gave possibilities. His brief words surprised Rev. Marshall, but she came forward and announced the last hymn. After the hymn she announced, "To all of you who are visitors, you will receive a formal letter describing our congregation and its work, and you are invited to have lunch with us today in the Fellowship Hall. The Ushers will show visitors the way. Two of Rev. Child's college friends, Randy and Joan Walker are visiting with us today. Recently Rev. Childs had the privilege of binding them in marriage. I'm sure they will be staying for lunch, so you will get to meet them."

Randy and Joan, like many others, stayed seated to listen to the postlude. Prior to the service she had noticed in the bulletin the Postlude was Bach's Fugue in G Minor. It was magnificent. It was a true celebration of a day well spent. When she complimented the organist on his choice of music, he said, "I am happy you noticed. Sometimes I feel the postlude is the least noticed part of the worship. I just try to give the people a lively going away gift." Randy had tried to beg off from lunch, but Leonard said to him, "You owe me."

"Okay, okay, we'll stay. Is that all right with you, Joan?"

"Sure why not, we were going to have peanut butter sandwiches. Why does Randy owe you?"

Randy and Leonard almost answered in union, "It's a long and boring story, and one we shall never mention to anyone."

While they were eating, several of Randy's clients came by to welcome them. Randy stood up straight when Mr. Ben Sparkman came by, "Well Randy, I've been thinking about you. Glad to have you here today. It wouldn't hurt you to come more often."

"How do you know what I do on Sundays, Ben Sparkman?"

"Probably sleep late with that beautiful wife. I would."

"Leonard has been our friend a long time, Ben," Randy said. "We spent many hours studying together in college and of course fighting. I thought he was going to be a lawyer, but I guess he got a higher calling."

"You can believe that. If he got you here, he's even better than I thought. Well, you're doing what you are called to do and doing it well. I am proud of you."

"That is a nice compliment, Ben. Thanks. Have you met Joan?"

"Yes I have. My Dear, when we met, you were sitting beside a man I despised. You are still very beautiful. I wish the best of everything for both of you, and I hope you are having the time of your lives. I miss Mary. My only regret is that we had done more things together and put business second." When he walked away, Randy said to Joan, "There goes a great man. Both he and his wife have been my clients for years. She was a realtor. Their realtor/lawyer marriage made a good combination. He keeps this church going. Leonard knows it, and so do I."

"If he is happy doing that, I think it's wonderful," Joan said.

After lunch Leonard invited them to sit in his office a while so they could talk. Leonard started, "You remember Bettye, don't you Randy."

"Of course, I remember. Leonard, have you even dated since she died?"

"Nope. Even God had to know Bettye was beautiful. Remember? She wanted me to be a lawyer, and was disappointed when I went to Seminary, but she sort of got used to living on bread and water. She loved her job at the capitol, so that money helped."

"Leonard, there is someone out there, maybe not like Bettye, but you could learn to love someone else."

"I have seen a few possibilities, but I cannot date members of my church."

"Leonard," Joan said, "I have the perfect person for you. Would you be willing to go on a blind date?"

"If she has your recommendation, Joan I would risk it."

"I'll make a call. What nights this week will work for you?"

"Are we getting that particular? Tuesdays or Thursdays."

She picked up the phone on his desk, "Margaret, are you busy this Tuesday or Thursday? I have someone I want you to meet."

"Not again, Joan."

"Yes, again. This time is different."

"Okay, Tuesday night is good."

"Is Tuesday night at 8:00 a good time, Leonard?"

He nodded and said, "Joan, you work fast."

"It's a no-tie evening, and dress is casual."

"Let him know how to get there, Randy."

When they left Randy said, "You're good, you know. Perfect. Tuesday can't get here fast enough. Margaret might put some zip into Leonard."

CHAPTER 17
Roger

Ms. Bee buzzed Randy's office, "You have an urgent call, a Mr. Roger Waddell."

"Roger, how are you?"

"Short and simple. Roberta died two weeks after you left. It was a peaceful death for her, but torture for me. She never complained of dying, only that she regretted we did not have enough time together. Your visit was a good diversion for both of us. It perked us up for awhile. I packed up some clothes and a few of her things, shook hands with the new owners of the inn, and left. They were so excited about getting started; it almost made me sick. I have been traveling around doing nothing, just roaming, getting away from any place that reminded me of Roberta. She was so lovely, and I loved her so much, but enough of that. At present I am in Memphis, staying where those ducks walk out of the elevator into the lobby. It's weird. They treat those ducks better than most people are treated. I am hoping to be in Atlanta in a week or so. Can you put me up for a short time? And by the way I need a job."

"The answer to the first question is yes, I can put you up for as long as you need. And second, you need job? Did you spend all your money? And what kind of job?"

"No, I have hardly touched my money, and I need a job that lets me work with my hands, and where nobody knows or cares how much money I have. I would like it to be temporary, maybe two or three months. Will you look around?"

"Yes, and I'll put Joan on it. Can you climb a telephone pole or lay asphalt?"

"Oh sure. No kidding, I need a job that helps me get rid of some of my frustration. Just have some options for me. Got it?"

"Got it, buddy. Looking forward to seeing you. When you get in town call and I'll give you directions."

That evening Randy said to Joan, "Guess who called me today?"

"The governor, wanting you to write his will."

"Not even close," Randy said, shaking his head. "Roger."

"Roger? Oh no, that means Roberta died. Oh, Randy she was so perfect. I will never forget her."

"Neither will Roger. He'll be here in a week or so. He wants me to help him find a job, something that makes him work hard. Some menial job, just to find peace."

"Why don't you ask Leonard or Margaret this evening? They ought to know something. Maybe she could use him to hang curtains."

"Or Leonard might be in touch with someone who lays hardwood floors or carpet," Randy said.

Leonard and Margaret

"Leonard arrived first, and insisted on looking around the condo. While Joan had him occupied, Margaret walked in unannounced. She still had a key.

She whispered to Randy, "Where is this new nerd she has set me up with this time. Cross your finger that I don't retreat."

"No nerd this time, Margaret. Leonard Childs was a college buddy of ours, and his wife died ten years ago, so she's not around to dump on you."

Joan and Leonard entered the room and greeted Margaret. "Leonard, this is the person I told you about, meet Margaret Tillman."

They shook hands. "My, you *are* dapper, where did they find you?" she asked.

"Be nice Margaret, I told him all about you a few minutes ago."

Leonard said, "Margaret, glad to meet you. I am a little bit rusty around women, so if I ask you the wrong questions just ignore me."

"I could never ignore you. So you know these two?"

"Only for years and years."

Joan interrupted, "Who wants wine? Three hands; three coming up."

"Leonard," Margaret said, "How do you like their condo. I mean how do you like the way it's decorated?"

"It's very nice. I like it."

"You are looking at my talents. I did the decorating. Now, how do you like it?"

"Margaret, it's beautiful. You are a very talented person. If you saw my house, you would have to carry most of my things to Good Will."

"She said to Joan, "And he has a sense of humor."

"Changing the subject, Margaret, have you been to church lately?" Joan asked.

"Why are you getting so personal, Joan?"

"Just answer me. Have you been to church lately?"

"Well, I went to the Methodist church two weeks ago for my little niece's Christening, and I went to your wedding several weeks ago. And I was baptized a Methodist. Oh my Lord, you were the preacher who married these two."

"You are correct," Leonard said.

"You were good. I'm so glad to meet you. Is this some kind of joke the two of you are pulling off?"

"No," Randy said, "Joan thought you and Leonard should get acquainted."

"And I am pleased," Leonard said.

"Are you now?" Margaret asked.

"Get over the pastor thing and let's have fun tonight," Leonard said.

The two of them went over to a couch and talked while Randy helped Joan set the dinner table. It was the first dinner Joan had actually cooked in quite a while. Randy came out of the kitchen and announced, "Dinner is served."

Joan turned on soft music, and everyone seemed to have a lot to talk about.

"This is great, Joan," Margaret and Leonard said at the same time, and they laughed.

"Thanks to you both. It was nothing: frozen casserole from the Fresh Market, bakery rolls, and fruit salad from the grocery store. Oh yes, dessert ordered."

"You don't have to tell all your secrets, Joan," Randy said.

"My kind of cook," Leonard said.

"You can't have her, she's mine." Randy said.

"Hey, I don't belong to anyone, right Margaret?" Joan asked.

"Women don't belong; they choose," said Margaret.

"How right you are Margaret. I like a woman who knows that," Leonard said.

"We are going to get along just fine," she said.

While Joan and Margaret were talking, Randy took Leonard aside and said to him, "You and I have an old friend whose wife died a few weeks ago. He will be here in a few days and he needs a job. Do you know of anything available?"

"Who is this old friend?"

"Roger Waddell."

"Did you actually say Roger? *The* Roger Waddell? The guy I punched? Randy, I don't know of any jobs for Roger."

"Leonard, Roger is still grieving! His beautiful wife, Roberta just died. He wants a menial job for a short time, one that will make him work hard, a job with long hours so he doesn't have to think. He owned the Cottage Inn Bed and Breakfast in Bar Harbor, Maine for several years and recently sold it. He told me he wants to work with his hands. I suppose it's to keep his mind from remembering. Since Roberta died he wandered all over the east coast trying to decide what to do with his life."

"Well, we could use an extra hand to help our Sexton. He's getting old and is about to retire. Would that be good? Maybe he could work until we hire a new Sexton. Goodness, Randy I'm embarrassed. From what I remember, Roger could own me."

"I believe a sexton's job will be perfect. It would give him a chance to clear his mind by cleaning up after people. You should have seen his place in Maine. He kept it up like the Ritz Carlton Hotel. I'll call you when he comes in. Don't blow his cover. OK?"

"Got you."

It could be said about that evening, "A good time was had by all." Leonard and Margaret found each other, and Joan and Randy found a lost soul a job.

CHAPTER 18
Roger Waddell

After a week, Randy said to Ms. Bee, "An old college friend, Roger Waddell will be coming in today. Let me know when he appears, and don't look alarmed when you see him. He's been through some tough times. Be nice to him."

"Have I ever been ugly to anyone?"

"I won't answer that question."

In about an hour, Ms. Bee went to Randy's office, "Your friend has arrived, and for your information we got along just fine," she whispered to him.

Roger was in an awful condition. He was bone thin, dressed worse than a hobo, and had grown a beard sprinkled with gray hairs. He came with very little luggage, having given away most of his clothes to street people. He even signed his car over to one of the men at the hotel and bought himself an old Ford. If he wanted to appear homeless, he certainly did.

"Roger, what have you done to yourself? Where is that Innkeeper Dude I once knew? Come on in. A handshake won't do; give me a hug. Would you like a cup of coffee or tea?"

"I am exhausted. A bed would be better, but for now coffee would be fine."

"Ms. Bee, please bring two cups of coffee, black. Roger, tell me where you've been and what you saw." She brought the coffee, "You didn't have to order two cups; I can count."

"Pay no attention to her, Roger. She corrects me all the time."

"The time on the road helped me realize that I am now solo. I went to some of the places my parents took me – from Vermont down to New York - where I stayed in a small hotel where I met with my father's lawyer and his broker. I discovered my parents where part owners of the hotel – a surprise. I saw two plays and hung out with some guy who worked at the hotel who felt sorry for me. He even took me to his place so his wife could feed me. Then Washington

D.C., Virginia, crossed over to Kentucky, and back to Nashville to see an old friend of my parent's. There was more, but here I am in Atlanta. I am not certain I have traveled enough, but I am weary. By the way this body is not as dirty as it appears. Thanks for agreeing to let me sleep over for awhile."

"Joan is excited about seeing you, and I have a possibility for a job. Do you remember Leonard Childs?"

Roger said, "The most promising guy who started off in law and walked away to enter the seminary, and the one who threatened to kill me?"

"The same guy. He said almost the same thing about you, 'You mean the guy who had everything, and walked away from law.' I told him about Roberta's death and that you need a job. With some reservation he has agreed to help. He says he can understand where you are. He lost Bettye several years ago. Of course, you do remember Bettye (Roger wearily nodded). Leonard had his first date this week. Joan set him up with a friend of hers who is an interior decorator, and I believe he is under her spell right now. Leonard is the pastor of a fairly large congregation here in town, and has a need for an assistant sexton, or perhaps created the need. According to Leonard their sexton is getting too old for heavy work and will be retiring soon. They need a temporary person until they can find an experienced sexton. He said it seemed impossible you would be working for his church, but he is going to set it up if you want the job."

"Sounds perfect, but I need a few days to make myself acceptable."

"You look like a bear. You might ought to get rid of the beard."

"Sure, why not."

"Ms. Bee, I'm taking Roger home with me. You've got it by yourself this afternoon; be nice to the clients." Randy was almost certain she gave him a rude sign.

When Randy and Roger got to the condo, he greeted Joan with a long hug, "It seems like yesterday when you and Randy came up. I love you both, but right now show me the bed." He slept for a day and a half. When he finally awakened he had no idea what day it was, the time of day, and barely remembered where he was. He heard someone rattling dishes, followed the sound, and ran into Joan. "Good to see you awake. I was about to knock on your door to see if you were alive. What can I get for you?"

"What day is it, or what time is it?"

"It's Friday, and almost 1:00 in the afternoon. You must be hungry."

"I will eat anything you have and maybe all of it."

He ate, had a shower, shaved, and didn't recognize himself in the mirror.

Where did I get all these wrinkles, he thought to himself. It felt good to be clean. Randy left a robe for him and a note: *Roger, when you wake up, you and I are going to the Mall to buy you some clothes. If you don't have any cash on you, I'll bankroll you for a while.*

He was ready to go when Randy got home. They found just what he needed at the mall. When Randy took out his credit card, Roger said, "Thanks for the offer, but I have plenty of money in my pocket." He produced a roll of bills, asked the clerk to dump his old clothes in the trash, and wore one of the outfits out of the store.

"I am uncertain about what a sexton wears," Roger said, "It might be some sort of uniform. If so, where can I get that sort of thing."

"I know a place."

Saturday afternoon, since no staff was in the office, Randy and Roger met with Leonard. "This looks like a college reunion," Leonard said. "It's been a long time, Roger. I had to laugh when Randy told me you wanted to work with your hands. I met with the property committee yesterday, gave them my request, and they approved it. Let me show you around. You can start Monday morning."

"Thanks Leonard, but remember I am your employee."

"Got it."

As they walked through the building, Leonard gave him a lot of information: The number of members, the size of the building, the staff, and introduced him to the sexton who was tidying up for Sunday.

"James, we have hired someone to help you, so you can retire. This is Mr. Waddell."

"Good to meet you, Mr. Waddell. These old bones are getting tired. I need to leave before they fire me. I'll certainly appreciate your help."

"James knows every inch of this building, having been here longer than I have. He doesn't like to admit it, but he can't do what he used to do. You'll be assisting him until we hire someone full time. Should you want supplies your contact will be a member of the Property Committee. Occasionally Sarah and I might want set-ups for different meetings or weddings. I will introduce her to you Monday."

"Sarah?"

"Rev. Sarah Marshall, our Associate Pastor."

James said, "You'll like her; she's the sweetest person. I'd do anything for her, anything at all."

Monday morning he rose ready for the new adventure. Randy and Joan laughed at his enthusiasm. "Hope you like your job, dear. Do good work so you won't get fired," Joan said.

"Thanks a lot, Mom. You would be surprised at the work I did around the inn. I will be okay. Well, let me get the old Ford started. Pretty soon I will be looking for a place and a car. Keep your eyes open."

"There's a two-bedroom available in this building. Would you like to look at it?" Joan asked.

"Let me think about it."

The first day of work went well. James pretty much told him what needed to be done each week. He was a jolly fellow, but much too feeble for the work. They got along fine from the very first day. Truth is Roger worked while James watched, but that was okay with both of them. "There is a lot of painting to be done around here," James said, "but we have to get approval from the Property Committee, and they're awfully tight with their money."

"I like to paint. James, you get the approval and I will pick up the paint."

"Good, my old back can't stoop and bend enough to paint." Coming down the hall was a beautiful woman. "Who is that?" Roger asked.

James said, "Rev. Marshall, come meet our newest employee. This is Mr. Waddell. According to Rev. Childs, he will be with us for about two or three months to help me out, that is until the church finds a new sexton."

"I am going to miss you, James."

"Thanks Ma'am, I think it's time for me to rest and get this old back in order."

"Nice to meet you, Mr. Waddell. If there is any way I can help you let me know. Welcome aboard, even if it's only for a short time."

Roger enjoyed the parade of people who came though all morning, and the work was just what he needed. By noon he felt like he had met a hundred people, including the children in preschool. He noted that everyone loved James, and different members had been doing his work for him the last few months.

"James had surgery recently," one of the members of the Property Committee said. "He needs to hang it up, and get well again."

"I am sorry to hear that," Roger said, "I will take the load off him for a while. By the way, a lot of places around here need painting. I believe I can find paint for a reasonable price. Do you think the Property Committee will approved it?"

"I'm sure we will. I'll call one of the members tonight."

"Here is the phone number where I am staying; let me know," Roger said.

Two months went by fast. Roger spent some time with Leonard and many of the other members. He was almost sorry they had hired a new sexton, but he needed to move on. Actually the Property Committee wanted to keep him, but Leonard told them Roger had made it very clear that his job was to be temporary. There was still two weeks until the new sexton would arrive. Because James had been sick so many days, Roger had the job by himself quite often.

In the meantime he looked at the condo, Joan suggested, but it seemed too large. He asked the manager about a one bedroom, and was told there were only two and three bedrooms, and that the one he showed him was the smaller of the two. He said to Joan, "Well, even if it may be temporary it would be a nice place to stay when I need it. Can you find a decorator to furnish it for me?"

"I know just the person."

"Let the decorator know that I do not want fancy. I want simple, neat and modern. I want to see the floor under every piece of furniture, and if it has carpet, pull it up!"

"I'll call Margaret and see if she can work you in her schedule."

"Is she the Margaret Leonard talks about?"

"Yes it is. Why?"

"Every time we get to be alone, he tells me about this lady he is dating, named Margaret. He even blushes when he says her name. Blushing at his age! She must be something."

"Hands off her, she's taken."

"I am not quite ready to put hands on anyone just now. Maybe one day the urge will return."

"I'm sure it will. Just get your mind and body in good shape, for now."

Roger painted several classrooms and hallways, making the place look much better. He noticed both minister's offices could stand a little jazz. They agreed. Leonard said he wanted to ask Margaret about the colors, and if Rev. Marshall agreed, he could paint their offices. He wanted to know more about Rev. Marshall and how she came to be in the ministry, but she always seemed too busy with something or someone. Well, that was okay. Finally he scheduled a meeting with Margaret to ask her what colors were proper for a minister's office. After she chose the colors, the property committee bought the paint.

While painting Sarah's office he took note of everything in the room, trying to get an idea of who she was. She liked books - that was obvious - and there were a few ancient figurines on the shelves. He looked closely at the two pieces of art on the walls, and he recognized the signature on one of them. There was a small couch that appeared to have been recently recovered, and he admired the expensive Oriental rug on the floor. Besides being educated, he noticed that she appreciates art, the classics, and nice furniture, items for persons wealthier than ministers. For some reason he could never capture her attention long enough to have a formal conversation. Well, that would have to wait until the new sexton arrived.

CHAPTER 19
Leonard and Margaret

"Have you noticed now often Leonard laughs lately? It's unlike him." One of the members said to another.

"I know why most men laugh a lot when they are single, but I have no idea if we can pin that on Leonard."

"Well, I outright asked him last week, and he said it was because he was happier than he had been in a long time, and when the time comes he would tell me."

"That's enough to hold me in suspense."

Leonard *was* happy. Margaret made him laugh. They were having so much fun seeing places neither had bothered to notice before. She had been too busy working, and he had made a hermit of himself for so many years, except when it came to church work. He needed the answer to many questions: How do people dates these days? What happens next? Is it wrong to love again? I feel like a young man, but I know nothing about Margaret. Has she been married before? What does she like? Would she marry a minister?

Margaret also stayed in a state of confusion: I'm dating a preacher! How did I get into this situation? Am I falling in love? He is so different, but kind of a stiff. We enjoy each other's company, but all he has attempted so far is holding hands. But we laugh a lot and eat out. Are we going in the direction of a long-term relationship? How it that going to merge with his church work? Do I have to be prim and proper? Can a pastor have sex before marriage? Do I wait for him to make the first move? My God, what am I saying? That I am ready for marriage again? Even I can't believe it.

When the phone rang Margaret jumped. "Margaret would you like take a couple of days off to go to a small inn Randy told me about. It's not far from here; it's called Maud's Inn. Randy has talked to the owner, a Mr. Fowler, and he can promise us privacy. I'm nervous mentioning this, but he says there is a room upstairs that looks out over the property that is pure heaven. The owner will bring our food up to the room if he needs to, and alert us if visitors drop in."

"Whoa! Slow down. Is this a secret mission, or something like that? Maud's Inn? Isn't that a strange name for an Inn? How could I turn that down?" Margaret asked. "I'll call my new client. I believe you know him. Maybe I can put him off for a few days. I think he is working at your church."

Leonard said, "So Joan told you he's working at the church. Are you going to tell him you're putting him off for me? I can't compete with him."

"Why should I be concerned about that, and why would he compete?"

"Never mind, pack a few necessities for a couple of nights. I can't believe I just said that? Is tomorrow about noon a good time for me to pick you up? Sarah has agreed to be at the office and take calls."

All night, he was so excited he hardly slept. This was an adventure he had dreamed of for so many years. He had heard an expression too often, but now he could use it, *I feel like I'm eighteen again*. Randy and Joan understood him. They knew that Margaret would be perfect for him. The next morning Leonard called Sarah to check on things before he left. "Everything will be fine," she said. "Just have a good time and let me take care of everything. You need this time away."

Leonard and Margaret laughed all the way to Maud's Inn, even after getting lost twice. She discovered that Leonard was directionally challenged. When they finally arrived, he was nervous. He said, "Wait right here; I'll be back soon."

"I'm Leonard Childs," he said to the man behind the bar. "I believe my friend Randy Walker called ahead for me."

"Good morning, Reverend Childs. Yes, he called. I'm glad to meet you." Holding out his hand he said, "I'm Charlie Fowler. Randy said he believes you have fallen in love, and need a few days."

Leonard said, "He's a tell-it-all. Margaret and I do need this time. Don't tell her, but I believe I'm falling in love. It's complicated."

"I understand complicated. You can be assured of privacy, and a warning of incoming intruders. Here is the key. The room is in the rear. You go right up these stairs."

"We have a little luggage."

"Better than Randy, he didn't bring any. I'll help you with it."

They went outside to get Margaret and the luggage.

"Mr. Fowler, this is Margaret Tillman."

"Nice to meet any friend of Randy Walker. I hope you find the room suits your taste. Come on in."

The view was exactly as Randy had told them, and the room was decorated as if had been planned for Margaret. She had no problem with the furniture and colors. "Leonard, this is perfect. I'm glad my mind doesn't have to redecorate it."

"Margaret, what makes it perfect *is* you are in it."

For a few moments neither of them knew what to do next. It was an awkward time. He began pacing. Finally Margaret broke the silence, "Come over here, Leonard. I have something to ask you, since you seem to be quite reluctant to speak. Have you fallen in love with me? If so, that is not a bad thing, you know. I've been waiting a long time for someone - someone different, someone who will accept me as I am. You must be thinking, 'Who is she?' So I will tell you. I was married when I was very young. The experience was a *big* mistake, and it turned me off marriage. My parents shamed me for not trying harder, but they had no idea what I was going through. Mom and I were estranged for a while. To tell the truth I decided never to fall in love again. I have money saved from my decorating business, so I'm not in debt. I have worked for some of the largest companies and finest people in town."

"Margaret I am not worried about your reliability, but I appreciate your honesty. I was married ten years and had no children. Bettye was sick most of those years. I wanted children, but it was not possible. After she died I gave my self wholly to the church. This is my second church. The church gives me an allowance for housing, and I am not in debt. Now that we have given each other a little revelation where do we go from here? I realized last week that I had come to love you, but I needed some time to reflect on it. It's a big step for me. Besides, I have about forgotten how dating goes. There's been a lot of dinner dates set up for me by church members, but none of those were the person I was looking for. I wanted to find someone who was exciting and interesting, and I believe that has happened. I want to take you into my arms and kiss you, but to be honest I haven't done that in so long I might be a little clumsy."

"First of all, I'd like to know what Bettye died of?"

"She was anemic for years, but she died of heart disease."

"So it was a long drawn out death?"

"Yes, for both of us."

"Well, Leonard, this is what happens next," Margaret said. She placed herself into his arms, and he kissed her. Margaret said, "That was a little awkward, so let's try it again." She was the aggressor, and he secretly wondered how many lovers she had been with. It became obvious to Margaret that Leonard lacked experience, as least current experience. Margaret though, *"He isn't just clumsy; he hasn't had sex in a long. My God, what have I gotten myself into?"*

Lying in bed, she initiated the contact by putting his hands on her breast, and then moving them to her legs, but he withdrew. Margaret said, "This is not working, Leonard. If this is not what you want, just say so." Almost in a fit of fury he lay on top of her and entered her, and finished quickly. "Is that what you want?" he asked. She decided not to speak. "Well, he asked, "Was that not good enough?"

Finally, she said, "That was not love; that was bad sex."

"I'm sorry. Maybe that's all I can do; it's been too long. Since you have had so much experience, you might have to teach me."

"What are you insinuating, Leonard? That I've slept with every man I know?"

"Oh no Margaret, I am so sorry. I have fallen in love with you, but sex has not been a part of my life for so many years. Maybe I should go to counseling."

"You want a counselor to teach you how to have sex?"

"No, of course not. If sex is important to you, I want to know how to please you. I love your laughter, your personality, your freedom around people, but if you want sex, you will have to be patient with me."

Margaret was afraid to speak. Suddenly she felt trapped and had thoughts about calling someone to come pick her up. *This man is married to the church. He has to be chaste. It's not too late to bring this to an end.* "Leonard, I believe we should end this trip and go home. You are not ready for marriage. I am very serious." She rose and started packing.

"No, please don't do that. If sex is important, I will be there for you."

"Leonard, if I have fallen in love with a priest that is not the way I want to spend the rest of my life. Yes, sex is important, not that I have had any lately, but I long for a good sexual relationship that comes from loving someone. I mean it. If you don't feel the same then we need to call this off before we go any further."

"Margaret, teach me what you know."

"Leonard, I don't like being a teacher. You may not believe it, but I'm not qualified. Maybe you should call a therapist."

"I'm serious, Margaret, I want to please you."

She hesitated to say what needed to be said, "Leonard, I made one mistake in marriage, and I am not about the make a second one."

"I'm scared of losing you," He said. "I don't want to spend the rest of my life without someone to love. Can we start over? Please come back to bed."

"Listen to me carefully," Margaret said. "You cannot live the rest of your life as you have. You have allowed the church to sterilize you. No, don't speak. Maybe you need to find someone else. Oh hell! Leonard, lie down. Put me in your arms like this. Now hold me tight and don't talk. Allow your body to feel my closeness until you began to sweat or until silence is unbearable. Then maybe something will click in your mind, bang on your heart, and say, 'this is wonderful, and I must have all of her inside and out.' If that doesn't happen, I will call someone to pick me up." As the tears fell down her checks she said, "Leonard, hold me closer and listen to me breathe. Put your ear on my chest. Listen to my heart. Caress me and kiss my tears away." He put his arms around her, wiped her tears, kissed her, and talked to her in whispers, "quiet now, everything is going to be all right. I love you." That night shall remain a mystery, but two persons slowly allowed the strange power of love to enter their bed. He wiped away her tears and hopefully his fears.

The next morning Margaret sat up in the bed and saw him sitting in a chair watching her. "Margaret do you have any idea what you will be getting into being the wife of a pastor?"

"Must you ask that question this early. It's so unromantic? The truth is, I have no idea. Don't you think I could ask you the same question? I'm in homes and in the privacy of many different kinds of people, both men and women. So, you will still be a pastor and I will still be a decorator, and we will be married. Hopefully we will understand each other's business and not get involved. How does that sound?"

"Pretty simple. Will you come to church or stay in your own church?"

"I guess I should be where you are, if your people can accept a Methodist, but just don't *ever* ask me to teach, sing, keep the nursery, or join the church."

"Now that is settled, when would you like to undertake the next step?"

"Is that a proposal? Maybe you can be little clearer than 'undertake.'"

"Let me put it this way, Margaret Tillman I have grown to love you, will you agree to marry me, share my life and all that I have?"

"Yes, Leonard I will, but *all that I h*ave is a little dated, don't you think? Oh, forget I said that. Last night was a beginning in our relationship, but we have a lot to do, don't we? On a very practical thought, there are a lot of people to tell. Surely you will want to tell your congregation in the proper manner. I want to have a party to break the news. How exciting is that? No, I want Joan and Randy to have a party, and then we will break the news. Hand me the phone. Let's call them. "Hello," says Joan.

"Joan, this is Margaret. Are you ready to have a party?"

"I love parties. Why do you ask?"

"Leonard and I have made a decision that will change our lives. We want you and Randy to give a party, so we can announce that we are getting married, and I don't feel one bit bad asking you to do that."

"Oh my gosh! This is wonderful news. You know we will. When do you want this party to happen?"

"We have two more days here until we will be back in town. Our present goal is to get to know each other better these two days. By then we should know if we can stand each other well enough to get married. I'll call you later."

"That went well," Leonard said. "Margaret, if you don't mind I would like to skip breakfast. I am a little tired. You go ahead."

"Not on your life. Get dressed, even if you don't eat, you can sit with me." Margaret began to think that the "morning after" might be a change of plans. Perhaps he was placing too much on what others would think, or maybe he is just scared. At breakfast Margaret kept saying that everything was going to be fine, and Leonard kept echoing her. "Leonard, our lives will be different, but we do not need to face every supposed conflict this weekend." And he responded, "You are right, as usual."

"Oh hell, Leonard. Let's go back to the room, put on our walking shoes, and go out in the woods." That morning they took off their shoes and played in a little brook, which Leonard had never done, counted the difference species of birds and animals they saw, which he had never paid attention to, and relaxed. At lunch they ate too much because everything tasted better. When it was time to go back to the city they were reluctant to part. Leonard said, "Margaret, it won't be long until we will be spending at least half of every day together. We will talk tonight and start our plans. I will try not to have a big smile when I back to the office. I love you."

"Wait a minute! Is that half of every day or twelve hours of night? Do I ever get a full twenty-four hour day? Forget I asked."

That evening Leonard wrote a poem.

LOVE IS MYSTERY

To those yet to experienced the pleasure,
love is like yelling poetry to the wind.
Though writers have tried to explain it,
language falls woefully short.
At twenty, a man believes in sudden maturity:
Living in the moment of the excitement,
having no previous understanding
how two persons grow old together.
At middle age love is a magic wand,

turning back the pages of years.
How can I explain it? Is there a word?
Ah, the word *peace* comes to mind:
Peace, unclear at twenty,
A sigh of relief at fifty.
So it could be said, love is finding peace.

CHAPTER 20
Leonard

The first day back in the office Sarah brought Leonard up to date on the happenings. Our new Sexton has arrived, and Mr. Waddell agreed to stay one week to get him accustomed to the tasks he is expected to do. I believe we might still need someone a few days a week to assist him, but Mr. Waddell said he is not that person. You will need to visit the Morrison's new baby girl. Two people are in the hospital, but going home today, and that is about all."

"Sarah, I need to make a few phone calls. Can you cover for about an hour?"

"Certainly, then next week, I need some time off."

"Done."

"Mr. Billings," Leonard said on the phone, "I need to have a short meeting with you. Are you available for lunch today."

"Sure, I will pick you up at twelve." Mr. Billings was Chair of the Board of Elders, and he was a man who could be trusted. He was not wealthy, having been an accountant his entire career, but he was honest and always worked closely with Leonard. He was the first person that should be notified of his upcoming wedding. After lunch Leonard said, "Ed, I need to tell you something, which shall stay between us for a few days. I have fallen in love, and am about to get married."

"Whew! I thought you were about to tell me you were leaving the church. Now I can listen to what you have to say. In love! Is there going to be a wedding soon?"

"We have a lot to do yet, such as get a license; have an announcement party, and of course, introduce her to the congregation."

"Leonard, I am so pleased. Who is this lucky woman?"

"Margaret Tillman."

"Margaret! She had a good reputation in town. She is a highly respected woman. You could not have made a better choice, my friend. I cannot wait to tell Marsha. She is going to say a lot of men are going to be envious."

"Fine. You may tell Marsha. Randy and Joan Walker are having a party for us as soon as we get the necessary papers, and I want you and Marsha to attend. Second, the Sunday morning after the party I would like for you to tell the congregation about our decision. Is that okay with you?"

"Will Margaret be in attendance that day?"

"What do you think?"

"Let me think about that. I'll ask Marsha what she thinks, since she understands things like this."

"All right, it's done. I am counting on your support."

"You will always have it."

Back at the office Leonard called Margaret, "You know we need to get a business license. Can we go sometime tomorrow?"

"Leonard, you just said business license. It's called a Marriage License."

"Did I say that?"

"Yes, you did. After lunch, I'll call Joan and tell her we will be ready for the party soon. What night is best for you?"

"How about two Friday nights away? I have to let Roger go today so I can invite him to the party, and of course Sarah will be there. Won't she be surprised? One day I dropped in on him while he was painting her office, and he was studying her room like a surgeon. I bet he could tell you everything in that office down to the names of the authors of every book."

"That's sweet."

"Do you have any objection getting married after a Sunday Morning Service?"

"Oh my gosh, how weird is that? Is that a practice of your church?"

"No, Margaret. I just thought it would be a good idea to allow my congregation to be involved. See you tonight."

Leonard caught Roger in the hall. In sort of a whisper he said, "I believe you need to end your position here by the end of the week.

I am about to be married in two weeks, and I want to invite you to the party. Get our new sexton settled as fast as you can."

"He has been a sexton before, so he is ready. A wedding! That is great. If Sarah is going to be there you need to give her the information why I was employed here. I do not want to be the one to inform her. People hate being duped."

"I already thought about that, so I will call her in after you leave."

"You and Margaret are lucky people. I will be there. And thanks for the opportunity to unwind here. It has been most helpful for me."

Leonard called Sarah to his office and told her about his plans, and that a date would be set fairly soon. "I'm not surprised," Sarah said. "Lately you have been happier than I've ever seen you. I'll be happy to perform the ceremony." Then he asked her, "What do you think about having the ceremony after a Sunday Service?"

"What a great idea. That would allow the congregation be a part of the wedding."

Leonard said, "Sarah, I need to tell you about Roger Waddell…

Leonard called Ed Billings, "The party at the Walker's will be next Saturday night on the 15th. We plan to get married the next weekend. You can announce the wedding to the church the morning after the party. Would you ask Marsha if the women of the church would plan a lunch after the service?"

"Sure, anything else?

"I have asked Sarah if she will officiate. She liked the idea of having the wedding after the service."

"I think that is a great idea. Our people will be so excited. I doubt they have ever attended a wedding on Sunday after worship."

The time went by too fast, but everything was falling in place, except deciding where they would live. It wasn't going to be a big problem; it was simply a matter of planning. They could do that later after the honeymoon. He would like for her to decide.

Leonard and Margaret came a little early to the party. Everyone else arrived shortly. The party was in "high gear" when Sarah entered and saw Roger. She walked over to him, "So you are a long-time friend of Leonard's?"

"I am an old college buddy. So are Leonard, Joan, Randy, Fredrick and Bob who will all be here tonight. I came through town, and needed some time to get my head cleared after my wife, Roberta died. Randy contacted Leonard and asked him to work me to death to help me get past my depression. Actually, I enjoyed every minute of it especially the painting. At least I am good at that."

"You did a good job in my office. Nice to see you again."

"I needed some down time to clear my head. I did not mean to deceive anyone, but living as a laborer was what I needed to help heal my mind and body."

"Laborers don't have the vocabulary you have, nor are they invited into the pastor's office so often. I didn't know what was up. I just thought you might be having a hard time, and Leonard was helping you out. He does that sometimes."

"Actually that is exactly what he did. I worked off a lot of frustration and worry by working hard and meeting nice people. I understand some of the folks miss me."

"Why sure. You were good, and they liked hanging around with you."

"Can I tell you a story sometimes? Roger asked."

"Not tonight; maybe some other time."

Roger made his way over to Leonard and said, "I am going to need some help from you. Sarah is unhappy that she wasn't informed on our arrangement."

"I'll take care of it. I should have told her."

"Good answer, old friend."

Leonard asked the people to sit so he could say something to them, and asked Margaret to stand beside him. "This a special night for me and for Margaret. We haven't known each other very long, but something sparked when we met right here in this room, and we are so glad these two fine people introduced us. Tomorrow morning Ed will announce to the congregation that we are getting married, and the next Sunday Sarah will perform the ceremony after the morning service. I hope all of you will be there."

Mrs. Peggy Williams said, "Oh, that is so nice. Congratulations. The Women of The Church will definitely have a feast after the wedding. I suppose there will be the largest attendance ever. We've never had *anything* like this at our church."

Leonard said, "Margaret, just in case any of you are not familiar with all of these people, let me introduce you. I understand my bride to be is the best decorator in town. (They applaud.) Everyone here has met Rev. Sarah Marshall. Without her my life would be difficult. Randy and Joan are old friends. He is an attorney and she is a writer. This is Roger Waddell, another old college buddy. His wife Roberta died, and he has landed here to start again. Bob Barnett and Frederick Winchester are also old college buddies, and this is Fredrick's wife Elizabeth. Peggy and Peter Stewart and Ed and Marsha Billings are faithful members of the church."

Margaret made her introductions, "Rose and John Stern, who own a successful travel agency in town, and this is Mary Ann Vincent, who has known me since high school. She is with Trust Company Bank. That just about does it. Let's eat."

The buffet was designed to sit to eat or stand to munch on the goodies. Roger whispered to Sarah, "You have heard about me; how about you?"

"There's not much to tell."

"May I drive you home?"

"No, I brought my own car tonight."

"Are you angry?"

"I liked you better when you were a sexton."

"Wish I had known that."

"We are not allowed to fraternize with employees."

"Did I say anything about fraternizing? I am not an employee anymore. You might try to be my friend."

"We'll see. I'll have to think about it."

"I will accept that possibility."

Randy said, "This has been great evening. I think it is about time we toasted the lucky couple: Here's to Leonard and Margaret whose lives are about to change drastically. Leonard, you have no clue, do you? Joan says that it is her fault she introduced you so don't blame me. (They laugh.) Joan, you are a great person for seeing possibilities in others, and I have always loved you for understanding me."

"Here, here," They all say. Others gave their tributes with just as much candor and laughter.

Marsha Billings whispered in Margaret's ear, "I believe it would be nice if you would be present at the service tomorrow morning, and you can sit with us. I'll wait for you at the back of the church."

'Thank you; I'll think about it."

Finally Roger stood and said, "Thank you Leonard for allowing me to work off months of frustration. You were a tough employer (Leonard laughed). Thank you Margaret for decorating my condo. I know both you and Leonard will be happy wherever you work and wherever you live. Thank you, Randy and Joan for putting up with me until I found myself again. If this is a true example of Atlanta people, I might learn to like this city."

Finally when everyone was gone, Joan and Randy sat awhile. He leaned over and took her hand, and said, "We know how they are feeling about starting over, don't we?"

"Yes, but I like to think we start over every day," Joan said. "I feel safe and powerful married to you. I've never felt that way before. I have a partner, a lover, and my children have a father and best friend all in one. I hope Leonard and Margaret will have that."

"Do we need to clean up tonight?"

"Well, we'll soak the dishes until tomorrow. You have something in mind?"

"Joan, I love you so much. Let the dishes wait. I want to make love to you like it's our own wedding night."

After they undressed Randy began kissing her, and played with her like a hungry teenager starving for his first sexual experience. Finally they came together, floating in sheets that were like waves. She wondered, *will it always be this exciting, this exhilarating*?

He said to her, "We have so much time to make up. I will always love you, every breath I take I will love you. That is an oath."

CHAPTER 21
Bob Barnett

The next morning, Randy delayed going to work to help Joan clean up. The phone rang, "Hello, this is Randy Walker."

"Mr. Walker, you have an emergency. Where in the hell are you?"

"Good morning, Ms. Bee. I love you too."

"No you do not, else you would be here. I have been holding Bob Barnett's hand. Get down here!" He said, "Calm down and be nice. I'm on my way."

He kissed Joan, and rushed off as fast as he could, "What is so urgent that Bob would not call me at home?"

When he got to the office he blew Ms. Bee a kiss, and said, "I have another life, you know."

"And so do I. He's waiting in your office." She whispered, "I am not used to seeing grown men cry. It makes me nervous."

"Bob, what's up this morning?"

"I need a friend, and you are the lucky one. Judy is giving Julia and me a lot of grief, and Julia is actually afraid of her. She has threatened to kill me, or herself, unless Julia chooses to live with her. Thank goodness school is out. Currently, we are staying with my parents out in Marietta. Even my mom and dad are concerned about their own safety."

"Bob, has Judy retained a representative?"

"Yes, but she isn't listening to him. Randy, I know her. She will kill me if I give her the chance. She is vindictive."

"If my dad were alive," Randy said, "I'd say he would be your best bet, being he was the meanest SOB in town. Since e isn't, you will have to trust a lawyer to represent you. Of course you know, according to the law in Georgia, Julia is old enough to choose to live with you. I don't believe she will change her mind."

"I know that, but Judy is putting her under a lot of pressure."

"Buddy, let's go outside of friends for a lawyer. I've known Georgia Parker a long time, why didn't you contact her? She is a good lawyer. Call her this very minute and ask if she will represent you, and find out if Julia needs her own lawyer. Go into my private waiting room, and make the call, now!"

Randy stepped into Ms. Bee's office and said, "I don't have an appointment until ten. Thank you for listening to Mr. Barnett."

"I am not a social worker you know, and it has been a long time since a man cried on my shoulder. I did not like it. I am not his mother."

"You were sweet to console him. Thanks."

"As long as that doesn't happen again. The next time if I look out the door and see a crying man, I will tell him to go away."

"Come on now, didn't you feel like you were just a teeny bit helpful."

"If you were my son I would send you to your room!"

Bob came into the room and said, "Georgia Parker will see me this afternoon after five o'clock or before, if she gets through earlier. Thanks Randy. I am both scared and embarrassed. This is a hard time for me and for Julia. Every day we are living with what will happen next?"

"Tell you what, come back at about 4:15, and I will drive you there."

"That won't be necessary. I have a couple of clients scheduled so I'll need to get back to my office." He stopped by Ms. Bee's desk and said to her, "Thanks for your help, Ms. Birkenstein."

"No problem," she answered.

"I heard that," Randy yelled.

The next morning Georgia Parker called. "Randy, I saw Bob Barnett yesterday, and he has *big* problems. I need some information. I do know the two of you are long-time friends, so would you be willing to fill me in?"

"Talk about complicated! I can do that, but it will take time. We are across town from each other, do you want to meet or phone talk"

"Don't we lawyers like to see some animation or brow lifting? You know, those sort of things," Georgia said.

"Okay. It's your dollar. I'll come to your office. When is a good time?"

"Tomorrow at noon for about an hour."

"Have a sandwich ready."

"This gal is liberated. Bring your own."

That evening Randy told Joan the latest in the Barnett chapter. She had been involved from the beginning, even before the beginning, so she needed to know the current events. "Randy, is there any possibility that Julia is really John's child? After all no one has seen the blood tests but Bob."

"Do you really want to know? I don't. But Judy still thinks Julie is John's child, and John must have believed it also. Bob believes she is his child, and says he has the proof. All this mess has put Julia in a complicated position."

"Judy still believes you have withheld the money she deserves. Frankly, I am a little surprised that John didn't leave her *something* in his will."

"I have wondered about that myself."

"Poor Julia. I wish she could get out of town for awhile."

Neither of them slept well that night.

Randy met Georgia the next afternoon. They knew one another because of bar meetings and other socials, and they had respect for each other's reputation.

"Nice to see you, Georgia. It's been a long time."

"Yes it has, and I see someone finally grabbed the most popular bachelor in
Fulton County."

"I don't know about that. I married the gal I loved since college, and I waited a long time for her."

"Why did Joan marry that bastard?"

"It's a long story."

"Okay, forget Joan. Give me a synopsis of Judy's problem.

"It can't be done in an hour, so I'm prepared to use short phrases."

"That's all I need. Start in short sentences, and give me time to copy."

"Here goes."

"John and Judy were high school sweethearts.

Judy had an affair with Bob Barnett, who was also in their high school.

John and Judy broke up.

Later John got engaged to Joan to get back at Judy.

Judy pleaded with John to break his engagement, but he wouldn't.

So Judy married Bob, though she loved John.

John married Joan, though he loved Judy.

After their marriages, John and Judy returned to their love affair.

Judy had a baby girl, named Julia. John believed Julia was his child.

John even visited her in the hospital *and* when she brought Julia home.

John must have told Judy he would leave her money to take care of Julia.

Not so, he left money to Julia to receive later in her life.

Judy does not know this.

Judy goes off the wall and accidentally shoots Bob in the leg.

Judy lost John and Joan got all the money.

"That is a quick synopsis of the mess your client is in. Judy nearly killed him once, and it could happen again. Julia, their daughter is a wonderful child, smart, in a private school, beautiful, and scared as hell right now. Bob says blood tests prove he is the real father."

"Oh, I do love good stories; they make excellent court cases. But this one is a doozy. Thanks, Randy, I'll take it from here. You're still as good looking as ever. Joan is one lucky woman."

"And so am I. Goodbye, Georgia and good luck."

"Dear Randy, you know luck helps, and I'm counting on it."

CHAPTER 22

Margaret and Leonard's Wedding

The church was packed. The ushers put chairs in the aisles, careful not to break the Fulton Country fire rules. Margaret and Leonard sat on the front row. The bride and groom, friends, and church Elders sat on the second and third rows. Leonard wore an afternoon tuxedo, and Margaret wore a beige ankle-length dress, with embroidered flowers around the neck, sleeves, and hem.

Rev. Sarah Marshall preached a good sermon, using the book of Ecclesiastes. The words, "For everything there is a time," were appropriate for any occasion. Leonard had said to her, "Please don't preach on matrimony. I realize I am putting you in a bad spot, but you can get a good message over otherwise. I have seen you do that many times."

After the sermon, the people stood for the Apostles' Creed, even those who didn't know it. Rev. Marshall motioned for the people to sit, and she stepped down to the front of the pulpit. She reminded the members and guests the church discourages taking pictures during the ceremony. She motioned for Leonard and Margaret to come forward and charged them on the meaning of marriage. "Are you ready to state your vows." They said, "Yes." The vows were read and repeated by the bride and groom. Rev. Marshall read a short passage from the Bible, and asked the couple to stand before the congregation, and promise to be faithful to each other and to God who created them. It was a short but meaningful ceremony. They had planned not to kiss, so it was a shock when Sarah blessed them, then looked at Leonard and said, "You may kiss Margaret now." The congregation applauded, and the service ended. One of the older ladies was heard to say, "I was afraid I was going to swoon."

As far as Roger was concerned, the only person standing in front of the people worth watching was Rev. Sarah Marshall. She was lovely beyond words. He longed to have conversations with her, but she seemed hurt not being in on his Sexton's job. Roberta, with her Jewish background, was not as beautiful as she was exotic, but Sarah was beautiful in the way she moved, her commanding voice, her face, and her smile. She mesmerized him with her intellect, and the way she cocked her head sideways when she was listening to people. Perhaps he would have a chance to spend some time with her during the reception.

Sure enough there was a feast in the Fellowship Hall, which was covered with garlands of flowers. Three elaborate cakes sat upon the table, but there was no official cutting. Those who could get near their pastor and his new bride wished them happiness and congratulated them. Others were satisfied to eat the sandwiches and cake. A small combo of church members played music for the occasion and a few people danced, even the children. One of the older ladies of the congregation said to Randy, "As long as I remember, we never had a pastor marry in front of their congregation. I am pleased that he included us. Leonard is a good pastor and a great preacher. We love him."

Roger moved around the room pretending to nibble at the fruit on his plate. He spotted Sarah sitting on the side. There was a seat vacant beside her, so he decided to take it before someone else did.

"Hi," he said, "You did a great job with the wedding. I could not watch the bridge and groom for listening to your words. Your diction is perfect."

"Oh Roger, you don't mean that."

"Yes, I do. You gave a beautiful message. It has been a long time since I attended a religious service or a wedding. I cannot believe I actually enjoyed it."

"Roger, what do you want from me."

"I want to sit beside you at dinner and learn from you. I am not quite ready for a relationship, but I would like for us to be friends."

"You are the strangest man I have ever met."

"I do not mind being strange. I do not know you very well, but I am determined to learn about you. Why not dinner this evening?"

"After this feast?"

"Who says we have to eat?"

"Okay, when do you want to pick me up?"

"Right now."

"Now? People are still here."

"Can we disappear?"

"I need to go by my office. Here is my address, meet me there in an hour."

"Is it a fake address?"

"Of course it isn't, ministers don't lie. Well, maybe they do sometimes, but I promise, it is the correct address."

"When someone says, 'I promise,' I believe them."

"Go away. Pick me up in one hour."

It was impossible for Margaret to remember all the names of the people, but she listened to every one of them. She knew some of the people, having had business with them. She remembered Charlotte Greene's red and white bedroom and the man-cave her husband, Boyd wanted for his artwork. His wife insisted on some sophistication in the design, so when it was finished he liked it. His work is already well known in the city.

She decorated the offices of a large legal group. Two of them are members of the church. One of them George Mackey whispered to her, "I can still see your fanny as you stood on the ladder hanging our drapes."

"Did you do that?"

"I did, once upon a time. One single man in our group said he was going to marry you, but looks like someone else beat him to it."

"Who was that?"

"Wouldn't you like to know?"

"I'm still a decorator, you know, and I plan to keep my customers happy. I won't bother Leonard's business, and he won't interfere in mine."

"Good. Knowing you, I'm not surprised. I do wish you a lot of happiness, and hopefully Jennifer and I can have dinner with you and Leonard sometime. We've been trying to pair up Leonard for a long time. I guess he had to do his own chasing. Good luck, Margaret I am happy for you."

As the people began to drift away, Roger went over to Leonard and Margaret and handed them an envelope. "Open it," Roger said. "It is a gift for a week at the Cottage Bed and Breakfast in Bar Harbor,

Maine, including airfare. I called the new owners, and they will be waiting for you to confirm the date for this Wednesday." Margaret hugged him, but Leonard said, "It's too much, Roger. I cannot accept such an extravagant gift, besides I prefer to make my own plans."

"You did me a tremendous favor, so I am returning one." Margaret jerked the envelope from Leonard, and said, "I can accept it. Are you going to stay in Atlanta while I fly to Bar Harbor, Leonard? Thanks, Roger we accept your sweet gift."

Joan and Randy went home and collapsed. That evening, sitting on their balcony, sipping wine, Randy said, "I wish we could go back to Bar Harbor."

"You know, Randy sometimes a place is not always as good when you get your wish for a second try."

"Well it was a peaceful time, but it did have a painful ending. I wish we could erase that part of the story. By the way, did you notice Roger talking to Sarah?"

Joan said. "A little female companionship will do him good. I don't see it as anything much, but at least he is willing to talk to a woman."

Randy said, "When David McKinney left Sarah his home and money, I knew she must be a special person. She took care of him, but I am certain she never *ever* expected him to leave her anything."

Joan said, "Roger is a good man. I'm quite sure he can take care of himself. I need a nap; it's been a long day."

"You go ahead, I have some things I need to read, and I might take the sofa afterward. I don't believe I can eat again for a week."

On Wednesday morning Joan took Margaret and Leonard to the airport. Talk was sparse. "A week is not a long time," she said as she let them out of the car, "but you will enjoy every minute of it." Leonard said, "I suppose." Margaret said. "Stop being a stiff, Leonard"

Chapter 23

Roger, Sarah, and Charlie

Roger and Sarah were in the car for some time without speaking. What was there to say? They hardly knew each other, and the knowing was a farce, though of necessity, until Sarah spoke, "Do you know where you are going, or could you be wandering?"

"We are going to Maud's Inn, a little place recommended by Randy. It is a rustic place not far from where we are right now. I am told the owner is Charlie Fowler, a member of an old Atlanta family. I called to tell him we are coming. Randy said it is a place to walk in the woods, sit on a balcony and watch the birds, talk about something or nothing, and Mr. Fowler will prepare us a light evening meal."

"That sounds interesting."

When they arrived at the Inn Sarah said, "You are right, this looks inviting - a walk in the woods and all this. Thanks Roger."

When they stepped inside, Roger froze. He had flashes of Bar Harbor, and became nauseated. Seeing his reaction Sarah thought he was ill. "Roger, what is wrong?" she asked.

"Give me a few minutes to calm myself and a place to sit." Sarah asked the innkeeper to bring him a glass of water. "Thank you. I am sorry to be trouble, but this room brings back vivid memories." Charlie Fowler and Sarah stood aside and waited for him to relax. Finally Roger spoke, "Randy Walker said he called to say we were coming."

"Yes, my business has improved since the Walkers stayed here. Welcome, I'm Charlie Fowler, the proud owner of Maud's Inn."

"Nice to meet you, Mr. Fowler. My wife and I had a bed and breakfast inn in Bar Harbor, Maine. When I walked inside I had a bit of nostalgia that threw me for a loop."

"You owned an Inn? That's great. Maybe you could come here more often and help me out."

Roger began to relax. "Do not say that unless you mean it. I am sorry, Mr. Fowler, please allow me to introduce you to the Reverend Sarah Marshall. She is a Presbyterian pastor of a church in Atlanta. I needed time away from all the excitement and asked her to join me."

"Nice to meet you both. You wouldn't happen to know Rev. Leonard Childs, would you?" Charlie asked Sarah.

"Why yes, he and I are ministers of the same church. I am the associate."

"He's a nice fellow. Then I'm sure both of you were at the wedding today."

"Yes," she said. "He and Margaret are perfect for each other. "

"They invited me, for some sentimental reason I suppose, but I couldn't get away for the day. Weddings are not my thing anyhow. I kind of got left at the altar once upon a time. Was it a lovely wedding?"

"Yes, and you missed a good meal afterward," Roger said.

"Just like a man," Sarah said, "He mentions the meal." They all laugh.

"What can I do for you, Mr. Waddell and Rev. Marshall," asked, Charlie. "Do you need a room?"

"No," Roger blushed, "Not today. We have no agenda. Do you mind if we walk around the place, and sit on the balcony that Randy mentioned, then perhaps have a light meal before returning to the city?"

"Sure, that would be fine. The woods are filled will many species of trees and flowers, and there are several trails that lead back to here, but don't go too far you might get lost. The stairway in the back leads to a room that is not occupied, so you may sit on that balcony. That will give you a good view of the area. I will have a light meal for you at seven. Is that okay?"

"Very good," Roger said. Mr. Fowler, who was Maud?"

"She was my mother. This was my parent's weekend home."

"They must have been dreamers."

"Without a doubt, Sir."

The woods and the sound of water running over silver stones brought relief to both of them that afternoon. They sat on the bank and watched as the sun slowly faded into another world. Roger said, "I have been thinking. I need to explain something to you. This place brings back both good and painful memories. The only difference is, my Inn was in the city and of course this Inn is far from any city. When I entered I was stunned for a minute. My wife, Roberta and I owned the Cottage Bed and Breakfast Inn in Maine. She was a lovely person," he said, shaking his head.

"When she died of breast cancer, I sold the Inn and traveled around the country for weeks until I could feel again. I have five friends in Atlanta. We all finished college together, so I decided to spend time with them. That includes Leonard, Randy and Joan. Leonard let me work at the church, which gave me time to decide if Atlanta was a good place to settle. The people at the church nurtured me and helped me heal. The harder I worked, the better I became. I am sorry; I do not mean to bore you."

"You are not boring me. I am a good listener."

"You are not going to believe this, but you are the first woman, besides Joan, who I have spent any time with since Roberta died. My invitation to you this afternoon was not an attempt to be forward, or rush into anything, but ever since I painted your office and saw the extent of your books and the orderly fashion of everything in the room, I thought being in your company would be nice. Is that all right with you?"

"It's perfectly fine. I was afraid you wanted to rush into something I am not ready for, but it's nice sitting out here in sort of a wilderness listening to the sounds of nature with someone who also enjoys it. I haven't had the opportunity to get away for months, so thank you for bringing me here. I don't go out very often. It seems I have tied myself to the church in a monastic sense, but today I am realizing there are other sanctuaries."

Roger paused, "Sanctuary. What a great expression for this place. Everyone needs a sanctuary, a safe place." They both were quiet for a while, gazing off into nowhere and listening to the sounds of nature. Roger said, "Sarah how did you get where you are today."

"It's not that interesting, but it's conversation."

"I have talked too much. Your thoughts would be nice right now."

"You must have had a wonderful marriage, Roger. Once upon a time I almost did. I haven't talked about this for a long time, but for some reason it seems appropriate now. I met the only man I ever loved while we were in seminary. We spent hours walking around the campus, studying together, and talking about our calling to be ministers. But right before graduation he told me he was having trouble visualizing both of us being pastors. He asked me if I would consider another area of ministry, such as a chaplain or a counselor. He could not imagine what kind of marriage we would have if both of us served different churches, or what would happen if we went to separate cities. It wasn't complicated to me, for I believed love conquered all things."

"So he wanted you to give up your dream?"

"Yes, he did. He was in love with me and angry at the same time. Both of us were miserable. One night he kissed me, held me by my shoulders, and said the most stupidest of words, excuse my grammar, 'I will always love you,' and walked away. Looking back, it may have been a sour attempt to keep the door open, or make me change my mind, or even a male's dream to make me continue loving him while he chose someone else."

"Where is he now?"

"He is pastor of a church in Atlanta, and has a stay-at-home wife who caters to his every need. I see him at meetings, and *it is not* my imagination, he still loves me. He has that dreamy look in his eyes and tries to talk to me, but I walk away."

"Do you still love him?"

"I have to admit, I used to tingle a few times when I saw him. I was hurt and angry toward him, *and* with God for a long time, but I was not about to give up my calling. No, I do not love him. I pity him for what he gave up. I love my work."

"Do you suppose you will ever find someone else?"

"I hope so. Do you ever think you might find another Roberta?"

"There is no other Roberta, but in time there may be someone. Did I just hear a bell ring? It must be dinner time." They both stood, as if they had been interrupted from a dream. Roger said, "I enjoyed sitting here with you. It was peaceful. I long for peace."

"Oh, yes, peace for me also. Thanks for introducing me to this place."

Since Charlie's other guests left that morning, Roger and Sarah were the only ones there. Sarah invited Charlie to share the meal with them, and he agreed as if that was the right thing to do. Dinner and conversation was interesting.

"I see stories in people," Charlie said. "I saw stress when you two walked in, and now I see a change in both of you. I like stories."

Roger said, "Our stories are simple: lost love, searching, finding peace."

"That's why I live in this place. That is exactly where I was," Charlie said.

Roger said, "You know Charlie, I like this preacher lady. No we are not involved. It seems we both are searching for something."

"I'm sure you will find it."

"Sarah, I like being with you and sharing stories. I want to take you around the world to see the places I have been. Then I want us to come back to this place and see Charlie again. How is that for friendship?"

"Whoa! Wait a minute! Something about that sounds interesting to me. Can I go with you? Please! Please!" Charlie asked.

Roger looked surprised, "Really?"

"Sure, I mean it."

"Well, why not? If Sarah can get several weeks off, and you can find a time to leave your business, I believe three persons, who barely know each other, would make an exciting trip. We should go. Come on, I am serious. Sarah? Charlie?"

Charlie said, "Boy, this is a quick friendship, but I like it."

Sarah said, "Quick is not the word; weird is more appropriate. But something about the offer intrigues me." Then as if talking out loud to herself she said, "Well, Leonard owes me. I can possibly get a month's sabbatical, but I'll have to see. It does sound exciting. Okay, I believe a month off can be justified."

"I am free and ready any time," Roger said. "Get your acts together and be ready to go. How does June 15th sound? I just picked it out of the air. That is almost two months away, so that gives me time to start planning an agenda. You can offer suggestions or just leave it up to me. I will need to make the flight arrangements at least two weeks ahead."

"Okay, okay! Sarah, get your time off! This is urgent," added Charlie.

"I will. Roger, I don't know enough to suggest an agenda, just do it yourself."

"Ditto," said Charlie.

"Charlie, do you have an innkeeper in mind?" Roger asked.

"Got it covered! When I moved here I inherited the nicest couple that live in a de-attached apartment, Mary and Robert Steele. She helps me and he keeps up the property. I couldn't handle this place without them. I also have a friend who recently left a restaurant in Atlanta. I'll call him tonight. One more thing, can we stay out of Germany? Too many memories there."

"Sure," Roger said, "Not my favorite place either."

Sarah said, "I haven't been this excited for years and years. I'll have to make a draw on some money and buy some clothes."

Charlie and Roger almost spoke at the same time, "Forget the clothes and the money. We will take care of that."

"Are you kidding me?"

"No, we are not. Come on, Sarah, this is a time of celebration. Charlie bring in your best wine and let us toast a threesome adventure."

"Here, here!" Sarah said, "but let's not call it a threesome."

"Sorry," Roger said. "Charlie, now that we have that settled I have a question."

"Well, questions are fine."

"That painting above the bar looks familiar. I saw it in a book somewhere."

"That belonged to my grandmother's family. The artist is Jean-Edouard Vuillard."

Roger said, "My parents loved art, and everywhere we lived, they always insisted we go to the local art studios or museums. How long have you owned it?"

"There is a story behind it, and it is long. I will read you something, if you have the time."

"I am at liberty to stay as long as I wish. How about you Sarah?"

"I'm interested that the two of you know something I don't, so it's all right with me to stay a while."

"Recently my grandmother, Margaret found my mother's diary. I have not shared any of it, except with her. I'll be back in a few minutes." When he returned he said, "Here it is. Let me read you parts of her story."

The two of them sat spellbound as Charlie read the tender words of his mother.

Maud's Diary

In all these years I have never written of my coming to America. Today I begin to write before my memory becomes darkened. I must do this for my son. I do want him to know of the things I have never spoken.

It was 1933 in Potsdam, Germany. A beautiful lady and I stood in a long line outside a crowded train station. The man who came with us handed her a roll of money and kissed me on my cheek. Later I learned he had given her some German Marks, and had bartered for a few American Dollars, which she tucked in her blouse. An older lady locked me in her arms and said, "Your new name is Maud, that is all, just Maud." After we boarded the train my companion repeated her words, "You and I must leave Germany forever. Remember, your name is Maud. You will have a last name when we get to America. If anyone tells you it is odd to have only one name just smile."

I was seven or eight years old and noticeably small for my age. I do remember that I lived in Potsdam. That day I was going somewhere on a train with an American woman whose name was Margaret. Adults did not include children in their plans back then, but I do remember my father was a professor. One night he and my mom carried me to a house, embraced me, kissed me, and left me. Leaving my home did not seem to matter, for most of the time it appeared I did not exist. The adults whispered any time I was near.

Looking out of the window of the train, trees and buildings went by so fast I became dizzy trying to follow them. Somehow I knew I would never see my family again, nor Germany. I was told not to be sad for I was going to American where I would be safe. There were long train rides for days and days. I don't remember how many times we changed trains or who the people were who helped us along the way.

After several days we were standing in front of the largest ship in the whole world: a ship going to the country called America. Policemen were tying to control the people who were pushing to get through to the other side of a rope. I doubted we would be able to board, but Margaret waved our tickets in the air, and yelled, "Americans!" An officer motioned for her to come forward. When she handed the tickets to the officer, he looked at me. "My daughter, Maud," she said to him. Then I saw her slip some money in his hand. He removed the rope, tipped his hat, and allowed us through. He would have noticed Margaret anywhere for she was so beautiful. Strangely, I remember that she was dressed in a white outfit trimmed in red, and she wore a blue wide-brim hat with a yellow ribbon flowing from it. Her long dark hair flowed in the wind. I was scared but proud to accompany her.

The trip on the boat was long and tedious. Our cabin was one stairway down from the topside of the ship. I could look out of a porthole and see the waves rocking us back and forth, but the most memorable times aboard the ship was my eating and vomiting. After days and days Margaret took me to a narrow walkway on the side of the ship to view the grand city of New York. "Look, Maud," she said, "We are in America where we will be safe. Soon I will give both of us another name."

I thought we had reached our destination, but we boarded a huge bus. Along the way the driver stopped only for us to go to the toilet and grab a bite to eat. I believe we were on the bus two days and one night until we finally arrived in the city of Atlanta, Georgia. A strange man, with a long beard, whose name was Levi, met us at the bus station and took us to his house. I tried to be nice, but I cried a lot, so Margaret slept with me until I got accustomed to the house and the surroundings. In a few weeks the man with the long beard and Margaret were wed and suddenly I became Maud Meyers. I suppose I was adopted, though no one ever mentioned that event. Levi looked too old for Margaret, but that did not seem to be a problem to her. Now I could go to school where I had to learn a new language.

Levi said America was going through some bad times, but not to worry; we would be safe.

We lived in Levi's nice home down town. He left every morning and returned at dark. I supposed he had a good business, but no one asked. Finally Mom, which I was told to call her, found employment with a local newspaper. She told me it was similar to the job she had before she went to Germany. In the evenings we had language lessons.

Page 29. The horrible war was finally over. Often I think of those relatives who hugged my neck when I left Germany, and who undoubtedly saved my life. I should not dwell on that for I am certain there are no answers.

Page 35. In 1948 I married Charles Isaac Fowler. His young wife died in childbirth a few years before I met him, and so did their little baby. I worked nearby in a bank owned by Levi. Charles and I used to see each other at the lunch counter at Woolworth's across the street. Though he was much older than I was, we fell in love. He told me that his mother was a Jew, so she wanted the name Isaac to be part of his name. He was always a good provider and a devoted American. We finally had a son, and named him after Charles, but called him Charlie. He was so beautiful. I wondered if he resembled my family. I would never know.

Page 57. We had been working six days a week and long hours through the years, so Charles decided we needed to find a place outside Atlanta that would give us relief from our retail business. The realtor found acreage near the Chattahoochee River within traveling distance of Atlanta. Upon viewing the land for the first time we were pleased and surprised to find an old hunting lodge in the woods. I remarked that one day it would make a great playhouse for our grandchildren. Using our suggestions a husband and wife architect team designed a building that resembled an old inn, and they hired a builder to make our dreams come true. In six months we moved to our summer home.

I wish to write about my beautiful home, as I sit inside it today. Upon entering our Inn, as Charles called it, one can view a large living area with small tables, sofas, and chairs spread about. There is an exposed kitchen with a bar and a storage room nearby. From this level, past the bar, we enter our suite. I love the expression our.

The architects designed a beautiful stairway that curves upwards to a balcony that has four small suites for our guests. They would have a nice view of the sunset in certain seasons, and could watch deer at the small creek that comes off the river. We furnished one of the suites for Mom, known always as Margaret, who comes quite often to visit. She taught Charlie to call her Margaret from the day he began to talk. I am forever grateful to her and love her dearly. On the back of the property Charles placed swings and stone benches, and he named our property Maud's Inn. Almost every weekend we came, and at least two suites were occupied with friends.

Page 70. Today is the first day of May. This morning I can barely see to write, for tears fall upon my cheeks. Charles was buried this week. We had seven wonderful years of retirement. I am beyond grief; I am devastated. He gave me a history and a future. I must go on for Charlie. Mom grieves with me for she knew how much I loved him. I must write more often for Charlie's sake. There is so much to remember.

Finally he stopped, "Perhaps that was too long. I'm sorry if I bored you. Shall we stop for coffee and dessert?"

"Oh, Charlie, her story is so wonderful," Sarah said, wiping tears from her eyes. "Her words come from a painful time in history. So many children did not make it to America. Yes, a cup of tea would be nice."

"I wish my mom had kept writing in the diary. There is so much I do not know about my relatives," Charlie said. "My Grandmother, Margaret, who I discovered was not really my grandmother, out-lived my Mom six years. She is the one who found the diary. She understood my mom's sadness, and stayed many nights here with her. In fact one of the upstairs suites was decorated solely for her. When Mom was dying, Margaret never left her side. I understand that now. They shared a perilous history of leaving German, and after I read their story, I realized they grieved for those left behind. Margaret told me that Mom often talked to her about her vacant memories. Margaret is the one who made sure that *My Name is Maud* was put on Mom's gravestone. She was the only one who knew my mother's real name, and she never told anyone, not even me."

Sarah asked, "Have you ever been to Germany?"

"Yes. That's when I found this painting. I never dreamed Potsdam was such a large city. I was rather depressed that I found so little information about my mother's family. They were simply erased from history, but at least I was walking the same streets where my ancestors had lived. I left my hotel the day before I was to leave, and walked to a nearby bookstore, having spotted it in my ramblings. I wanted to find a book to read. From the back of the store came a voice, 'Good afternoon, how may I help you?'

"I told him I was looking for something interesting to read while on the plane back to Atlanta, Georgia." The man extended his hand, 'I am the owner, Walter Schmidt. I hope you had a nice visit.'

"I gave him my name, and told him I did not find what I came to discover. I had too much hope and not enough luck.

"He said, 'I am very sorry, would you like to tell me what brought you here? Americans always have such nice stories.' Well, It didn't seem to matter, so I gave him a short history of what I knew of Mom's past, from her diary, and of my decision to search for her history. I said to him, I don't understand why, but my grandmother gave my mother a new name as she was leaving Germany in 1933 with a lady named Margaret. I was told her father was a professor, and her mother was a Jew from a family of means. When I stopped talking, there was long silence. Mr. Schmidt rose from his chair, went to the phone, returned, and handed me a paper. 'These people may be able to assist you. It is permissible to talk about this now, but it wasn't in the late 40s,' he said. 'Here is a name and address. I can call ahead for you, but you may desire an interpreter, so if you wish, I will drive you there when I am through here. Perhaps you would like to go through the shelves while we wait.'

"At the door of a house in mid-city, Mr. Schmidt flipped the polished door knocker several times. A young woman came to the entry and motioned for us to enter. Without a word we followed her to a room were five persons sat drinking beer. The room was so dimly lit it was hard for me to focus my eyes. I remember a musty aroma that must have come from the elaborate rugs on the floor and the heavy drapery. I noticed one of the walls had shelves from floor to ceiling and on the shelves were probably a hundred books. I turned toward the street side, where we entered, and saw a large piece of art in an unbelievably beautiful frame. After accepting a beer and some salty crackers I sat in the chair someone pointed to. I don't remember tasting the beer or the cracker, for all eyes were focused on me. Finally I asked, has Mr. Schmidt informed you why I am here?

"The only person to speak was an elderly lady. When one of the men started to interrupt, she raised her hand to hush him. 'I see you have brought your interpreter, but I speak English, Mr. Fowler. Yes, Mr. Schmidt has informed us of your reason for coming to Germany.' After an uneasy pause she continued, 'if I remember correctly Maud was your grandmother's name. I was twelve years old at the time, and your mother was the only child of a seminary professor and a young nurse. After they were (she paused) taken away, your grandmother entrusted their daughter to a woman who was living in Germany at the time. She was an American Jew.' She paused. 'Your mother's name was Christel. Yes, that was her name. Her father was Professor Kappel. Everyone knew him. He was a Gentile, but his wife was a Jew. I forgot her name. It was so long ago, you know.'

"Do you know where my grandmother lived? I asked. There was no answer. Believing they did not understand the question, Mr. Schmidt repeated my words. Suddenly no one was looking at me.

"Finally the old lady answered, 'yes,' then paused. 'You are visiting in what was their home. I hope you have not come here to reclaim it, Mr. Fowler, for we have purchased it legally.'

"I knew of no words to respond, so I stood and looked around the room, thinking and wondering if this furniture belonged to my family. I asked did my family own that painting? Mr. Schmidt had to repeat the question. 'Yes' the woman answered. Then I will take it since it belongs in my family. I am sure you did not purchase it *legally*. Mr. Schmidt removed the painting for me. No one moved to stop him.

"All eyes were diverted from me as I stood frozen. I memorized every detail of the room and made a vow never to forget every inch of it. I turned and left. Thanks and goodbyes were definitely inappropriate words. Mr. Schmidt followed me into the street. Nausea rose fast in my stomach, and I vomited into a trashcan fastened to a light pole. I should have been pleased, for I found more than expected, but for some reason depression gripped me. I began to think of how many people lost their heritage and their homes. I need to go home, I said to Mr. Schmidt. I have seen enough. Mr. Schmidt drove me to the airport the next day."

"Wow, Charlie," Roger said, "What a story."

"Yes it is. My parent's Inn meant more after that trip. I decided to make it a place of joy, a place where people could come to rest and revive. The painting you asked about, is the one that hung on my relative's wall in Germany. It is a reminder of how unlucky my heirs were, and how fortunate I am. My mother would be so happy."

"And it appears you have done a great job. I hope to be here more often," Sarah said. "All right boys, two months isn't long. Let's get busy. Thank you, Charlie for sharing your story with us, and many thanks for this lovely visit. I will never forget the story of your mother."

Roger spoke, "What happened in your family's situation was the story of many people back then. Your mom's soft expressions in the diary brought out the Jewish blood in me, and both angered and healed me. I was protected from all that history." He paused and rubbed his hands together as if washing them. "I must read more about that period of history. Thanks Charlie for your hospitality. I am looking forward to spending more time with the two of you."

CHAPTER 24
The Court Room

Bob spent a restless week. He waited for Georgia Parker to call. He and Julia received several threatening calls from Judy. She demanded to see Julia, but Julia refused to go. She accused Bob and his parents of corrupting Julia against her.

At last Georgia Parker called him at his office, "I got some information from Randy and processed it in my mind, so I have an idea of the situation. We need to meet pronto. When can you meet with me?"

"Let me look at my calendar. I can mark off tomorrow afternoon. How is that for you?"

"I'll make it work."

Bob went back to work for half a day. He asked one of his best clients to use another lawyer for the time being because of his family's crisis, and he seemed sort of peeved. Mark Richards said, "Bob, I have been knowing you for several years, if something is wrong explain it to me. You and I are more than client and lawyer. I don't want another lawyer. Whatever is happening, I can wait awhile if I know you are not just blowing me off."

"I appreciate that, Mark. By now you should know that my marriage has been in shambles for a while to the point that Judy shot me in the leg. She is seeking divorce and custody of Julia. I will see that she never sees my daughter again. I have retained Georgia Parker as my lawyer."

"Wow! You got a good lawyer there. I'll hang with you, Bob, and if there is any way I can help you, call me. I have a lot of respect for you."

"Thanks Mark. You know how lawyers can drag this out, so this could be awhile. If it takes too long, you feel free to get help with Frederick Winchester."

"He's a good man. Thanks for the referral."

The hearing was almost over before it started. Judy was no longer being held at the hospital ward. She appeared in court with her lawyer, a Mr. Wallace who seemed helpless. Georgia tore him apart. The Judge listened to three character witnesses and dismissed the others. Judy was told to stay away from Bob and Julia, and to continue to seek counseling.

Judy exploded, "I have a cousin who has money, and I will fight this." Bob whispered to Georgia Parker, "He died, but she doesn't know it."

Bob was granted custody of Julia. Judy stood, waved her fist, and began to yell. The Judge had the bailiff remove her. He addressed Georgia Parker, "Do you believe your client and his daughter feel unsafe at this time?"

"Yes, Your Honor they do, especially Julia."

The attorney for Judy Barnett asked to approach the court, "Your Honor, there seemed to be an uncertainty about the paternity of Julia Barnett. Can that matter be brought up at this time? Mrs. Barnett would like Mr. Barnett to prove he is Julia's legal father, and we don't want this brought up in front of Julia."

"Ms. Parker, what do you say?"

"We have no problem proving she is my client's daughter, I have the blood test papers right here, Your Honor," Georgia Parker said. The Judge took the medical report and examined it. "Who asked for this report?"

"My client did," Ms. Parker answered. "He and Julia had the blood drawn while he was in the hospital after being shot in the shoulder by his wife."

"Who does Mrs. Barnett believe the father is?"

"Your Honor," Georgia asked, "Do you really want this courtroom to know?"

The judge demanded that both lawyers come forth. "Speak quietly Mr. Wallace, who is this other person?"

"John Randolph."

"And why does she suspect that?"

"They were young lovers in high school, and continued their association long after they married others."

"Mr. Wallace, why do you not accept this medical report?"

"Mrs. Barnett would like to request another blood test in her presence."

The Judge said, "Do you mean she does not trust this medical report?"

"She does not, Your Honor."

The Judge said, "This test was made at a reputable hospital, and I know the person who signed this. I don't believe he would falsify a report. So the answer to your request is *no*, Mr. Wallace. Does that satisfy everyone?"

"Yes, your honor," Georgia Parker said.

"No, Your Honor," Said Mr. Wallace.

Outside the courtroom, Georgia said to Bob, "I do not believe you and Julia are safe. I suggest we hire security around the clock to protect you during the daytime at your office, and do the same at your parent's home. A guard will be required for Julia. I know a good female who will take the job. I have used her before. I'll call her right now, and I will call a company to start guarding the home of your parents. Where is Julia?"

"She's at the gym. They have been told not to allow her mother to pick her up. I believe she will be glad to have the security."

Georgia made a call, and had a guard sent to gym immediately. "I believe the judge is having a monitor put on Judy, but they don't always work. Just be careful, this could get nasty."

Randy and Frederick met Bob as he left the courtroom. They could see he was a bit shaken. Randy grabbed his arm, and whispered, "Calm down buddy. Let's old college boys go for a quick let-down-lunch. I know the exact place, and it will take us long enough to get there for you to settle down."

Randy called ahead and Charlie Fowler was waiting for them. "This is a place I go to recover, and I brought Joan here once. Bob, it can be a place for you to go and feel secure." They did everything to calm Bob except using old college yells. Finally they saw that he had relaxed, especially knowing Julia would be safe.

Bob said, "I will be glad when this is all over and so will my parents. They have always lived a quiet life except when my brother and I were at home. This is upsetting everybody."

"Bob, you need to get back to work as soon as possible. You need that interaction with people. You are a respected lawyer; don't lose that contact."

"Thanks boys. Too bad Leonard, Roger, and Joan aren't here."

"For God's sake don't ever have Leonard and Roger in the same place for very long. They might cut loose at each other. As for Joan, this is boy's day out," Frederick said. By the way, who was Maud?"

"We should ask the Inn Keeper," Randy said.

———

The next morning, Bob rode out to Marietta to see his parents. When he arrived he saw the guard sitting in a car so he identified himself. This whole mess had put pressure on his parents, so he needed to find a way to settle them down. They greeted each other and sat around the table drinking coffee.

Bob said, "It went well in court. Of course, I didn't speak to Judy, so I have no idea what to expect next. I have to make certain both of you and Julia are safe for the time being."

His father said, "Bob, we will do what we have to do in this situation. We just want you to be careful. You don't have to sleep on the couch in your office; come on up here. We have plenty room."

"Don't worry I have some clothes at the office, and being there makes it easier on me for now. I need to pick up Julie today to see how she's doing. She's at the school gym practicing basketball with her team.

"Oh, she is the sweetest child. She could stay with us forever, but I know she needs you," said his mother.

———

"Bob drove up to the school gym. He and his security guard met Julia's school guard and started walking up the steps. Two blasts exploded, and all three of them fell to the ground. In an instant an old blue truck skidded away, but not until one of the guards got the tag number. Bob looked to see if everyone was all right, and saw his guard lying on the ground holding his leg. Then Bob felt his shoulder, and realized he had been shot. In a few minutes two Police cars rushed in. One guard flagged down another policeman, and gave the driver a tag number and the kind of truck. One of the officers ran up the steps into the school to keep anyone from coming out. One ambulance came and another was called. The ambulance with the guard left, and Bob was put in the second ambulance. Bob told the technician, who was trying to stop the bleeding, "I am not leaving until someone goes inside and gets my daughter."

"Sir, we need to get you to the hospital, now!"

"No, I will not leave without my daughter. She may still be in danger."

"Okay, I'll get someone to find her." In a few minutes Julia and her guard were in the ambulance with him, and they were on their way to the hospital.

Julia held his hand all the way. She kept saying, "You're going to be all right, Dad. You have to. Don't you close your eyes, I want to see you wink at me."

Trying to make her laugh, he said, "Honey, I've got to be more careful, first the leg and now the shoulder, this is getting to be a regular war. When we get to the hospital, call Mr. Walker. His number in the address book in my pocket."

The driver asked, "What hospital do you prefer?"

"Piedmont."

"Piedmont it is."

———

"This is Ms. Birkenstein, how may I help you?"

"Ms. Birkenstien, this is Julia Barnett. I need to speak to Mr. Walker. My daddy has just been shot."

"Good Lord, honey; hold on. Mr. Walker, I know you are busy with a client. Are you about through?"

"Just about, why?"

"Julia Barnett is on the phone. She says her daddy has been shot, and she needs to speak to you."

He said to his client, "Do you mind if I take this call? It's an emergency."

"Oh yes, go right ahead."

"Julia?"

"We are in an ambulance, Mr. Walker. My dad is on the way to the hospital. He wants you to call his lawyer and let her know that he will be at Piedmont Hospital. Also call my grandparents, and make sure their guard is still there."

"What the hell, Julia?"

"He was shot at my school, and one of the guards was injured, but the other guard got the license number. They said it was an old blue truck. "

"Okay, I'll get right on it." He told his client there had been a shooting, and he needed to get to the hospital as soon as possible. "We are about through here, anyway. Your estate planning looks good to me, but there are a few other things we need to discuss about it, especially concerning how your divorce will affect your estate. Can I call you later and set up another appointment to finish all this? You have already done a great job getting everything together. Will you be available tomorrow or the next day?"

"I can be here anytime, after all I'm retired. I hope your emergency is not too bad."

"I've been knowing you a long time, Fred. I'm sure you know Bob Barnett. He's been shot, and I need to get to him."

"Good Lord! Shot? How serious is it?"

"I don't know yet."

"I've played many a golf rounds with him. He and I are friends. Yes, go take care of him. What a mess he's in. Tell him hello for me. Randy, if I can help with anything, please let me know."

'There is something you can do. When you get home see if there is an old blue truck in the Barnett driveway. That's the only description I have, and if there is, get the tag numbers."

"Oh, my god, I wonder if it's my truck. Okay, I will hurry home, and call you later."

CHAPTER 25
The Hospital

Joan was in the hospital lobby when Randy arrived, and the lobby was covered with police officers. Randy identified himself and Joan, and one of the officers accompanied them to the emergency room waiting area. He was told Bob and the guard had lost a lot of blood, but both would survive. When Julia saw them she crumbled into Joan's arms.

"Roger said to Julia, "We will wait with you until your dad gets out of the operating room, then we will take you home with us. He is going to be okay. Julia, you are old enough to know things are going badly. You can stay with us for a while until we can figure out what is best for you. What is the phone number of your grandparents? I need to call them."

Julia said, "I realize what a mess my family is in. I'll do what you say. I like you and Miss Joan, but I'm used to staying with the Winchester's."

"You can't go to their house tonight. Someone may be looking for you there. We live in a condo, and it is hard to get past our guard."

"I don't know why anyone would want to hurt me and my dad, but I guess anything could happen."

"Now we have nothing to do but wait. Joan, I'm going to ask the guard to get us a sandwich. Okay?"

"Sure, that might help. I can't believe I'm hungry." The sandwiches came, and the three of them found an anteroom with a table.

Joan tried to think of things to say to Julia to get her mind off the tragedy. "Julie, what are your plans after graduation?"

"I'm going to the University of Georgia and hopefully to medical school."

"What a great future. What made you decide to go into medicine?"

"My friend, Mary Anne has a bad heart condition. One day I told her, "I'm going to be a cardiologist. I will find a way to cure you. Of course that would be a long way off, but she said she would wait for me if she could. If I can't help her I would like to help other people like her."

"Wow! I believe you will."

After two hours the doctor came out of surgery. "Mr. Barnett's surgery went fine. They are getting him prepared for the recovery area, and he will have to spend a few days in the hospital. The shotgun did a lot of damage to his shoulder. I suggest you go home and come back in the morning. He will be in recovery over night, well perhaps longer."

Randy said to Julia, "Call your grandparents and tell them you are well taken care of for the night. After you're through let me speak with them. Julia handed the phone to him, "Hi, this is Randy Walker. I'm sure you've heard by now that Bob was shot. He has a pretty bad shoulder, but he is in recovery. Joan and I will take Julia home with us tonight. If you need us, here is the number to call. Do not give this number to anyone, not even the guard, and if you have floodlights leave them on all around the house. I'll call you in the morning."

"Thank you for your help, Mr. Walker, we have been so worried. Please keep us informed."

Glad to be home, Randy was extremely frustrated. He went into the bedroom and shut the door. If he knew how to pray, it would be a good time to try it, he thought. He knew Joan would respect the closed door, so he sat in his old red leather chair and tried to block out the confusion of the day.

Joan found Julie a pair of Cassie's pajamas and sat with her in case she wanted to talk. Julia said, "I don't know why my mother is doing this to us. I've heard the rumors about her and Mr. Randolph, and I am sorry if that hurt you. I knew she was gone a lot at night, but I always had Daddy there with me."

"Julia, I believe your mother is ill. Perhaps when all this has settled down, she can get help."

"Do you think she shot my daddy tonight?"

"I don't think so. She may have hired someone else, but we don't know."

"This is so confusing. Is it all about me?"

"Not entirely. There are many problems in the marriage of your mom and dad. Do you want the truth?"

"Yes, ma'am I'm old enough to hear it."

"I'm sad to say this. There have been many rumors about your mom and my former husband, Mr. Randolph. Well, it has been discovered that the rumors are actually true. Your mother and Mr. Randolph believed you were his child. Now that she knows better she is angry with everyone, but she is not angry with you. She is confused because the man she loved did not keep his promise to make things right by leaving her money to raise you. "

"Did they really love each other?"

"Your mom and Mr. Randolph were high school sweethearts, but something tore them apart, and they married other people."

"Were you angry at her and Mr. Randolph?"

"Not any more. I am happy now and married to a man I really love, the kind of man I hope you find one day. Your daddy is a dear man. He wants you to have everything, and he will do whatever it takes to give you his love."

"Thanks, Miss Joan. You don't have to stay with me, I'm okay."

"Sweetie, don't call anyone. Your grandparents know where you are, but we don't want anyone else to know. This is a safe place. Not a soul can bother you while you are with us."

"Thank, Miss Joan. Good night."

The following morning Randy left early, and got to the office before Ms. Bee arrived. He needed time to think. The phone rang, "Mr. Walker, your wife gave us your number. We have arrested a young boy who was in the truck, and it appears Mrs. Barnett will be arrested when we can find her."

"Officer, I have an idea. Check the house of her neighbor, Mr. Fred Mills. Don't ask me why; it's just a hunch. Call me back if you can."

In a few minutes his phone rang again. "We found Mrs. Barnett, and are considering what to do about Mr. Fred Mills. Thanks for the tip. We don't know whether he is involved or not, but we will soon find out."

Randy left a message to Ms. Bee, "I am headed to the hospital. Look over Mr. Fred Mills estate planning, and see if you can find anything unusual; maybe I missed something. I'll call you later."

The nurse allowed Randy to see Bob, "But don't stay long," she said, as she was moving away. Bob was awake. He had tubes and wires all over him. "Bob don't try to talk too much. I have Julia and she's at the house with Joan. The police are trying to put things together. You rest today, and after you get in a room, I'll be back. This had gotten to be a terrible mess. I just hope we can all get through it. I believe Julie is going to be fine. She's been through a lot these few days, but she's so much like you in sorting through the details."

Slowly Bob talked, "Julie wants to be a doctor. Maybe, she'll change her mind and become a lawyer, take over my practice so I can go to some far-off island and disappear."

CHAPTER 26
The Arrests

The next few weeks were bedlam, and the newspapers and the media contributed to it. The reporters did their usual jobs of throwing all sorts of information around which kept everyone in confusion. A boy named Kip Jones was in jail, but there were rumors that other arrests were apparent. Later they brought Mr. Fred Mills and Judy Barnett in for questioning, and the two of them were not allowed to see each other. Judy hired another lawyer, Kip was appointed one, and they released Fred Mills, finding no evidence to detain him. It was going to be a long and nasty situation. All anyone could do was wait.

When Bob was released from the hospital he and Julia went back to his parent's house to allow Bob a period of recovery. Bob did not like being in the spotlight, but somehow the press found them. They camped out in the street. Randy called him, "Here's what I think. It appears Judy was hoping to become involved with Fred Mills, possibly to convince him to get rid of you. He admitted they had become somewhat friendly, but denied having anything to do with the shooting. Judy must have gotten his housekeeper's son, Kip to help her. It is a fact; the boy was driving Fred's truck. The police aren't saying how Kip Jones is involved, or if he has given any information. Bob, my advice to you is to find a safe place for Julia to get out of Atlanta until the publicity dies down. Can you think of anyone?"

"I have been thinking about calling my brother, John. He and his family are living in London. We visited them a couple of years ago, so let me get in touch with him. He has two children, a girl in college, and a son fifteen. Let me see what I can do."

In a few hours Bob called Randy, "I just talked with John and told him the whole story. He said I should put Julia on a plane, and they would take care of her and show her a good time. Will you take care of getting the ticket and taking her to the airport?" "Yes, I'll be happy to do that. Tell your parents to get her ready. I'll send Joan to pick her up. Pull one of the cars out of the garage so Joan can pull in, and tell Julia to pack the minimum in one bag. Give her a credit card so she can buy what she needs over there."

"She has a card. My brother, John already suggested that she travel light. They will take her shopping."

Joan arrived to find cars everywhere, hardly leaving space for her to pull in the driveway. She decided to stay a while to give the impression she was not in a hurry. It was obvious to her that Julia had been crying after being told she was going away. Bob and her grandparents finally convinced her that leaving was the best thing for her. Thank goodness Bob kept their passports in his office. He called his secretary to tell her to get Julia's passport ready for Joan to pick up.

Joan and Julia backed out of the driveway and waved at the reporters. One of them held a mike up to the window, trying to get an interview, but she ignored it. She didn't rush, and no one seemed to be following her.

That evening Randy and Joan put Julia on a plane bound for London with all sorts of instructions, "Don't tell anyone your name. Sleep or watch the movie. If anyone asks why you are going to London, just say you will be studying there. Should they ask where, say your uncle is making the preparations. You are so beautiful some good looking guy might ask if he can see you sometime while you are in London, just say 'I'd rather not' no matter how good looking he is. Have your uncle call *me*, not your daddy, when you get there. I'm sure he has an international phone. Right now you may not believe you are doing the right thing, but you are. All your dad's friends will be supporting him, and we will get him through this. If I got into trouble he would be the first person to come to my rescue. Remember this, he is sending you away for your safety. You might want to find a school and take some courses that can transfer to your school here."

"Thanks for all your help," Julia said. "I know everyone thinks this is the best thing for me. You have made me feel better about leaving. I will miss my daddy and my grandparents. I am worried about the pressure they are going through, because my grandmother is not very well. I don't want all this to make her die."

"Your dad will take care of them," Randy said. "In a few days this will be old news, and the reporters will move on to something else."

The next day John Barnett called Randy from London, "The package arrived in good shape. I know our family will enjoy everything. Let's get back to each other soon."

"Glad you called. Share everything with the family," Randy replied. He thought to himself, *just like war times, codes could be valuable.*

CHAPTER 27

Roger, Sarah, Charlie

The month of June arrived fast. It seemed like a good time to be leaving Atlanta, for both the weather and the shooting were hot news. Roger hated confusion; he wanted life to be perfect. *What a neat idea, the three of us traipsing around the world with no worries, except where to go, where to stay, and what to see.*

Charlie's caretaker took him to Roger's place. Margaret picked up Sarah, met Charlie and Roger outside the condo, and drove them to the airport. She didn't feel well, but having a task helped her.

"Now, don't you get in any trouble running around all over the Continent. I can't come over there and get you, so remember who you are," Said Margaret.

"Yes, Mother," they said together, and laughed

They were able to reserve three seats in a row, which made it easy to talk about what might be exciting in Lisbon and Madrid. After Spain it would be Athens, then Rome, and Venice, or plans could change.

"I know a little bit about these places," Roger said, "But I do not wish to be your tour guide. When we get to a place we may decide to see something completely different than I planned. Be prepared for anything. In some of these places we may be able to get suites, and in others it may be one room. Sarah, are you okay with that?"

"I don't suppose either of you will harm me, so I'm game. You can turn your backs while I dress. Now, the bathroom is the only issue."

"Who said there were going to be a bathroom?"

———

As they approached Madrid, Sarah began to think about her life. *Here I am on a plane with two men I hardly know. There was no way I was going to tell Mom. She would have attempted to convince me this is definitely not a good social idea. I feel like waving to her, my ex lover, and the church, and yelling, here I am, the new me, on a trip I never imagined, going to places I've only read about, and with two men I hardly know*! *Eat your heart out Tony Sterling. I've topped your non-offer, and I am sitting on top of the world.*

She turned to Roger, "You are making my dreams come true. Thank you." And to Charlie, "Who are you? I believe I'm going to find out soon."

Charlie said, "Go, preacher woman, it's about time you and I discover there are other ways to live, and you, Ole Roger are going to show us."

"Amen," he said.

Looking out the window Charlie's mind drifted back several years ago when he flew to Nashville to marry Rose Phillips, the girl of his dreams.

We met in college, and promised to love to each other forever. Dad became ill, so I went back to Atlanta to take care of him, causing me to miss a full semester. The week of the wedding Mom hired a caretaker to stay with Dad while we headed to Nashville carrying relative's wedding gifts packed in suitcases. Two nights before the wedding I can still see her face and hear her voice, 'I can't go through with this wedding, Charlie," she said. 'I don't want to leave Nashville and move to Atlanta, and besides you left me to take care of your dad, so I figure you'll always love your family more than me.' But the blow that hurt the most, 'besides, there might be someone else." I was stunned. I said, why didn't you call me before I made the trip, and she said, 'I thought what I had to say should be said to you personally.' I have no idea where I found the courage, but I remember the exact words I said to her, and I'm still proud of myself: Then get all those presents you unwrapped and pack them back into our personal suitcases today! And you can take care of the personal hotel bills my mother and I incurred, since you reserved them in your family's name. I needed to say this to you personally. Oh, how I remember the look on her face when I turned and walked out. He laughed out loud.

"What's so funny, Charlie?" Sarah asked.

"I'm just laughing about what I told the gal who left me at the altar."

"Want to share?"

"Never, never."

Roger was thinking: *I hope this trip means as much to them as it does for me. It has been years since I traveled out of the States. Dad would announce to my mom and me, 'get packing, I have business' in Rome, Japan, Israel, or wherever, and there we would land where I had to learn another language and customs. I bet those Japanese were surprised to see me dressed up in their native clothes. That is so funny now. I just went with whatever they wanted to do. Well, except for one incident. Wow! What a childhood and look how I turned out.*

"You two will never know how many places I landed as a kid. I thought we were a normal family. I guess that is why I turned out normal."

"In whose opinion?" Charlie said.

"I think I'll keep a journal," Sarah said.

"What a great idea. You can do it for us too."

"Lazy, lazy, you two."

Finally they deplaned, waited for their luggage, and walked off into an adventure. A new world awaited them.

CHAPTER 28
Margaret

Back in Atlanta Margaret was thinking about Roger, Sarah, and Charlie, wishing she could have gone with them. Instead, she was vomiting into the commode. Leonard yelled, "you are going to the doctor today. I can't believe this has gone on as long as it has. I'll call Joan and ask her to take you."

"No, you take me."

"Not today, Margaret. Call Joan."

"I'm not married to Joan, remember, and don't remind me that I married a busy preacher!"

"I'm so sorry, but I have two couples coming for wedding counseling."

"Maybe you and I should have had counseling before *we* married." He tried to kiss her, but she pushed him away, "Get away from me."

Joan picked her up and was shocked how bad she looked. "What in the world have you been eating? You look terrible. Just tell me where to go; we need to get there as soon as possible."

"Dr. Annette Nelson is one of my best friends. You know where her office is. She has agreed to work me in. I have no idea how long that will take, but I brought my vomiting tub just in case."

Joan waited and waited for Margaret to come out of the room. When she appeared she was ashen. "What in the world is wrong with you?" Joan asked.

Dr. Nelson was right behind her, "She is pregnant! This lucky lady is pregnant!"

"And at my age," Margaret said, crying.

"Margaret, you are only thirty-nine. Don't you remember?"

"Yes, but…"

"Oh, I know," said Joan, "The congregation will discover their preacher actually has sex at home." Finally everyone laughed. "Let's go by the church. I want to see Leonard's face."

Riding to the church Margaret said, "Joan this is a private thing."

"Not any more; I just noticed you're already showing. You're not getting fat; there's a baby in there. Okay, I'll wait outside the door and put my ear to it."

"He's going to be upset. He's too old to have a baby around the house. When I go into labor I can hear him now, 'what? You are in labor! Call Joan, she can sit with you until I get there.' "

"Margaret, forget all that and just tell him. Don't make up the ending before he hears about the beginning."

———

When they arrived at the church Joan waited outside the room. She heard Leonard yell, "Are you serious? Tell me again. I want to hear it again and again."

"I'm pregnant and it's all your fault," Margaret said, as she sobbed.

Then he yelled, loud enough for God to hear, "I'm going to be a father," and ran out into the hall yelling, "I'm going to be a father!"

People came out of their offices. "I'm going to be a father, shake my hand."

Margaret said, "Of course I had nothing to do with this."

Everyone hugged, kissed, and cried. It was a good day in the office.

His secretary began spreading the news to a few select persons, and the excitement continued by phone. She thought about inserting the news in the Sunday bulletin, but of course everyone would know by then.

———

Joan waited for Randy to get home to tell him the news. For some reason she was depressed: "What is wrong with me? I'm happy, but jealous. I do wish I could give Randy a child of his own. I wonder if Cassie and Rick can fill that vacancy in his life. No, that's not the same."

When Randy opened door Joan started crying, "Margaret is pregnant, and I wish it were me. Am I jealous, Randy?"

"Maybe not jealous, but definitely delirious. Just be happy for Margaret and Leonard. You and I are lucky, especially me. You have given me two children, and after grandchildren come I'm going to teach them so many things they're going to look exactly like me."

"Oh, Randy we would have had a beautiful child."

"If he or she looked like you that would be true. Stop crying, Joan, you and I have more than I ever dreamed of, and if Cassie decides to share an office with me, I might get to see our grand baby more often than you."

"You wouldn't dare!"

"Nope, just kidding. You think Cassie will choose to come to Atlanta and practice?"

"I will tell her she has to. After all who's going to look after us when we are an old married couple?"

Randy said, "I have an idea. In a few weeks why don't you and I go to England to visit Julia. By that time she will be so familiar with the city she can be our tour guide."

"I'm not sure this is a good time. Ms. Bee will be mad at you, besides there is too much going on right now. We will have to choose a time when Cassie can take over. Why don't we wait and see if she decides to go into practice with you?"

CHAPTER 29

Randy and Joan

Sitting on the balcony after dinner, the city of town Atlanta looks alive even at ten o'clock. It is a beautiful sight to watch all the lights and cars streaking past. The only negative sight is what cannot be seen: the city lights hide the stars. "I went by to see Mom today," Randy said. "I had business in that area. She and Pearl must be having their second life. They are young again. You will not believe all the things they do. Pearl has three new painting commissions and Mom is her agent and bookkeeper. They live off Mom's money and have fun with Pearl's money. I have tried to buy one of Pearl's paintings, but she and Mom will not hear of it. They want to give it to us, so I may have to go through their agent. They both appear to be in good health. I must take you to their condo, but they are so busy we may have to make reservations."

"Don't you remember? I picked them up for lunch one day. Everyone in the restaurant seemed to know them. Talk about feeling like an outsider! By the way, we got a card from Roger today."

"Who sends cards anymore?"

"Roger. Anyway, he said Sarah is the recorder of their trip. She sent a lot of photos. Let's go back inside and look at them."

"Wow, look at Sarah," Randy said. "She looks different, more Bohemian with that rag around her head. There, the three of them together. Wonder who took that picture?"

"Some wayward tourist I suppose."

"Is that Greece or Rome?""

Who cares? They're having a ball. Charlie always acted so business-like, but look at him now. He has on shorts and a tee shirt, but not Roger he dresses like his mommy taught him. The three of them act as if they've known each other for years."

"I wish I could get a picture of Margaret's stomach so they could see it. Maybe they don't know yet," Joan said.

"Whoa! Sarah is kissing Charlie or maybe just hugging. You think the church members know about this?"

"Look! Here are more pictures from Madrid, Milan, Venice, Rome, and Cyprus. Then a note, 'Roger left us today for business elsewhere. Charlie and I will fly home on Tuesday. Roger said he would be home a week later. We cannot believe how fast a month can slip by. Joan, it would be nice to see you, but we can get the bus into town if it is not convenient for you to meet us at the airport.'

"Randy, I will bet Sarah is having the best time of her life. She looks free and excited. This is the Sarah I would like to know better. Is it my imagination or does Roger look older?"

"Joan, Roger is still grieving. He told me before he left that he likes Sarah, but as a friend not as a lover. By the way Rick called me today. He and Colin are having problems. Their relationship is not working out the way he thought it would be. Colin saw him talking with some woman, and made an ugly scene about it. Can't gay men be friends with women?"

"I would think so, but what do I know about gay relationships? Now you really are his dad when he talks about his sex life with you."

"He's coming home this weekend, so maybe we'll find out what's wrong. Joan, I'm more concerned about Bob than I am about Rick at this moment. Where does he go from here? We've been friends a long time, but I don't know how to help him."

"We can't solve his problems. Your friendship means a lot to him, and he trusts you. Sometimes I believe your relationship with Frederick, Bob, Leonard, and Roger is some kind of plural marriage. You would do anything for each other. Women have relationships like that but men rarely do, or at least that's the way I see it. Why don't all of you get together when Roger returns and make some sort of plan?"

"That's a great idea, but don't forget you are also part of this friendship. Tomorrow I'll call Frederick and Leonard and get started on it. Thanks, Joan. I love you. You know worry tires me more than hard labor."

"When have you done hard labor?"

"It was just an expression."

All the unsettling events had taken a toll on their time together, but their love was stronger than ever. Randy enjoyed teasing her, and was still excited just being in the room with her. Tonight he started with the top of her head twirling her hair into curls and traveled to her toes. "You are perfect," he said. "As long as you think so," she answered. "Even your hands are sensuous - the fingers of a pianist." One at a time he put them in his mouth. "*Surely no one ever started with fingers*," he thought. She brought him toward her and found his ear. There was no turning back. Maybe the phone rang; maybe it didn't. Troubled friends; forgotten. Their mouths met. There seemed to be no urgency on his part, just a natural progression, but she could wait no longer. She invited him into the region were children are created, and far inside to the spot where passion bursts into flames and every inch of the body participates with a quiver. She wasn't certain about him, but for her the sensation lasted for hours - a constant reminder that she had freely given her body to be invaded. Side by side they nestled on top of the covers. Words were not needed. Why try to explain thoughts that went far beyond any language?

The phone rang early the next morning. Joan answered. Rick said, "Mom, can I speak to Dad?"

"Sure; hold on." She waited while they talked.

After hanging up Randy said, "Everything is okay with Rick. He and Colin have come to an understanding, and Colin has moved out. From what I gather their relationship has been rather rocky a long time, so this decision is good. Jealousy never makes a good marriage."

"Surely they were not thinking of marrying!"

"No, I was speaking figuratively. I should have said partnership."

"Changing the subject. Randy, have you heard anything new about the shooting?"

"A little. Judy was released on bail, but the poor kid, Kip Jones remains in jail. If this goes to trial, I will almost bet Judy is involved somehow. We'll have to wait and see. Kip had been working in the yard for Fred and his wife, Mable for several months.

When she moved out, Judy sort of moved in and out. They talked in front of the kid as if he was too dumb to hear or understand, a mistake many people make. The gun was Fred's, and it's doubtful the kid had ever shot a gun before. His mother said he had never been smart. She took him out of school when he was twelve, but she absolutely believes he would not have hurt anyone unless he was provoked into it. The local opinion is that Judy would be held responsible in some way. The whole episode continues to make good fodder for the media. That's about all I know."

"Well, that was a mouth full. You learned a lot."

CHAPTER 30

Charlie and Sarah

Joan had agreed to pick up Sarah and Charlie at the airport. She didn't know either one of them very well, but she was happy to do it for Margaret. Driving from the airport, she tried to fill them in on events. They had heard that Margaret was pregnant. Someone had written them about the shooting, so there was not much left to tell. Sarah said, "Roger said to tell everyone not to worry about him. He was going to Israel to see the relatives of Roberta. We offered to travel with him, but he said he needed to do that on his own. Roberta must have been a special woman."

"She was very special. She was one of the most exotic persons I have ever met. I am not sure he will ever get over her," Joan said.

"That is what Charlie and I decided. But he was delightful the whole trip. He knew more about the places we visited than many authors know. He made our trip exciting and educational. Can you believe this? When we were in Cyprus we ran into a guy Roger knew when he was a teenager. We were walking down the street when Roger spun around and yelled, 'Whoa! Justin, is that you?' 'Roger? No it can't be,' the guy said, and they embraced. After Roger introduced us we sort of stood aside for a few minutes and watched the reunion. 'Wow!' Justin said to us, 'this is hard to believe. Roger and I were like brothers. Our parents kept their heads into odd books and lively discussions most of the time, so we hung out together. This is unbelievable! All of you must come to my home for dinner tonight. Sasha is a wonderful cook.'

"It was a perfect ending to our trip. Justin and his wife Sasha prepared a delightful meal; a meal like nothing I have ever eaten, and I'm a pretty good cook myself. Roger asked Justine if he would be willing to make a trip back to Israel with him, and he agreed without even thinking about it. So they took us to the airport and here we are."

Joan said, "Randy will be disappointed Roger did not return with you. He has planned a meeting with friends to help Bob Barnett out of his mess, but I suppose it can wait. It has been rather tense around here, and we have no idea how this shooting situation is going to work out. It's good Bob's daughter Julia is in England staying with his brother and family. Anyhow, I'm glad the two of you are safely home. Sarah, I enjoyed the photos you sent. Your writing made me jealous that I wasn't tourist number four. Back to work for all of you and hopefully new adventures."

"Thanks, Joan," Sarah said. Looking toward Charlie she said, "Charlie and I have something to tell, so you are the first to know. We have become good friends, which means we may see more of each other. Right, Charlie?"

"Yes, I believe so. It wasn't the romance of being on foreign soil and seeing exotic places. At first I thought Roger had interests, but he said his interests were not romantic. I said to him, you are a crazy, man. He answered, 'and you are lucky; you have my blessings.' I said, well thanks, I guess."

Sarah said, "One evening, I talked to Roger about Roberta. He can't imagine being able to love like that again, but I believe he will one day. I reminded him how all three of us had shared feelings of being left behind, but of course his situation was different. Right now, I have to get back to being a pastor and Charlie has to return to the best little Inn in state of Georgia. In the meantime we have to find time to be together to see if what we felt on our travels was real. Sometimes being in exotic places can play tricks on emotions."

"Back to the grind for me too," Charlie said. "Sarah, I have no doubts what we experienced is the beginning of a great relationship. If what we felt during our travels was real, it will be just as real here."

Joan said, "I hope you know that I write love stories, so yours might make a good book. Give it a try and keep me informed." They laughed.

CHAPTER 31

Roger falls in love

Roger and Justin knew exactly where they wanted to go: a little café near the Yarkon River. It was a peaceful time when they were young. They both had applied for colleges without ever attending any public schools. Justin's twin sister, Rosa would stay with their parents a little longer. Being a girl they wanted her to mature, so they put her in a small school in Tel Aviv. Both parents had written letters to colleges about their schooling and travels, and had no doubt they would be admitted to any college. Roger and Justin had their own doubts. They had discovered girls, and life was beginning to mean something else. Now that the two of them were together again, Roger was thinking of an experience they had on the banks of the River many years ago.

A crowd of girls kept drifting by, trying to get our attention. Finally, Justin offered them a seat, but only two of them Roberta and Sasha decided to stay. Both had dark hair, full lips, and thick eyebrows. Roberta was tall, but Sasha was the talker. Not that Roberta was shy, but she didn't get many words in against Sasha's monologues. Both Justin and I were smitten. For three weeks the four of us could not be separated. My parents were not pleased, for they wanted nothing to interfere with my education. My father said I would be in the States soon, and there will be plenty of girls for me to date in college. Justin's parents were not as strict, as long as the girl was Jewish.

I admitted to Justin that I had never had sex, and wondered if this was the time the event was supposed to happen, especially if two people were in love, and I was definitely in love. Justin admitted the same, but Sasha was a free spirit, and he guessed by her kisses, she was familiar with the process. One afternoon while sitting near the bank of the river, the desire and the moment met. The girls made a picnic lunch and brought along blankets. After the meal Justin and Sasha took one of the blankets and found a private place.

I was certain it was the time, so I kissed Roberta on the cheek, and she brought our lips together. She lay on the blanket and motioned me to lie beside her. We were past the kissing stage when I pulled away. I told her that I have never gone further than this before.

"Then I will show you," she said. "First you start with my breasts. Then you will know what to do." Playing with her breasts excited me. The only breasts I had ever seen were pictures in those magazines I saw across Europe – the ones I hid from my parents. She raised her skirt and I felt an urge that could not be described. I fell upon her and entered the most blissful place on earth. With regret, I remembered my father-to-son talk, "Son, there are certain things between a male and a female that must remain untouched until marriage." I asked him how does one know? "You will know," He said. Now I wondered why my father had kept this exciting experience from me. But I was in love and that made everything right.

The next day I pleaded with my parents to allow me to delay going to America. I told them I would be alone, and would not see them for a long time, and besides I have met this girl. I was so young and terribly inexperienced. I thought if they just saw her they would change their mind, but when I looked at the tickets he handed me, I knew they would never meet her. I was to land in New York, and a family friend would meet me and take me to the College of William and Mary. Since I had an equivalent of two years of private instruction, I would be entering as a junior. My father looked toward my mother and nodded his head for her to speak. She said, "It is settled then, we will meet you after you finish your undergraduate courses, then you will enter their law school and make us proud." Growing up, how did I miss the fact that I was to become a lawyer?

Again, I pleaded for them to reconsider. I reminded them I had always been a good son, and learned so much from our travels and my lessons. I promised I would go to college later. As near angry as I had ever seen my father, he said to me, "You will be leaving tomorrow; you must have your education. Hopefully we have taught you well, my son. We trust you and we expect you to trust us. You may see this girl tonight, but tomorrow you leave. We love you and know what is best for your future."

That evening I told Roberta my parents said I was to leave in the morning. She said, "I understand. In Israel we are taught to obey our parents, but we have not, have we? My father asked me if you were Jewish, and I told him I would ask you. Are you Jewish?" I was afraid of losing her, so I told her I was not a practicing Jew, but I had studied the Torah as I studied all other religions. I did not tell her I was only part Jewish. I asked her if religion mattered to her. She said to me, "A Jew is a Jew with or without practicing religion." I did not understand her answer. She must have noticed I was puzzled, so she said, "I am a Jew but not an Orthodox Jew." Well, I had learned a lot from my parents, but never about that division of Jews. We made love again, as if it would the last time. And we cried in each other's arms.

Late that night my parents awaited my return. Again, I begged them to allow me more time. My father asked me if I had given away my virginity. I told him I was in love, without answering his question. "That does not answer my question!" He shot back at me. Never before had my father been angry with me, but now he was also disappointed. He claimed they had given me too much freedom and apologized they had not instructed me in such things. My mother said I would forget the girl in time, and she cried. I had never seen her cry, and it made me mad. I asked my father if he had a girl before my Mother, and he told me that was of no concern to me. Both my parents believed education was the most important part of my life. The next morning I left for America.

———

"Roger! Roger! Come back to me. I know where your thoughts are, and I don't blame you. We will look for her family tomorrow."

The next day they rented a car and traveled to the village where Roberta was born. Justin told Roger that both of Roberta's parents had died, and the old grandmother, Paula lived with Roberta's brother and his family. Also a granddaughter, Joanna lived with them. Roger grew anxious as they approached the house, "I am frightened. They will know I did not keep my promise to return, and they will ask me to leave."

"I do not think they will be rude to you."

A beautiful young woman answered the door. Roger was speechless. He fell backwards, but Justin braced him. It was like seeing Roberta again. A gentleman came to the door to see if there was a problem. Justine said, "Greetings. Remember me? I am Justin, and this is Roger Waddell. We have come to see Roberta's family. Tell your family Mr. Waddell is fulfilling a promise he made to Roberta before she died." An older woman came to the door, "I know who you are, Mr. Waddell. I am Roberta's grandmother. She told me you would come one day, and so this is the day you change our lives, huh?"

"I am sorry, I do not mean to change your lives. I loved Roberta. I did not want to leave Israel, but my parents had other plans for me. With God's help we finally met again. We had a wonderful marriage, and I miss her terribly."

"It had nothing to do with God, Mr. Waddell; Roberta went looking for you," the grandmother said. "Roberta said you would come one day. Joanna, come here," she called out. "This is Mr. Roger Waddell. He is from America. He is your father."

Without hesitation she said, "So nice to meet you Mr. Waddell." But Roger could not speak. He asked for a chair, for he was about to faint. Justin found the chair and steadied him into it.

"Are you disappointed?" The grandmother shouted. "What is the matter with you; cannot you speak? She is the one you put in Roberta's belly. Look at her, how beautiful she is. We knew this day would come, that is why Roberta told you to find us."

"Why was I not told of her? Why? Why?"

"That was the way Roberta wanted it. She feared she would lose you again. We have kept her secret, until this moment. A child without a father is not a shame here, Mr. Waddell. Joanna is loved by many people, and has been educated in the finest schools. She was the envy of her class with the money and clothes sent from America by Roberta. She is very proper, and she is a teacher."

Gaining composure, Roger said, "I must tell you, there is no way I would have left Roberta if I had known about you, Joanna. I met your mother by accident years ago when I was uninformed that sex can bring babies. She is the only one I have ever loved, and that is the truth. She was a most remarkable person."

"My grandparents always told me I was a special person, a child born of great passion. Do not fear, Mr. Waddell I will ask nothing of you, but to be your friend."

"No! No! We cannot be friends! You are my child! Having found you I will love you forever. I want you to live with me, not because you are a child of passion and look like your mother; you are my blood. Yes, I am stunned, but other than loving your mother, meeting you is the most wonderful thing that has ever happened to me. I have a child! A beautiful young woman has come into my life again. Yes, I am disappointed that no one, not even your mother, told me you existed. She had her reasons, besides she knew my parents would never accept her. I had planned to go back to Israel, but after college and law school and a very short law career, my parents became ill, so I flew to New York to care for them. That is when I met your mother again. We were so in love. Oh, if only you had been with her. I am overwhelmed. My insides cry out for all I have missed. Justine, I have a child!"

Justin said, "Enough! Enough! This calls for a great meal. Where can we find a place to have dinner?"

"You are always thinking about eating," Roger said. He turned to the grandmother and asked, "Is there a good place around here to eat?"

"You are in good place. I will prepare a good dinner for all of us, and we will celebrate the rebirth of this family. Justin, how is Sasha?"

"What a woman, and three babies," He said. How about that!"

"You should not have moved away. Sasha belongs to Israel."

"Oh, no! Sasha belongs with our children and me, but she has never forgotten your family and her friends here."

Roger looked at Justine and asked, "So you knew?"

"You should not ask me that; I will not answer."

While the dinner was being prepared Roger and Joanna went into another room to talk. "My mother always told me my father was a fine man, a man of great learning and wealth. She said he had obeyed his parents and left for America, but one day the two of us would meet. Thank you for keeping her promise."

"I want you to come to America with me. There are many places you can teach, and there are those who would like to meet my child, the child of Roberta. Will you consider going back with me?"

"I have thought about finding my father for years, and this meeting is just as wonderful as I had hoped, but I have a place here. I would like to visit someday, if I may."

"Of course, but I am disappointed. Maybe you will consider later. I will fly over here and travel back to the States with you, or send you the airfare anytime. You will enjoy my friends, and I will take you to see the little Inn in America your mother and I owned. There is so much we need to know about each other."

"I have kept a journal. One day I will allow you to read it," she said. At age six, I made the first entry, and there will be an interesting entry at the end of this day."

Dinner was announced. Roberta's grandmother made the dishes from items already in the house, plus a few veggies from the little garden plot in the back yard.
Everyone bragged on the dinner, which pleased the grandmother and her son's family. There was a lot of laughter every time Roger blundered through a question. Justin whispered to Roger, "My friend, you are most anxious to learn too much too soon. Today you must be patient and enjoy the occasion."

"But there is so little time," Roger said.

"There is plenty of time later; just relax."

When it was time for Roger and Justin to depart, Roger broke into tears. He promised to come for Joanna during her short break from teaching, and she agreed to go to America for a visit. Roger wanted to offer Joanna some money to buy herself something, but Justin said, "Bad timing, my friend; you will insult them."

"But it will be a gift."

"You do not know her well enough to give her a gift, besides her grandmother will not allow her to take it."

"I hope you are right."

"You do not need to be the rich American to them. You are her father, and she has just met you. Your presence is joy enough. They will laugh behind your back if you offer money."

Roger kissed the grandmother and shook hands with her son, Paul and thanked him and his wife, Mary for their hospitality. He stood by the door with his arm around Joanna, and thanked the family again, for he was reluctant to leave. The trip back to the States was long.

CHAPTER 32

Margaret and Leonard

Margaret's pregnancy was never perfect. "I'm too old to have a baby," she said over and over. Leonard paid little attention to her whining. He was always working, so it was up to friends to take her back and forth to the doctor and shop for her.

Wednesday morning Margaret told her assistant to finish most of the work she had contracted to do, because she was just too tired to get out. She began feeling pain in her stomach, but surely it was not labor, for it was not time for the baby to be born. Suddenly she felt a thrust of water running down her legs. She had never demanded that Leonard leave his work, but this time he had better come home. She called the church. "Rev. Childs your wife is on the phone. She said it is an emergency," his secretary interrupted.

"Tell her I am in a meeting right now." When the secretary told Margaret she was furious. "You tell him to pick up the damn phone."

Rev. Childs, she needs to speak to you, and wants you to pick up the phone." "Excuse me, it's my wife."

"Leonard, my water just broke, I need to go to the hospital!" she screamed.

"Could it be the flu, or an upset stomach? I'm in a meeting right now."

"Did you not hear me, you dim-wit, my water just broke? You had better come home now or you will never see this baby!"

By the time he arrived, she could not stand; she was already in labor. He called an ambulance and got her into the hospital. Leonard called Joan, "Could you come to the hospital to sit with me? Margaret is in labor, and I am a coward." Finally Joan arrived and the two of them waited. A nurse came to the room and asked if he would like to be present for the birth of his child. He looked toward Joan for support, but she pretended to be reading a magazine. He said, "I don't think it is necessary for me to be there." Joan said, "Of course he would like to be there." He looked sick. The nurse picked up his arm, checked his pulse, and said, "Pulse okay; come with me."

About two hours later, Leonard was brought back into the waiting area. "We have a baby boy, but he is very tiny, though he yells like a wild cat. They have taken him to some place to check him out, and he will be in an incubator for a while. The nurse said I could see Margaret when they put her in a room. I thought I was going to faint, but Margaret yelled at me like a mad woman, 'you had better not be a coward and leave me, don't you dare! You stay right here and sweat with me. You hear me?' " Joan couldn't quit laughing.

"I am serious. The doctor said, 'now Margaret, don't be too hard on him, he's used to being in control. Give him a little slack.'

" 'Slack, hell!' she said. She looked at me, 'you caused this, so you need to have this pain too, and don't you faint on me.' I said to her, Margaret, don't tell all our secrets. I'm not going to leave, but if I vomit, I hope it isn't on you. 'you'd better not vomit, either' she yelled, 'hold my hand.' She is fine now, and the baby looks perfect. Thank you, for being here for us. I've baptized a lot of babies, but I didn't imagine what the parents went through to get them here. How could I have been so dumb to allow Margaret go through that procedure?"

"I won't answer that *dumb* question, and I believe the event is called labor not *procedure*. Have you and Margaret settled on a name?"

"We agreed if we had a boy we would name him Michael Leonard Childs, Jr., and we will call him Michael. Joan, I have a lot to learn."

"I don't think you need me anymore, so I'll be going. Maybe you should call your secretary and give your members the good news. I imagine they will be celebrating this occasion, but you need to stay here with Margaret!"

"Yes ma'am!" he said with a salute.

———

Joan was tired, but she decided to stop by the office to see Randy. She always enjoyed talking to Ms. Bee, and for some reason she hugged her. "Well, what caused that?" Ms. Bee asked.

"I'm afraid it's too hard to explain. Margaret just had a baby boy, and it brought back memories. I wish I could have given Randy a child."

"He doesn't need a baby. Get over it. He's got you and your children. What's the matter with women today? I survived with no children, and I feel blessed."

"Oh, you would have been a good mother."

"Just between you and me, I have a child, but he doesn't know it. He is still that young lawyer coming in and ordering me around. First time he did that I set him straight and told him, you do your job and don't try to do mine and we will get along just fine. I love him, but don't let him know it."

"Did I hear my beautiful wife?" Randy called out.

"There are two of us in this room, couldn't you include me in that 'do I hear?'" Ms. Bee asked.

"Ms. Bee, I tell you every day how important you are to me."

"But you never call me beautiful."

"Well, that has been my mistake, from now on you are The Beautiful Ms. Birkenstein, but you must call me handsome."

"Never, it would go to your head."

"See there, Joan. She won't return the favor, what should I do with her?"

"Do not put me in the middle of this. The two of you call each other whatever you wish when I'm not here," Joan said. "Margaret had a baby boy today, and they named him Leonard Michael, Jr."

"That seemed like a quick pregnancy to me," Randy said."

"The baby was early and is in an incubator right now, but he's going to be fine."

"Leonard with a baby; I can't imagine. I guess we will have to go see him baptize his own baby," Randy said.

"Why do you say it like that? We don't have to, but we will."

"You still have a lot to learn, Mr. Walker," said Ms. Bee.

"And you are still teaching me."

"You've got that right."

"Lovely Ms. Bee," he said bowing to her, "I must leave with my wonderful wife and take her out to dinner.

"May I come?"

"Someone has to close up the office, and you are it."

"Then go play and leave me alone."

They dropped by the hospital on the way to dinner. The nurses had allowed Margaret to hold Michael for a while, and Leonard was watching. "Here, Leonard hold Michael," Margaret said, "Show the Walkers you know how?"

"But I don't know how," he said, "I might drop him."

"How many babies have you baptized? Did you ever drop any of them? If you don't take him, I'm going to pitch him to you."

"Okay, okay. Hand him to me. Hello little Michael, I am you daddy."

"Put your hand under his head."

"He's so ugly, he's beautiful."

"Don't you ever say that about our child! I bet you looked just like him."

"We are going to leave you two so you can figure out how to hold a baby.
Don't be too hard, Margaret, I understand it's natural for women," Randy said.

"Who says so? You wait and see how good a Dad I'm going to be," Leonard said.

"Well, that was a lovely evening," Joan said. "I wanted to hold him, but I was afraid I might not return him to his mother."

"Hold on, Joan. We've been through this already. You and I have two children. We don't need a baby to fulfill our lives. Don't think like that."

"Thank you. I got a little dreamy back there. We have two kids, and don't let me forget that."

"I have a question," Randy said. "Are all babies that ugly at birth?"

"*No* baby is ugly at birth, just different."

"Got ya."

CHAPTER 33

Randy and Ms. Bee

At the office the next morning Randy's head was swimming. So much was going on, he felt his work was not his priority. He dared not ask Ms. Bee; she might agree. Bob had obtained an uncontested divorce from Judy. Their daughter, Julia enclosed a notarized letter for Bob to use at court, if necessary, saying she preferred to live with him rather than with her mother. It wasn't necessary, since she was old enough to make the decision, but she wanted him to have the information in case he needed it. She was still in England waiting to finish the courses she had started.

Since Randy was Fred Mill's estate attorney, he called him to ask how he was doing, and if he was seeing Judy he needed to back off, for there was a possibility she would be arrested. Mr. Mills agreed, though he said it wasn't much of a relationship. Randy made the comment to Ms. Bee, "They seemed the most unlikely couple. Poor Fred, he had no idea what he was getting into." And she answered, "That is none of your business."

"Yes, ma'am, just don't hit me."

"Be nice to me, or I'll call your mama."

The trial for attempted murder, driving without a license and other insignificant issues, was scheduled to begin on Tuesday, since Monday was a holiday. Randy felt sorry for Kip Jones, but realized the boy had the best lawyer for his case. Thank goodness for that one factor. He hated confusion. He had an urge to take Joan and get out of town, but he needed to stay and support Bob. He wanted Roger to get home soon so the group could get together. Group? Well, I guess we are. He was going through Roger's latest notes to them, and said out loud, "A daughter!" He ran into Ms. Bee's office and said, "What the hell is Roger talking about? What daughter?"

"Calm down, Mr. Walker. It is not like you to interrupt my silence. Who? What are you talking about?"

"Roger! Roger Waddell! Your rich buddy who comes in here and kisses you every time and tells you how beautiful you are. He discovered he has a daughter."

"He does not kiss me. He embraces me. There is a difference."

"Look here, he has a grown daughter who lives in Israel."

"How does someone discover they have a daughter? I thought there was only
one way that could happen."

"You are so right, Ms. Bee, and that happened years ago when they were both very young, but nobody ever told him she existed."

"That is so sweet. He will make a good daddy. I'm certain he can make up for the time he didn't know her."

"Wait, he says he will be here tomorrow. Does he mean today or our tomorrow? This is great news. If she looks like Roberta, oh wow! He's been depressed since she died, but now he has a new purpose. God is wonderful."

"Leave God out of this; you don't know what God does.

"I'm learning, Ms. Bee; I'm learning."

"Get back to work, you're behind already."

"Can I whistle while I work?"

"If you must."

"By the way, Ms. Bee your favorite child, Cassie has gotten permission to attend the trial. She's hoping to pick up some experience, studying young Robert Sanders. I hope she doesn't like it so much she will decide to go into criminal law."

"So, you want her here in the office with you? Hold your tongue, women are allowed to choose their own careers, I believe."

"Right you are again. I haven't flipped; my lips are zipped. How do you like that for a poem?"

"You have most definitely flipped a lid. (The phone rings) Wait a minute. Hello Mr. Waddell! I've heard of your good news. Yes, he's right here. I will." She hung up. "He is getting a cab from the airport."

"He should have called me, I would have picked him up."

CHAPTER 34
The Trial

The court appointed attorney for the young boy had planned to plead Guilty by Reason of Insanity, but changed his mind to not guilty. The boy wasn't very smart. He had no money, no father, and a destitute mother, so it would be a challenge to any lawyer. Usually the court appointed some lawyer on the bottom of the list, but this time a young lawyer was appointed that intended to do his job.

Robert Andrew Sanders, Jr. was the son of a prominent Atlanta lawyer. Randy told Joan, "It has been said, he was raised with a law book in his hands and groomed to follow his father. He isn't as cocky as his dad, but he is smart, careful and exciting to watch in the courtroom. He tends to be excessive in the research on his clients, and appears to have the wisdom that most young lawyers don't acquire for years. He's handsome, quick, courteous, and single, and the District Attorney knows him well."

The Trial

The people in the courtroom stood as Judge Brown entered. The jury panel had been picked the week before, so everything could proceed in order. The district attorney, Mr. Frank Lauder gave his opening statement of the charges: attempted murder, fleeing the scene of the crime, speeding, and driving without a license. Attorney Sanders questioned the District Attorney's charges and announced his defense. He planned to show that Kip Jones was a young boy caught up in a net of conspiracy.

The District Attorney called the witnesses who were at the scene of the crime: The security guard who identified the tag number on the truck, the arresting officer, and the two victims, Bob Barnett and the security guard, Richard Wilson. The arresting officer said,

"As soon as I turned on my siren the boy stopped, and he didn't resist arrest. I yelled at him to get out of the car, and he started crying."

"Your witness, Counselor."

"Officer Morrison, did the boy say anything at all."

"No, not a word, but he was crying."

"Did you handcuff him?"

"Yes sir, I did. I said to him, son do you know you are in a lot of trouble? And he answered, 'Yes Sir.' "

Next, Bob Barnett testified, "I was at the school to pick up my daughter, Julia. No, I did not know the boy personally, but occasionally I have seen him working in Mr. Fred Mills' yard. Mr. Mills is my neighbor."

"Mr. Barnett were you wounded, and did you have surgery?" The District Attorney asked him.

"Yes, I was wounded. I had surgery on my right shoulder."

"How long were you in the hospital?"

"Three days."

"Your witness, Counselor."

"Mr. Barnett, can you move your shoulder?"

"Yes, very well. The doctor did an excellent job."

"Did you recognize Kip Jones as the shooter?"

"No, I did not. Everything happened so fast."

"And have you ever had a conversation with him?"

"No, he was usually working in my neighbor's yard, and never looked up to speak."

"Thank you. No more questions."

The District Attorney produced three character witnesses who knew the boy. One witness was Fred Mills, who employed the boy's mother as a housekeeper. He characterized Kip as shy, backward, possibly retarded, and unschooled, but he was good help in the yard.

Attorney Sanders stood to object. Looking at his notes he said, "Your Honor, using words such as shy, backward, and retarded are subjective. Those impressions can influence a jury. Are we judging this boy by his character or whether he has committed a crime?"

The Judge said to the District Attorney, "Mr. Lauder, have your witness refrain from the use of subjective examples. Let those expressions be struck from the record."

The District Attorney continued. "The defendant, Kip Jones was speeding, driving without a license, shot two men who were seriously injured, and fled the scene of his crime. His mission was obvious: to kill. Only one witness has had anything good to say about him, that he was good help doing yard work. This is an open and closed case of guilty."

Attorney Sanders rose, "Your Honor, is the District Attorney speaking his closing statement at this time?"

"Mr. Lauder, shouldn't you have saved that for your closing statement?"

"Perhaps it would appear, Your Honor. I was stressing the facts for the jury."

Since the opening statements and the prosecution had taken so long, the Judge dismissed the court until the afternoon session. He faced the jury, "You will be taken to a room, and lunch will be brought to you. There will be no discussion among you concerning the trial since you have not heard all the evidence. A bailiff will be outside your door. If you should need his services, knock on the door."

In the afternoon session, Attorney Sanders called a psychologist, Dr. William Simmons, to the witness chair. "You have met with Kip Jones. Would you tell the court about your visits?"

"I met with Kip Jones three times. Kip is an under-developed young man who has been deprived an education by the school system and his mother. He is neither retarded nor un-teachable; he has Dyslexia. It appears the school system failed him miserably, and his mother was in no position to argue with them. In many ways, for the past four years, Kip has remained a twelve year old to her. She has protected him, and he goes with her to the places she works as a housekeeper. He shows mechanical skills, and can remember exact lines of television shows and sentences people have spoken."

"How did you come by these revelations?" The District Attorney interjected.

"Don't keep interrupting the defense," the Judge said, "But you can answer the question, Dr. Simmons.

"I tested him, but I was never alone with him. I asked Dr. Jeannette Edwards, a well-respected expert in that field, to also test him. She is here in the courtroom today."

"Your Honor," The District Attorney interrupted, "I would like to have the opportunity to have the expert of our choice to test him."

"I don't believe that is necessary," the judge replied. "These two psychologist have been in my courtroom before, and they are tops in their field."

"Thank you," Dr. Simmons, is there anything else?" Attorney Sanders asked.

"Yes, he was never aggressive while he was being tested. When I asked him why he agreed to talk to us he said, 'because you're older and smarter than me.' He is a person who believes in the authority of adults."

"Thanks you Dr. Simmons," Robert said.

The Judge said, "Does the District Attorney have any questions?"

"Yes, Your Honor. "Dr. Simmons, were you given any information about the seriousness of the action this boy has taken?"

"I will have to say I read the Atlanta Constitution. It was in the headlines, if you remember, but I tested Kip Jones without prejudice, the way we have tested many children and adults."

"Do you believe he is capable of knowing right from wrong?"

"I'm sorry, sir, I was not asked to consider that question?"

"That's all for now," the District Attorney said.

"I'd like to call Kip Jones to the chair," Attorney Sanders said. He was sworn in.

"Kip, did you know Mr. Bob Barnett?"

"No sir, but I know he lives next door to Mr. Mills, where my mom works."

"Then why did you shoot him and the security guard?"

"I promised never to tell."

"Who did you promise?"

"I promised never to tell that either."

"Had you rather go to prison than to tell?"

"You mean be locked up?"

"Yes, that's what a prison is."

"I don't want to be away from my mom. She needs me."

"Then you will have to tell the Judge *and* the jury why you shot those people and where you got the gun."

"I don't want to get anybody in trouble."

"You are already in big trouble, Kip. You know that don't you, son?"

"Yes, Sir I do."

"You are going to be in more trouble if you don't talk to the Jury and the Judge." Attorney Sanders waited. Kip paused, and appeared to be deciding how much to tell. "There is this lady; she is nice to me. She showed me a gun, and put some bullets in it, and asked if I'd like to shoot it. I told her no ma'am! But she said, 'you want your mama to keep this job, don't you?' And I said, sure. She said to me, 'can you keep a secret?' And I said, of course. I have lots of secrets."

"Is that all?" The District Attorney interjected.

"Sit down, Mr. Lauder," the Judge said. "Mr. Sanders will let you know when he is through. Proceed."

"This lady said there was a man who was hurting her, and he ought to be shot. And I asked her, has he hurt you bad? And she said, 'very bad. He might hurt you and your mom if he knows you are helping me.' No, I said, we can't let him hurt my mom. She said, 'then you will help me?' I said, Okay. She said, 'I just talked to someone and they said this man is going to pick up his daughter from school. I know where that school is. If I tell you, will you shoot him for me?' And I said, I ain't never shot a gun, and she said, 'it's easy. You just point it at someone and, *bang*.'

"Will I get in trouble? I asked. 'No, you're child,' she said. I never hurt nobody, I said to her. She said, 'okay, I guess your mom can't work with Mr. Mills anymore and neither can you.' I said, that's not nice, my mom needs this job; she ain't got no money. And she said, 'if you do this for me, I will give her some money.' I said, you sure nobody will come after me? And she said, 'no, you just drive away. You can use Mr. Fred's truck, but if you tell anyone it will be bad for your mom. Do you understand?' I said I don't like this at all. It ain't right to shoot people. And she said, 'no one will ever know.' I said, I will always know. I don't think I'd better do this. And she said, 'why did you steal that money off Mr. Fred's dresser?' And I said, I don't know nothing about any money on Mr. Fred's dresser.

'Well,' she said, 'the money is gone, so I guess your mom must have taken it. So I will have to call the cops to arrest her.' And I said no! You can't do that! I'll do what you say. I can't let my mom be arrested; my mom is a good person."

The courtroom was silent. Even the Judge seemed to be speechless. He asked the District Attorney if he had any questions."

"Yes, I do. Judge, can the court order this boy to reveal the name of the woman?"

"Son," the Judge said, "You must give us the name of the woman who asked you to shoot Mr. Barnett."

"I can't let my mom go to jail."

"I promise you, before this court, your mom will not go to jail."

"All I ever called her is, Miss Barnett. She lives next door to Mr. Fred. She's always been nice to me, but I feel bad that I had to do this."

"Mr. Lauder, do you have any more questions?" Asked the Judge.

The District Attorney stood, "How old are you, son?"

"I'm sixteen," Sir.

"So you had never *ever* shot a gun before?"

"*No,* Sir. I ain't never held one before."

"Do you go to church?"

"Yes Sir, every Sunday and sometimes on Wednesday night."

"Do you know the Ten Commandments?"

"Yes Sir, every one of them, by heart."

"Tell me, do you know the 6th Commandment?"

The boy said, "Just a minute Sir," and counted on his hands. "The sixth commandment is, *Thou shall not kill.* I'm sure of it."

"So is it a sin to break the 6th Commandment?"

"Yes Sir, but I was obeying the 5th Commandment? You shall honor your father and mother. It comes before the 6th Commandment."

The people in the courtroom stirred a little. Some of them laughed.

Judge Brown said, "Order! Is that all Mr. Louder?"

"Yes, Your Honor."

"Will the lawyers come to the bench?" He leaned over to them and said, "Let's go into my office."

The judge sat behind his desk, and Mr. Lauder and Mr. Sanders stood. "We have been presented with a dilemma. Mr. Sanders, you used emotion to save you client. I don't usually like that, but it is done. Mr. Lauder, you stepped on your own foot. If I were you, I wouldn't bring up the Bible again. This boy is socially immature, and not used to making decisions, except when it threatens his mother, his only role model. There was a crime committed, and there has to be some punishment under the law. That is, unless we find him incompetent. Mr. Lauder, what say you?"

"It is hard to believe a sixteen year old could be so uninformed, but the jury will believe he was forced into protecting his mother. If we dismiss the charges we do not solve the crime. And I cannot convict this boy with this jury. Half the jurors were wiping tears. I almost cried myself. But I believe he has to learn what he did was a bad thing. Mr. Sanders, had he told you the name of the woman?"

Atty. Sanders said, "No, he would not, but I believed he would if we put him under pressure. Your honor, this boy needs help, and going to jail will not give him the help he needs. I would like to get the boy back in school, but first I will see that he spends time with a specialist to catch up on reading and a lot of other things. I believe Dr. Jeannette Edwards will be interested in helping him. I don't know how long it will take him to catch up, but I believe he can do it."

"Let's go back in the court room," the judge said.

The Judge addressed the jury, "You are dismissed. Do not discuss today's proceedings with anyone. You will reconvene tomorrow morning at 9:00."

Cassie had been in the courtroom all day. She stayed behind when everyone left. She walked up front to where Robert Sanders was stuffing papers in his brief case. "Hi, I'm Cassie Randolph, but I'm thinking of changing my last name to Walker, dropping Randolph. Now that I have made that stupid introduction, I want to say I admired your work today."

"Thank you, Miss Cassie Randolph, maybe Walker. That wouldn't be Randy Walker, would it?"

"Sure is. I got out of my classes this week to watch you. I thought you might teach me a few things."

"Did I?"

"I was impressed. I know my dad would like for me to come into business with him, but I haven't decided yet." There was a long pause. "Well I had better be going. Nice to meet you."

"Wait! Do you have plans for lunch? Maybe you would like to study me some more."

"As a matter of fact I don't have plans. Where can I meet you?"

"No meeting place, just follow me. I'll bring you back to your car after lunch."

"I don't have my car. I came with my dad, and I'm supposed to leave with him."

"He was in the courtroom?"

"There he is. I'll just wave at him to go away."

"I can take you home. I have nothing planned for the afternoon. Let's go to The Four Seasons, it is nice place for lunch. I have been there a couple of times, and always wanted to go back."

"Okay with me."

When she waved at Randy he came over to them. "So you are putting your father off for another man?"

"Hello, Mr. Walker nice to see you," Robert said. "I'll bring her home later. I hope you don't mind."

"Does she look like a teenager? Have fun, both of you. Drop in and meet Joan before you leave her at the door."

The afternoon passed too fast. The food was delicious, but they couldn't eat fast because there was so much to talk about. Cassie was thinking, *he is so easy to talk to. I like him.* He was thinking, *why haven't I met her before?* "Are you coming back tomorrow?" he asked.

"Wouldn't miss it, got to report back to my professor. You were marvelous."

"I don't like to hear words like that. I am too new at this. When I see my father he will sit me down and let me know what I should have done."

"He wouldn't!"

"He was in the courtroom, and yes he will."

The lunch lasted until late afternoon, and the evening with Joan and Randy was lovely. During the conversation Cassie said to Randy, "Dad, what did you think about Robert's work today?"

Joan answered for him, "Cassie, never ask a lawyer to critique another lawyer's work especially while they are face-to-face. They never tell the truth, or they are jealous and give suggestions. Perhaps you could ask, how do think the trial went today."

"Wow, I have a lot to learn. Don't answer my question, Dad." Cassie said.

"Personally, I believe the trial went well, and you did a great job, Robert. As a young lawyer you did the right thing by not making the District Attorney look too bad. You were well prepared. He was not, and he knew it."

"Thank you, sir."

When Robert was leaving he asked Cassie, "Lunch again tomorrow? After all, you are coming back to study me."

"Why not?"

"See you then. Sit in the back of the courtroom so I can't see you. You might distract me. Good night."

"What is this, Cassie? What about Arthur?" Joan asked.

"Who? Oh, him. I forgot to tell you, Arthur isn't in the picture any more."

"So much for sharing."

"Mom, Arthur doesn't even come close to Robert."

"Watch out, Cassie lawyers are slow to act," Randy said.

"We know, don't we, Mom?"

"Go to bed; you have to get up early."

"Yes ma'am. Going to court tomorrow, Dad?"

"Had enough. You can tell me about it."

The next morning the judge sat before the courtroom, and said to the jury, "Kip Jones committed a crime, but under threat of harm to his mother, his sole provider. I agree there must be restitution. He has spent some time in Juvenile protection, which may have seemed an eternity to him. He could be sent to prison and receive parole, but it is doubtful he will receive the training necessary to get a high school diploma. Someone has agreed to help him do that. I found him quite intelligent and brave in the situations he has been exposed to. I met with the two men who were injured, and they both agreed the charges could be dismissed, except for the driving without a license. I will decide the penalty. Mr. District Attorney, have Mrs. Barnett arrested immediately."

"Yes, Sir."

The Judge dismissed the jury, and thanked them for being good citizens by serving in the capacity of a juror.

Attorney Sanders said to Kip, "Do you know what just happened?"

"I'm not sure, Sir," he said.

"The charges against you have been dropped, except driving without a license. I am sure you will have to pay a fine for that. You and I will meet with your mother, and find a way to get you back in school. I believe you are a smart boy, but you need a formal education. You can *not* make a living doing odd jobs for people."

"I know that, Sir."

"And don't you drive any more. I'm surprised you even knew how to drive. It will take you time to catch up with your peers in school, that is, young people your age. The next few months you will study as never before. I have a lady who is willing to help you with your dyslexia. Before you can do anything you must learn to read. A person cannot survive in this world without being able to read."

"I understand, Sir. I'll work hard. Thank you for helping me. When I get some money I will pay you."

"What will please me better than money is claiming your right to an education. Do you understand me?"

"Yes Sir, I will work hard on that."

Robert and Cassie went to lunch at a café on Peachtree Street. Robert said to Cassie, "Would you like to meet my parents?"

"So soon?"

"I told them about you last night, and my mom wants to meet the girl I have invited to lunch two days in a row."

"You told her?"

"Yes, I did. I haven't invited a lady out to lunch in months. It is a big deal for me and for them. I think she was beginning to believe I might be gay."

"I would be glad to meet your parents, but the rumor is your father is a grizzly bear. Should I be afraid?"

"He can be tamed, which mom hasn't tried. You might be the one to do it."

"Count me in. Just let me know when, so I can doll up."

"You don't need to doll up. I'll talk to them and set a date, and call you. Why don't we ask Joan and Randy to come also?"

"Sure, I'll ask them and let you know."

"My father has a lot of respect for both of them. Cassie, I know this is going to sound forward, but I have to say this. I have enjoyed these last two lunches with you, and hopefully you have felt the same. I know you must finish school, but I am going to miss you. I've been floating on air and not sleeping very well at night. The truth is, I want you here with me."

"Robert, school will be over soon, and I am already scheduled for the bar exams. Maybe we should put off the dinner with our parents until a later date. Can you come up for the weekend and help me prepare? By the way, I still haven't written my paper about your work in this trial, which has to be turned in as soon as I go back. Perhaps I could also add a postscript to the paper such as, *he was wonderful, and so were the lunches we had together, and he kissed me on our second date*."

"Well, I had better get busy to keep you from telling a lie."

The cafe froze in time as he rose from the table, took her hand, pulled her to his body, put his arms around her, and pressed their lips together. They stood a long time until they realized the people in the café were applauding. They bowed to the crowd, and someone in the back yelled, "Way to go Robert!" They turned around, and saw Judge Brown. Both he and Cassie said, "Thank you, Your Honor."

CHAPTER 35
Judy Barnett

The Sheriff and a deputy rang the doorbell at Judy Barnett's house. There was no answer. As instructed, they rang the doorbell at Fred Mills house. Finally, he opened the door. "Is Mrs. Judy Barnett visiting you?"

"No Sir, she is here sometimes, but not today. She lives next door."

"We have a warrant to search her house, and also yours, to find her."

"You may come in and feel free to search, but she is not here. I haven't seen her in a couple of days." They called the two deputies in the second car, and they began the search. Mr. Mills gave them a key to Judy's house. She was not found inside the house, garage, or the out buildings, and there was no car in the garage. "Do you have an idea where she might be?"

"No, I do not. She usually keeps pretty much in touch with me, but not today."

"If she calls, or you see her, tell her the police are looking for her. Here is the number to call. Mr. Mills, I'm told that you should be available also."

"Am I under arrest?"

"No sir, just stay in town and be available."

———

It was dark, and raining so hard Judy had problems seeing the road. Her plans were to stay off the major expressways, because she feared someone would spot her. She knew by now Kip Jones had incriminated her in his testimony. "I might as well have shot the gun myself," she said out loud. "Why did I trust the boy? I depended too much on his ignorance. Never again will I trust anybody, never!" She slapped the steering wheel over and over with the palm of her hand. "Wherever you are John Randolph, I hope you are rotting in hell. You ruined my life. Even when you were dying, you didn't call me. Did you even think of me or did you hold *her* in your arms and ask forgiveness? There were so many things we could have done together instead of sneaking around. You led me to believe you would leave her. You promised! You promised me! You were a bastard, that's what you were. Maybe I will join you in hell. But first I have to get to Tennessee to see an old friend there. Maybe I have enough gas and won't have to stop until I get out of Georgia, at least get out of these mountains. I'm never going to set my feet in Georgia again. There is nothing left for me. Who wants the house? Let it rot. Oh, Julia, my Julia."

The driver of the truck was shaken. He told the policeman, "When I rounded the curve, there was a car right in front of me, and on my side of the road. There was no way I could stop that truck. I called you as soon as I could stop. I'm lucky. I could be down that bank with the driver. I feel awful. I need to sit down. Have you found out who is in the car?"

"According to her driver's license, she is Judy McKinney Barnett. I have made a call. Excuse me just a minute while I answer this." A voice on his patrol radio said, "There is a lookout for her. She is wanted in Atlanta for attempted murder. Bring her in."

"I'm afraid that will not be possible, at least for the moment. We haven't even gotten her out of the car. It's a mess. Wait a minute. The officer down below just hollered that she is definitely dead. The driver of the truck isn't hurt, but he is shaken up a bit. I just saw him vomiting."

"Officer, call me back when you have confirmed everything."

"Will do."

The morning news bulletin in Atlanta was shocking: *Judy McKinney Barnett, who was wanted for the attempted murder of her ex-husband and a security guard, has been found dead in an automobile wreck in the mountains of North Georgia. The driver of the tractor-trailer said he rounded the curve and there she was on his side of the road. She was born and raised in Atlanta, and was the daughter of Mildred and Gilbert McKinney who are deceased. She was recently divorced from Attorney Bob Barnett, and is survived by her daughter Julia Barnett. There has been no attempt to contact either of these persons yet. We have been told her body will be returned to Atlanta in a few days. Stay turned for more information.*

Bob Barnett called Randy; "I guess you have heard the news by now. I got the call around midnight. Someone here in Atlanta gave me as a contact. The news is on the television by now."

"What news? We're just having breakfast."

"Judy was killed in a traffic accident in North Georgia last night."

"Good God! Where are you Bob?"

"I am in Marietta with my parents. There are reporters in front of the house. I can't imagine how they knew to be here. I went out on the driveway and asked them to leave. I tried to assure them they probably knew more than I did."

"Call the police, and ask them to clear the reporters to give your parents some relief. I'm coming to pick you up. Have you called Julia?"

"Not yet. My parents and I are trying to decide how to tell her."

"Don't call her yet. I will be there in about thirty minutes. Joan, listen up. Turn on the news! Judy is dead. I'm going to pick up Bob. Call Frederick and Leonard, and if Roger gets in, hold onto him. I'm going to bring Bob and his parents back here."

By two o'clock in the afternoon they were assembled at Randy and Joan's condo. Bob's parents chose not to come since the police had cleared their street. Elizabeth came with Frederick because she had a good relationship with Julia. Roger came in, expecting to give a full report on his trip, but Joan asked him to wait until after the meeting.

He gave her a big hug, and said, "Anything for you, Joan. I am in love again, but I can wait to tell you about her."

Randy began, "I have gathered all of us today because we are tied together in a long friendship that has bound us together for years. Of course all of you know that, so I really didn't need to say it. Surely you have heard the news by now. There are several things to consider. First: When and how to tell Julia? Bob is most concerned about that. Second: How do we handle this situation with Judy's death, especially for Julia's sake, and perhaps yours Bob? Third: According to the police her body will be coming into Atlanta in the next couple of days. There will be transfer bills, and then her burial."

"I will take care of all those items," Bob said. "Right now help me decide how to tell Julie. She has to be told."

Frederick said, "Julia is a smart child, but the distance is going to upset her. Also, she is enrolled in school and needs to finish. I believe she should be told, but encouraged not to come home for a while." Elizabeth agreed with him.

Roger said, "Why not let her decide? She could fly home and then return."

Leonard said, "She was alienated from her mother, but Bob, it may be she would want to support you. Do you want her with you?"

"I am quite capable of taking care of this by myself. Perhaps I am the one who should go to England to be with her."

Randy said, "What a great idea! Call her and give her the news, but tell her you will be coming over there, and give her an approximate date of your arrival."

Joan said, "Bob, I like the idea that you will be the one who does the traveling, and it will give you a chance to get away from here for a while. Your parents may want to go with you."

"I doubt that. They do not fly, but perhaps they would go north Alabama to visit her sister. Let me say something. I don't know of many situations that compares to the unity in this room. We are family. We are always there for each other because we love each other. I could never take advice from anyone who would not be able to consider all my faults, and who also can see the good in me. Your support is appreciated more than I can tell you."

"Thank you. Tell us what you want to do," Randy said.

"I would like to call Julia now. Will someone find out what time it is over there. Julie has known all of you since she was a baby, so she will understand this meeting. If anyone wants to talk to her I think that would be a good idea." Randy said, "There is no problem with the time zone."

Bob used the phone he bought to keep in touch with Julia. "Hi Julia, all your most favorite people are in the room with me. They want to say hello." And each person gives a greeting.

"Sweetheart, I have some bad news. Your mom had a bad accident. She was rounding a curve on the wrong side of the road up in the North Georgia Mountains, and was hit by a semi."

"That's terrible," Julia said.

"That isn't all," Bob paused, "She was killed instantly," Bob said.

"Daddy, why was she up there?"

"She was running away from the police. We discovered she had asked a young boy to kill me, thinking her troubles would be over."

"Are you all right?"

"Yes, I am fine. I have great support here."

"Daddy, even though she was my mother, we had a poor relationship."

"I know Honey, and I hate telling you about this since you are so far away."

"Should I come home to be with you?"

"You know, I would rather come over to see you. It will be good for me to get away for a while, and besides I need a rest. You can help me relax and show me around, but first I have to bury your mom. Since she caused the accident there will be no trial, but probably a hearing. The truck driver was really shaken. I have spoken to him, and he will be all right. I'm most grateful for that. I will come when everything is settle here."

"Are you sure?"

"Yes, I am absolutely certain that is the best way for both of us. I don't want you to miss any school. Tell your aunt and uncle about our conversation. They can be your sounding board until I arrive."

"How long do you think?"

"I am not sure right now. I have things to take care of. I will call you in a couple of days. I love you."

"Julia," said Elizabeth, we all think it's a great idea for your dad to go to England, and I am looking forward to the day you will finish your schooling and be here."

"Thank you, Miss Elizabeth. I'm looking forward to being there too. I love all of you, and many thanks for supporting my dad."

"Bye, bye, Julia," all of them responded.

"You were great Bob," all the friends were saying.

Joan said, "Roger, it is nice seeing you again. I want to know about this new love of yours. I believe this would be a good time to go on to another subject, but don't say a word until I make tea and find some snacks."

Roger said, "This is a rather awkward time, but Joan is right, some good news will be good. When I was a teenager I met a girl in Israel. She had a strange name for a Jew, Roberta, but it was the name her father chose when she was born. We had a wonderful but short time together. Well… we did more than just hang out, as some might say. I was definitely in love, but my parents did not approve of me getting serious with any girl, so they sent me to The States to attend college. I never forgot her. Years later we met in New York, and in a few weeks we were married. We had a wonderful time together until she died of breast cancer. That is a very short way of bringing you up to date.

"My boyhood friend Justin and I went back to Tel Aviv to find her parents, as I promised Roberta I would do. When a young lady answered the door, I almost fainted. Justin had to stop me from falling. She was a younger copy of Roberta. I will make this brief. She is my beautiful daughter, Joanna from that very short relationship I had with Roberta in Israel. For some reason Roberta choose not to reveal her birth to me. The grandparents have educated her to be a teacher. When she has her next break I will fly over and bring her here for a visit. Hopefully, she will decide to live here. You will meet her, and perhaps she will fall in love with you and this country. End of story."

Joan and Elizabeth were in tears, and the others hollered after hearing his story. Everyone was excited to see Roger so happy. Elizabeth said, "Your story is like a fairy tale and so beautiful. All of us will make her welcome. "Yes, yes" the others.

Randy said, "Roger, you are a lucky man. I look forward to meeting her."

Bob said, "Thank you, Roger for bring some good news."

After a short period of silence Leonard said, "Back to the previous conversation, "Bob, it's time to conclude this discussion. Do you want me to go with you to sign for her body and help you with the burial plans?"

Bob said, "Leonard, I would be happy for you to be with me when I pick up her body, but I don't want a service; it could become a zoo. I am sure Julia would appreciate a short prayer for her mom, and please no one else there for the burial except the two of us. It would be awkward."

"I will be glad to do this for you, and I can go anytime, Leonard said."

The night had been rather somber until Roger told his story. It is always good to follow bad news with good news. Roger stayed for a while to catch up on all the events since he had been gone. He had not seen little Michael yet, and that was a priority. He also wanted to get together with Charlie and Sarah. During the weeks of the trip he noticed they were becoming close friends, but no romance was visible to him. Finally he said, "Folks, I am very tired, please excuse me. I hate you are having all this trouble, Bob. Let me know if there is anything I can do."

Later, when they were alone, Randy said to Joan, "All this commotion and emotion has cut into our time together. I am exhausted, but it wonderful to see how all our friends come together in a crisis. You are the most important person in my life, and I want nothing to interfere with our happiness. We need to settle down a bit, and taste each other's breath. Wouldn't you say I am right?"

"Yes, you are," Joan said. Something inside of me leaps when I see you leading your friends. They trust your advice, but you are right, I want the passion we have for each other to be our priority. Let's leave the cleaning up until tomorrow. Take me into your arms and lead me to bed, but this time prepare me for sleep, for both of us are exhausted. What we need is seven hours of unconscious relief from tragedy. I should hate Judy, but all I can think of, even though she betrayed my family, is what a waste of life. I feel so sorry for Bob and Julia. I hope they can get on with their lives. I am so grateful our friends trust your leadership."

It was a lovely evening. No one else in the world existed. There was no need for words. The closeness of her body went through every pore in his body. God! What a woman. His heart pounded faster as he held her. Earlier in their relationship, he could not be this near without thinking of sex, but for now he was silent and thankful to be the luckiest man alive. "Yes," he said to her, "I believe our bodies are telling us we need rest tonight."

Three days later Atty. Bob Barnett and Rev. Leonard Childs stood beside Judy Barnett's grave and pondered the events of the past months. Leonard said, "Lord, this is the end of strange events which have brought tragedy to Bob and his family. Only you know if Judy Barnett was close to insanity. Only you know the reasons for her actions. Once she had a beautiful daughter, a marriage, a lovely home, and parents who now welcome her in a grave beside them. Once she was a lovely woman who played the piano, loved to play tennis, and attended church. Lord, forgive her transgressions and bring her family and friends peace. Be a constant companion to her daughter, Julia and to Bob, and bring happiness to them in their upcoming reunion. Amen." They left before the internment.

CHAPTER 36

Cassie and Robert

Robert wanted to cancel his appointments and head out, but there was one he couldn't push aside. His father dumped all the cases he didn't want onto him, especially this one. Both of them hated custody cases, and the situation with the Griffins was complicated. The wife filed for divorce, accusing her husband of using excessive punishment on their daughter. Their firm had agreed to represent the father, Mason Griffin. Robert was not quite sure why.

At the first meeting with Mr. Griffin Bob began to understand a little about his disruptive and destructive daughter, Suzanne. His mind wondered as he sat behind his desk listening to Mr. Griffin. *What do parents do with a wild daughter? But what is considered wild these days? Is there any excuse for using a belt on a child, and when is punishment against the law?* After meeting for about forty-five minutes, Robert ended their long conversation, "Mr. Griffin, I need to do some research on what constitutes abuse. Does your wife have any pictures of the supposed abuse to your daughter?" *My brother and I were given the belt quite a few times when I was growing up. Of course that is not something I should say right now.*

"I have no idea about pictures," he answered.

"See if you can find out. I have a trip to make, but I will be back Monday morning. I would like to see you and your daughter some time next week. Make an appointment before you leave."

It seemed like months since he and Cassie had met; yet it was only three weeks. He was on his way to visit her for the weekend. He felt a little silly glancing at the bouquet of flowers on the seat beside him. *The last time I gave flowers to a female was the orchid my mother bought my date for our high school prom, and I stuck the girl when I tried to pin it on her gown. Her mom had to help me. How embarrassing.* Do *men bring flowers any more? Maybe I should throw them out the window. Why am I so excited and nervous? I wonder if she feels the same way I do. I never figured I'd meet the person I could fall in love with in a courtroom. I could marry this lady. What am I thinking? Anyway this is about the time I usually get dumped - It's been nice Robert, but I'm not ready for commitment yet. No, she's not like that. Cassie Randolph, maybe Walker, is something else. I want this to be a perfect weekend, but nothing is ever perfect. I believe I'm at her address. Well, here goes.*

He stood in front of the door thinking of his mother's words, "Now try to be nice to the girl, Robert." He rang the doorbell, and Cassie came to the door. She grabbed him around the neck and kissed him. "What took you so long?"

"Wow! Let me go out and come in again. I will say hello, Cassie, and you will invite me in. I will say do you like flowers or am I old fashioned? And you will say, 'hello Robert, welcome to my apartment; throw the flowers away.' I like your way better; let's try it again." This time he grabbed her.

"Flowers?" She asked. "Where are the flowers?"

"In the car. They almost got dumped along the way."

"Go get them, and we can place them beside mine." He got the flowers out of the car, and took a quick look around the apartment to get an idea what kind of woman she was. There were books and papers everywhere and a couple of stray coffee cups sitting around. The art on the wall was interesting, and he noticed there were no curtains on the windows. He found a blue chair and fell into it. He always liked blue. "It's been a terrible three weeks, but it seems like months since I have seen you. It was just the wrong time for my father to pitch too much my way."

"Hell-o! Forget the weeks and your father. You are here now."

For two days she did make him forget Mason Griffin and his father. The only time they talked about law was helping her study, but even then between kisses. He was comfortable with her. He was falling in love with a person he hardly knew. How was that possible?

Driving back to Atlanta, late on Sunday afternoon, there was a moment he crossed the line between being with Cassie and his work. He wanted to mark the place on the highway. He had decided his first objective was to arrange a meeting with Suzanne Griffin. She held the key to the whole case, so he had to find a way to get her into his office with only a child advocate accompanying her. He spoke with his dad and he agreed that would be the best move. *Wow, he agreed with me.*

The meeting was arranged while Suzanne's parents waited in the reception area. She was a lovely young lady, mature beyond her age. She sat up straight in the chair, was not chewing gum, and did not appear bored. She had beautiful eyes that could mesmerize any young man. She told him she was an excellent student, and was on the tennis team and debate team, and her advocate confirmed she was tops in her classes and definitely college material. When Robert addressed her, she paid attention. "Suzanne, what do you want to happen in your family?"

"I want the battles in my family to go away," she said. "My parents are worse to each other than to me. I admit dad hit me with a belt, but mom made too much of it. They are the ones who need to go to counseling, not me. To tell the truth, if they divorce, I would choose to live with my dad. My mom can be a bitch at times. They are so bad for each other that it's hard living with them. They are the ones who should go for counseling, not me. They need to decide whether to try to make a go of their marriage or quit." After a few more questions Robert said, "All right, let's call your parents in."

When the parents were settled, Robert challenged them to repair their relationships. "Do you want me to set the scene of what would happen in an open trial, and how it would hurt your family?"

"No, that is not necessary; I think we know," Mr. Griffin said. Mrs. Griffin just shrugged her shoulders. Robert asked her, "Mrs. Griffin, do what do you think?"

"Right now I don't give a damn. My daughter hates me, and my husband is against me. I get it; I don't belong in this family."

Mr. Griffin said, "Then I think we are through talking."

"Just a minute. I have some suggestions. Suzanne needs to see her advocate frequently, and I hope the two of you will seek counseling." Robert gave them the name of a counselor he knew. He saw little hope of the marriage lasting, but miracles do happen.

Two weeks later Mr. Griffin called to say he and his wife had seen their counselor once, and Mrs. Griffin agreed to drop the child abuse accusation. Their lives would not be interrupted by a trial, thank goodness. Robert wished him luck.

After the call, Robert slumped in his chair with his head in his hands. *Is that what marriage is like? How can two people sink so low in their relationship? Even after seeing the worst in marriage, I still want children, but I hate family law.*

CHAPTER 37

Roger, Sarah, and Charlie

It was Saturday morning. Roger decided he wanted to spend the day with friends, so he called Charlie. "Charlie, this is Roger. I have been missing you and Sarah. Would you like me to pick up Sarah and come out?"

"She's already here. Come on, we have been talking about you. Business is slow, so it's a perfect day to sit around. The grounds are beautiful today. Flowers are blooming everywhere." Roger had not relaxed since he left Israel, so he knew the Inn would calm him.

As he was told, the grounds were covered with wild flowers, and the place still reminded him of Bar Harbor. They greeted each other with lingering hugs and kisses, and the aroma of coffee filled the room. He told them what happened after they left each other, mostly about finding Joanna. "What? A daughter? Tell us more."

"She is so beautiful and I am a father! *And* she will be coming to visit soon."

After the surprise, they spent time reminiscing about the best places they visited and the people they met. "Enough traveling," Roger said. "What is going on?"

Charlie began, "Well, as you probably realized, we enjoyed each other's company, and we will see where our relationship leads us. Sarah is quite an individual, and I believe she thinks the same of me."

"Certainly I do," Sarah said. "Roger your idea was so wonderful; it changed my life. I was so burned out with church work, I had considered asking for a year's sabbatical to hide out in a commune. Out travels were beyond what I could ever have imagined, and I want to thank you for all you did for me. One day, somehow, I am going to find a way to repay you."

"No paybacks please. Everything ended well for all three of us. I do hope the two of you are meant for each other. I love both of you."

Charlie said, "We haven't used the word *love,* yet, but it lingers in my heart. Sarah, could it be possible that we not only enjoy each other's company, we have become fond of each other?"

"I thought you would never bring that up. Yes, it is possible, but I am not going to worry how we work it out. If it is meant for us to be with each other, everything will fall into place, but I am happier than I have ever been."

"I am so excited for both of you. What can I do to hurry this along?"

"You can't fix everything, Roger. However, Charlie and I decided we want you to be a part of our lives, and we must meet Joanna. She is going to love this Inn. I thank you for introducing me to Charlie's little haven. What is stamped in my mind forever is three strangers, sitting on these chairs, making that quick and lasting decision to get out of town. You found your Joanna, and Charlie and I found each other. Surely we cannot ask for more."

"Sarah, the tenderness I see between you and Charlie is real. Do not linger too long seeking providence to tell you what to do. One day the two of you will create a family, and I dare say both of you believed that you never happen. Am I right?"

"Roger, how right you are. Sarah, one of these day I want to wake up in the morning and see you beside me. I want to have babies with you. My life will be complete if you will love me. Is it too soon to ask if you would consider marriage?"

"Charlie! Let me think about this. How will we do all this? You out here, and me in Atlanta?"

"So you don't believe what you said earlier, that things will work out?"

"Oh, Charlie, I do believe that. We can work it out. Am I repeating myself?"

"Yes, you are," Roger said.

"Roger, are you a part of this?" Sarah asked.

"I am. *We* are waiting for your decision."

"*We*? What is this *we*, Roger?" Sarah asked.

"*We* made a life-changing trip together. *We* have a relationship. *We* trust each other. *We* are getting older by the minute, and w*e* cannot expect everything to be perfect. That makes *me* a part of this *we*."

"Dear, dear Charlie, I trust you and I do love you. Can we envision spending a life together? Roger is that a good enough response?"

"Do not ask me; ask Charlie."

"Well, okay. Charlie, is that a good enough answer?"

"Yes, Sarah it is. Isn't this going to be wonderful? Roger, grab the camera over there, and make our proposal picture, so I can send it to her church tomorrow."

"Now, Charlie I can take care of that myself," she said.

"You know," said Roger, "This old Inn has a lot of memories for so many people. I plan to take Joanna to see the Cottage Inn in Bar Harbor her mother and I shared, and then bring her back here to see this special place. Well, it is time for me to be going. I want to see Leonard and Margaret's little boy today. Oh, only if I had held my own baby in my arms. Damn it! I missed all those events. Do not let that happen to either of you. Charlie, I am glad you have this little haven, it is definitely a lover's nest."

"You are so right, Roger. Come again and help us make decisions."

"Any time, any time."

CHAPTER 38

Roger, Margaret, and Leonard

Roger called Margaret to see if it was a good time to come over, she said, "Yes, I'll call Leonard and tell him he has to be here pronto. God knows, if I don't call him, he'll find something else to do."

"Is he giving you any trouble? I will beat his ass for you if you want me to. He is lucky to have you and Michael."

"Come on. You can take care of Michael while I fix supper."

"Do you mean that? I might get a speeding ticket. Will you pay the fine?"

"A rich man begging from a pauper, not going to happen."

Roger arrived in a short time. He noticed that Margaret had gained a little weight, probably from being pregnant. She was nursing the baby, and Roger asked if he could watch. "I have never seen a baby nursing. It is a mystery to me. Maybe I can picture how it was when Roberta nursed Joanna."

"Sure, why not."

"Oh my, Margaret, I am watching pure nature. Just think the food of life is flowing through your body into his. At this moment I wish I were a woman."

"Well, it's not the easiest thing at first, but I got used to it. Leonard told me about your daughter Joanna. Don't pine, Roger. You still have time left to be a good father. It's going to be exciting watching you with her."

"When you are finished, may I hold Michael?"

"Sure, here is the burp rag. When he spits on you, it will be a reminder of what you missed. Don't be so scared of him, he's limber. Just put both hands under his head and lay him on your knees."

"Hello Michael, this is your uncle Roger. Margaret, he laughed! Do I look that funny?" She chose not to tell him it might be gas.

Leonard arrived while Roger was still holding the baby. "Margaret," he said, "You have given our baby away. Don't get sticky fingers, Mr. Waddell. You've got your own now. Just because she isn't a baby, you can't have mine."

"Leonard, you lucky dog, a beautiful wife and a son. Maybe I will have a grandchild one day, and I have hopes he or she will have an American father."

"Planning her wedding, huh?" Leonard asked.

"No, I want her just like she is until I get used to her. She is *so* beautiful my head swims just thinking of her."

"Give me my son, you've put him to sleep. Wake up, son it's your daddy." Michael squinted his eyes a little, but didn't wake up. "Can we ask Roger to go home now, Margaret?"

"No, I have invited him to experience my cooking. Making draperies I'm fond of. Cooking I detest. I need to get back to work soon to feel successful. Leonard can pick up food better than anything cooked in this house. Look how skinny he is."

"I tell you what I am going to do for you, Margaret," Roger said, "I am going to call this company I know and order ten complete meals sent to you."

"Great! When will they start coming?"

"You don't need to do that, Roger I can help her," Leonard said.

"Be quiet, Leonard you don't have time to help me, besides, it's a gift, and a gift of food is exactly what I need, unless you are going to start cooking," Margaret said.

"Okay, Roger throw your money around if you want to."

"Listen, Leonard *do not* be an idiot. You did a favor for me letting me work at the church to get my head straight, remember?"

"Well, go ahead this one time, then we are even."

"Margaret, I think I should be going. I have let things slide since my trip overseas. Let me take you up on a meal later. Call me if you need anything."

"Thanks, Roger, maybe Leonard will be more cordial another time. I think a lunch appointment would be good for both of you."

Leonard walked to the car with Roger. "Stay out of Margaret's life. The last word Bettye uttered was 'Roger.' I don't intend for that to happen here."

"I am sorry about that, old man but that was not my fault, so do not blame me. If she had married me, her last word might have been, 'Leonard.' Maybe we should have been her harem. I got over her years ago, and maybe it is time you did also. Go back inside before I get angry and punch you."

After Roger left, Margaret said, "Leonard, you surprise me, and not in a good way. You have known Roger for years. It seems you would remember the old times and appreciate him, or forgive him, whichever one is appropriate."

"Margaret, I don't feel like fighting; I don't even want to eat. I believe rest is what I need more than food. Forgive my behavior. Kiss Michael good night for me."

"Go on to bed. I'll check on you later after I put Michael down."

CHAPTER 38
Leonard

Entering his condo, empty of the people he loved, Roger was alarmed how bad he felt. He was shocked by Leonard's actions and confrontation. What could be wrong with him? He has a beautiful wife and a baby, yet he does not seem to connect with them. His last comment must mean the old memories are flooding back. It has been years since Bettye died. She thought she was marrying a lawyer, but he turned into a preacher, and she was not even a Christian. I had feelings for her myself. Looking back, Leonard was the one who was obsessed with her. I should have told her that I did not love her. The gal I left behind in Israel still haunted me. Blame my parents on that. What an idiot! I do not know if it was my love for them or my fear of them. I just obeyed, like I had always done. Leonard needs to talk to someone, but I am definitely not the one listen to him.

He sat down to contact Joanna when his phone rang. "Roger, come back here now! Leonard has just left in an ambulance, and I need someone to look after Michael."

"What is wrong with Leonard? He was not at his best behavior, but I thought it was because I was there."

"Stop talking and get over here!"

He walked in the house just enough time for Margaret to show him some bottles of milk in the refrigerator she had pumped from her breast. "If you are uncertain of what to do, like changing a diaper, call Joan or Elizabeth." As she was leaving she yelled, "You have to warm the milk, but don't get it too hot."

"Do not worry about us. Go!"

He waited for Michael to wake. "Changing a diaper cannot be all that hard, Michael. I just have to made a triangle and pin it. One pin ought to do. Whoa, you have two pins. Do not cry while I figure this out." He put the diaper on, but it fell off when he lifted Michael. "Okay, let me try this again, fold here, then here. Now I see why two pins are better. Let me go see what food you have in the fridge. 'Warm,' she said. Running hot water over the bottle will take care of that. I would have made a great father, Michael." Then a sound came from the diaper. "Phew, Michael what is that odor? Oh no, I have to do it all over again." Putting his pride aside he decided to call Joan. "Hey, Joan I need some help here. Leonard is in an ambulance, and Margaret is close behind, and I am playing at babysitting. I need some advice."

Joan said, "Slow down; what's the matter?"

"As I said, an ambulance is transporting Leonard to the hospital, and Margaret left. I am tending to Michael. I managed to put the diaper on, but it appears he has soiled it. Help me out here."

"Is the diaper a disposal diaper?"

"How do you tell?"

"Is it paper or cloth?"

"Well, it is not cloth."

"Take the diaper off, roll it into a wad, then clean his bottom with a wet towel, and put another diaper on, and throw the old one in the trash. It will take me twenty minutes to get there, so take care of him the best you can in the meantime."

She arrived to find Roger sitting in a rocker chair feeding Michael a bottle. "So what happened to that fearsome guy I heard on the phone?"

"I just discovered I might have been good at this after all."

"How did you get this job?"

"It is a long story. Call the hospital and find out want is going on." She went into another room and called the waiting room and Margaret answered, "Margaret, what in the world is going on?"

"I don't know. They haven't let me in the inner sanctum yet, but I think he had a heart attack."

"I'm here with Roger and everything is all right. If you need something to do, call Elizabeth, and ask her to come sit with you."

"Good idea. I'll call you later."

Elizabeth arrived just in time for Dr. Mark Williamson, a friend of hers and a member of Leonard's church, to come into the waiting room. "Margaret, Leonard is in serious condition. On the way here, the technician had to re-start his heart several times. My partner is with him now, but I need to get back in there. I will let you know how he is as soon as I can. Hi, Elizabeth I'm glad you are here."

"Thanks. I plan to stay as long as she needs me."

"Let me say this to you, Margaret, you should call one of the elders of our church to come."

"Thanks for the advice, but I believe a friend is better right now."

"What happened, Margaret?" Elizabeth asked after the doctor left.

"Leonard was grumpy all evening. To tell the truth, when he saw Roger, he was quite uncivil to him. I couldn't hear what they were saying outside, but Roger left without eating dinner with us, and Leonard stormed back into the house and went to bed. After the ambulance left with Leonard, I called Roger to come back and take care of Michael." Margaret called to see how Roger was doing. Roger said, "Do not worry Joan is here with me, but I managed to change a dirty diaper and warm the milk all by myself. Everything is in control. Call me if there is any change."

"Roger, it looks bad. I'm so sorry he was nasty to you, but now I realize he was not feeling well."

Joan took the phone from Roger, and said, "I just got a call from Randy. He's probably walking in the hospital's door right now. If Elizabeth needs to go home, Randy can stay."

"I might need both of them," she answered. Two hours passed. Elizabeth said, "I believe it would be appropriate at this moment if we pray, considering we haven't heard anything for quite some time."

Margaret said, "I wish I knew how to pray, but whoever hears me might say, 'Where have you been all these years.'"

Elizabeth said, "I *have* been praying. I just talked to Frederick, and he's decided to come sit with us. He's a deacon at our church, so I bet you he is praying." Frederick arrived, and the three of them waited. The door opened, and when they saw the expression on Dr. Mark Williamson's face, they all rose. "I'm sorry, Margaret there was nothing more we could do. His heart just stopped beating, and we tried everything to start it, but he didn't respond. I am sorry to be the doctor to pronounce my pastor dead. Elizabeth, here is Rev.

Sarah Marshall's number. I believe it is time for you to call someone from our church."

No one moved or spoke, for there was nothing to say. Finally, Margaret began crying, and so did all the others including Dr. Williamson. He said, "Margaret, Leonard was such a good man and a wonderful pastor. He was so happy finding a wife and having a son. This is not fair to you and Michael, and the church members are going to be devastated."

"Can I see him?"

"Yes, come with me; I will take you to him."

"Mark, you are right, there is nothing fair in all this. Leonard was so excited about having a son. How could God do this to him?"

"Margaret, don't blame God. Leonard was a workaholic, and he accomplished more than was expected of him. He is going to be missed by a lot of people."

"I just wish he had accomplished more for me and his son."

The room in the emergency room was cold. She leaned over to Leonard and put her hand on his chest, and said, "Michael will never remember you Leonard, and I will never forgive you for dying. You worked too hard and spent too many hours with your members. I missed so much of you in those long evenings I waited supper for you. I waited for years to meet someone like you, and now you are gone. We had great plans, you know."

"Margaret, Michael will remember him if you talk to him about his father. Just keep reminding him what a good person he was. Now is not a time for you to be angry. It is time to grieve, but not in angry."

"People grieve in different ways I am told, but I don't know how. I think being angry helps me right now. Surely, you know what I mean."

"Maybe, but these next few days will require you to face a lot of people. Listen to them, and learn how to live again."

"You are sweet, Mark. Wait! What do you mean I will have to face a lot of people?"

"Margaret, the people in our congregation will want to grieve with you."

"I guess they do, since he spent more time with them than he did with me and Michael. Someone needs to take me home. I want to hold my baby. Who takes care of what has to be done now?"

"I will call a few people, and we will handle everything the way you want it. We have to move him to a funeral home, and you have papers to sign. Get someone to take you home, and you and I will talk tomorrow."

"I know absolutely nothing about funerals in the church. Get someone to take care of everything, and I will pay them."

"Margaret, don't think about money right now. I'm sure the church will take care of the expenses and preparations. Don't worry about it; go home."

———

Frederick went home. Elizabeth got the keys from Margaret, and drove her home, and Randy followed in his. They would go back later and get Elizabeth's car. Randy called Roger and gave him the bad news. "Roger, you realize this is the first one of us to die. This is kind of scary."

"You bet it is. Should we let Bob know? Of course he is in England, but I believe he needs to know."

"Let me think about it. I do not want to interrupt his vacation. He needs it."

———

Margaret dreaded going into her house. Leonard would not be at the bedside of a parishioner tonight, and he would not be coming home. It was a weird thought. She felt someone had stabbed her in the stomach. She vomited in the yard, and was not too alert when they put her into bed. Joan stayed for the night, and Randy went home to decide whether to call off his appointments for a couple of days. Then he thought, "Maybe the best thing to do is work."

CHAPTER 39
The Wallace Kids

"You're late again," Ms. Bee said, as she met him at the door. "Three persons are waiting for you. They came in together, but they *do not* have an appointment."

"Tell them to wait. Leonard Childs died last night. It has been a tough evening."

"You mean your friend, the pastor?"

"Yes. I don't know if I'm fit to see anyone."

"Oh, then you won't like this crew. Go to your office, it might be good for you. You might have something to say to these idiots," She said.

Before he was seated at his desk the three of them paraded in.

Ms. Bee followed them, "I'm sorry, Mr. Walker, they got past me."

"Apologize to Ms. Bee, Billy. She runs this office, not you."

"Nobody tells us what to do," he said.

"Never mind, I'll take care of them, but only because of their mother."

The oldest son, Billy was the bully, "You gave our mother bad advice. Our business is none of your business. We don't think she's capable of managing her property."

"Wait just a minute. First of all you have no business bursting in here, trespassing on my property without an appointment, and besides you weren't polite to Ms. Birkenstein. She should have called the cops. Hell, forget it, I know who you are, the self-centered leeches, the Wallace kids. Wanda Wallace, WW your dad used to call her, what a woman! Yes, I advised your mother to do as she wishes, but I sent her to another lawyer so I would be able to testify against you. And you can bet if you take this to court, the judge will bust your buts. Your mom, you don't deserve to say that word, is a smart lady and capable of defending herself. I *do not* wish to hear from any of you, so leave my office, or I will call the cops."

"We don't believe you know our mother well enough to say what is right for her," responded.

"Let's see, I have known her since I was a little boy. Billy, she even spanked you and me one time for fighting. You were a bully back then, too. My advice to all of you is if you need money get a job, and quit trying to rob your mother." He rose, opened the door, and called, "Ms. Birkenstein show these people out."

"You haven't heard the last from us."

"Oh I'm sure of that, but remember this, not a one of you is smarter than your mother. Perhaps her only failure was not teaching you respect. If you father were alive he would disinherit you."

Ms. Bee peeped in his door and said, "I must say," Mr. Walker, "You were splendid; I heard it all."

"So you were listening? Good. You might have to report how despicable they were. Can you believe them? Their father should have smothered them at birth."

"Now, now, that would be murder. Perhaps the courts could do something similar like banishing them or allowing *her* to disinherit them."

"What a great idea! That wasn't a good way to start a day. Get me a cup of hot, strong coffee. You might need one yourself."

"Yes, Your Honor."

"Cut the comedy. I need to ponder on the life of Leonard Childs."

He held the cup in his hands, and everything in the office disappeared.

We were seniors in college. Both Leonard and Roger were interested in the same girl. God, Bettye was beautiful, but she was definitely an airhead. She "played" both of them. One day Leonard and Roger came to blows. Frederick and I had to tear them apart. I told Roger how childish he was, and Frederick sent Leonard to wash his face. We took Roger aside and told him he could do better. He needed to step aside for Leonard. Frederick grabbed him and said, "What's the matter with you, Roger? Find a girl with brains." Roger got the message. In a few months Leonard married Bettye. After graduation he entered law school, but at the end of the first year he left law school and entered seminary to become a pastor. Bettye never recovered from the blow. Frederick predicted she would be helpless and Leonard would be her savior. How right he was.

CHAPTER 40
The Funeral

Randy came into the house, poured a glass of wine, and sank into the sofa. Joan was talking on the phone. He had never felt so tired, so useless, so vulnerable, and *so* old. Joan said, "I'm talking to Cassie." Randy looked up but said nothing. "What? You want us to come to supper with the Sanders? Cassie, aren't you moving a little too fast?"

"Mom, this is serious. Surely you are not surprised."

"No, not really, but for the next few days we cannot schedule anything. Leonard Childs died yesterday, and a lot of people are grieving, especially Randy. You remember Rev. Childs. He was the pastor who married us, and we have known him for years. Are you agreeable to wait awhile?"

"Sure, Mom. Tell Dad I'm sorry about the two of you losing your friend, and that I said neither of you are *old*. He can't be old; you just birthed to him. Mom, I'll be finished here in three weeks, and Robert has already been helping me study for the bar exams. I am prepared! It won't be long before I'll be back in Georgia. You and Dad won't have to worry about helping me bring my things home. Robert has agreed to rent a small truck."

"Well that's nice of him; thank him for us. I'll see you then.

Joan told Randy about the call, and he said, "Do I have to have dinner with Bob Sanders? He is about as obnoxious as a bull."

"Is a bull obnoxious? Couldn't you call him something else?"

"Okay, then Mr. Obnoxious. My mom used to say he was uppity. I knew the day Cassie met Robert Junior at the Kip Jones' trial he was already gaga. Two dinner dates in two days and he was hooked. This whole thing has gone too fast."

"Let's see. You grabbed me from behind, kissed me with passion, and told me you had loved me for years. I knew you wanted to throw me on the bed and make mad love. Yep, I knew it. I bet they can't top that!"

"You got me there."

Roger called, "Joan, the funeral plans are being made. Their governing body wants the funeral to be at the church. They call it a Celebration of Resurrection, not a funeral. Margaret objects to having a church funeral; she wants something more private. She said, 'the very idea, allowing people to watch me grieve offends me. I know how that goes: People watch the survivors to see how they are *taking it*.' I told her that she has to consider that the members of the church have known him longer than she has, and they will also be grieving. She finally agreed with me. Will you see if she will talk to you?"

"Thanks for the information. I'll call her now."

"Margaret, this is Joan. Roger is worried about you. How can I be of help?"

"I'm so sorry. I know I'm being self-centered bitch, but I can hardly breathe. Roger did help me understand a bit, but I haven't had time to know those people, and Leonard had a long relationship with them, so I'm not going to complain about anything else. They are being so kind taking care of everything, and one of the Elders has been especially nice. He has called me several times getting my opinion and telling me what everyone is doing to get this event together. Can you believe there will be a dinner afterward? Who can eat at such a time? It's sort of cannibalistic, like eating the dead. I can't even think about smelling food much less eating it."

"Margaret! Don't think about such things. Go along with these people so they will have an opportunity to grieve for their pastor."

"Just to be more comfortable, Joan can you find me one of those hats that has a veil in front? At least I can to be able to hide my face."

"You can have the one I used."

"Thanks, Joan. They *are* trying to be helpful. One of the Ladies of the church called and asked me to bring Michael, and she would have someone standing by to take him to the nursery if he cries. I had been wondering about that, so I told her how nice it was to call and offer to help."

Margaret did not get her wish for the casket to be brought down the aisle with Leonard's friends as pallbearers. Seems the church elders thought it would work out best if a family burial was first, and a celebration of the deceased's life at the church afterward. That is the method some of the churches have started. Margaret said, "Someone told me there is a theological reason to do it that way, but it is probably so the people can have a meal without waiting for the family to return from the burial. So be it. Leonard is not going to be buried beside his first wife. Roger and I thought it best to buy a new plot. Poor Bettye is not left alone; she is buried in a plot with her parents."

It was a solemn graveside service. Rev. Sarah Marshall, who was very close to Leonard, gave the last rites. She read a short passage of scripture and thanked God for Leonard's honesty, hard work, and his trust in God and the Church. When the words, "Ashes to ashes, dust to dust" were spoken, Margaret felt a chill run through her bones. Suddenly she could hear her mother's reprimand, *Never, never step on a grave. It will bring you bad luck.*

"So this is how we will all end," Randy whispered to Joan. "Not attractive words for ending one's life."

"Get used to those words; death happens to all of us," Joan whispered. "Surely you don't believe that our bodies will fly away right up to the heavens, do you?"

"Sounds like a better method to me. I still don't look forward to it. Maybe I'll go like Leonard – quick."

"And not say goodbye to me. You'd better not."

After Rev. Marshall finished, the funeral director allowed family and friends a few moments to reflect, pick a flower off the bier, throw dirt on the casket, or whatever gave them closure, then ushered them away to the waiting congregation.

The church was expecting so many to attend they had a television screen installed in a couple of the large classrooms to take care of the overflow. One of Leonard's closest colleagues, the Rev. Phillip Doss was asked to give a meditation, and two other pastors, plus Sarah, were on the podium. The organist played Massenet's Meditation from Thais after the family and friends were seated. Roger was carrying Michael, who must have been fed just before, because he slept the whole time. The choir sang two beautiful songs as pictures of Leonard, doing various things around the church, were flashed upon a screen. Margaret could hardly breathe seeing how handsome he was when he first came to the church as a young pastor.

Each pastor took a short part in the service. Sarah read the scripture passage from Leonard's first sermon to their congregation, which was given to her by the church historian. After the benediction, she gave the invitation for everyone to stay for lunch after the organist ended with the procession. Margaret's only request was relayed to the organist. She wanted the service to end with Felix Mendelssohn's March of the Priests.

After the organist finished, the family was led into the Fellowship Hall. There was no receiving line. People simply mingled as they spoke to Margaret and to Leonard's friends who were identified by boutonnieres on their lapels. Michael became restless, so Margaret asked Roger to take him to one of the ladies. "Tell her there is a bottle inside the diaper bag." About five ladies came forward, but Roger gave him to a lady who was especially nice to him when he worked there.

Margaret pretended to eat, but she wished there was a sin-eater she could call on to eat her food. She remembers her mother talking about that weird guest, who would be asked to slip in and eat a table full of food to forgive the sins of the deceased, or maybe today it would be her sins; she wasn't sure which. What she didn't realize, she wasn't expected to eat anything. She was a grieving widow who could do as she pleased. After dinner, Roger and Joan escorted her around the room to thank a few people for the service and the food.

It was a tiring day, but not yet through. Their small group agreed to gather at Randy and Joan's condo to settle down and play with Michael. It was amazing, and a little eerie, how much he resembled that young preacher on the screen. There was a lot to discuss, but some things could be taken care of later, such as getting Margaret settled in the right place. Of course Margaret had not thought about that.

Bob arrived back in time for the funeral. It was a good time to greet him with enthusiasm, and listen to his experiences in England. Bob said, "The trip was the best temporary place for me. Julia and I traipsed around the sights of London like she was a British citizen, and my brother's wife and children were excited to have me there. They were beyond gracious to me the whole visit. Julia will be home as soon as her studies are finished. Both of us are grateful for your support. The other news is, my realtor called to tell me I have a contract on my house, so I will be looking around when Julia is here to help." His information was a positive diversion. When he finished, no one spoke for a few moments. They were all watching Michael. Roger broke the silence, "Margaret, tell us how can we help you?"

"I'm a capable business person, but I don't feel like it today. Confusion is the best description I can think of, but I do not feel helpless. One thing I am sure of, I will not stay in that house."

"We realize that," Joan said. "Perhaps this is not a good time to think about all the things you have to do."

"Margaret, do you mind if I take you home, and spend a couple of days with you? I will be glad to help you find a realtor and assist you with Michael while you talk care of some necessary projects." Roger asked.

"Roger, I don't want to take up your time. I know you want to go see Joanna, but whatever time you have before that, I will accept."

"Then I will stay the night with you and we can talk in the morning. Good night everyone; I will keep you informed." Slowly everyone left, and the room became quiet, as if the air was taken away.

Finally, Randy said, "Joan, I feel a depression coming on. I suppose that is what happens when friends start dying. We all feel responsible for Margaret, but she is a strong person – much stronger than Leonard - and she will definitely land on her feet." "Randy, this is not time to feel sorry for us. We have to live the life we are given, and tomorrow I am going to begin doing that, and so are you. You have a business, and I have started another book. I believe we need to get away for awhile after we meet the Sanders."

"Oops, I forgot about that less than exciting event. Call Cassie tomorrow and set up a time; let's get it over with. We haven't heard from Rick lately? When we don't hear from him, I tend to think he is not doing well. I'll call him tomorrow, but let's have two glasses of wine and go to bed. Lately it seems that going to bed is a time of recovery for us."

It had always been exciting getting in bed with each other, but tonight both were daunted by the events of the day. The bedroom was a place to make love, a place to share secrets, and a place where sex comes naturally, but tonight death crept into their lives making it awkward. Randy said to Joan, "This kind of day may come more often as we and our friends get older. I can't put aside the events of the day and focus on anything else. I am just hoping I can find sleep through the tragedy."

"Then let's do the usual after a nasty day," Joan said. "Let's kiss each other with the most passionate kiss as if we just made love. First put your ear to my heart and count the beats to make certain I am alive, then look into my eyes and remind me how lucky we are. Only then can I find sleep."

"Can I also sing you a song?"

"Save it for breakfast, she said."

"Goodnight, love of my life. Your heart beats sixty-five times a minute, your eyes are still brown, and your lips are inviting. See you in the morning."

CHAPTER 41

Roger and Margaret

Before Roger put Margaret and Michael to bed, he said to her, "We will talk in the morning. Presently rest is what you need." When they were settled, he placed a call to Joanna. It took three tries before he connected. At last, "Joanna, is that you?"

"Yes. Shall I call you *Father or Dad*?"

"I would like either, but since Father is formal, you may call me that until we become more familiar with each other. I want to come for you as soon as your school break takes place. When will that be?"

"In two weeks I will have a month's leave. I have been so excited about going to America, but I was afraid you would not be able to make it."

"Absolutely nothing could stop me. If I should become ill, I will send someone else. Are you all right with that arrangement? Give me a firm date so I can buy my ticket and both our tickets back to the states. We can get your return ticket later. (He was so hoping that ticket would never be bought.)

"I will be ready," she said. "You can plan to spent the night here. My uncle will take us to the airport."

"Thanks for the offer, but I will arrange a return flight to the states, so I will want you to be at the airport, ready to go. We will not be going directly to Georgia. I have planned a side trip. It is time for me to get away from a recent tragedy. One of my friends died a few days ago, and tonight I am at his house taking care of his wife, Margaret and her baby, Michael. He is beautiful, but I bet you were even prettier. I will call you about the time of arrival, and hopefully you will be waiting for me. I have to change planes once. By the way do not bring a lot of clothes; we will purchase what you need after your arrival."

"Oh, that sounds lovely. Goodnight, Father." She did not catch the words, side-trip until later. H*ow exciting, another surprise.*

Margaret was up and in the kitchen before Roger rose. He came in to find a full breakfast, and Michael on a pallet playing with some plastic rings. "He's teething," Margaret said. "He'll chew on anything so I bought these for him. I'm glad he is on the bottle now; no bites any more. Come sit, we have to eat."

"Margaret, this breakfast looks great. I do not believe I ate enough yesterday to count as food. Thanks for letting me sleep."

They ate in silence. There was so much to say, and no way to start the conversation, but it had to be done. "Margaret, does Leonard own this house or does the church?"

"Leonard bought the house with a life insurance policy he had on Bettye, and the church had been giving him a housing allowance for years. There is a small mortgage. Roger, I have no intention of staying here, so today I am going to call one of my realtor friends and put it on the market."

"Where will you go?"

"I'm not leaving town. I have a good business, so I'll find a place and settle in as soon as possible."

"How can I help?"

"You have been so good to me already, Roger, but I have to do this on my own. I sold my condo when I moved in here and have not touched that money, so I have plenty of cash to buy another place, and besides Leonard had a life insurance policy with the church. I will have that, and Michael will have his Social Security."

"Would you like for me to see if there is a unit for sale in our community?"

"It certainly wouldn't hurt, but I won't be expecting everyone to baby sit. I have engaged a woman who will keep Michael during the day. She has even agreed to take Michael to the homes where I will be working, if I want her to."

"Margaret, that's great! You have good business sense. You are going to be all right. Now let me tell you my news. In two weeks, I am leaving for Israel to bring Joanna to America."

"Wonderful! Roger, you are going to be a fine father. I am looking forward to seeing the daughter of the beautiful Roberta."

"You are not going to believe this, she is truly another Roberta. I tell you, I almost fainted when I saw her. She can stay a month, but I am hoping she will make this her home."

"She must; she needs to be with her father."

"Call your realtor while I clean up the kitchen. If she is like other realtors she will arrive shortly, so I am going to leave now. I will call around to see where condos are available and let you know."

Jeanette Morris came by that afternoon. She knew the house well, quickly appraised it, and took the listing. "This house should sell quickly in this area. Just in case, I hope you can find another place soon."

"Roger, one of Leonard's friends is going to help me." That must be him on the phone now."

"Margaret," Roger said, "There is nothing available where I live, but I will keep looking. If the house sells right away, you can stay in my condo for a while."

"Nope. When Joanna comes the two of you will need your time together. I'll find a temporary place if I have nothing by the time this place sells."

"A temporary place is not good for you right now. Joanna and I will not be home for at least two week. I am taking her to see the Cottage Inn her mother and I owned in Maine, and we will rent a car and drive back to Atlanta so she can see a little bit of the America she has dreamed of. Anyway your house cannot possible sell and close in two weeks. Ask the realtor if there is anything that needs to be done to the property, and have her hire someone to take care of it?"

"I have already asked her about that, and she has agreed to do a once-over before she leaves."

Roger went by again before he left for Israel, but he saw that Margaret had everything in order, so he said to her, "I am getting ready to set out for Israel, so I will not be available for a while. If you need anything call Joan and Randy." Not long after he left an elder from the church called Margaret and asked if he could drop by. He arrived shortly, so he must have been in the area. He brought a small gift for Michael.

"Mrs. Childs, we want to know what you need, and how we can help."

"Thank you. I know the members are grieving, so I hate to ask anything of you, but one thing has come to my mind. If you can help me claim the insurance policy Leonard had with the church I would appreciate it. Also, maybe you can ask his secretary to pack up the personal items that are in Leonard's office. If there were any items the church would like to have just have her call me. Does the church own the furniture in his study?"

"He bought the desk, chairs, and pictures himself from his allowance."

"Then, let that furniture remain. If the next pastor does not want it, use it somewhere else in the church."

"Are you certain? I do think there is one painting you will want to keep. It is a painting by a well-known Atlanta artist, Pearl Hoffman, and there is a chair, not a desk chair, but a lovely piece of furniture you should definitely keep."

"Thank you for telling me that. I do want the painting and the chair. Would you like for me to have someone pick them up?"

"I will personally bring the painting and chair to you. I have known Pearl for years. She is quite an artist. You may not know this – she is Randy Walker's aunt."

"Oh, thank you. Your folks did love Leonard. I am grateful to the church for all you did during the last few days. I could not have made it through without your help. Please let the people know. I will write a letter after I get settled."

"It is going to be hard to replace Leonard, but I believe there is someone in our system that will be perfect. Rev. Marshall has agreed not to accept another position until we call a new pastor, and we will compensate her well."

"Sarah is a wonderful person. Leonard enjoyed working with her."

"There is one more item. Many memorials have been given to the church in honor and memory of Leonard. Also a group of anonymous donors have given a fairly large sum of money, and requested it to be a scholarship fund for members to use for their undergraduate college degrees. The Board of Elders is placing all donations into that fund, which will be called The Leonard Child's Education Fund. Also the Church will continue Leonard's salary and housing allowance to you for six months. Even if you should sell, the money will help you in relocating."

"My goodness, what a generous gift! I am stunned and happy the people of the congregation decided to do that. Thank you for coming by. I do appreciate your concern for me and Michael."

"Let me say this for our members, we wish you happiness and prosperity for many years. You brought excitement to Leonard and gave him a child. He told me Michael was the thrill of a lifetime. I am indeed sorry he passed, and that he will not be here to see Michael grow up. Should you decide to remain a part of the church, we would be happy."

"I am not certain about that, but thanks so much for all you and other members have done for me, and for dropping by today."

CHAPTER 42
The Sanders

The stifling heat and visible pollen of the late summer causes Georgians to hibernate far too much. Only a swift thundercloud can clear the yellow dust from the air, but around the first of September the dust will be gone, just in time for children to be shut up in their classrooms. When the leaves finally break out in brilliant colors in the Fall, it will take your breath away, and even more so in the mountains of North Georgia. The trees decorate themselves with gold, yellow, and red colors only Mother Earth can design. For a couple of months the roads are over crowded with people getting relief from the summer heat, looking for beauty in out of the way places.

Randy finally agreed to visit with Robert's parents. The Friday evening visit with the Sanders came too quickly for him. In the car Joan was humming and Randy was grouchy. They were not going to the mountains or to one of the new shows at the Fox Theater. They were going to meet their future in-laws. An evening with Bob Sanders was sure to be torture. He was wishing they were meeting Cassie and Robert Junior for dinner, far away from where they were headed.

"Joan, if I get any feeling they don't like Cassie I am going to leave."

"What could possibly be the reason they wouldn't like Cassie?"

"Bob chooses the persons he enjoys, and he has very strict rules. He couldn't stomach your ex-husband. They almost came to blows in court a couple of years ago."

"Nobody ever told me about that."

"You probably didn't follow court events."

Joan said, "I never had an inside to John's business."

"One-time Bob asked me, 'Isn't Hoffman a Jewish name?' Being shocked that he knew my mother's maiden name, I said, probably, since my mother is Jewish."

"How did he know her?"

"He knows Pearl more than my mom. After a remark he made about Jews at a charity event, Pearl refused to sell him one of her paintings, and they haven't spoken to each other since."

"Okay, Randy let's not talk about prejudice tonight, besides as far as I know Cassie doesn't have any Jewish blood."

"By God, I wish she did. Don't worry, I promise to be on my best behavior. Should I have worn a tux?"

"I don't believe this is a tuxedo event. Well, we are here. Suck it up."

Young Robert met them at the door. "Thank you for coming tonight. This is an exciting time for me. The day I met Cassie my life was changed forever. I love her, and can hardly wait for her to become my wife."

Randy said, "I could tell at the courthouse there was something happening. You were noticeably gaga. Am I right?"

"Yes, sir, you are. I know this appears to be fast, and my parents feel the same, but they will come around. I love Cassie. She is everything I ever dreamed of finding in a woman."

"Sometimes fast is good," Joan said. "Randy and I waited too long to be with each other."

Randy said. "I love Cassie. I just want to make certain you do also."

Joan said, "Randy, calm down." Looking toward Robert, she said, "She has only been his daughter for a while, yet he is already quite possessive, as you can tell."

"I can understand that," Robert replied. "Come on in. Let me get you a glass of champagne." He pointed toward the French doors, "They are outside on the patio."

"Well, well, Joan and Randy Walker," Bob Sanders said holding out his hand, "Looks like we got rhythm here between our two children. It is a pleasure hosting you tonight."

Randy said, "Thanks for the invitation. If your son is as good in marriage as he is in the courtroom, all will be well."

"Let's quit being so formal, this is my wife, Grace. Grace, meet Joan and Randy Walker." Grace said, "Joan, I do believe we have met before."

"Yes, we met at a luncheon at the Swan House. Nice to see you again."

"Joan hugged Cassie and said, "My little girl has met her prince. I am so happy for you sweetheart."

"Mom and Dad, come sit down. I could hardly wait for you to get here. Robert and I want to tell you about our plans, and want you to be a part of everything." They all sat and waited.

Finally, Robert said, "Since I was raised in the Episcopal Church, and Cassie has a preference for the Presbyterian Church, we have decided to find an alternate place for the wedding. We want to open that discussion now." Nobody spoke.

Standing by Robert, Cassie said, "We want our parents to talk with us tonight, and help us find a suitable place. Okay, you can start any time."

Grace was the first to give a suggestion, "Well, there is always the country club or the Ritz Carlton."

"Are we expecting a large crowd?" Joan responded.

"We do have a lot of friends who would be invited," Grace said.

"Mom," Robert said, "those are two places we thought of, but turned both of them down. They are too impersonal, and besides we don't want a lot of guests, just close friends and family. Keep thinking."

"I don't like the country club idea either," Bob chimed in, "They claim to be accommodating to its members, but they stick everyone of us for a lot of cash." Robert look amazed that his father would say such a thing.

"No, I'm serious, son. We have been to a lot of weddings at those two places, and there is nothing sacred or sweet about them."

Joan said, "I believe you are right. I feel the same." Grace did not look happy.

With a little hesitation Randy said, "I'm sitting here thinking of a place called Maud's Inn out on the Chattahoochee River where the moon and stars can be seen at night and the food is terrific. The surroundings are romantic and perfect for a wedding."

Robert said, "Tell us more about Maude's Inn."

"I'll do better than that. Tomorrow, being Saturday, if it is convenient I will rent a limo and we can all go out to Maud's Inn on the Chattahoochee River."

"That sounds rather charming," Grace said. "Bob, let's do it."

"My dear, if you want to see this place, I'm ready to go." He said.

"Then it's settled," Cassie said.

"Grace said, "Enough wedding talk for now. Mary has planned a wonderful meal, and she has agreed to stay and watch us eat it, to make certain we enjoy it. She had been with us almost thirty years. Cooking is her talent."

"And Mrs. Sanders has invited me to the wedding."

"And you will not have to cook," Bob said with a laugh.

The air was light, the conversation interesting, the food was delicious, and two families blended quite well. On the way home Joan said, "Couldn't have been a better evening. What made you think of Maud's Inn?"

"Oh, you know."

"Oh yes; I do know. Sneaky, aren't you?"

"I'll call Charlie when we get home, and tell him to put on the charm."

———

Robert took Cassie outside to have some time alone with her. They sat in the swing on the gazebo porch. He said, "Well, that went well. I hate to say this, but I was a little bit tense. Sometimes my mom is a little stuffy and dad tends to be a bit critical, but the most unusual words that took place this evening, were spoken about Mary. I am pleased my mother invited her. She is like family to me."

"I'm pleased too. Our parents were gracious, and my new Dad behaved. Robert, I don't know why I'm thinking of this, but since we are talking about families, what happened in the Griffin Case? It sounded like it was going to be a disaster."

"Funny you should ask about that, it's been on my mind a lot lately. I met with their daughter and her advocate. She had a different story than either of her parents. What a dysfunctional family! I can't imagine how the kid has survived. She is going to stay with her grandparents until her parents work out their differences - the father quits hitting and the mother stops bitching, but I imagine a divorce is in the future. I met the grandparents during the hearing. Both are around late fifties and exceptionally nice people. They are taking Suzanne to Europe this summer. Would you like to guess what the girl's mother said when they told her about the trip?"

"I can guess: Why aren't you taking me. I'm the one who needs to get away. "

"You are too good. Those were almost her exact words."

"Case solved?"

"Suppose so. They paid me a lot to get to that conclusion. But the whole thing was definitely a bad example of marriage."

"What are you saying?"

"Nothing really. I know our marriage will not be perfect, but if and when we have children, I hope we always love each other as much as we will love them."

"I believe we will. My birth father was a cold, distracted, uninvolved, and unlovable man. My mom should have left him. I don't know why she didn't. Having seen that side of marriage, I want nothing like it. I love you Robert. We'll do well together."

"I know we will. I suppose I got a little depressed dealing with the Griffin family. Lawyers are not supposed to get personally involved, and I'm not going to let it happen again. I do love you Cassie. I only wish we had found each other sooner."

"Cheer up, Robert. We will be good friends and good parents. You are right about not getting so involved with a client. You'd better take me home so we both can get a good night's sleep to deal with our parents tomorrow."

"Good idea. Cassie, if you please my mom, I'll give you a hundred-dollar bill."

"I'll take that offer."

Driving out of town on Saturday morning, conversation was light. Limos can make anything impersonal. Suddenly they all noticed that outside Atlanta the leaves were already beginning to color. It was either an early fall, the heat, or lack of rain. Cassie said, "This is magnificent! If we like this place, we have to get married before the leaves fall."

"It can be done," Robert said. As they drove onto the property, he could hardly wait to get out of the car. He grabbed Cassie, and the two of them wondered off. Charlie's caretaker found them, and showed them the way to the Chattahoochee River.

Inside the Inn Charlie had refreshments waiting. Without any warning, Sarah came into the room. "Sarah!" Randy said, "It's nice to see you again. What a surprise.

"Charlie called and told me you were coming, so I couldn't resist, could I, Charlie?"

"She's a part time fixture around here, but with Leonard's death, I might not get to see her so often." They introduced her to Bob and Grace.

Bob walked around inspecting everything, then wandered outside. When he came back inside he said, "Grace, I like this place. What do you think?"

"It's cozy, but it won't hold a lot of people."

"Good, then we don't have to worry about paying back obligations." Grace did not look happy.

Robert and Cassie returned, holding hands like children. Robert said, "We have made a decision. This is the place we want to remember the rest of our lives. What do you think, Dad? Mom?"

Bob said, "Well said, son. So let it be. You *are* good Randy." He looked at Charlie. "Let's see, Charlie Fowler. I knew a Mr. Charles Fowler in Atlanta who had a son named Charlie. Oh, you are that son?"

"I am indeed. Many people in Atlanta had dealings with them at one time or another. When they died, I inherited this property, and haven't left since."

"Ah yes, they were nice people. You have a good investment here, Mr. Fowler, good indeed."

The afternoon went fast. Cassie and Robert gave a wedding date six week away, and it was fine with Charlie. "Do any of you want to spend the night after the wedding?"

"Joan and I will, I'm certain. Charlie, reserve us a room," Randy said.

"We might also stay," said Bob, "Right Grace?"

"I don't know…Maybe…I am a city girl. Can we talk about that later, Bob?" Bob laughed, "Money and comfort does terrible things to people."

"Mr. Fowler," Cassie quickly interjected, "Robert and I will be back in a few days to make the arrangements. How many people do you think we can invite?"

"Forty-five guests*, including* the six of you. Here is my card."

Randy said, "Rev. Marshall, "I don't believe our children have a pastor to marry them. Would you be available?"

"If the bride and groom asks me, I would consider."

"Kids, you have a minister here, you'd better grab her," Randy said.

"Oh, that would be nice," Rev. Marshall." Cassie said. Would you consider?

"Under two conditions. I will meet with you at least twice, and give me those dates as soon as possible. Do you agree? Here is my telephone number."

Robert said, "We agree, don't we, Cassie?"

"Yes, thank you, Rev. Marshall.

As they walked toward the limo, Robert slipped Cassie a hundred dollar bill. He was sure she could tame his mother, so he put it in his pocket that morning.

After returning home, Randy said, "All the way home Bob seemed pleased with everything, but Grace was noticeably quiet. No telling what happened when they got home. I've always thought Bob was a snob, but I just met a bigger one."

"I'm glad to get the plans started. I don't like things drawn out. You rascal, Charlie knew exactly which room to hold for us. I can hardly wait. Let's pretend we are in that room tonight. I remember every detail. Can I have a rerun?"

As soon as they undressed, Randy led her to the bed, "Mrs. Joan Walker, what is your pleasure tonight?" After visiting the Inn, where they first made love, she was more desirable than ever. There was electricity in the room.

"Mr. Randy Walker, you can start at my lips and travel down. You never know what you will find when you go south."

He felt her body with his eyes closed. By now he had memorized it. He found her breast as firm as ever, and her nipples ripe.

This is the stomach that would have held my children, and this is the place where they would have entered the world. After all these years of waiting, I am the luckiest man in the world

Then he entered the place that makes two lovers one. Afterwards he fell asleep with one arm across her chest, so she could not escape.

Morning came too soon. She raised her head and said, "I should be up planning the wedding. Did you hear Cassie come in last night?"

"What night?"

"Mom," came the call from the kitchen, "breakfast is almost ready. Don't you think you have slept long enough?"

Randy said, "Who slept?"

CHAPTER 43

Wedding plans

The days were flying past – two week, just like that! The phone rang.

"Joan, this is Roger, just want you to know Joanna and I are in Maine, and will be traveling south in a couple of days. Do not expect us anytime soon."

"Roger, Cassie is getting married in four weeks. I hope you and Joanna will be here by then. Sarah has agreed to perform the ceremony."

"We will certainly be there before then. Have you heard from Margaret?"

"Yes. She sold her house. She bought a condo a block from here. A Mr. Johnson died, and his family did not wish to keep his condo."

"Poor Mr. Johnson, but good for Margaret. Can we get everyone together when we get back? He knew what he meant by *everyone*. I want all of you to meet my beautiful daughter. Joanna, say hello to Joan Walker, also a beautiful person."

"Hello to everyone. I am looking forward to meeting the friends my father speaks of quite often."

"We will definitely get together when you arrive. Let me know the date as soon as possible. Have fun along the way."

"Got to go, Joan, time for lunch."

As soon as she hung up, the phone rang again. It was Bob Barnett. "Hi, Joan. Julia came in late last night, and we are shopping for a place to live. Wish us luck. Both of us want to locate somewhere between Atlanta and Marietta. We have Cassie's wedding on our calendar."

"Good for you. Roger just called. He and his daughter Joanna are in Maine. He wants us to get together as soon as they arrive. We can have one big party. I'll call you. Drop by any time, and we'd like to hear about Julia's adventures."

The date for the wedding was arriving fast, but there was not much preparation for the families to handle. There would be no flowers to buy, no decorating to do, only a list of people. Joan called Grace and reminded her of the forty-five persons capacity. She responded, “I will honor those directives.”

“Thank you, Grace. I am looking forward to being with you again.”

“I am also looking forward to seeing you. I will get my list to Robert so he and Cassie can send invitations. See you later.” Joan panicked. *Invitations! I forgot about invitations.* She ran to Cassie’s room, and said, “We forgot about invitations.”

“No invitations. We are calling instead of sending invitations. That way it is not so formal.”

“Has Robert told Grace?”

“He will tonight. Hold your breath.”

“Are you wearing a gown?”

“I will wear something like a modest cocktail dress, and Robert will wear a suit. Mom, don’t worry. Everything is going to work out just fine. The inn doesn’t call for fancy. Don’t you agree?”

“I do. You never believed in being fancy, anyhow. Go for it! I’m surprised you aren’t wear pants. Grace would faint.”

“Wait a minute, I didn’t think about pants.”

“No, Cassie, no pants.”

CHAPTER 44
Rev. Sarah Marshall

It was late Friday afternoon. Sarah was in her office making some last-minute work for the Sunday Worship Service. She was stretched beyond her endurance, doing the work of two pastors. She and Charlie had fallen deeply in love, and she wanted more time with him. They saw each other twice a week, which was not enough, but for the time being it had to be. She was excited that a committee had called an interim Pastor, but she would not be able to take the position for a month.

She and Charlie were comfortable with each other, and he had begun to enjoy her friends as well. He was ready to marry, but the time wasn't right. She knew he was her chance for happiness, and both of them wanted to start planning for their future. Her thoughts were interrupted by the telephone. At first there was a silence, then a voice said, "I hear you are seeing someone."

She immediately recognized Tony's voice. "That is none of your business, Tony. Have you been nosing around in my business? I promise, you will regret it. How did you know I am at the church?" Looking out the window she saw his car in the parking lot. Thank goodness the doors were locked.

"Sarah, listen to me, don't do this. We missed our chance once; let's not do it again. I will get a divorce so we can marry. I made a bad mistake letting you go. We can both forget the past and start over. My wife knows I am still in love with you, but she has been willing to accept the situation for the sake of my ministry and our children."

"What a self-centered idiot you are. Get off this property, go back to your wife, and beg her to forgive you. She deserves better. Now listen to me. Forget you called me, and *never, never*, *ever,* call me again! If you do, I will report your harassment to your Elders. And quit spying on me."

"You wouldn't do that. You are just angry with me."

"Why should I be angry with you? I don't even know you any more. I am in love with a wonderful man who accepts me as I am. I trust him and he trusts me. I could never trust you. I feel sorry for you."

Sarah hung up the phone and laughed. She was proud of herself for keeping control of her voice. She said out loud, "Thank you, God for having been jilted. It was a powerful lesson." She called Charlie, "I just received a strange call from Tony Sterling. I've mentioned him to you a couple of times. He is the guy I told you and Roger about. Somehow he heard about my relationship with you, and begged me to get back with him. He was irrational, saying he would get a divorce, and that his wife knew about me. I threatened to report him for harassment if he didn't get off church property and never called me again. It was unsettling for me."

"Did he sound like he was drunk?"

"No, but he was irrational, and sounded desperate. The whole thing caught me by surprise, and I am angry." Holding the phone she walked over to the window. "Charlie, he hasn't moved his car!"

"Call the police. Do you want me to come over?"

"No, that will not be necessary, we will be together tomorrow, and I can wait until then. Charlie he is getting out of his car!"

"Stay right there. I am going to call the police. Wait for them." It was only a few minutes till the police arrived, but Tony slipped away when he heard the sirens. Sarah felt it was safe, so she picked up her keys and met the policemen in the parking lot. She gave them a description of Tony's car. After a short conversation, they asked her if she wanted them to follow her home, and she thought that would be a good idea. After she went into her house the policeman moved his car about a block from her house and stayed about an hour.

Saturday was a wonderful day for Sarah and Charlie, despite the phone call on Friday. The autumn air was invigorating. The first time they made love, they had been uncertain of the ethics a pastor should follow. It was awkward, and they both apologized, then they laughed together. They were literally swept away into some foreign oasis where the water was fresh, the land was productive, and the Inn and the church were far, far away. Both had waited so long, but for now the wait was a different kind, Tuesday and Fridays. On Tuesdays they met at her house. On Saturdays, Sarah always had to leave the inn early to get ready for the Sunday services. One day they would be in their own home, and it would be sweet without any theological reasons whether their unity was right or wrong. Charlie was a good lover - and deliberate, and there was a wild streak in her that both thrilled and amused him. He loved her so much, but it was impossible to tell her just how much. She enjoyed feeling his hands on her, and she loved his kisses and his tenderness. They knew they were meant to be together.

Sunday morning she should not have brought the Atlanta newspaper inside before going to church. She slipped the plastic cover off and laid it upon the table, and almost went into shock when she saw the headlines: *ATLANTA PASTOR KILLS HIMSELF. The Reverend Anthony Sterling, a local Presbyterian Minister shot himself. His body was found yesterday...* Sarah dropped the paper, and called Charlie, "Have you seen the paper?"

"Yes, I have. I just finished reading the article. He shot himself in his car, late Saturday afternoon, about a block from your church. He may have gone by the church again to see if you were there. Thanks heavens you were not in the building. Are you all right?"

"Yes and no. What he did was not right. I have no words for how this makes me feel. Do you think he was trying to punish me?"

"Listen, do not read the article before services this morning. I called Randy and gave him a short overview of the situation. I will meet you at their place after church. My caretaker and his wife are able to take care of things here. Are you listening? Please do as I ask."

"I will, Charlie, I will. Maybe I was too harsh on the phone with him. No, I wasn't. He invaded my privacy. I am sad for all this, mostly for his wife and children. But killing himself on *Saturday*? He left a bad, bad, memory for his congregation."

"Sarah, you are not the culprit in the situation, neither are you a victim. I'm just grateful you were not at the church late yesterday. He could have killed you as well as himself. Get control of yourself, and preach a good sermon today. If anyone asks you if you have read the paper, you can truthfully say you saw the headlines."

"Yes, I suppose that will work. See you later. I love you."

"You have no idea how much I love you. Bye now."

The buzz around the congregation was definitely about the suicide. Thank goodness the Elder, who was the liturgist for the day, would have the Morning Prayer. Sarah asked him to include Rev. Sterling's family and his congregation in the Prayer.

The crowd was slim since many families had gone to the mountains for the weekend, and Sarah did not blame them. She got through the service without any emotions. After the benediction, she informed the people she would be away for the afternoon, but if they needed her for an emergency, they could reach her after 8:00 in the evening. As the people left the service, several members asked if she knew the minister who had shot himself, and she answered truthfully, "Yes, I knew him. We were in seminary together, and I saw him occasionally at quarterly gatherings of Atlanta pastors and elders."

———

Joan and Randy's place was a haven for them. Sarah was able to talk about the previous relationship with Rev. Sterling, and about the phone call. "Joan, thanks for inviting us to be here with you today. I had a fear that someone who knew me from seminary days might drop by my house. What can I do to help with lunch?"

"Randy picked up our lunch at one of the cafés. We both thought it would be good to spend a quiet afternoon away from the Sunday crowds."

———

For a while their world was small and intimate, but the phone interrupted their meal. Randy answered in the bedroom. It was Frederick, "Randy do you know the whereabouts of Rev. Sarah Marshall?"

"Sure. She and Charlie are here with us. Why?"

"Do not turn on the television. You know how the reporters find out everything. They have discovered the last person Rev. Sterling called was Sarah."

"Good God! How?"

"You are a lawyer, figure it out. The reporters are trying to find her. Call that Elder that you and I know, a Mr. Billings, and asked him to meet me at Greene's Drug Store right away, because some reporter may be watching the church. We will be at your place as soon as we can. If it seems like I am offering myself to be her lawyer, I am. Tell her not to talk to anyone."

"Sarah, two people will be here in about thirty minutes, Frederick Winchester, our friend who is an attorney, and Mr. Billings, an Elder from your congregation. Listen to me. Frederick is offering to be your lawyer, and your Elder needs to know what's going on."

"Why? What has happened? Why do I need a lawyer?"

"The news reporters have discovered Rev. Sterling's last call was to you."

"Oh no! This can't be happening!" she said."

"Everybody calm down. We'll have our coffee and cake, and wait. Sarah, you have nothing to worry about, unless you denied knowing him to anyone."

"When I was asked this morning, I did not deny knowing him. I even had the Liturgist mention his family in the Morning Prayer."

Frederick and Mr. Billings arrived. Of course they had discussed the reason for the interruption of their Sunday afternoon. They sat together in silence for a few minutes. Mr. Billings appeared to be uncomfortable. Sarah introduced Charlie to him, "Mr. Billings, this is the man I hope to marry one day, Charlie Fowler. He is the owner of an Inn near the Chattahoochee River."

"Nice to meet you, Mr. Fowler, you are a lucky man."

"Sarah," Frederick began, "Let's get down to business and talk about your phone call from Rev. Sterling."

"First of all," Sarah began, "It was a very unexpected call. Tony Sterling and I were engaged in Seminary, but he could not comprehend how both of us could be pastors, so he asked me to give up my calling. I refused and we parted. It wasn't long before he married someone else, and I have to admit I was crushed at the time. At church related meetings he tried to talk to me, but I ignored him. On the trip to Europe with Roger and Charlie I became a new person, freed from Tony Sterling's hold on me. Then on Friday afternoon, when I was at the church working on the Sunday service, came this desperate call. I don't know how he knew I was there. He may have seen my car. He was rather rude, almost demanding, and definitely serious. He said he knew I was dating someone. He begged me to stop and get back with him. He said he had made a bad mistake and would divorce his wife, because she knew he would always love me. I told him I would report him to his Elders for harassment if he did not stop spying on me. He kept interrupting and appeared to be serious. I told him to go back to his wife, if she would take him, and ask for forgiveness. Then I hung up. Let me say right here, I never want to tell this to anyone again."

"Too bad you didn't record the call," Frederick said.

"I never record a call. I respect people's privacy."

Frederick asked Mr. Billings, "What have you to say?"

"I believe my pastor handled the situation very well. His call to her was improper, especially being another minister. The fact that he killed himself does not involve her in any way. He must have been a weak man trying to put off his misery onto her. I do wonder how the press got a hold of his phone. Anyway, I will call a meeting of the Board of Elders and lay some groundwork on this. Sarah, you are our only minister at this time, and we trust you and love you. Mr. Winchester, I would like for you to be at that meeting."

"Sarah," Frederick said, "I am sure there is no reason for me to say this, but I will. *Do not* talk to anyone about this. Allow Mr. Billings to do what he must, and let your Elders protect you. You are not the first woman a man regretted dumping, but few of them put a gun to their head. Sorry to put it that way, but remember I am a lawyer and I know too much."

"I understand the situation. Tony Sterling has put two churches and me in a delicate situation. Leonard's death delayed Charlie and my wedding, and now this. Mr. Winchester, your advice is excellent; our Elders are quite capable of handling this."

"Nice meeting you, Mr. Fowler," Mr. Billings said. "I knew your parents. Good people. I am happy for you and Sarah. We'd be mighty proud to see you some Sunday mornings."

"Thanks for the invitation, Mr. Billings. Weekend guests pretty much take up my time, but perhaps I'll be able to attend soon. You know, I haven't heard Sarah preach, yet. Right now my caretaker and his wife are handling things so I can be here with her."

"You're a good man. I'd like to see your place. Frederick says it's a nice place."

"Word gets around, doesn't it? You can come and sit on our porch anytime."

"My wife and I just might do that."

Randy said, "It's also a very romantic place, right Joan?"

"You know it is."

"Now let's don't get too personal here," said Mr. Billings, and they all laugh.

Sarah dreaded going to work on Monday morning. Every step she took was as if her body was gravitated to the ground. When she arrived all eighteen Elders and Frederick were assembled. They stood as she entered. Her first fear was she would break into tears, but instead she was speechless.

After opening with prayer, Mr. Billings began, "Rev. Marshall, I have informed our Elders of our meeting yesterday. They are humbled to be privy to your dilemma and are sworn to secrecy. We need to develop a plan for you and the church members that will keep incorrect information from floating around in the congregation."

"All I can think of saying is, I am grateful for your support."

"Rev. Marshall," Mr. Billings began, "Your attorney, Mr. Winchester met with us this past hour to form a carefully written statement that would not bring discomfort on either you or Rev. Sterling's family nor both congregations. Here is what we have, and if there is any thing you would like to change, feel free to suggest. Please read the statement Mr. Winchester."

Rev. Sarah Marshall received a phone call from an old friend, Rev. Anthony Sterling late Friday evening. They had known each other since seminary. At one time they had planned to marry, but after graduation they went their separate ways. He may have called her Saturday evening, believing she was a colleague who knew him well enough to understand him. Their conversation was not long, but she heard nothing that made her believe he was suicidal. Her final suggestion was that he should go home and talk to his wife before he made any life-changing decisions. She was unaware he killed himself until she saw the headlines in the Sunday newspaper. Their entire conversation was personal, so there is no need for us to repeat it. Our prayers go out to the family of Rev. Sterling and the members of his church.

"All of you are so amazing; I could not have written it any better," Sarah said. "I am grateful for the careful wording. Since all of you have sworn to uphold the honor of your sacred positions, I will tell you this in confidence. Somehow Rev. Tony Sterling thought we could return to the relationship we had in seminary, and he was willing to leave everything if I would agree. I was shocked that he would contrive such a situation. I cannot imagine any minister willing to make such a proposal that would shame his or her family and embarrass the people of the Church of Jesus Christ. I am in love with a wonderful man, Mr. Charlie Fowler, and I would never jeopardize our relationship."

Mr. Billings said to the Body of Elders, "I met Mr. Fowler last evening, and he is so like his father." And to Sarah, "We wish the best for you and Charlie. We will have some help for you soon, and you can fulfill your dreams."

"Mr. Billings, surely your must know that the ministry is the first part of my dream. Charlie and I will work out the other part."

"We have not completed our meeting yet, Rev. Marshall. We are granting you a week's paid leave, including two Sundays, from your duties at the church, and that will not be part of your scheduled vacation leave. Under this kind of stress we feel this is best for you and for the congregation. A retired minister will attend to the necessary situations and preach for you. Your home is also too available for intruders. May we suggest that you go out of town for the duration? Do you think the Inn on the Chattahoochee would be a good place to hibernate?"

"I believe it would be just the place. How nice of you to think of that."

"In your absence we will direct all your calls to the temporary interim, so don't even think about calling for your messages."

"Thanks to all of you for your support. I will expect your continued prayers while I am away." The church secretary came to the door and said, "Sorry to interrupt, but there is a drove of reporters outside asking for Rev. Marshall." Frederick rose from the table. "I will talk to them. Any of you who wish, come with me, but Rev. Marshall, you remain inside."

Frederick addressed the reporters, "Folks, may I have your attention? I am Attorney Frederick Winchester, and these men and women are Elders of this congregation. I realize you are trying to do your job, but you are treading on sacred ground at this moment, even blocking the way for the nursery school children and their parents. A statement about Rev. Marshall's connection to Rev. Sterling will be released to the Press this afternoon." They all started asking questions at once. He said, "I hear the questions you are hollering about. There *is* no bloody relationship. There is only sorrow for a minister who chose to end his life in a horrible way, and who of us can understand why? In his misery he chose the quickest way possible. This is a sad, sad situation, and I hope there are no reporters at Rev. Sterling's home or his church. *My God*, try to be courteous at this sad time."

"Why does Rev. Marshall need an attorney?" One of the reporters yelled.

"Doesn't everybody." Frederick responded.

"It just seems suspicious to me."

"Then you are an idiot. You have no foundations to make that statement." Gradually the reporters left the parking lot when Frederick went back inside the church.

Sarah chose to spend the night with Joan and Randy. Two of her staff followed her to the condo. They drove around about fifteen minutes in case a reporter was on their trail. Joan asked them in, but they needed to get home to their families.

Later that evening Joan rode over to Sarah's house to retrieve some items she needed to take to the Inn in the morning. When a car pulled up behind her she called the police, and remained in the car. Two teenage boys came up to her window and yelled, "Rev. Marshall, we would like to talk to you. Please roll your window down." When she refused, they began taking photos. About that time a patrol car drove up behind Joan. One of the policemen said to the boys, "What in the hell are you two doing invading someone's privacy. You idiots, this is not Rev. Marshall. She's probably in New York by now. Lady, please stay in your car. What are you boys doing out here pestering this lady?" It was silly but he asked, "What media are you with?"

"We are not with any media. We just wanted to get a scoop like everybody else is trying to do."

"What do you mean, 'a scoop'?"

"We were going to sell our interview. People do that all the time."

"Not this time. How old are you? (No response) Let me see your drivers' license. Good lord! You both are only sixteen! Why are you roaming around at this time of night? Don't answer that. Give me your parents' names." At first they refused, but he threatened to put them in jail if they didn't comply with his instructions. He asked for their parent's phone numbers. One of the officers called Mr. John Trace, "Do you know the whereabouts of your son Daniel is tonight?"

"Sure. At his friend, Jonathan's house."

"No, he is out here, pretending to be a reporter, harassing a woman they believed to be Rev. Sarah Marshall. If you don't come and get him, I might have to put him in jail."

"Tell me where, and I'll be right there."

The other officer made the same sort of call to Mr. Will Jenson. While they were waiting for the fathers, Officer Webster said to them, "Boys, can you imagine your mother driving up into her driveway and being approached by two strange teenagers this late at night?"

"No, sir," both of them said, at once.

"Boys, I am trying to give you a courtesy lesson to avoid giving you time for trespassing and harassment. Think about it, and don't ever do this again. Where did you get that expensive camera, anyway?"

Timothy Jenson said, "It belongs to my mother. She likes to take photographs. She's quite good at it."

"Then learn from her. I bet she doesn't go around knocking on car windows, and snapping pictures."

"No, sir. I'm sure she wouldn't do that."

Both fathers arrived within two minutes of each other. They saw their sons leaning against the car with their heads down - a pitiful sight. They introduced themselves to the officers and hugged their boys.

"Thanks for coming so quickly, I'm Officer Webster, and this is Officer Greenblatt. Here are their police reports. Your boys will have to report to a Juvenile officer, the date is on the report. I am a father myself - two sons and a daughter. If they lied *to me* about their whereabouts, I might put them in home detention until after their hearing. I'm going to keep their licenses, and after the hearing I will give them to the two of you. Gentlemen, take your sons home. I believe they need a little instruction. Have them write an apology to this lady, whom they thought was Rev. Sarah Marshall, but she is her friend Joan Randolph Walker. Send their letters to me at the police department, and I will give them to her. Whose car is this?"

"It belongs to my son Timothy," Will Jenson said.

"Then let him drive it home. It doesn't need to stay here all night, but you stay right behind him."

"Good God, Timothy," Will Jenson said, looking at the police report, "Did you have to choose Attorney Randy Walker's wife to harass?" After the boys got in the cars, Officer Webster pulled the fathers aside. I believe your sons have learned a valuable lesson, so don't be too hard on them. I am thinking of my two sons, and what I would do. Perhaps you can take away privileges. Kids hate that."

"Thanks, officer. We appreciate your advice. You've helped us already by scaring the hell out of them. "Hi, Joan sorry about the whole thing, give Randy my apology," Will Jenson said.

"Thanks, Will. Timothy's grown so much I didn't recognize him."

After they left Officer Webster went over to Joan's car. Hi, Joan, you are as pretty as ever. I haven't seen you since, I don't know when, but I've been keeping up with you. How's Randy doing? Tell him I said hello."

"I believe the last time we met was when our daughters graduated from high school. You know Randy?"

"Everybody worth their salt knows Randy Walker, and that's the truth. Our orders were to drive by here often to protect Rev. Marshall. I'm glad we were close by. Mind if I ask what you are doing here?"

"I'm picking up some items for her, so she can get out of town for a rest. Thanks for looking after her house. I bet you didn't expect to find two sixteen year olds prowling around."

"You can never tell any more. They just wanted to get in on the excitement. I might have done the same thing when I was sixteen, and my daddy would have put the belt to me good. Where is Cassie now?"

"She just finished law school, and is getting married soon."

"You don't say. Who is the lucky man?"

"Robert Sanders, Jr."

"Oh, Lord, I hope I never have to go to court against his father."

"And how is George Anna?" Joan Asked.

"Out of college, teaching in South Carolina. Not married yet, but close.

"Well Joan, we will sit here until you get the things you're after, and one of us will follow you home. This whole mess has gotten out of control."

"Thanks, George. Tell Anna hello for me."

"Will do."

When Joan returned home Randy asked, "What took you so long?" She started telling the events of the evening, but at times, she couldn't talk for laughing so hard. "Actually I found it sort of interesting that two sixteen year olds were trying to get a scoop to sell." Finally she got through it. "By the way George Webster said tell you hi. How do you know him?"

"It's a good story, but not as good as yours tonight." He left it at that.

The next morning Joan followed Sarah out to Maud's Inn. Sarah asked her to stay for a couple of hours, but she said, "Thanks, but no thanks, the two of you need some quiet time, and besides I'm sure you have a lot to talk about. Sarah, call me when you are ready to go back to town."

"Thanks, but things should be settled down by then."

Chapter 45
The Wedding

The group (Cassie, wickedly started calling them "the clan") had a small gathering, a week prior to the wedding to listen to the adventures of Julia, who had grown up while away, and Joanna, who was even lovelier than they had imagined. But the center of attention was Michael, who reminded them of Leonard. This intimate gathering gave them time to catch up. There was so much to tell, and all of them were good listeners. Now they all could attend Cassie's wedding and revel in new events in their "family."

All their friends were there for the wedding, including Roger's daughter, Joanna and Bob's daughter, Julia. Frederick and Elizabeth also brought their daughter, Molly. The three girls stayed together the whole day. Rick agreed to be the chauffeur for Randy's mother, Ana and Aunt Pearl. They had become a second family to him. He always went by to see them when he was in town because they entertained him and made him laugh. He pulled Randy aside, "They are so funny. Ana says to Pearl, 'You aren't going to wear *that* are you?' Pearl answers, 'Sure, why not? I always wear pants. Do I have a decent dress in that closet? What do you think Rick?' I said, "Ana, I think Pearl looks great, and you look great also, so let's don't argue? 'Who's arguing,' both of said, at once."

"That's A&P for you. They have been doing that for as long as I remember, but they love each other." Randy said.

Most of the autumn leaves had fallen because of the heavy rains, but the scenery and surroundings were still lovely. Both Roger and Bob looked rested, and more contented than they had been in a long time. Though Sarah was the minister, she helped Charlie and his caretakers with the Preparations. She thought: *Not long from now, someone else will be the minister, and Charlie and I will be the bride and groom, husband and wife. That sounds so nice.* She shivered thinking about it. She also thought it odd that she and Charlie seemed to have gradually merged into "the group," and perhaps the first outsiders to penetrate their close friendship.

Grace and Bob Sanders looked younger and most elegant in their Sunday best, taking Robert's suggestion not to overdress. The guests, she and Bob invited, were impressed with Maude's Inn, and it pleased Grace. Many of them would later choose the Maud's Inn as a place to get free of city life. Randy told Charlie, "One day you're going to have to expand. The word is getting around."

"Can do," Charlie answered, "Yep, can do."

The wedding was in the lobby. It was crowded, but who cared. Some of the guests sat on the steps to the balcony, or the few chairs available, but most of them stood the fifteen minutes of the service, keeping their wine glasses in hand, just the way Cassie and Robert had envisioned. Before the service, after everyone stopped talking, Robert and Cassie told their guests how they met. "I spied her in the courtroom. She almost made me forget my arguments, and I could sense her presence even when I was facing the judge."

Cassie said, "There was no doubt about it, he was more interesting than my assignment. I knew my dad was watching me that day, so I pretended to be writing, but I couldn't take my eyes off Robert." Someone interrupted, "Oh how sweet."

Robert said, "Continuing on. I fell in love on the second date, and after being apart for two weeks, I took her flowers on our third date." All the guests said, "Ahhh." He said, "And that's all you need to know. So let's continue."

The traditional vows were short and reverent. Sarah ended by asking them to stand face to face while she read a poem written by Cassie for the occasion.

I dreamed of being lucky
        of finding Love
        in foreign lands
        plucking history from the wind
        washing my feet
        in the River Rhine
        walking the streets of Paris.
But the Forum of Rome
        and the mountains of Switzerland

were not my destiny
In the oddest place of all
he walked back and forth
across a courtroom floor,
and with his eyes said, "Hello."

Dreams are not always found
in far away places,
nor in our imaginations
I found my love
in the city of Atlanta,
the gateway of the South
I will always love you, Robert
yesterday, today, and forever.

Everyone responded with applause, and Robert looked into her eyes and said, "So you are not only an artist but a poet. One of these days I shall respond to that poem."

Rev. Marshall ended, "May your love always be special, creating an image to others who desire to take this step. Now, turn around and go kiss your parents as a thanksgiving for raising you, and then declare your love to each other by sealing this service with a kiss."

"How beautiful," Grace was heard to say after Robert kissed her. When Cassie kissed Joan and Randy, they did not want to turn her loose. Then without a second thought Robert grabbed Cassie and kissed her, "That is for marrying me." Randy followed his lead and kissed Joan. Then others in the room starting doing the same with their partner, even Charlie came forward and kissed Sarah.

Rick headed for Cassie. "Sis, thanks for sharing your life with me. You know I will always love you," then he kissed her. "Is your friend, Colin in the past?" She whispered to him. "Yes, definitely. Our arrangement didn't work out. I need a lot of time to think about what I want to do, and who I want to be, so I am telling Mom and Dad tonight that I am going to spend a few months in Paris."

"Why Paris?"

"It's a long story, no time to tell you everything now, but it will be good for me. Pearl has friends there. I'll be staying with them. Does that sound crazy?"

"No, it doesn't. I have no doubt that you will be a great artist. Pearl recognizes your talent, so I'm thankful she's spurring you on."

"Thanks again, sis."

After all the movement around the room, Cassie and Robert stood hand in hand while Robert addressed their guests, "Our wedding could not have ended any better. Thanks to all of you for sharing this day *and* your kisses with us. And we thank our parents for being generous with their time and their money. (Everyone laughed.) Mr. Fowler gives you the privilege of roaming around the grounds of Maud's Inn, and he wishes that you taste the food his staff has prepared. He doesn't want any leftovers." The people lingered and danced to the music of a small combo, drank the wine, and laughed all the way back to Atlanta.

Cassie and Robert left soon after the wedding to make their flight on time. Randy and Joan's wedding gift was transportation to Maine and five days in the Cottage Bed and Breakfast. Finally only Randy, Joan, Sarah, Charlie, Rick, and his two passengers were left. "Sarah, it is your turn next," Joan said.

"Yes," Charlie interrupted, "It's about time."

"Mom, Dad, I must talk to you a few minutes?" Rick asked.

"Sure, come over here and sit," Randy said.

"I will stay at your condo tonight after I take A&P home, but tomorrow I am headed to Paris."

"Paris! Why Paris?" Joan asked.

"I need to work some things out. Pearl has American friends who live there, and they have invited me to stay as long as I wish. She was so excited calling them, for a fleeting moment I thought she would be going with me. She is encouraging me to paint. Don't worry, I *am not* going off the deep end." Joan was shaking her head. "Really, Mom I'm fine. I just need a change of scenery."

"Well go for it," Randy said. "Keep in touch with us at least once a week. That will make your dear dad and your sweet mom happy."

"Will do. Thanks for understanding."

"I'm not sure about all this. I know you have the money and the time, but should we worry about you?" Joan asked.

"Sure, if you want to."

"Thanks for permission. Have a good time and learn something, anything."

"Dad, will you help me get the sisters in the car?"

"Be back in a few minutes, Joan." After they helped the sisters into the car Rick and Randy stood beside the car and talked. Joan could see Randy with his arms around Rick.

Joan and Randy helped the caretakers and Charlie clean up the place. Finally, they went upstairs to their quiet haven. Randy said to Joan, "We have been so lucky. You make me forget about the past, for my real life began when you married me. Today was so special. Did you notice how Cassie introduced us as Mom and Dad? That was worth a million dollars to me. I am the luckiest man alive."

They sat out on the balcony, holding hands and watching the sun disappear.

Randy cut the silence; "There's something mysterious about the sun leaving parts of the earth in darkness. I've never thought much about it, but I need to rise earlier in the mornings and watch it return, and be thankful. Oh, I'm aware the earth is a sphere that rotates, but I claim ignorance. Science takes all the poetry and majesty out of nature, and we wind up not appreciating the things of the world that are so perfectly planned."

Joan said, "Thank you, Randy for those beautiful words. When I was little my Sunday school teacher used to read the creation story to our class in such a dramatic way, I could almost visualize it happening. She would clap her hands and say, 'Children, look out the window, see the grass and the trees God created.' And on and on she would go creating the waters and two great lights – one to rule the day and one to rule the night. Her animation was so captivating and so beautiful."

"Will you read that story to me one day, the way your teacher did?"

"I will, I promise."

CHAPTER 46

Maine again

Cassie and Robert arrived at the Cottage Inn Bed and Breakfast in Maine about dinnertime. It was as lovely as they had imagined. The owners, Joyce and Ralph Templeton were very attentive. Joyce delivered dinner and wine to their room as soon as they were settled. "Breakfast will be at nine in the morning. You can come in your robes if you wish and dress afterward. In a day or so, we would like you to give us the latest news about Mr. Waddell. We enjoyed their visit, and his daughter is so lovely."

Cassie said, "Thank you for the wine. Tomorrow we want to walk around to get an idea where we are. We would like to explore the area to see if Roger and my parents were exaggerating, *and* we do have a lot to report about your former guests."

"In the office you can select all the information you need. You might not get to see everything in such a short time, but be sure to visit the art studios. As far as shopping and places to dine, there are many and easy to find."

In an hour they were well fed and totally exhausted. They had not been intimate for several weeks, so they knew the event *most special* was to end the day celebrating their wedding and the beginning of a new life together. Robert kissed Cassie with a new passion. There was a special thrill knowing she was now his wife. "We've had a long day, but there is a lot about you I don't know, and secrets we haven't shared. I would like to know everything - what you like or can't stand - so I won't get in trouble. Tell me about your growing up years and what you absolutely can't abide, but I keep wondering why we never ran into each other in Atlanta."

"Atlanta's a big place, and there's not much connection between high schools, except maybe sports. Growing up I couldn't wait to get out of Atlanta, but now I can't wait to get back; it's home."

"I will never want to forget the day I looked across the courtroom and saw you. I knew you were the person who was going to change my life. I want to have that feeling the rest of my life."

Cassie responded, "The rest of our lives is, hopefully, a long time, but we will never forget that day, will we? By the way I do like flowers, so you can bring them home anytime. *But* maybe a string of pearls is better in a nice little box hidden among the flowers."

"You sound like a lawyer making a point, but I got that one: *pearls*."

"When I was in the courtroom, I was taking notes, but I was also sketching the young lawyer that seemed to have such charm, and who knew exactly what he was doing. I still have that drawing. I'm planning on framing it."

"You were doing that? Are you some kind of an artist?"

"One might say that I am or hope to be. You never noticed those two watercolors on my wall?"

"You did those? Wow, I've married a beautiful and talented lady who has studied law, and who is also an artist. I have no idea why I am so lucky. Do you have other talents I haven't heard about?"

"Yes, I am a romantic. I inherited that from my mom, but tonight show me how much you love me, and I'll be forever yours. No matter how many times you have held me in your arms these last few months, I have waited for this moment to hear your voice speak three words to me as your wife, *I love you*."

"Love is not only a word, it is an action," Robert said. "I love your intellect, your beauty, and your laughter. I love your tenderness and your body lying close to mine. Every time I kiss you and make love to you my whole body tingles for hours. When I touch your breasts I want to hold them forever, and I can't wait to see our child nursing them one day."

"Whoa, not so fast! I'm not ready to think of babies."

"Okay, your breasts belong to you, but you can share them with me, right?"

"This conversation has given me a thrust of desire and a need to explain it. This is a night I never want to forget. I am in a far away city with my husband who has become my best friend, so I want to remember this room, the food we eat, the sites we will see this week, and the sweetness of your hand touching mine. We made a commitment today, though we walk through sorrows and pleasures, we will do it together. Let us always remember our dreams are ahead of us. I love you."

"You have my promise; I love you." They expressed their love with a passion different from all other times. Always before, in their relationship, sex and intimacy was grabbed for lack of time or energy. This time they pushed everything aside to arrive in a world where only the two of them existed. Afterward, they turned to face each other. He said, in a whisper, "You have taken my breath away. I cannot form the correct words, but isn't fate wonderful?"

"Then be quiet, and think only of our joy and love for each other. Be grateful that my professor sent me to study a case, and you were the lawyer appointed to handle that case. It was not fate, it was providence."

"So what is the difference?"

"Fate happens regardless; providence is planned."

"Oh."

CHAPTER 47

Margaret

Margaret was settled into her new home. It was supposed to be an exciting event, but depression struck her, and it hurt. Michael was asleep and she realized she was so tired it was even painful to walk. *My God, I'm starting all over again and with a baby. Everything is supposed to be in order at my age, but my life is not. Those who care about me are saying that I did good getting this condo and selling all the furniture I didn't want. The couple that purchased Leonard's house was allowed first choice of what I didn't want to carry with me, and they were so happy it made me sick. For heaven's sake what is wrong with me? I hated that house. Roger and Joanna were a lot of help. Michael is not the way to my heart. Right now he is a burden. I don't know how to begin again.*

The church made good on all their promises to Margaret, and someone called her frequently to see how she was doing. When word got around that she was accepting new clients, she had so many calls she became overbooked, and even that frustrated her. Thank goodness she had Rebecca (Becky) Williams to help her. Becky was divorced, had no children, and her references were excellent. Those three characteristics meant she could focus on Michael. Besides caring for Michael, she became somewhat of a secretary, answering the phone when Margaret was away and was good at booking appointments. Eventually Becky stored her furniture, moved in with Margaret, and slept in Michael's bedroom. When Margaret's work was nearby, Becky would take Michael and let him play on the floor while she helped Margaret. Her talents for scheme and color were impressive. She was the best thing that had happened to Margaret in a long time.

Roger and Joanna visited Margaret frequently, always bringing presents for Michael. It appeared that Joanna was having the time of her life. One day, while they were visiting, Margaret asked her, “Joanna, do you have to return to Israel? We have all come to love you. It’s going to be difficult to give you up.”

“My father also has those wishes,” she said as she looked at him. “In my mind I am trying to see what is best for me and for him. I converse with my grandmother frequently, and I am always glad to hear of my brother’s family. Yesterday I called her, and for the first time she did not speak of missing me. She said to me, ‘your brother and I have great love for you, and you will always be a part of us, but you are where you belong, in America, with your father.’ She did not mean that I no longer belonged to them. She does not want me to depend on my brother’s family for happiness.”

Roger said, “I want you to make this your home, but you are the one who has to decide what is best for your life.”

“Father, I have a wise grandmother, and she is always right.” She hugged him and wiped the tears from his eyes. “While I was in your state of Maine the presence of my mother was real, so real I had memories of the short time I had with her. I missed her, but my grandmother would not allow me to grieve. When I would cry or complain she always said in Hebrew *that’s life*, or *life is good*, and that settled all arguments according to her philosophy. Now I realized how desolate you must have been after my mother’s death. This is not the time to leave you, and I am sure my mother did not want to leave you, either. Since I am both part of her and part of you, life will be better for both of us. We will call my grandmother tomorrow and she can notify the school. But I can be certain they have replaced me, for I have been away too long.”

“Today you have given me the greatest of gifts. No words can express my feelings at this moment. I am indeed a fortunate man.” All three of them danced around the room, and even Michael clapped his hands. “Margaret, are you available this week to take Joanna shopping for clothes?”

“Nope, I think you should do that. I don’t like spending other people’s money, except when they hire me. Besides, the two of you will have fun shopping.”

“But I have no idea what woman wear.”

“Joanna knows what she likes. Let her decide.”

“Okay, okay. Tomorrow we start. Margaret, when will you have time to decorate Joanna’s room?”

"*Now* you are hiring me, but I'll need your help, Joanna. Be thinking about your expectations, like colors and kind of furniture you prefer." Joanna said, "Furniture, simple like my father's, but rooms with accents of bright shades of yellow, blue and green. Those colors that make me happy."

"Okay, I believe that is sufficient information."

After Roger and Joanna left, Margaret collapsed on her bed and sobbed. She felt abandoned again. She began to cry like she had never cried before. Becky sat beside her and held her hand, "Margaret all the events of the past few months have happened so quickly, you have not had time to recover. You don't want your friends to feel sorry for you." There was no answer. "Well, do you?" No answer. "I suppose it's time we find a way to rescue you."

"We! You say it so sincerely."

"You have a lot of friends. They pop in every now and then because they are worried about you, but they have their own lives. You have to connect with who you are *now* and find joy in the new you. You have never used the name Mrs. Leonard Childs in your business the whole time you were married, so you are still Margaret Tillman. Am I correct? Reverend Childs was beloved by his church members, but he did not leave them a gift. He left you the greatest gift, Michael. You must never see Michael as a burden. He is a beautiful gift! You have to be concerned about doing the right thing for him, but you must also decide what is right for you."

"Mothering is supposed to come naturally, but I don't believe I have those skills. God knows I never thought about developing mothering skills."

"Soon it will become natural," Becky said. "Just you wait until he begins to walk and talk. You won't feel like the only person in the room anymore. All you need to do is put him in your arms more often, put kisses all over him, and he will be fine."

"Is it really that easy?"

"No, but it will help. The main point is that you love each other. He is not your former husband and he is not you. He is a beautiful son God has given to you. When you think of him as the best gift ever, you and he will be fine. As a mature mother you can teach him things better than if you were a twenty-year-old mother. Pretty soon he will be helping you decorate."

"Now you are a prophet."

"Why not?" And they both laughed. Margaret grabbed Michael off the floor, kissed him and said, "You are my gift; the prophet has spoken. We will be all right." She turned to Becky, "We need to get out of town. Where would you like to go?"

"Are you asking me to choose?"

"Choose. Anywhere. Think of a place we can walk around and stroll Michael, and enjoy art studios and eat out."

"Savannah! Let's go to Savannah," Becky said, "It's a great place for walking. Let's cancel our appointments for next week and reschedule them. I am certain everyone will understand."

"Well, Savannah here we come! Becky, find us a good hotel that will accept a toddler, a nanny, and a widow."

"We are as good as gone," she said. She made some calls. "Done! We are registered for the day after tomorrow in a suite with two separate bedrooms. Let's get our things together."

"So soon? I have a lot to do."

"We will do it together," Becky said. "I will make some calls tonight, and then we will finish cancelling appointments in the morning, so do your thing."

"My thing?"

"Think Margaret. Get yours and Michael's *things* together. Don't carry too much, we can buy some items there if we need something."

"How did you get to be the boss in this situation?"

"I inherited it. Some lovely lady with a beautiful baby boy knew she needed help, and she gave me the job."

"You are taking this prophet title seriously. A whole week in Savannah! Oh how good it will be to get out of Atlanta. Becky, the last time I left the Atlanta area was when Leonard and I went to Maine on our honeymoon, and that was not a good trip. Leonard was surly all the time. One night I threw a shoe at him when he called his church. He didn't do that again. I should have gone without him."

CHAPTER 48

Savannah, Georgia

Driving into Savannah was like entering a city in a foreign country. Everything in the city looked preserved like pictures on a post card, and the houses were different that any she had ever seen. Margaret said, "Maybe Atlanta would look like this if Sherman had not burned it." She didn't expect a comment; she was just thinking out loud. When they arrived at their lodging, Margaret stepped out of the car and sniffed the air, which felt and smelled like the sea - a little stale and a bit damp, but it was just what she needed: a place where she would be a visitor and no one would be waiting on her to finish her work. She said to Becky, "Did I fall asleep when you decided to leave the States?" Becky laughed at her, but she was pleased.

The accommodations Becky had chosen were perfect. Their suite had adjoining rooms with their own bathrooms, and both rooms faced the Savannah River. Becky insisted that Michael stay in her room so Margaret could get plenty of rest. It was the first night Margaret slept without interruption. She woke early in the morning feeling rested. She peeped in on Becky and Michael to find them still asleep, so she dressed and went down to breakfast by herself.

"Is this chair taken?" A familiar voice behind her asked.

"Bob Barnett! What in the world are you doing down here?"

"I could ask you the same question. Mind if I sit with you?

"Of course I don't mind. I'll answer you first. Michael's nanny, who has become my long needed secretary, nanny, and assistant, thought getting out of Atlanta would do me some good. This past year has not been the best of times for me, but when I woke up this morning I felt free, so I left Becky and Michael and escaped. She has saved my life."

"I am here for a meeting," Bob said. "Something akin to continuing education on legal issues. Must keep up with the constant changes in law, you know."

They finished eating, but lingered and finally moved to the lounge to continue their conversation. Talking, with no clients on their minds, they seemed to have a lot to say. "Margaret, you are an interesting women, and quite funny. I don't believe I have laughed so much in years. Are you busy tonight? If not, would you like to go out with me?"

"I need to ask Becky if she minds staying with Michael. Can I call you with an answer in a little while?"

"This is my room number. I'll be looking forward to your call, so hopefully I'll see you tonight."

"I need to call Becky before I go up. Becky, what can I bring you for breakfast?"

"I've already ordered room service for us. I fed Michael a little bit of my grits, and you cannot believe how he ate. Both of us are full and happy."

"Okay, I'm coming up."

That afternoon Margaret and Becky strolled up and down River Street pushing Michael in the stroller and eating too much candy and drinking sodas. Becky said, "It's been almost twenty years since I was here with a person who did not appreciate its old weathered looks. It looks the same. Savannah must have a great historical preservation organization; it never changes. I like that about this place."

"I will not ask who you were with, but if you like it so much we can come more often, or you can find us other vacation spots. We need a change of scenery every now and then. By the way, I met an old friend at breakfast. Do you mind if I have dinner with him?"

"Him? Sounds interesting. You go ahead. I've walked enough today, so I'll call room service for dinner."

Margaret said, "I think we brought enough food for Michael. You know, he truly is a beautiful child. I can't believe I have such a handsome baby. You should see my baby pictures, Becky. I'm surprised my mom and dad took me home with them."

"This child is going to make the ladies scream. That is my prediction, and I can't imagine you were an ugly baby."

Excuse me while I make a call. Bob, this is Margaret. Yes, a good day. Tonight will be fine. Can we meet in the lobby? Seven? See you then."

The afternoon had given Margaret the free moments she never seemed to have. Becky took a nap while she played with Michael, kissing him, and trying to teach him to kiss her. He laughed every time she kissed him, but when she put him up to her face, the best he could do was slobber. She felt lucky snuggling him close to her. Since he had been taking the bottle, she was not always tired. Finally she fell asleep with her arm around Michael. The last thoughts she had were Becky's words: kiss him a lot, and you will learn to love him. She was indeed a prophet. He was the most precious baby, and she had fallen in love with him.

At seven, Bob was waiting. "I've made reservations at Elizabeth's on 37th" he said, "A restaurant you will enjoy. I hope you are as hungry as I am."

"I skipped lunch this afternoon so I could get fat eating the candy we collected on River Street. You probably know more about this city than I do, so I'll accept your choice.

Elizabeth's was perfect – interesting on the outside and cozy and rich in inside. Margaret looked around appreciating the vivid colors and the elegance of the dining room. Their waiter was both handsome and efficient, and the meal was the best food she had eaten in years. They ate and talked about anything and everything. She was trying to remember when she felt so good and so free. It came to her mind that Leonard didn't know a good meal from a bad one.

Bob leaned over to her and said, "Margaret, I'm going to be quite forward, after all we are not strangers. Would you like to go back to the hotel and come up to my room? We can talk, listen to music, or whatever happens."

"Bob, I would love to. I was hoping this evening would not end too soon."

They entered his room, though it was actually a suite. “Do lawyers always get this kind of treatment when they have meetings?” she asked.

“If this room was a dump I wouldn’t have asked the best known decorator in Atlanta to be my guest.”

He came toward her, took her hand and began dancing to the magic music of James Taylor from the tape he inserted. Then he put his hand her chin and kissed her. Her head began to swim. No one had ever kissed her with such passion. She wanted to back away, but her body would not run. She needed this. It had been so long, so very long.

Bob was surprised at himself. He wanted to be intimate with Margaret from the moment he sat down at breakfast with her, and it had been a long time since he even wanted to have sex with anyone. He took her by the hand and turned toward the bedroom. In sync they removed their clothes and fell upon the covers like two starved pilgrims. No words were necessary. They entered another world, one where passion is understood, and no questions asked. The rhythm between them was unbelievable, both trying to make up for lost times.

When it was over neither of them spoke. It was a communion of relief, and no words were necessary. Side by side they lay, breathless from their encounter. Margaret was the first to rise to find the bathroom, and when she returned, he rose. But both came back to the bed, and embraced with the same fervor. It was as if they were rediscovering the anatomy of the opposite sex. They searched for the exotic places, each one of them thinking, *It has been so long.* Margaret sat upon him, and pushed him inside her, and he cried out, “My God! My God!” He looked at her and said, “Margaret, this can’t end here, you are absolutely wonderful.” Finally she rose, washed herself, then returned to the chair where her clothes were draped over the back, and slowly and sensuously redressed. He couldn’t take his eyes away from her as she replaced each piece of clothing over her body and ran her fingers through her hair several times.

She is beautiful and exotic, he thinks.

She leaned over and kissed him on the lips, “Bob, it was wonderful. I am astonished at how wonderful. We have to find out if we were two starved travelers, or if this night means more than that.” She kissed him and said goodnight.”

"Please don't go, not yet. We need to talk."

"No, we must think about whether such passion leads to commitment, or if passion is enough for us. I can't put into words what it meant to me. It was a wonderful evening, Bob." She blew him a kiss, and left.

Bob surrendered to helplessness and abandonment. He sat on the bed paralyzed and cursed himself for not blocking the door.

Back in her room she could hardly breathe: *What is wrong with me? Why did I leave? But why didn't he stop me?* She closed the door, and stood with her back to it, trying to catch her breathe: *Someone has to know what I felt the last few hours.* "Becky, are you asleep?"

"No, I thought I would wait up to enjoy some adult company."

"Becky, it was a wonderful evening, the kind of encounter women dream of. I've known Bob for a good while, but only casually. He and Leonard went to college together. He turned me, or I turned myself, into a woman of pure passion, and I am not embarrassed to speak of it. We were instantly drawn to each other. He wanted to talk about what happened before I left, but I couldn't. I don't know if it was passion that mattered most or the beginning of a great love affair. I need to know. How will I know?"

"Do you realize you have been breathless from the moment you came into the room? That speaks well of what happened. I don't think you will know until you are together again. It's simple: It was an unbelievable act of passion or it was two persons starving and finding each other in the right place. That's what I think."

"Those words again? Do I make the next move, or will he?"

"Who knows, but it will happen. Take it slow."

"Have you ever been in a sexual situation where you completely lost all inhibitions?"

"No, but I wish I had. Margaret, let it go. I don't believe it matters who makes the next move. I just love seeing you so excited. I've discovered the real Margaret."

CHAPTER 49
Sarah and Charlie

The meeting of the Elders was on Monday evening, and Sarah was prepared.

When she walked into the room, she noticed someone present she barely knew, but that was not too unusual since they were without a senior minister. After the preliminaries Sarah asked to hear from the Search Committee about the arrival of the Interim Pastor. The chair of the committee said, "We have secured the position. Rev. Dr. Jessica Johnson will be here in three weeks. Her expertise and training have made her suitable for Interim Ministry. She is well qualified and excited about coming."

"That is great news," Sarah said. "I would appreciate it if the Property Committee will begin getting her office ready. Also the Personnel Committee will produce a letter to put in the bulletin for Sunday. Let's continue with the committee reports."

The Chair of the Elders said, "Not just yet. The New Church Development Committee Chairman, Rev. John Moss is waiting outside the door. He may have a proposition for you. I'll invite him in."

"Reverend Marshall," Reverend Moss began, "We have been thinking about developing a new congregation. It will not be immediate, perhaps a year or so, but the possibilities look good. We would like to recommend you for the position of organizing pastor, but in the meantime we hope you will remain with this congregation for a while longer, especially helping the new Interim Pastor get settled. Starting a new congregation is an interesting adventure, and besides it is not too far from a nice little Inn for which, I understand, you have a fondness. We have had an offer of land. There are several families in the area, and more development for residential housing is expected. We are not asking for an answer this evening. We have discussed this at length, but there are many preparations and legal issues before the building can begin, and the committee is not putting any pressure on you, because this is going to happen with or without you. A meeting with several of the residents is scheduled for this coming Thursday, and we would like for you attend."

"It sounds interesting. Yes, of course. Let me know the time and place."

The rest of the meeting went as planned. Afterward, several of the people showed their support of Sarah with expressions such as, "We have been praying for you lately. Sorry about that unfortunate experience. We are proud of the way you handled the situation."

Mr. Billings said, "Rev. Marshall, if the committee's proposition is something you would consider, you may find time to marry your Mr. Fowler after all."

"Thanks to all of you. I am going to have to process all this. After the meeting on Thursday, I will know more."

She was unsure how to tell Charlie the news, so she chose to wait until after the Thursday meeting, but she couldn't help wondering how he would feel about it. They had led separate lives for so long, meeting when they could, and each time fraught with some pressure. She wasn't sure if this new position would set them apart even further. She saw marriage as a definite change in their relationship, and was uncertain how he would accept all the interruptions she had in the ministry. Starting a new church takes time and money, and of course residents, so she had a lot of research to do before the Thursday meeting. Arriving home she was still in a panic thinking of the changes she would be making, so she called one of her friends, a recent organizing pastor of a church in Northeast Georgia, and he agreed to meet with her the next day.

Thursday came too quickly. She met at the church with twenty people who desired to have a church in their area, and was pleased how passionate they were. They even talked about securing a place to worship in the event the process would not happen fast. The meeting had just started when Charlie walked in, "Hello Rev. Marshall, I hope these people have convinced you to consider this new congregation."

"Charlie, what are you doing here?"

"I am planning on being a part of this congregation, if that's all right with you."

"Of course, of course," she said without thinking.

Nothing final was decided at the meeting, but there was a lot of excitement. She realized creating the church was going to be a slow process, and she still had a lot to do where she was, but she felt a new adventure and position would be good for her.

After the meeting she said to Charlie, "You were the biggest surprise of the day. Did they contact you?"

"No, it just happened. Some of the locals were having lunch at the inn a few weeks ago, and I heard them talking about how they were still traveling into Atlanta to attend their churches, or not going at all. One of them said, 'I don't know why we can't have a church in this area. There are a lot of people out here within a fifteen-mile radius.'

"The problem is *land*, Phillip, *land*. It's expensive and probably not available,' said one of the women.' I asked them what church they attended, and three of them were Presbyterians, so I said, I happen to own a good bit of property out here. Phillip said, 'well, Mr. Fowler, what are you saying?' Maybe some of my land could be available, I said. The same guy said, 'you may have the answer, Mr. Fowler. Let's put a bug in the right person's ear and see what happens."

"You are a sneaky person," Sarah said. "Just think I chose not to tell you about the meeting, and you are part of the whole plan."

"Yes, I was a little disappointed, but I understood. The best news is there are no visitors at the inn, so I can be at your house for a few hours tonight. Let's go."

Later that evening Sarah said, "Charlie, I love you dearly, and I need to say this, I am ready to get married. Right now we have time together, but it is sort of staged, if you know what I mean."

"I know what you are saying, but I don't think the word *staged* speaks for our relationship. Even when we are apart, I am thinking of you. We make the best of the time we have together, and we are as far apart as the telephone. How will it be when we are together every evening? I think we will talk about our day instead of our week. I would like that. Our love is so great we shouldn't be living apart. I want to see you come home exhausted from your day and look at the meal I have prepared. I want to watch you struggle with parishioners and live to tell about it. I want every bit of you I can have. Right now, I cannot move to the city, and this is too far for you to commute. So how do we do otherwise at this time?"

"It's useless to consider it, and that frustrates me."

"Hold on for now. Years from now we will look back and be proud of our commitments. Tonight let's rally and enjoy each other. I admit I don't like seeing you so tired, but you can make it and so can I."

"Thanks. I suppose I have to get some of these feelings out in the open occasionally. Charlie, I swear to you. I have never loved so fiercely. There is one thing I need to say, I want a child one day, and I don't want to be too old when that happens."

"Now we are talking about children! Okay, okay, I agree. I hope we have twins."

"Don't say that; think of me! Okay enough is enough. Before we get to triplets let's change the subject."

Charlie said, "I love you and always will. That is a promise you can write in the margins of your Bible. Would that be sacrilegious?"

"Charlie, you would be surprised what people write in their Bibles, especially teenagers. I promise you; tomorrow I will write *Charlie loves me* in my Bible. Just for my information, do you have a Bible?"

"I do; my mother's Bible. It's mine now, so gotcha there. You can't read it."

"Why not?"

"It's in Hebrew."

"Then, perhaps one day you can read it to me."

"You're too old for me to read to you. Since she was a Jew, she insisted that I read some of the old stories to her at bedtime, like the creation. But David was her all-time favorite character. I made a sling shot and practiced killing giants. I maimed a few trees around our house.

"Could we compare that with me jumping off a shed with a cape on, pretending to be Wonder Woman? I nearly killed myself." He couldn't stop laughing for a while, "That is too amazing," he said.

"Come to church Sunday, if you can. The choir is singing a special song at my request. It is a lovely arrangement of Duke Ellington's Come Sunday."

"Duke Ellington wrote sacred music?"

"Wait and see."

CHAPTER 50
Cassie and Robert

Their five days at the Cottage Inn in Maine was more fun than Randy said it would be. They visited several galleries on their walks, but bought only two pieces of art to remind them of their trip in years to come: A small painting from a gallery on Main Street, and a hand-blown vase with all colors of ocean blue. A couple of sweaters were necessary, since they had not come prepared for the weather. And for sure, they ate far too much seafood. Robert said, "Some of these chefs need to move to Atlanta." It was impossible for them to decide what had been their favorite café or restaurant.

Their visit was ending too quickly, and they finally set aside time to sit down with the owners, the Templeton. Ralph said, "Tell Mr. Roger Waddell we appreciate all the business he has been sending us, and that we are growing fast. We are booked pretty far ahead."

Cassie said, "Let me tell you about our friends you have entertained. It took over an hour, but they seemed to enjoy all the stories, both good and bad.

"We are sorry to hear about Rev. Childs' death," Joyce said. "Do not leave until we give you a gift to take to his child. And it is so wonderful Mr. Waddell found his daughter. You know we got to meet her. She is so beautiful. Tell Joan Walker we finished reading her latest book. She is a gifted writer. All of you must have a wonderful time in Atlanta."

Cassie said, "Atlanta is a neat place. There is something for everyone, but I hope we will be back here one day. In this place there is a feeling of history and a sense of being laid back. In Atlanta we are always pushing ourselves to the point of panic. When we get home we will fill Roger in about our time with you and hope it makes him homesick, but since he found Joanna, he could be happy anywhere.

"We were married at Maud's Inn on the Chattahoochee River, which is not far from Atlanta. If you ever decide to go south to

Atlanta, call Roger. He said that inn reminds him of yours. Thanks for your hospitality. This has been more than we ever expected. I can see why Roger not only grieves for Roberta, but for himself."

———

Back in Atlanta, business was waiting for Robert. Cassie took the last legal step to get her Attorney's license, which she passed. She had decided to tell Randy that being in practice with him is what she had wanted to do. He could teach her so much and it was the kind of practice that would not require her to be in the courtroom very often. She and Robert agreed to stay in the Sanders' guesthouse on the back of their property until they found a place they wanted to buy. It was private and cozy, and elegantly designed. Cassie asked Grace, "Your guest house is a beautiful place. Did you design the house and interior yourself?"

"I worked with a local builder, and contracted with an Atlanta designer concerning the interior. She is the best in Atlanta."

"Would that be Margaret?"

"Yes, she is a smart woman."

Robert and Cassie admitted there was sadness about leaving each other that first Monday morning after being together so much. Both sensed their lives were about to take separate paths. Their careers were about to engulf them, but they were grown up now, and besides adults were supposed to contribute to the community by using their talents. Cassie wasn't as excited as she should be. A little black cloud formed over her as she dressed for work. When they embraced, she cried. "Look at me," Robert said. "You are going to have a great time. Take these words to work with you: Being an attorney is exciting. The clients will fuel your energy. Some people will knock you off your feet, some will bore you to tears, and some of them will warm you heart. You have a big heart, perfect for all occasions."

"Thanks, I needed that, but I am going to miss you all day."

"I guarantee you, in three hours you will forget those words."

She arrived at work to meet Ms. Bee face to face. "Good morning," she said. "Is this the approximate time you will arrive every day?"

"No, Ms. Bee I will try to be here by 9:00. Is there a problem?"

"I just need to know; I prefer a steady routine."

"Ms. Bee, I am glad to be starting my career here. You and Dad will teach me a lot. I am ready and willing to learn."

"Well spoken, Mrs. Sanders. Well spoken. You and I will get along fine, but if you get too rambunctious, we may have to hire another person around here."

Randy came around the corner, "Don't pay any attention to her, she can handle both of us. I guess we'll have to raise her salary to make her happy."

"Don't talk about me as if I am not present. Money does not cure everything, Mr. Walker; respect does. I'm old enough to paddle both of you. Time is being wasted. Go train this child to her work, and let me do mine."

About mid-morning, the phone rang, "May I speak to Cassie Sanders?"

"May I say who is calling?" Ms. Bee asked.

"Mr. Sanders, her newly-wed husband."

"Remember Mr. Sanders, I was there."

"Oh, yes ma'am, I remember. How are you handling the new partnership?"

"That is a personal question. I don't even know the answer myself, and if I did I certainly would not reveal it on the phone."

"Yes ma'am, I know you wouldn't. Ms. Birkenstein, may I have the privilege of speaking to my dear wife."

"Yes, you may. One moment. Mrs. Sanders, there is a man on the phone claiming to be your husband. Should I tell him to wait or go away?"

"Thank you, Ms. Bee, I hope you were nice to him. I will take it."

"Mr. Sanders, she just asked me if I was nice to you. Well?"

"Yes Ma'am you were a jewel, and I do love your sense of humor, he said."

"Somebody around here needs one," she said.

"Hey Cassie, how is it going?"

"For the first day, I'm up to my ears in learning, but I'm enjoying it."

“Guess who just called?” Robert asked. “Who?” She answered.

“Kip Jones. I suppose we could say the young boy who brought us together. He asked me to pick him up for lunch. He sounded so grown up.”

“Are you going to meet him?”

“Sure, I’m curious. I’ll let you know how it goes.”

CHAPTER 51

Robert and Kip

Robert picked up Kip after school. What a surprise! He was well dressed and most polite. "Jump in Kip. What would you like for lunch?"

"Wherever you have time will be fine with me, Mr. Sanders." Robert drove to a diner on Ponce de Leon. It wasn't over crowded, so they would be able to have conversation. After they ordered Robert said, "Tell me what you have been doing these past few months."

"I'm still spending time with a tutor, and I am learning how to read and speak properly. I wish I had known about dyslexia years ago; reading has become much easier. None of my courses have been difficult, and I am never bored with my lessons. My mom still works for Mr. Mills, and he's a lot nicer to her than he was before. You know what I mean by *before*. I still have time to mow his yard, but now he takes care of the plants while I mow. I think we have become friends. You are not going to believe me! The school has decided that I can go into the eleventh grade next year. That's how good things have been, and I have you to thank for getting me out of trouble and saving my life."

"Wow! You have quite a lot to tell me. I'm so glad things are going well with you, but don't give me all the credit. To tell the truth, you did me a favor. During your trial I met the woman I love, and we are now married."

"Really! That's great. When can I meet her?"

"You will, but I hope it is not in a courtroom."

"You bet your life it won't be. Mr. Mills is paying me good, so I have saved some money. I understand that you were appointed to represent me, so I want to begin paying you back. Here is $50 to start."

"Oh, I've already been paid. The court always pays the lawyer. You and I sort of stomped that district attorney didn't we?"

"Yes sir, we did. Even though the court paid you, I feel it's my responsibility to pay you for representing me, and I will get more money over time."

"I do appreciate it, especially since you earned it, but I was paid by the courts, so taking your money would be unethical. Thanks, it was a generous offer."

"No, I am the one who should be thanking you. I would be in jail if it weren't for you. My tutor thinks I should make plans to go to college, so she wants me to start some of the courses to get me approved. I'll be doing that next year. My mom says she's proud of me. Mr. Sanders, I do have a favor to ask. I want you to talk to my mom. My dad hasn't been around since I was two years old. Somehow he heard about the trial and wants to come visit us. My mom and I don't want him to come. He will take my mom's money and hit her again. She said he threw me up against the wall the day he left, and he didn't come back to the house. She thought that made me retarded. We need to know what to do. If you have time, can I take you to see her? She's at Mr. Mills' house every day now."

"Sure why not, but I need to call my office, first."

They rode over to the Mills' house, and flashbacks came back about the Barnett case. He knew he would never forget all the events around that tragedy. Kip was a lucky boy to have gotten out of that mess, or maybe he had a lucky attorney.

Mrs. Jones came to the door and asked permission from Mr. Mills to allow them enter. "I hear you may have a problem, Mrs. Jones," Robert began. He paused after seeing Mr. Mills. "Good afternoon, sir. I hope you don't mind my visit. Kip seems to be worried."

"Mrs. Jones may need your help again," Fred Mills said. "I suggested that she talk to you. I don't want her to be troubled by this scoundrel. She's a good woman and a hard worker, and I will be glad to pay you."

Mrs. Jones said, "I'm so embarrassed. It's been years since I heard from my husband, Lester. I thought he was most likely dead. He's nothing but trouble. We, that is Kip and I, want to know if there's a way we can keep him from hurting us?"

"I'll do the best I can. First point, if he contacts you again tell him you have a warrant against him, and that he will be arrested if he comes near you. I will call my office when we get through and ask my secretary to get a warrant. Second, a warrant does not keep a criminal from finding you; so keep your doors locked even here at Mr. Mills' house. Do not open the door to anybody, because you may not recognize him after so long. Third, if you even think he's at the door call the police immediately. Kip, does he know where you go to school?"

"I don't think so, but I can't be sure he hasn't followed me."

"I will contact your principal and give him a copy of the warrant."

"My principal is a woman, Mrs. Thompson."

"Okay, I will see that Mrs. Thompson receives a copy of the warrant. You are not to come out of your classroom unless she summons you. Do you understand? Does your school have a guard on duty?"

"Yes, sir I understand, and we do have a guard."

"Mr. Mills, will you agree to take Mrs. Jones home in the afternoons?"

"Definitely; she is a valuable employee."

"Better yet, if I remember correctly, you have a garage apartment. Would you agree to move them in there for their safety."

"Of course."

"Is it furnished, and is there a phone?"

"Yes, to both questions."

"Mrs. Jones, you and Kip bring what clothes are necessary, and leave your house for a couple of weeks. Mr. Mills, when you pick them up drive around for at least thirty minutes. Stop at several places and look around. If you see anything suspicious call the police. On second thought, I will go with you to get their clothes right now if you are available."

"Yes, I am available."

By the time they got back to Fred Mills' house it was almost dark. "Mr. Mills can you get someone to take Kip to school? For a few days I would like for you to stay here while Mrs. Jones is working."

"Sure, I have a friend who will help."

For some reason Robert was worried. Mean people seem to have a second sense about things other people never think about. But he had done what he could do.

Two days later, about noon, there was a knock on the door at Fred Mills' house. Mrs. Jones peeped out the window, and there was Lester. Mr. Mills came around about the same time and called the police.

"Open this door, Mildred, I know you're in there. Get out here or I'll knock this damn door down, and I'll shoot the first person I see." About that time the police rounded the corner. Lester shot at the door, then turned and shot at the police. Both policemen opened fire at the same time, and Lester fell to the ground.

"Mrs. Jones, stay inside. I'm going out," said Mr. Mills. About that time a policeman came to the door to ask if they were all right. "When your lawyer gave us his name the other day we looked up his record, and found he's wanted in two states for robbery and murder. Wanted no more; the guy is dead. He had a gun and a knife on him so he meant business. We'll get him down to the morgue for positive identification. I believe all of you are safe now."

"I'm going to call the boy at school, and let his principal know there is no need to be on the look-out any more," Mr. Mills said. "Thanks for getting here so fast. My housekeeper is going to be able to settle down now, and to tell the truth I've been as scared as she was."

Inside Mrs. Jones was shaking, "Is he really dead?"

"Yes, he is dead. You don't have to worry any more."

"My boy is *sure* going be glad. Thank you, Mr. Mills you're a good man. We'll be moving back to our house tomorrow."

"I've been thinking what would be best for you and the boy. It makes more sense for you to stay in the garage apartment. Since you are renting your other place we can clear out what you need, and you can remain here if that is all right with you."

"Yes Sir it is, but we don't want to be any bother. I know my Kip will be happy. You've been so kind. I want to thank you for being so kind to him."

Mr. Mills picked up Kip from school and told him the whole story. He was so stunned he was unable to speak. "That's all right, son you and your mom are safe now, and she has other news for you."

Kip ran into the house, and fell into his mom's arms. "I wish I had been here to help you."

"We did all right for ourselves. He won't bother us anymore."

"Thank you for helping us, Mr. Mills. Have you called Mr. Sanders yet?" They shook their heads, no. Good. I want to call him. He'll be glad."

When they finished moving into the garage apartment, Robert came by to say hello. Mr. Mills took him up to the apartment where the four of them had a toast with ginger ale. Kip said, "I'm going to owe you a lot of money, Mr. Sanders. You might have to wait 'till I finish my schooling so I'll have enough."

"Son, consider your debt paid. The news that you and your mom are safe is better than money. Get in touch with me every now and then to let me know how everything is going."

"I will, sir. My Mom and I thank you again, and I wouldn't mind having lunch with you sometimes. The next time it'll be my treat. I still have that fifty dollars."

"It's a date; just let me know."

Robert practically danced down the stairs. Some things do work out for the best. Kip didn't owe him a dime. Because of him he had the greatest prize of all.

CHAPTER 52

Freddie Winchester and Celeste Murray

The following weeks slipped by as fast as summer passes for school children, and soon it would be Christmas. So much had happened; it was hard to put it all in perspective. The only family that seemed normal in all this confusion was the Winchester family. Their children Freddie, Jr. and Molly were ideal children, and Molly was like a sister to Julia during all the problems with her mother. Frederick's law business was thriving, and Elizabeth was a dedicated worker at their church and a regular volunteer in the Children's Hospital Auxiliary: two of her many obligations. That was before...

Freddie called from Las Vegas. "Mom, sit down. Celeste and I have something to tell you."

"No hello, or hi, or I love you?"

"Mom, you know I love you. We want you and Dad to be the first persons to know, Celeste and I got married."

"What! Why did you do that, Freddie?"

"Mom, Celeste and I have loved each other for long time, and you know her mother would stop her marrying me. There is something else, I'm going to be a father."

"Wait a minute. You are throwing all this at me too fast. Did you decide to get married because of the pregnancy?"

"Mom, what kind of question is that? Celeste and I have been talking about marriage for a long time. At first we thought we would wait until after the baby is born. Mom, help me out here."

"How can I help you, Freddie?"

"Support our decision."

"Oh, Freddie, I could never be mad at you. You know I love you and we will love Celeste. I am happy for you. Come on home. All of us need a hug."

"Call Dad and tell him for me."

"Call him yourself. Get him out of whatever he is doing, and tell him what you told me. *Now*! Freddie."

"Yes Ma'am. I'll call as soon him as we hang up. See you day after tomorrow."

Celeste Murray is a classic southern beauty, spoiled and bronzed in the sun, and she never has to prove anything by entering beauty contests. She is the daughter of one of the most respected families in the professional circles in Atlanta. Her mother, Doctor Louise Hamilton Murray is a college professor, and her father, Doctor Thomas Jackson Murray is an Orthopedic Surgeon. The Murrays live the life they can afford, country club, charity balls, and members of the largest Episcopal Church in Atlanta. Louise Murray will not only be hurt, about her daughter marrying a Black Boy, she will be embarrassed that it would bring shame and limit her friendships, and it makes no difference to her that Freddie's mother is white.

Louise Murray had made it plain to Cassie that she wanted her to marry young Robert Sanders, Jr. She was devastated when he married Cassie Randolph.

The Winchesters have been surprised and hurt by her attitude. Frederick defended Dr. Thomas Murray successfully in a malpractice suit, and they are both members of an exclusive male fraternity in Atlanta. Frederick had discouraged Freddie from dating Celeste because he knew it would cause tension in the two families. "But we are in love," Freddie would say, as if that make everything all right. So problem is, how to reconcile four adults who are about to become grandparents. Molly was offended that the Murray's were prejudiced, "People should be able to marry whomever they wish," she said to her mother. "Weren't her parents aware Freddie and Celeste dated in college? Racism! I hate it. I looked in the mirror the other day and wondered whether I'm black or white. None of my friends have ever asked, and besides, they don't even know that Dad has a Black mother and a White father. The whole thing is stupid. Oh yes, will their baby be known as *mixed?* Whoever invented such terms? Mom, you have to talk to these people! You and Dad will not be upset that Celeste is *white* will you?"

"No! Have you forgotten that I am white? What's the matter with you? Molly, wait until Freddie and Celeste get back. We will talk to them and see what they want to do."

"Where is Dad? I want to know what he thinks."

"When he comes home, ask him. He married me, didn't he? What do you expect him to say?"

"Damn, sometimes I forget Dad is somewhat black. Mom, how crazy is that."

"Pretty damn sweet, Molly, but I don't like your word somewha*t*."

Frederick called, "I just got the call from Freddie. I'm coming home early. Do you know if Celeste has called her parents?"

"I don't believe she has. She is probably afraid to call them."

"Elizabeth, I asked Freddie and Celeste to come on back to Atlanta instead of staying another night. We need to have a good plan. To tell the truth, since they have been dating I had a premonition something like this would happen. Her family is going to be happy. We had parents who supported us. Thank you, Elizabeth for marrying me. I love you."

"Oh, Frederick, we were meant for each other. Don't get too worried about the Murray family. Maybe they will be happy about the child."

"Pray, my dear Elizabeth, pray. This may get difficult. How is Molly doing?"

"She's a little up tight. She doesn't want to see Freddie get hurt. I wonder if Freddie called Tommy, Celeste's brother. They have been friends a long time. Maybe he can help the situation."

"This is more than a situation, Elizabeth; this is a crisis."

As soon as they hung up, the phone rang. Molly answered, "This is Tommy Murray, Molly. I need to come over to see your family."

"Sure, come on. Did Freddie call you or something like that?"

"Yep. I'll be there soon." He had been in their home so many times he always got a friendly hug from everybody. "Hi, Miss Elizabeth. I hope you are doing well. When Freddie called I told him I would try to be here when his Dad gets home from work. I just pulled in behind Mr. Winchester."

"That's sweet of you. Are you worried about the situation?"

"No, but my mom will be livid. Dad will eventually take everything into consideration; he is a compromiser. He hauls my mom out of the situations she gets herself into. I'll bet you twenty dollars, when she finds out they are married, she will demand the marriage be annulled. And believe me, it won't matter about the baby. She'll blame everything on Freddie."

"Daddy," Molly yelled as Frederick walked in the door, "Isn't it great you are going to be a grandfather?"

"Of course, honey, of course. Hello Tommy glad to see you here. Do you know if Celeste has called your parents?"

"I don't believe so. She's the type to confront them face to face, and enjoy it when mom faints onto the sofa; not literally of course."

As soon as Frederick was settled with a cup of coffee, Molly demanded, "Okay, let's talk. What is going to be the plan?"

"Molly, don't go so fast," Elizabeth said. "Let your dad get settled, and let's hear what Tommy has to say."

"I had a feeling they were going to do this," Tommy said. "Freddie and I are pretty close, but I knew he couldn't tell me because it was a family issue."

"Tommy? You could have told me." Molly interrupted.

"Then you would have been in the same predicament I was."

"Let's don't try to plan tomorrow," Frederick said. "I don't believe there is anything we can do but wait until they are home. Tommy, did you take them to the airport?"

"I did, Sir."

"Can you pick them up tomorrow?"

"Yes Sir, I had planned on doing that."

"When you get back, if you can stay for a one-sided family meeting, it might be help for us."

"Let me think about that after I talk to Celeste."

"That's a fair answer," Frederick said.

"I'll be leaving now; all of you are such nice people. I am proud my sister and I are going to be a part of this family."

"I hope that doesn't mean you have your eyes on Molly," Frederick said.

"Daddy, why would you say something like that?"

"Well Molly, you never can tell," Tommy said, and gave her a punch on the shoulder.

Freddie and Celeste arrived at the airport at 4:00, and Tommy was there to greet them. "The two of you have stirred up a hornet's nest for sure."

"Why? Do Mom and Dad know anything?" Celeste asked.

"Not yet, but you have to tell them before someone else does."

"I'm dropping the two of you off at your house, Freddie. I have been asked to stay, but I believe going on home is the best thing for me to do. The less I know, the better I can negotiate for you later, Celeste. You understand?"

"Sure, Tommy; see you later."

Molly greeted them at the door, "Get in here you naughty people. You could have let me know. Mom's in the kitchen, and lunch is ready. Dad's in his room answering a phone call."

"Welcome home, kids," Elizabeth said, hugging both of them. Should I introduce both of you as my children, or Mr. and Mrs., or what?"

Right now I am officially Celeste Murray Winchester, and Freddie has also agreed to add the hyphen to his name. It's a new thing with people our age."

"Oh, that's good, Celeste; maybe that will please your mother," Molly said. "Men don't change their last names, so why should we have to change ours."

"Celeste," Elizabeth said, "Your parents have to know."

"I realize that, but I want to tell my father first. He understands me. One day I tested him. I asked him if it really mattered to him who I married, and he said, 'I just want you to make the right decision that will make you happy.' But my mom is a different story; she will be happy as long as I live the way she wants me to live. I have no idea how to approach her." Frederick came back into the room. Celeste asked, "Mr. Winchester, will you call my father for me on his business phone? Here is the number."

"I'll be happy to call him. Dr. Murray, this is Dr. Frederick Winchester. Good. Thank you. How about you...yes, it is…I have someone here who needs to talk to you."

"Daddy, this is Celeste, are you in a place we can talk privately?"

"Hold on a minute, let me walk outside to the patio. Okay, what's on your mind, sweetie?"

"Daddy, will you be very quiet and listen to me while I tell you something?"

"Are you in some kind of trouble?"

"No Daddy, I'm in love. Freddie and I flew to Las Vegas and got married." There was a long silence. "Daddy, are you all right?"

"Well, I was a few minutes ago. Why did you do that?"

"You know why. Mom would never approve."

"And you thought I would?"

"Yes, Daddy, I believed you would. You and I understand each other."

"Tell me how this came about."

"Daddy, this was the only way, really it was. Mom is blinded for what's best for me. I knew she would never approve of this marriage."

"You are right about that. She is going to put me *and* you through hell."

"Daddy, you are going to be a grandfather!"

"Marriage and baby all in one phone call? Is there anything else I will need to check my blood pressure."

"Do you think we should come over right now? Mom has to know sometime."

"I suppose now is as good a time as any, so come on. Maybe you should give me time to take a tranquilizer."

"Daddy, I didn't know you took tranquilizers."

"I don't, but I'm going to find one."

"Tommy, where are you?"

"I'm up here in my room, Dad. You need me?"

"Are you hiding? You usually stick your head out when I call you."

"I *am* hiding, but if you want me to, I'll stick my head out?"

"No, I'll just come up. Did you know about Freddie and Celeste?"

"Only recently. Freddie called me from Las Vegas, and told me. I had a remote idea what they were planning. I didn't want to tell you. I felt it was Celeste and Freddie's responsibility. We have a problem, don't we, Dad?"

"Stay with me, son; we'll get through this."

"I'm sorry, Dad. But it couldn't be much of a surprise, since they have been dating off and on for three years, but mostly at college. Dad, you should see them, I hope I can find someone who feels about me the way Celeste feels about Freddie, and he loves her so much. Can you accept their decision, Dad?"

"Right now I have to handle your mother. You and I should be prepared for anything, but remember when they approach your mom don't try to handle my job. Okay? I'll handle it the best way possible."

"Yes, Sir. I know you will, Dad. I love you. Mom has always been hard to understand. There are times…

"I know, don't say it. Anyway, don't try to define your feelings at this moment."

"I understand, Dad."

Tommy met Celeste and Freddie at the door, and whispered, "Dad is okay. Come on in."

"Mom!"

"Celeste! What is this boy doing here?"

"Mom, remember I love you, so listen carefully to me. I love Freddie Winchester. I have always known we belong together."

"Stop it," she yelled.

"No, Mom, I won't stop. We are married, and we are going to have a baby."

"No Negro…

"Louise, stop it; don't say that." Thomas yelled.

"No, I will not stop! We will have this married annulled, and she can get an abortion or that half-black baby will be put up for adoption!"

"Mom, you can't do that. We are adults, and we love each other."

"What do you know about love? Do you know what a life you will have?"

"Sure, I do. I have married into a happy, successful family. Both Freddie and I are professionals and make a good living. My dad is a well-known doctor, and my mother is a college professor. She works with all kinds of people, but sadly she's a very prejudiced person. I have no idea how she associates with Asians, Blacks, Indians, and all sorts of people at work. She must fake it all day."

"Why, you little slut, you…" Celeste stepped back to avoid the slap.

"Louise, stop it! Do not complete that sentence. You will be sorry. Think about this: For the rest of your life you will be denied access to you daughter and her family, while Tommy and I visit them and play with their child."

"In that case, the two of you can move out of *my* house."

"I beg your pardon, I believe this is *our* house. And I am going to tell you something I have never revealed. My parents did not want me to marry you because your father was a small-time accountant and your mother was his bookkeeper. My parents couldn't possibly see them dining at the country club and playing golf."

"You're lying."

"Call my sister if you don't believe me. But I married you, and my parents learned to tolerate your family. Now, you can accept Freddie into our family, or face the consequences."

"You don't have the guts to have consequences."

"Oh yes I do. Tommy, come here. Take Freddie and Celeste out back."

He began, "Louise, I have created a monster by marrying you, and I should have known better. I don't intend to live with a monster. You will pretend to accept this marriage until you can accept it. You will be civil to Freddie, and we will call on Elizabeth and Frederick Winchester, or I will call on them, and you can file for divorce. You will *not* attempt to destroy this marriage legally or by gossip. My God! Louise, Celeste is your daughter. She is smart, beautiful, and strong - strong enough to accept happiness where she has found it. The decision is up to you."

"Obviously you have made your decision, but you cannot force mine. I will never accept this marriage, so forget your threats."

"Maybe you didn't understand. If you are not willing to accept this marriage, call your lawyer tomorrow to start divorce proceedings. I can't wait for you to tell the judge why you are getting a divorce. You probably won't have a job anymore."

"My skills are more important to the school, than my beliefs. Why should they care that I don't want my daughter married to a nigger."

"Stop saying that! How many students do you have in your classes that are not white? They will be knocking on the President's door to get rid of you. I am asking you not to get a divorce, but if we do divorce, you will be the losing partner."

"You aren't that cheap."

"Oh, I'm pretty cheap right now. Have I lived all these years with you not to realize how hateful you are?" He turns and walks toward the patio. "Freddie, welcome to our family, that is mine and Tommy's family. I am sorry about Louise. She grew up in an environment that never learned to accept Blacks and Asians, and has followed in her family's footsteps. I remember taking her father, Mr. Hamilton to lunch when Louise and I were dating. He was a belligerent racist and refused to have lunch in a café where Blacks were dining. To this day, I regret walking away to find an acceptable restaurant for him. I thought time and social events would change Louise, but now I realize she has kept this hatred deep inside until this situation today. I apologize, but I can't change her. I am happy for both of you. How can I help celebrate this double event with you?"

Freddie said, "Let's allow a few weeks to pass, then we will think of some way to get together. One of my dad's best friends, Joan Walker will be happy to plan an event for us. We are not going to keep our marriage and our baby a secret. That is how sure we are of our love. Celeste and I have talked about repeating our vows in a religious ceremony, later on, with my family's minister. I am sure we can arrange it. We'll let you know."

"Tommy and I will be there."

From upstairs Tommy said, "Don't count on Mom, she hates losing face. I suspect she will go about her life as usual, and like a good Southern lady of yore, never talking about it, and never changing her opinion. I'm sorry."

"Tommy, thanks for your help; you are a true friend. I don't want to turn you against your mom, but you do what you have to do."

"Brave statement, old man, but having a mom like her does not change my friendship. Sis, you are my hero, and I'm so glad you have found happiness. Go girl, I love you."

"Thanks Tommy, I love you. Dad, thank you for understanding. You know I love you. I don't know what is going to happen between you and mom, but I will stand beside you."

"I know you will. Now go home. You do have a home for her, Freddie?"

"Yes Sir, I do. Here's my card. It has my business and home phone."

"Love you, Celeste," Tommy yelled out. "I'll call you in a few days."

"I'll wait for your call." She stepped inside the house and yelled, "Goodbye Mom. Sorry you are disappointed in me." No answer.

Freddie said, "I can't believe I gave him my card. What was I thinking?"

"It looked sort of sweet to me," Celeste said.

For Elizabeth, the previous night felt like a bad dream. Everything was so normal in their household, until Freddie and Celeste's marriage changed everything. They came back by the house, and gave the details of the evening. Both Frederick and Elizabeth cried. It was the worst moment in any of their lives. It had been a long time since Elizabeth had heard of that kind of prejudice. When she and Frederick married all their close friends and Frederick's legal associates came to celebrate, and the members of their church were also there. Now she realized how unbelievable that was. But today she needed a friend. Joan was someone who would do anything for a friend, so she decided to call her. "Joan, do you have plans for tomorrow?"

"None I can't change. Do you want to come over here, or should I come there?"

"I'm in desperate need of a change of scenery. I'll come over there."

"That will be fine. I'll call Randy, and tell him I got a better deal for lunch."

"Thank you, Joan. I'll be there after Fredrick leaves for work."

The next morning Joan was waiting. When she opened the door Elizabeth burst into tears. It was so unlike her. "Elizabeth, what's wrong? Come on inside. I have brunch ready, but it will wait."

"It's a long story, Joan. I hope you have time to listen."

"I do have time, and I insist we do it at the table. I bet you haven't eaten anything today."

"You are right about that." She poured out her anger to Joan. "My child has been rejected and humiliated. He is handsome, bright, and hardworking, and has never been in trouble. Why would anyone find the need to crush his spirit with so much bitterness? I thought about calling my pastor, but he would probably tell me to forgive and forget, and I do *not* need that sort of instruction. If I feel this bad, Frederick must feel worse. And Molly? She got so mad we had to stop her from screaming. She wants revenge, and can't understand why we aren't going to war."

"I can understand why she feels that way. This is going to be hard for her. How are you going to help her?"

"I don't know. She is impulsive and hardheaded. This past year at the Naval Academy, she was out to save the world. I don't want to kill that spirit; it will get her through life. Freddie doesn't have that sense of spirit, and he admires Molly."

"Molly is like you, Elizabeth, strong and independent. Your mom and dad must have been wonderful and caring people. Did they accept Frederick right away?"

"Yes they did. They had friends all over the world, and thought Frederick would be a good husband and a good provider. *Provider* is such an old fashion expression, but they actually said that. I guess they wanted me to continue to have all the things they had provided for me and for my sister. They were not rich, but they sacrificed for us, and they were good role models. His military career carried us to places I may never return, but it was the best education anyone could ever have. I believe Molly is trying to follow in my dad's footsteps by going to the Naval Academy."

"You have a great family, and you will get through this. Right now focus on your strengths. You don't have to solve Freddie's situation. He will come though this and make you proud. I can only imagine how much you hurt for Celeste. I bet she feels like an orphan after the terrible things her mom said. Being a mother I have a hard time believing Louise Murray could be so cruel. But you have to let Dr. Murray take care of that side of the family."

The telephone rang. "Miss Joan, this is Freddie. Is my mama over there? I have been trying to find her."

"Yes, she's here. I'll give her the phone."

"Good God, Freddie! No, this can't be. Where are you? I'll be right there. Joan, Celeste is in the hospital. Freddie says Celeste has lost the baby. Can you drive me there? I'm so mad and hurt, I might run over a policeman?"

"Sure, come on. Let me grab my purse."

"Freddie said Celeste's father is on the way."

Freddie and Dr. Murray were standing outside Celeste's room. Both of them were in tears. "I am so sorry, Freddie; I know who is responsible for this."

"Dr. Murray, she cried most of the night, and cursed her mom in between sobs. Here they are. Mom, thanks for coming. Hi, Miss Joan, thanks for bringing Mom. This is not good, Mom, this is not good. We were so happy about the baby. Last night when we tried to sleep she said, 'I am the daughter of a devil. How can I live with that?' I couldn't believe she said that. Cassie believes her mom willed our baby to die. I have to change her mind. Help me!"

"Son, we will get through this. Louise probably wishes I would die, but she cannot hex anyone. There is a powerful God between your family and Louise."

"Mr. Winchester," a nurse said, "Your wife is calling for you. Stay with her as long as you want. Dr. Murray, I'm sorry about your daughter. You can allow the ladies in later."

"Dr. Murray, this is my friend Joan Walker," Elizabeth said.

"I've seen you many times at events, and I know your husband, Randy, and Bob Sanders, the father of your son-in-law. Small, small world, isn't it?"

"Yes it is. Randy and Frederick went to college together, in fact, there were six of us who practically lived together, and now we are all in Atlanta, except Rev. Leonard Childs, who died."

"How nice to have close friends."

"Dr. Murray," the nurse said, "Your daughter wants to see you."

He tried to compose himself as he took Celeste's hand, "Honey, I am so sorry. How is my girl?"

"Not so good, Daddy. It hurts that she did this to me. How can I ever love her again? She has hurt me and Freddie, and we will not go near her again."

"You do not have to decide on that right now. Focus on healing your body and your heart, and hatred is going to hinder that process. Concentrate on life with Freddie, the person you have loved for so long. That will help heal your body so you can start anew. Think about this, the child you lost helped you and Freddie make a decision you had long delayed. Perhaps the next child will bring happiness to a settled husband and wife who have seen enough sorrow."

"Oh, Daddy, you always have the right words. Your words heal."

Freddie brought Elizabeth and Joan in, "Thanks, Mom for coming, and thank you too, Mrs. Walker. Mom, you won't be a grandmother yet, and Molly won't be an aunt. She is going to be hurt. But Dr. Murray's has helped us a lot."

Elizabeth said, "Celeste, would you like to stay at our place for a few days? I don't think Freddie knows how to cook, and you will need food to help recover."

"What about it, Freddie?" Celeste asked.

"I think that's a good idea. And Dr. Murray you are welcome to come and be with us anytime. Mom is a great hostess."

"Thanks for the invitation, but another time. Right now I have a lot of things to take care of."

Freddie was on the bed with Celeste. Joan bent over and gave him a kiss, "I have watched you grow up. You are from a good family, and you will be a good husband. Look at the two of you, so young, so beautiful. I'm envious. Thanks for allowing me a few minutes with you."

"I just talked to Molly," Elizabeth said, "She's having a fit. It's a couple of weeks before she returns to the Academy. Celeste, Molly said for you to get home so she can give you a little TLC for a few days."

Dr. Murray said, "I need to move on for now. Celeste, we'll talk later."

Thomas Murray entered his house that had been his shelter for years, but it meant nothing now. He felt like a broken man who had just lost an heir. "Is that you, Thomas?" Louise asked, "Where have you been?"

"At the hospital. Celeste just lost her baby boy."

"Good, maybe Celeste will come to her senses. It's good the half-breed died."

"Did I misunderstand you? What did you say?"

As she entered the room she said, "I said it's good the half-breed died!"

"That's what I thought you said. Get out of my way. Get your things together. I am putting this house up for sale this week. I will lend you enough money to find a place, and I don't want any more conversations except in front of a lawyer."

"You can't do that, this is common property."

"That doesn't matter. You have no idea how much it doesn't matter. You will not contest our divorce. If you do, all Atlanta is going to know what a bitch you are. Tommy will stay here tonight to make certain you don't burn the place down. Tomorrow he will take you to look for a place to live. Do not come back here without finding something that you can afford on *your own* salary. When this house is sold, I will send half of the profit to you, and don't forget to take what furniture you need. Don't leave anything in the house that reminds me of you. As far as I am concerned, Tommy doesn't have to speak to you, except in a business manner. I'll do everything I can to keep you from ruining his life also. Tommy, I know you are listening, understand?"

"Yes, Dad I understand."

"Tommy, help me get some things together. I am going to a hotel after I go back to the hospital. I'm sorry to put all this on you, but right now Celeste and I need you."

"Dad, I'll take care of the house and get Mom resettled. It's about time I find a place of my own. I don't like this house anymore. If I fall in love with someone who is not a White southerner, I might get the same treatment. The fact is, I had a few dates with Phyllis Wingo, whose parents are Asian. I guess that would be a no-no around here, right, Mom?" No answer.

"Probably," Thomas said."

Freddie was still at the hospital when Dr. Murray arrived. Celeste had been given a sedative so he and Freddie talked in the hall. "Dr. Murray, after you called me, I talked to Joan, and she said you are welcome to stay with them tonight instead of trying to find a hotel. She and Mr. Randy are nice people."

"Yes, I have known them for years. Tell them thanks for me, but I need to be alone tonight. I'll call you tomorrow." He decided to spend the night on the couch in his office. He would be ready for work the next day.

He had never been in his office past midnight. It was eerily quiet, even his steps echoed down the hall. How many patients had he comforted there? How many times had he said *everything is going to be all right* to a patient? He needed someone to say those words to him tonight, but there were no voices, not even his.

The next morning Thomas Murray put in a call to Georgia Parker. "Georgia, I may need your services. Can we meet for lunch tomorrow?"

"What's up Thomas?"

"I'll tell you at lunch. See you at noon. How about the hospital cafeteria?"

"Wow, such an intimate location."

"Don't make light of it; the food is actually good."

"I'll be there."

Freddie and Celeste drove to his parent's house. Frederick, Elizabeth, and Molly greeted them, and for a few days it was a shelter for them. After Freddie returned to work, Celeste stayed a few more days. Molly hated leaving, but had to return to the Academy.

Three weeks later, Celeste reported to work, but her heart was not in it. The manager of the firm suggested she take another two weeks off, but she refused. "Send me out on a job. I'll dig my heels in, just wait and see. I need to be busy."

"Being busy is not work. You will have to focus on this project, else you take the time off until you *can* focus. I can't afford any mess-up on this contract. You will work with Jim Moss on this project, and bring us an opinion on the situation."

"I'm ready today if Jim is."

"He is ready. Jim, come to my office," he yelled into the phone. "You are the leader in this project. As soon as you and Celeste bring us an analysis on the situation, we can proceed."

"Will do," Jim said. Let's go Celeste."

"It's good to be back to work," she said.

CHAPTER 53
Cassie

Robert and Cassie met Joan and Randy for dinner at The Fish Market. Cassie had followed the drama of the Murray family. She and Celeste had not been close friends, but Robert knew her well. Cassie said, "Robert you were supposed to marry her? How did that not happen?"

"You came along and got me."

"Did I do that, or did you tempt me?"

"Regardless of the continue flattering invitations from her mother, I had no intentions of dating *or* marrying her."

"Okay, that's enough," Randy said. "We don't want to get in an argument about who had the best courtship."

"Mom, what have you heard from Rick? It's been months since he left. I think he has forgotten me," Cassie said.

"He's having a ball. Pearl sent him to the right people, and those ladies are treating him like a son. He won't be coming home any time soon. According to what I read from his emails he has found his calling, and he will remain in Paris for quite a while. He is improving in his art lessons, and has sold a few small paintings. I told him he owes me a painting. I don't know where the two of you inherited your talent, but it wasn't from me. What happened to your painting, Cassie?"

"Robert and passing the bar."

"Don't blame it on me," Robert said, "You really should work on your art." To Joan he said, "I saw the paintings she had in her apartment, and had no idea she was the artist until I asked her who painted them. I had to *make* her hang them after we married."

"Dad, will you ask Ms. Bee if I could set up an easel in my office and paint in my spare time?"

"I'll let you ask her, and I'll crack my door to hear her response, 'who has spare time?' "

"Mom, she's a killer. I think Dad is afraid of her."

"You bet your life I am, and I don't intend on getting her dander up."

"Robert, Ms. Bee is the color in our office. As gruff as she is, she is so funny. I think she likes me, but she treats me like a child."

"Well, you are to her, Joan said."

"Mom don't side with her, she wouldn't like it."

"Cassie, are you and Ms. Bee ready to handle the office for awhile?"

"Why, are you retiring?"

"I believe I said, for a while."

"Sure, what's up?"

"Your mom and I are going on a trip."

"Since when?" Joan asked.

"Since I got the tickets to Scotland."

"Really, Randy. Scotland? Why there?" Joan asked.

"Adventure and a celebration of your new book. But let me finish. After a week in Scotland, we will spend some time in Paris."

"Wonderful! Have you told Rick?"

"Yes, I have. The ladies are making room for us in their apartment."

Cassie turned to Robert, "Of course you will help me out if I get in over my head at the office?"

"Estate law? I'm not equipped. You can always ask Ms. Bee."

"And she is equipped," said Randy. Whatever, do not try to tell her what to do. She will let you have it. Just hand her the papers. So, it's settled, we will be leaving in exactly twelve days from today, and will be gone for two weeks. Cassie, will that give us enough time to get you ready?"

"It's now or never, so my answer is *yes*. I suppose it's time to start earning my pay. Robert, don't plan anything those fourteen days. Mom, I heard you had a great book-signing event. Congratulations, I'm so proud of you."

"Thanks, Cassie. I'm about out of characters for now, so I'm going to rest for a while. Maybe a new inspiration will knock me in the head in Scotland."

After they got into their car, Robert said, "I am so proud of you Cassie. You are going to be a great lawyer."

"And I want to be a mother someday. That's why I chose estate law so I wouldn't have to go to court very often, remember?"

"Court will happen, occasionally. Just keep good records, and if the clients will allow it, record your sessions. It is much easier to get a transcript than having Ms. Bee take notes. And motherhood? I would like to wait at least a year. I can't afford to share you right now. You bring so much excitement to my life; I want to revel in it."

"I'm sorry, I did not mean *immediately*. I don't believe I want a baby on my lap while I'm interviewing clients, but you and I will make lovely children."

"I have to tell you something. Yesterday, when I went by to see my parents, Mom ask me, 'are you going to give me a grandchild before I get too old?' She was thirty-two and Dad thirty-one when they married, so add my brother's age to that, and you get her point."

"What about your brother Timothy? You never talk about him."

"I don't think he will ever marry. Mom and Dad have no idea he is gay, but one day he is going to have to tell them. I honestly believe they will be accepting. Mom has some bohemian cousins, and they get along fine when they spend time together. She says they make her laugh. Like them, Timothy is a clown. Dad *could* have a hard time with it, but who knows?"

"You never told me Timothy is gay. I told you about Rick, why didn't you say something then?"

"Forgive me, my dear wife, for avoiding the issue. I do have a hard time with it sometimes, but I love him."

"You would love Rick too. He is so smart and very talented. I have confidence he will become a well-known artist. My father called him a sissy most of the time. Of course my father was rarely home. I'm surprised he was there often enough to get my mom pregnant twice. I want you to get to know Randy's Aunt Pearl; she should have been his mother. She has always treated him like her son because she knew his father was a jerk. As the story goes, Pearl had a lover once, a gal from Chicago, but she died in a car accident, and supposedly Pearl never dated anyone else, but who really knows? She and Randy's mom are sisters and the best of friends. No one else could live with either of them. Robert, you have a lot of history to learn."

"Wow, Randy is a lucky person. I saw him watching us in court. I sensed he would my chop my head off if I touched you."

"Did you really think that? He would have been so pleased."

"Well, that may be overstated, but I did have a fear of him for a few minutes. I felt like a sixteen year old trying to approach him to ask you for a date."

"Oh, that's *so* funny. He is a good person, and has always loved my mom. It is a long story, and sometime on a cold winter night I will tell you their story."

"I can't wait to hear it; I'll pray for snow."

At home that night Robert grabbed Cassie into his arms and was reluctant to let her go. He said to her, "I lie awake at night thinking what might have happened if you had not been in the courtroom that day. No girl I ever dated was the for-life partner I was looking for. I had begun to feel my destiny was to be a bachelor. There was someone out there for me, but in all of Atlanta, I couldn't find her. One day you just appeared. You are not going to believe this, but the moment I turned around to make a point, or something like that, I saw you. I knew you were there to find me. I'm not sure how I made that conclusion, but I did."

"That is so sweet. Sometimes I wonder who the real matchmaker is. Some say it is simply a matter of fate, others believe a higher power is involved. I like to believe it's a God thing. If that sounds corny, that's all right."

"Cassie, you have no idea how much I love you. I want to shower you with gifts, take you on trips, and show you off to my friends who have been trying for years to set me up with dates."

"Robert, you don't have to do any of those things…well, I could use a new car. I've been driving that Chevy for years now. I'm kidding, of course. I can buy my own car. By the way, I have no idea how much I'm being paid. I guess I'll have to ask. I digress. Robert, you are everything I ever wanted, smart, handsome, personable, and damn good at a respectable vocation. I am the one who hit the jackpot. Can we hush talking now, and show each other how much love we have."

Robert seemed timid when they undressed together, but he loved watching her. Sometimes he felt awkward approaching her when beginning their prelude to intercourse. He wanted every time to be different. This time she finally realized that she was to be the aggressor. She began by doing all the things she wished he would do. Finally when his passion clicked in, he seemed to forget who he was and became the lover she was teaching him to be. Afterward as they lay entwined, he said, “Thanks for bringing me around tonight. In appreciation, this coming weekend will be our first adventure at an automobile dealership.”

“Wow, I can hardly wait.”

“I’m sorry I broke the fervor of the moment.”

The next morning Cassie got to work early, hoping to beat Ms. Bee.

Damn, she is already here: Maybe she can read minds, like Dad said.

“Good morning, Cassie, or should I address you as Ms. Sanders.”

“Between you and me, Cassie will do. For clients Ms. Cassie Walker-Sanders.”

“That is a mouthful, but I like it. There’s rhythm to it.”

“Thank you Ms. Bee. You will be Ms. Birkenstein in front of clients.”

“You and I will get along fine. Just fine. Here are some papers to read before your day starts. These are concerning the persons Mr. Walker is working with at the moment. And they may be carry-overs while he is gone. We have two couples coming in this morning. I believe it would be important for you to sit in on the meetings. You will introduce yourself, of course.”

“Of course.”

“On your desk you will find some material on house rules concerning estate attorneys. Try to get those read before Mr. Walker leaves for Scotland. I’m certain you studied most of that in law school, but check off the items you are not clear about, and we will go through them.”

“Thank you, Ms. Bee, I’m sure this will be a great help. Are you going to give me a test?”

"Don't get smart with me. I have one of those in the office already."

Cassie walked over and kissed her on the check, "You are a dear, and I am looking forward to working with you."

"Goodness gracious, go to work, and let me be."

"Ta, Ta."

When Cassie left the room, she saw Ms. Bee touch her cheek and smile.

The phone rang, "Mr. Walker, Dr. Thomas Murray is on the phone."

"Randy, this is Thomas Murray."

"Greetings, what can I do for you?"

"I understand you're a friend of Georgia Parker, and I can't seem to get her to return my calls. I set up a luncheon date, but she called my office and cancelled it. Can you help me out?"

"Well, is she out of town?"

"I'm not sure. I may be getting the run around."

"Let me try her and call you back. This is Randy Walker, is Georgia in?"

"Just a minute, Mr. Walker."

"Hi, Randy. Long time since we talked. How can I help you?"

"What's wrong with not answering Dr. Murray's calls?'

"Are you kidding, his wife is also trying to get to me."

"Are you serious? Listen Georgia, if you had to make a choice between the two of them, could you possibly take Thomas?"

"I don't know. It's going to be nasty. I've got other important things to do."

"Then let's put it this way, maybe you shouldn't represent either of them."

'That's what I've been thinking."

"Who is the best divorce attorney in town?"

"Robert Sanders, Sr., without a doubt."

"Good God, he's my son-in-law's father."

"You asked me for the best; you got it."

"Thanks, let's have lunch again."

"Randy, don't tempt me, you're married, remember? Oh, hell, let's have lunch."

"You are a dear, Georgia."

"But not dear enough, huh, Randy?"

"Georgia, why don't you call Bob Barnett, and take him out to lunch or Roger Waddell?"

"Both are nice looking, but both have baggage."

"What do you mean, baggage?"

"A daughter to come between us."

"And both of the girls are smart pieces of baggage. They could use someone like you for a mentor."

"Thanks, ole buddy, I'll have to think about it."

Randy made the call, "Thomas, this is Randy. Your wife has already called Georgia Parker, and she is not taking either of you. She suggests you call Robert Sanders, Sr., and I think that would be your best bet. Tell him both Georgia and I recommended him."

"Good idea. Thanks, Randy, will do."

"Good luck, Thomas."

CHAPTER 54

Molly Winchester

"Mr. Winchester, there is a call from your daughter."

"Molly, how are you?"

"Dad, I'm all right, but in trouble."

"What in heaven's name could be your trouble?"

"One of the midshipmen came into our quarters and attempted to rape my roommate. I came to the door after playing nine holes of golf, and I heard someone in the room talking. My roommate was saying, 'don't do this; this is not right.' And a male voice said, 'I can't wait any longer. I know you want me.' And she said, 'no, I don't! Go away now before we get in trouble. I'll yell and someone will hear me.' Then I heard what sounded like a scuffle, so I opened the door. I yelled for him to stop, but he said, 'make me.' He was on the bed on top of my roommate, so I swung the eight-iron like a baseball bat and hit him on the back. He jumped up, and hit me on the jaw. I hit him again, a little too low; well, you know where. He fell to the floor and was doubled up on the floor screaming. I called security guard to come get him. People were standing in the hallway when the guards got here. One of the guards yelled, 'Get back in your rooms, and don't say anything about this; we'll take care of it.' They lifted him and took him out, and the other guard turned around and yelled to us, 'the two of you are confined to your quarters.'

"I yelled at him, why are we in trouble? We have a right to defend ourselves. Then he said for us not to report the incident, he would take care of everything after they got Stoddard to the clinic.

"Susan wants to drop the whole thing, but I refuse to do that. I believe the school should know about this. You might need to come up here. My roommate has several bruises, and my jaw is already sore. I took pictures of the injuries, but I don't believe Susan is willing to stand behind me. Like I said, she just wants the whole thing to go away."

"I'll be up there tonight. I need to call another lawyer, and hope she can come with me."

"See you later, Daddy."

"Georgia, this is Frederick Winchester. I need your help immediately."

"Why am I so popular this week?"

"A midshipman tried to rape Molly's roommate, and Molly hit him with a golf club; you know where. A guard took him away, and the other guard is trying to get them not to press charges. I need to go up there."

"Frederick, you just punched a soft spot. I'm going with you. Give me time to cancel some appointments. I always keep a change of clothes here, so pick me up as soon as you can."

He called Elizabeth. "Elizabeth, I have to go on a trip, do I have to tell you why?"

"Yes, you should."

"Molly is in trouble. A third class midshipman tried to rape her roommate, and Molly hit him with a golf club. Someone is trying to get them not to press charges. I just called Georgia Parker and she is going with me. There is enough going on here with Freddie and Celeste for you to stay. Can you trust me to take care of this?"

"But wouldn't my being there help her?"

"No, she doesn't need a mommy right now, she needs a lawyer."

"I know you are right, just keep me informed. I love you."

"And I love you. I'll call you later."

They arrived at the Academy around midnight, and almost had to fight someone to get on campus. Frederick said to the sentry, "We are here to give assistance to one of the midshipmen."

"Who might that be, sir?"

"Molly Winchester."

"One moment, sir. I have to make a phone call. You cannot see her, Sir. She is confined to her quarters, besides no one can enter the residents without permission."

Georgia said, "Call the person you just talked to, and give me the phone. Hello, this is Georgia Parker, a lawyer from Atlanta.

Would you like for me to call an Admiral in Washington. I know a couple of them. In fact, I just defended one of their sons last year. Do you want me to make that call?"

"No, Ma'am, but I need to call someone first." He made the call, and another midshipman came and escorted them to Molly's dorm.

Molly and her roommate, Susan Matthews, were waiting. Susan had marks on her arms, neck, and a swollen lip. Molly had a bad bruise on her face. "Well, this is the pits, isn't it, Dad? Thanks for coming. Susan, this is my Dad, Frederick Winchester, and Dad, this is my roommate, Susan Matthews. Susan is from Mississippi."

"I'm so sorry for both of you. I'm just glad you were not hurt any more than you are. Let me introduce you to your Attorney, Georgia Parker. I want both of you to listen to her."

Georgia said, "What has happened here is not appropriate, in fact, it is against the law. Susan, Molly said that you just want it to go away. Why do you want what happened to you go away?"

"I just don't want any trouble. Everyone in my family is so proud I am at the Academy, and I don't want to shame them."

"Then we will inform them so they can be involved. Susan, let's call your parents so they can hear our conversation."

"Mom, this is Susan. Can both you and Daddy get on the phone?"

"Mr. and Mrs. Matthews, this is Georgia Parker. I am an Attorney from Atlanta and a friend of Attorney Frederick Winchester, the father of Susan's roommate. There has been an incident…no, your daughter is not in trouble. A midshipman tried to rape your daughter, and her roommate stopped him."

Georgia Parker held the phone so the parents could be heard, "Oh, my gosh," Mrs. Matthews said, "I can't believe that could happen there. I am in shock."

"Mrs. Matthews, rape can happen anywhere. Molly called her father, and we came up as soon as possible." Georgia listened to their concerns for Susan, how she has always been a good child, and how glad they were that Molly had called them.

"Do we need to come up there?" The father asked.

"That is not necessary at this time," Georgia said, "but I need your permission to question Susan and represent her."

The father said, "If you feel this is necessary, we will approve that. Is she hurt?"

"Yes, several bad bruises and scratches. Molly photographed her injuries. We will see that you get a copy. Just to let you know, we are taping this conversation."

"Susan, did you encourage this midshipman to enter your room and have sex with you?" Georgia asked.

"No Ma'am, I did not. You may not believe this, but I have *never* had sex with anyone. When I do, I want it to be right."

"So this wasn't the right time?"

"Definitely not, and besides we did not have sex, he just tried to."

"So he tried to rape you."

"Rape is such a dirty word."

"Whatever he was trying to do, did you tell him, no?"

"Several times."

"Did you let him in your room?"

"He knocked on the door, and I said come in."

"Do you let anybody who knocks on the door come inside?"

"I've never worried about it before."

"How do you know this guy?"

"I've seen him several times around the Academy grounds. He is usually with a group of people. We are all fairly sociable here. One day he said to those around us, 'this gal is smart and pretty,' pointing to me; too bad she is in the Second Class.' Another guy said, 'lay off her; she's a real southern girl and you're a damn Yankee.' Everybody laughed. And this guy said, 'yep, your beauty is a curse.' I said that's not a nice thing to say to me. One of my friends said, 'let's go. I don't like the conversation here.' And as we were leaving this guy whistled."

"Does this guy have a name?"

"John Wilson Stoddard."

"Susan, are you injured?"

"Yes, Ma'am, but not terribly. I have a bruise on my neck, my lips, and one of my hands."

"Molly, are you injured?"

"Yes Ma'am, Stoddard gave me a pretty good punch in the jaw."

"Susan, did you try to defend yourself?"

"Yes Ma'am. I did pretty good, too."

"Molly, when you came in and saw what was happening, what action did you take?"

"I had just finished playing golf, so I grabbed my golf club, the eight iron to be exact, and hit him in the back with the handle of the club. Then he jumped up and hit me in the jaw. I pushed him away, got a good grip on the club, and hit him way below the stomach. Well you can guess where the club landed. He fell to the floor, and was screaming. I made a call, and told the guard to get here fast, that I had knocked Midshipman Stoddard to the floor because he was trying to rape my roommate. I told them to hurry because he was in agony. They were here in a few minutes, and one of the guards took him out. The other guard, Midshipman Wilson told us not to tell anyone; they would take care it, then he said, "you are confined to quarters.'"

"Mr. and Mrs. Matthews, that's all we are going to do now. We may need you later. I'm going to give Susan the phone so you can talk. Sorry you had to hear about this tonight."

Mr. Matthews said, "We are glad for your assistance and so happy Molly came in at the right time."

"Here's Susan."

Frederick said, "It's awfully late. Georgia and I will find us a place to rest, and we will be back in the morning. Do not let anyone in this room unless it's a school official, but even then do not answer any questions. Refer them to your lawyer, Attorney Georgia Parker from Atlanta, Georgia. We will see you in the morning."

The next morning, Georgia and Frederick had to go through the same routine again to get admission. They arrived at the dormitory to find a group of people standing in the hallway. Frederick opened the door, and some lady with a mike pushed in Susan's face, was trying to question them. Molly said, "You have to contact our lawyer if you want information."

"What's going on here? Who are you, " Frederick asked?

"I'm here to get a statement."

"Who called you? How did you get into here? This is none of your business."

"Any news is my business," the reporter answered.

Georgia said, "I just make it my business, get out! Someone call the Superintendent."

A fellow midshipman said, "I am a friend. When I saw all these people, I pushed myself inside to see if I could help Molly and Susan."

"Everybody leave except this midshipman, and don't come back," Georgia said. "We need some order here."

In a few minutes there was a knock on the door. "Who is it," Georgia asked?

"The Superintendent. May I enter?"

"Yes sir," Molly said, and without hesitation, she and Susan stood at attention. He was there about thirty minutes, the time it took for Frederick and Georgia to tell the story of how they were called, and how they got in the building.

"I assure you we will get to the bottom of this and will not need your services," he said.

"I'm sorry, sir," Georgia said, "One of the guards has already tried to get Molly and Susan to forget this happened. And some reporter was here."

"The guard had no right to do that. I will see that the young man is accountable for his actions, and we have a process for that. How did a reporter get inside?" Turning to his aide, he said, "Find out who that reporter was and how she entered this building. I want to know immediately who let her in."

"Frederick said, "I can assure you, Sir we will be following this incident. My daughter, Molly loves this Academy with all her heart. She defended a midshipman who was in the process of being raped. I'm sure you know that attempted rape is a crime."

"Yes, I know, but the midshipman may have a different story, and I will need to hear both sides to make a decision."

Frederick said, "Sir, I am putting in a call to my Congressman who nominated Molly for this duty. He knows her and respects her, and if we have to, we will call the person who nominated Susan. Both of them might want to be present when you interrogate these midshipmen."

"You are overstepping your authority here?"

"Sir, Attorney Parker and I drove all the way from Atlanta to protect the reputation of two of your midshipmen who have been told, by at least one person, they did not need to report an attempted rape, that they will take care of everything. You know what that means, don't you?"

"I'm puzzled why anyone has the authority to say that. Who was that person?" Looking toward Molly, he said, "Give me a name."

She said, "Midshipman Jonathan Wilson, Sir."

"Good God, how do you remember that?"

"I am a very observant person. The Navy has taught me well."

"Well said, Midshipmen Winchester. Report to the infirmary, and then to your classes."

The next morning the Superintendent's aide summoned all parties to the office, including those who took the midshipman to the infirmary. Even the injured Midshipman was brought in. Frederick and Georgia were not allowed to be present at the meeting. The midshipmen rose as the superintendent entered the room. He addressed the group, "We are here to discuss a situation concerning Midshipmen Winchester, Matthews, Stoddard, and Wilson. Pay attention! The answers you give today are important to the Academy and to your tenure here. At ease! Midshipman Stoddard, "What were you doing in Midshipman Matthew's room?"

"I just wanted to visit her, Sir," he answered.

"While visiting her, was trying to have sex a part of that visit?"

"I had not planned it to be, Sir."

"Let me remind you, there were two people in that room, and I am ordering you to tell the truth."

"I'm sorry, sir; things kind of got out of hand."

"Well, now we are getting to the point. Did you try to force Midshipman Matthews to have sex with you?"

"I don't remember much, sir. I mainly remember being hit in a bad place by Midshipman Winchester."

"Are you saying the bruises on Midshipman Matthews and Winchester are not the injuries you gave them, when things kind of got out of hand?"

"I don't want to leave the Academy, sir. I want to apologize to Midshipman Matthews and Winchester."

"Do you know what attempted rape is, Midshipman Stoddard?"

"Yes, Sir, I know."

"Would you say your actions *kind of* constitute attempted rape?"

"Sir, I don't want to use that word. I thought she had affection for me, after all she let me in her door."

"What word would you use, Midshipman Stoddard?"

"I don't know, Sir. There must be a better word."

"You laid on top of a midshipman, bruised her neck, her lip, and her hand, and punched another midshipman who tried to stop you, and you think there is a better expression than attempted rape? And Midshipman Stoddard, when someone knocks on your door at this institution, do you ever think you are going to be harmed if you let them in?"

"No, sir."

"Stand aside, Midshipman Stoddard."

"Midshipman Wilson, why did you tell the midshipmen not to report the attempted rape, and that you would take care of the situation yourself?

"I'm not sure I said those exact words, sir."

"Then what were *those exact words*?"

"I told them no need to worry, I would take care of it, and take Midshipman Stoddard to see a doctor. Sir, I don't remember saying not to report anyone."

"And did you call any superior about this situation?"

"No, sir."

"How were you going to take care of it?"

"I didn't have any immediate plans at the time, sir."

"Why didn't you take the two female midshipmen to see a doctor?"

"They were not on the floor in agony, sir?"

"What was your impression of the them when you were in that room? Did you check their injuries? Why did you tell them to stay in their room?"

"No, Sir I did not check their injuries. I was just trying to keep everything quiet, sir?"

"Oh, my God, you did not think they would report the incident, did you?"

"Sometimes women don't, sir."

"You make me ill; stand aside. He pointed to his aid, "Take Midshipmen Stoddard and Wilson to their rooms, immediately! Take away their phones, and have someone stand at their doors to keep anyone from leaving or entering. I will have a ruling later. Midshipmen Winchester and Matthews, I deeply regret what happened to you, and I have no pity on your intruder. I am going to mull over their punishment for a few days, and get back to you. I regret you did not come to me, which may mean you felt I would not believe you. That is not a good example for others in your situation. You both have a good record here, and I apologize for what happened to you."

"Sir, may I speak?" said Midshipman Matthews."

"Certainly."

"Sir, Last night I spent several hours mulling over what happened to me. May I speak frankly, sir?"

"Why not, there's no one in this room but the four of us."

"I want to do what is right for all of us involved, Sir. Do I have your permission to offer a suggestion?"

"Might as well, Matthews; I'll hear it." He turned to the aide, "Include this conversation in your papers."

"Sir, first I want to apologize for not calling the proper authorities. I believe these midshipmen learned a powerful lesson, and I would hate to see them expelled from the Academy. Dismissal is a life-changing punishment. Also, I want to be a good example to other midshipmen. I've learned a lot from this incident, and I have no intention of covering up what happened to me. I do believe we - meaning you, Molly, and I - ought to find a way to save Stoddard and Wilson's careers."

"How so, Midshipman."

"Sir, Molly and I would like a private, sincere apology from the two midshipmen. I believe a public apology given to other midshipmen, orally and in writing, would be the punishment they deserve. Over a period of time, after they complete whatever tasks you assign them to do for amends, the Academy could consider whether they would erase this incident from their records, pending the two of them stay out of trouble. Perhaps erase is not a good word, Sir. You probably have a better one." She paused. "One more thing, Sir. I believe their families should be notified of their conduct and their punishment."

"Midshipman Matthews, I will take your suggestions in consideration. You are dismissed. Midshipman Winchester, you are dismissed. I expect the two of you to be an example to others of the correct manner an incident should be reported."

Yes Sir, we consider that an order."

Before Frederick and Georgia left for Atlanta, they gave the Superintendent the transcript of the interviews and copies of the photos that contained the pictures of Molly and Susan's injuries. (They had copies made at a local drug store.) It was a long way back to Atlanta.

Four days later, all the principals of the attempted rape, Midshipmen Matthews, Winchester, Stoddard and Wilson were ordered into the Superintendent's office. Phone connections were set for the parents and their lawyers.

The aide announced, "Ladies and Gentlemen and Midshipmen, after much deliberation this meeting is called to render judgment to an incident that happened in the room of Midshipmen Matthews and Winchester. Attention!"

The superintendent said, "After much thought and meetings with the Chaplain and the Commandant of Midshipmen, I have come to a verdict. Midshipman Matthews has asked for a less harsh judgment than dismissal from this Academy. I must admit, at first I thought little of her suggestion. But after informing certain authorities of the legality of her suggestion, I now issue these orders. Midshipmen Stoddard and Wilson step forward.

"Midshipman Wilson, you will apologize to midshipmen Matthews and Winchester, and make a public apology of what you should have done upon entering the rooms of Midshipmen Matthews and Winchester on the night in question, and you will word your speech without mentioning the names of Matthews and Winchester. In your statement, written and oral, you will address the issue of what it means not to make a proper report when you are called to assist someone in peril, whether it is on the grounds of the Academy or on the battlefield. You will remain at the academy, but on probation with limited privileges, which will be discussed later. Have you anything to say at this time?"

"Yes, Sir. I apologize to Midshipmen Matthews and Winchester. What I said to them undermined respect and integrity. It made me untrustworthy in their eyes and in the laws of this Academy, and I sincerely apologize."

"Midshipman Wilson, never *ever* try to take the law in your own hands."

"Yes, Sir. I understand."

"You may step back."

"Midshipman Stoddard, you are despicable. If it were up to me, I would send your but home in disgrace, but Midshipman Matthews believes the Academy can find some value in allowing you to stay. She has asked that you be allowed to remain at the Academy, because she realizes being forced out of the Academy would affect your entire life. If that is not the spirit of forgiveness, then nothing is. I would hope she would not be so kind to an enemy in combat. But you are not her enemy; she feels sorry for you. I would rather be whipped than have someone tell me they are sorry for me. You will also make private apologies to Midshipmen Matthews and Winchester, and a public apology to the Academy, in which you will not mention the names of Matthews and Winchester, and you will be on probation for one year. Your behavior must be, without question, exemplary in every way. You will in no way harass Midshipmen Matthews and Winchester nor any other midshipman. Also Midshipman Matthews has asked that your crime be written as attempted sexual contact, since both of you dislike using the common term *rape.* She does not like the idea of everyone thinking she was rape victim. Midshipman Winchester still has a visible sign where you punched her. I hope you realize that two important Atlanta lawyers would have put your ass in jail, don't you?"

"Yes, Sir I do."

"I am putting out a report that I want you shunned for a whole month. I have never before given a shunning to any person, but you deserve it. You will eat alone, and you will sit apart in class. You will also have guard duty three nights a week for three months. Keep your but out of trouble, or you *will* be dismissed from this Academy. Do you understand me?"

"Yes sir, I do?"

"Now, your apology. Go ahead."

"Midshipman Matthews, I deeply regret my shameful attack upon you, and I am grateful that you saved me from expulsion. Midshipman Winchester, I am sorry that I hit you when you were trying to defend Midshipman Matthews. I don't know what I was thinking. I must not have been thinking at all. I realize I cannot undo my willful actions, but I respectively ask both of you to forgive me. I will do everything in my power to regain your trust in me. One day I hope we can become friends. Is that satisfactory, Sir?"

"It is for now. I want you to turn your life around, and some day, make the Academy and your parents proud of you. You realize you have been given a gift by these two midshipmen, don't you?"

"Yes Sir, I do, and I am extremely grateful."

The aide said, "Attention. Dismissed." After the superintendent left, he thanked the parents for their time and disconnected the phones.

Molly called her father when everything was over, and he seemed pleased the way it was handled. "Tell Susan, I'm proud of her."

"She told me she had been raised in the Lutheran church where forgiveness is a sacred gift, and her parents were also pleased the way she handled herself. I wanted to hang Stoddard up side down by the feet. What an idiot! Maybe I need to find a church. Dad, did you call Granddaddy?"

"I did, and he is so proud of you. You need to call him sometimes. The best thing you and Susan can do now is to settle down, focus on your studies, and when you have time write Georgia Parker a note. I'll send you her address. She is one smart lawyer."

"Dad, I observed that in her quick action. Sometimes I wonder if I would like to go into law with the Navy. I'm going to look into it. How would you like for me to be a part of Navy Judge Advocate Generals Corps?"

"You can be whatever you want to be. If being a JAG lawyer is your dream go for it."

"Thanks, Dad. Give Freddie and Celeste my love."

Midshipmen Stoddard and Matthews made public apologies for actions. Their words were sincere and well written.

It took a while for Molly and Susan to settle down, and both experienced a mild depression. The word had spread, and that didn't make it easy on them, but they had each other and multiple tasks to complete. They returned to class without any disturbance from their peers, but they both had trouble sleeping. Susan said to Molly, "I wonder if this is what it feels like after you come out of combat - weary, stunned, angry, and glad you weren't killed?"

Molly said, "You've given our experience a good assessment."

CHAPTER 55

Scotland and France

It was time for Randy and Joan to leave for Europe. Randy was certain Cassie could handle the ordinary business while he was gone from the office. He saw how she had taken to the work the last few weeks and how much she enjoyed it. Best of all, the clients liked her, and Ms. Bee was fond of her, though she would never admit it. He and Joan were ready to get as far away from Atlanta as possible.

He brought Cassie up to date on the Wanda Wallace situation. Her children had decided to take her to court. "I would like for you to call her, and get to know her. Her kids want to rob her and declare her incompetent. As mean as they are, they might even try to kill her. Well, probably not that. She and George spoiled their kids rotten, and now they are paying her back. Her lawyer, Bob Barnett and I are on the same page in her defense. You will learn a lot about greed from this case."

"Do you expect their case will come to court before you return?"

"No, it's scheduled sometime in the fall. Ms. Bee has knowledge of all our clients. Don't hesitate to ask her to help you. If any new clients ask for an appointment, go ahead and see them, and have her sit in to take notes, or you can record the session if you get their permission."

"You and Mom have fun, and don't worry, I do have the availability of a fine lawyer just in case I need legal advice."

On Tuesday, Randy and Joan flew out of Atlanta for Scotland. Their expectations were not set in stone. It was past time to get away to meet strangers, eat at odd places, and see a new part of the world. They both held hands on the plane and slept for hours. Arriving in Edinburgh, they inquired about a hotel, and were taken to the fabulous Balmorals, an exotic place to learn the hospitality of the Scots. They spent most of their time walking about town visiting museums and other historical places, and definitely overeating. Then for two days they rented a driver to take them out of the city to tour castles, farms, houses, and a few small towns. Everywhere, people were pleased to greet them. As a surprise their driver took them to visit a relative of his who lived on a farm about fifty miles north of Edinburgh. The next day they visited a family who owned an inn. The couple and their two children prepared a good meal for them with lots of wine and showed them around their farm. The lady suggested to them a couple of places they should visit in town. The next day their driver took them to a small store to meet a writer who owned the place, and Joan purchased one of his books. It was their willingness and their driver's knowledge that enabled them to learn about a country they had only read about. They could have stayed a month, but it was time to leave for Paris.

Rick met them at the airport. At first they didn't recognize him, for he had grown a full beard and was so thin he appeared much taller. Driving into the city Joan asked him about finding a good place to stay. He said, "You will be staying with Pearl's two friends, Gracie and Frankie who have been looking forward to your coming, perhaps even more than my expectation, and they insist it would be an honor for you to stay with them. Believe me, you are going to enjoy them. Sometimes I imagine I am talking to Pearl, for they are so alike. Plus, they take care of me as if I am their son."

The ride from the airport to the flat was a lesson in history, Rick being the professor. People were everywhere. Along the way men and women were painting and selling their art on the spot, much like Randy had experienced in New Orleans on Jackson Square. Venders were hawking their vegetables right up to the window of the car. Some drivers on motorcycles scooted in and out of lanes so fast, Joan was certain they would be hit, but Rick just laughed. Ladies were hanging out the windows talking to the people below. One could imagine they were acting out for the new visitors from America, but Rick assured them what they were seeing was not unusual.

Finally they arrived at the flat, and were greeted with much hugging and kissing. Frankie said, "So you are the parents of this fine man. Thank you for sharing him with us. We are so proud of him. He has agreed to sleep on the settee while you occupy his room. Don't mind the clutter of this place, we don't spend our time cleaning, as you will see." Rick showed them his room, which was filled with canvasses, paints, and paintings. On the wall was a grouping of paintings, and they could see how he had progressed, because it was the same painting over and over. It appeared he had learned a lot and was proud. "Thanks for your hospitality. We don't want to disturb your lives, but first of all I want to say that we appreciate your taking care of our son," Joan said to the women.

"He's no problem, no problem at all. We are just so proud of him, yes we are. His work is finding acceptance in many places. Just you wait and see. But first we must have hors d'oeuvre and some wine, or tea if you wish. Rick, help Gracie with the refreshments while I get your parents settled," Frankie said. "The snacks will carry us over until we have dinner at our favorite café."

As they were sipping their tea, Rick said, "I was going to wait until you leave, but I cannot hold this back any longer. Close your eyes, I'm going to show you the painting I did for you." He brought out an easel covered with a linen cloth and sat it before them. Then in the manner of a flamboyant artiste, he removed the cloth *ta da!* The room was silent, and Joan and Randy were speechless.

Two girls on the steps of a flat
dressed in their Sunday best
are playing with their dolls.
Two women, chatting from above
are sweeping off their tiny porches
and cursing the hot weather.
A boy is paused on his wooden scooter
with both hands on the handles
and one foot on the pavement
his eyes open wide, his jaw dropped,
searching for courage
to ask, "May I play with you?"
The colors are difficult to identify
The reds are muted
The yellows have a dash of orange
The blues are bathed in black and brown
And there is a hint of purple on the steps.

A perfect portrayal
of imagination and desire
on a perfect Sunday afternoon.

Frozen in Time,
Richard R. Walker

As they studied the painting, Joan and Randy were speechless. Tears filled their eyes, and they embraced their son. "It is lovely beyond words," Joan said, "And I cannot believe it belongs to us." Randy said, "Son, you are that little boy, am I right?"

"Yes Sir, you are right. Aunt Pearl called my first paintings *flat* because of the colors. I have been studying with a French lady who said the same thing. She made me experiment over and over until I got the paints right. I've learned so much since I have been here. Aunt Pearl would be happy."

"Pearl is not the only one," Randy said. "I'm so glad she insisted you come here, but I want to know one thing, why are you so thin? Are you eating?"

"Why do men always think about food?" Joan asked. "You're quite thin, but you don't look unhealthy."

"Frankie and Gracie have to make me stop my work to eat, and they are offering me food all the time."

"He will be okay once he finds exactly what kind of artist he is," Frankie said.

"We are certain he can be one of the greatest, and so is his teacher. She is "handing him off" as the expression goes, to another teacher soon. You just wait and see. I must tell you, he has become our son also. How are Ana and Pearl? Be sure to tell them we miss them, but I don't believe we will return to the states any time soon."

Randy said, "Both of them never stop long enough to grow old. Pearl had predicted that coming here would help Rick."

Soon they were on their way to the café. Walking in the door they were welcomed by the owner, and their table was ready. Joan turned to one of the walls and saw the art. She turned toward Rick. "Yes, Mom those are my paintings."

The proprietor said, “Maybe soon one of them will not sell, and I shall have it for my own. Please say so, mon ami.”

“Don’t let him fool you,” Rick said. “I’ve already given him a painting, else he wouldn’t allow me to hang my work here. He pretends to be my agent. He sells the paintings, and takes the money for me. That way I don’t look like I’m pandering.” He leaned over to Joan and Randy and whispered, “I believe he keeps a little aside for himself, but that’s okay.”

Every day was special. That afternoon they did a long tour, but seeing the Arc de Triomphe from afar was the highlight of the tour. Joan Said, “It is so much grander than I imagined it would be. I’m surprised the Germans didn’t destroy it. It is most magnificent!” Rick said, “Hitler had no idea of destroying it. His dream was to conquer it and own it.” Randy said, “I can see why.” Rick introduced them to as many areas as they could see in such a short visit. He enjoyed watching their faces as they tried to remember it all. It was amazing how much he had learned about the city in such a short time. Joan remarked, “Paris is not exactly a city, it should be a country. There is so much to learn, I’m mystified. It would take months to learn everything.”

“You are right, Mom. I took French in college, but I realized how little I learned when I came here. One has to speak the language to be accepted by the people.”

They noticed Rick wore a coat all the time and had a cough. Randy suggested that he find more time to relax. He said to him, “You don’t have to learn everything about painting in a year. You are working too hard, so slow down. You have already proved you can paint. Take some time to relax, and see a doctor about that cough.”

“I promise to see a doctor after you leave, I don’t want to waste a minute away from you and Mom. You have to know, I have no plans to return to the states, for this is where I discovered who I am and what I am supposed to do with my life. I paint like a Frenchman, and that might not go over in Atlanta.” Randy decided not to look at Joan, because he knew she was not happy.

The only time they rested were the few hours of sleep each night. On the day they were to leave, Joan stood in the middle of the parlor trying to paste all the images in her mind: the quaint smell of the tufted furniture, the aroma of bread from the bakery down the street, the sounds floating up from the sidewalk, her son standing at the easel, Frankie and Gracie bustling around the room, almost ancient rugs on the floor, and the paintings on the wall in Rick's room showing his progress in the past year. She was so proud of him.

Randy went into the kitchen to thank the women, while Joan finished packing. He whispered to Frances, "How is he?"

She leaned close to him, "He is under the care of a doctor."

"Take care of him. If you need anything let me know."

"We will take very good care of him. Don't worry about that." He slipped her an envelope of money from his jacket, and she tucked it in the pocket of her apron.

Joan came into the room, "We are packed and ready to go. I know Rick is in good hands with the two of you. Make him see a doctor for that cough."

"Yes, we will take care of that. He is very special to us."

When they were on the plane returning to the States, Randy said to Joan, "We have some kind of son there, don't we?"

"Oh, he is such a good person, and I love his art. Are you sure Rick packed his painting well? I want it to reach Atlanta in one piece."

"He did. He probably does that quite often. If we crash, it might even float in the ocean."

"Don't say such a thing."

After Joan and Randy returned from Europe, the weather was particularly miserable. Randy went to the office the day after they arrived. Both Mrs. Bee and Cassie were glad to see him. After formal greetings, he and Cassie drifted into his office. She said to him, "I am so glad you are back. We've had four new clients, and Ms. Bee and I handled them quite well. She was most helpful getting me adjusted, and we have someone coming in today. I wonder why clients would even think about venturing outside."

"I'm proud of you, Cassie, and glad to have you aboard. Now I won't worry about the clients when your mom and I decide to do something. Can you take the next client while I talk to Ms. Bee? Tell her I would like to see her."

"Will do." She whispered as she was leaving, "Ms. Bee and I closed shop one day and went out to lunch." She did a thumps up and winked. "Okay, I get it." He said.

Ms. Bee was smiling when she entered. How unusual. "Welcome home, Mr. Walker. I hope your trip was pleasant."

"We had a wonderful time, and Rick has become quite an artist. I hear you and Cassie worked well together, so do I need to be brought up on anything?"

"The papers on you desk will bring you up to date. I sat in with Cassie for her first client, just to make certain she was prepared. I did not have to do that again. She has performed quite well while you were away, and the clients like her."

"I'm so glad. Do you think we need to hire another person to help you?"

"I don't believe that is necessary right now. Cassie does her own cleaning up, so I still only have one person to take care of."

"Don't be smart with me; you might hurt my feelings. I love you too. Go to work."

"Yes Sir. Good day."

The winter was long and tiring with rain and more rain. In December the sleet fell and marooned cars on the main expressways. It has been said that Atlanta will have at least one bad sleet storm every January, but it rarely snows. When sleet or snow falls from the sky, traffic is a disaster, and a few street-people are known to die in their thin blankets. The Yankees who have moved south laugh and make statements like, "You don't know what bad weather is," or "Your kids get out of school after an inch of snow; you've got to be kidding, right?" A person has to be born in the south to understand that snow is for northerners.

Residents long to see the first bloom of dogwood, redbuds, and cherry blossom trees, an indication that spring is finally present. The trees are stunning from Macon to North Georgia, producing pollen that makes the air cloudy. Those who have allergies just have to bear it, so they dream of summertime, when a quick rain is a gift from heaven. Little children used to play in the heat and think nothing of it, now they huddle inside in air conditioning. Well, maybe not all of them. In mid-summer many counties have summer camps for the kids, and almost every part of the city has churches that offer Vacation Bible Schools on different weeks, so parents can parade their kids to every one of them. In the summer movie theaters should advertise *for children only*. If an adult is expecting a quiet theater with enough popcorn and coke to last for over half the movie, they'll have to wait for school to start back. That is when the north Georgia trees begin putting on their best show of the year. In the clear, crisp air they turn from green to shades of yellow, red, purple and brown almost overnight. The people in Maine and Vermont say they have the prettiest trees in the fall, but the folks in North Georgia don't believe them.

But it was still winter in Atlanta, and Randy had a lot of work to finish. The faces of Wanda Wallace's kids nagged at him day and night. He had to find a way to stop them, that is, he and Bob had to find a way to stop them. "I hate greed," Randy said to Ms. Bee while they were working on some of Mrs. Wallace's papers.

"Then stomp the kids," she said. "You have my permission."

"Well, thank you, Ms. Bee," he said.

CHAPTER 56

Wanda Wallace (WW)

Randy was prepared for war with Wanda Wallace's sorry children, so he met with Bob Barnett to discuss his planned strategy. The hearing would be in civil court. They knew the lawyer for the Wallace children was new and inexperienced. He would attempt to prove their mother was incompetent to handle her own finances. So Bob and Randy spent most of their time finding information on the current state of her children.

The long-awaited hearing began with both attorneys giving their opening statements to the court. Since Bob and Randy had already guessed the petition of the Wallace kid's lawyer, they were not surprised, so they agreed to sit quietly and let him hang himself. The first person their lawyer called to the stand was the oldest son, Billy Wallace. "Tell the court why your mother is incompetent to handle her finances."

He said, "She spends our inheritance unwisely and foolishly. Dad worked hard for his money, so we don't want to see her waste it."

"Do you have any proof of her being wasteful?"

"Yeah, she spends a lot of money traveling all over the world, and spends too much money on herself and charities. She even said to us that she might spend all of it, since it was hers to spend."

"Do you have proof of this spending?"

"Her estate attorney will not reveal facts to us, but we know about the traveling and the constant redecoration of our home place."

"No more questions."

Bob Barnett rose to question him. Did your father leave a will?"

"Yes, but he may not have been in his right mind."

"Did a psychiatrist or a psychologist tell you that?'

"No, we just know he wasn't himself."

"How do you know that?"

"He was sick a lot."

"Do you believe your dad and mother loved each other?"

"I suppose they did. They were married a long time."

"You suppose? Did they argue a lot?"

"No, dad just did what she wanted to do."

"Has your mother been declared incompetent?"

"No, but she should be."

"Why do you believe you and your siblings should have her money?"

"We could use it."

"Do you have a job?"

"Right now I'm unemployed. I'm not able to work."

"Has a doctor declared you are unable to work?"

"No, I haven't asked any doctor to do that, yet."

"Is it a fact you play golf frequently? Is that true?"

"Yes, it's good exercise for me."

"You also belong to a country club, don't you?"

"What has that got to do with anything?"

"Where do you get the money to do that?"

"My wife works."

"She makes enough for you not to work and for you to play golf?"

"No she doesn't. I borrowed some money."

"How much did you borrow?"

"That is none of your business."

"Answer the question," the Judge said.

"$20,000."

"Let me see, you borrowed $20,000, and gave your mother as the person to pay if you failed to meet the payments. Isn't that right? Why did you borrow the money without her agreeing to be responsible?"

"She should be happy to help me. I'm her oldest child."

"So, the money your parents worked so hard to earn, the money you want to take from your mother, will be used to pay your bills that have enabled you to belong to a country club and play golf? Your honor, I have no more question for this oldest son."

"Step down, Mr. Billy Wallace."

His attorney stood, "Your honor, I would like to have that testimony stricken from the records. He was goading my client."

"I don't think so, Mr. Jenkins. I believe the questions were honest, as were your client's answers," the Judge responded.

"I call to the stand Margaret Wallace Thompson," their lawyer said.

"Mrs. Thompson, do you have anything to add to the testimony of your brother?" Mr. Jenkins asked.

"I believe my daddy would have wanted to give money so my kids could continue their education. He wanted them to succeed. I don't have the funds for them to attend a private school, but my mother refuses to help.

"What did she say when you asked her to help your children?"

She said, "Get a job and pay for their schooling yourself."

"Did you get a job?"

"I have children at home, and I have to tend to them."

"Did your parents pay for your education?"

"Yes, but I believe daddy was the one who insisted on that."

"Your witness, Mr. Barnett."

Bob Barnett began. "Mrs. Thompson, correct me if I am not correct. I believe you have three children, ages 19, 22, and 26, so I don't believe you have to stay home with them. Why would you say that?"

"They still need attention."

"Are they disabled?"

"No, they are lazy."

"Does your husband work?"

"I am divorced, and all I get is a little alimony."

"Why doesn't your ex-husband support your children's education?"

"He is out of work right now. If my mother would help us out, we would not be in this fix."

"Are you in good health, Mrs. Thompson?"

"Yes, why do you ask that?"

"Then why are you not working? You have a college degree."

"I was raised to be a lady, and I should not have to work."

"Is your mother a lady?"

"Yes, I believe she is."

"Didn't she work in your father's business for years."

"Times were different then."

"No more questions. Your Honor, may I approach the bench?" Bob asked.

The Judge motioned both lawyers to come forward. "I see no need to call the third child of Wanda Wallace." Bob said. "I have the same questions for her, and I expect the same answers."

"Let's do it anyhow; I want to hear what she has to say," the Judge said. "Mr. Jenkins call the younger sister."

"Jeannette Wallace, come forward."

Mr. Jenkins asked, "Do you have anything to add to your brother and sister's testimony, or should I ask you the same questions."

"Shoot away, I don't care."

"Has your mother ever supported you?"

"Yes, she got me out of trouble a couple of times."

"Are you grateful for that?"

"Sure, she can spend money when she wants to."

"Are you angry at her for not giving you money?"

"No, not angry. I just don't understand her hoarding all our money."

"Why would you say, 'our money?'"

"Well, children should be taken care of, even if we get in trouble when we are older, and she has the money to do it."

"Your witness, Mr. Barnett."

"Mrs. Wallace, how many times have you been married."

"What does that have to do with anything?"

"I'll ask you again, how many times."

"Four."

"I believe your mother bailed you out of jail when you tried to run over one of your husbands. Is that correct?"

"I wasn't trying to run over him, he got in the way."

"Did your mother give you money for an abortion?"

"I'm sorry, that is my private business."

"Let's put it this way, did you have the abortion?"

"No, I thought it would be wrong to do that."

"Were you pregnant?"

"I found out I wasn't pregnant."

"Did you return the money to her?"

"I don't remember."

"Let me help you. She gave you a thousand dollars, and you did *not* return it.

You spent it on drugs, and you were arrested."

"She is the reason I need a psychologist. She was too hard on me. I hate to see her waste Daddy's money when we could all use some."

"No more questions."

The judge motioned for both lawyers to come to his quarters. "Mr. Jenkins, it appears you are not very well informed about your clients. Have you received any money from them for this trial?"

"No Sir. They said I would be paid after they got some money."

"How long have you been an attorney, Mr. Jenkins?"

"This is my second case, Your Honor."

"You have not done a good job. I could call a mistrial because of your inexperience, but I won't. Your clients have lost their own case. It is obvious they are not responsible persons. I really don't know whether they are stupid, or just plain arrogant. Mr. Barnett, I realize you would be calling their mother, Mrs. Wanda Wallace to the stands, but I doubt you need to. I will hear your closing statements.

Closing statements were as the judge expected, quick and redundant. It took the panel exactly thirty minutes to get settled and give a verdict. They sent word they were ready. "Mr. Foreman, what say you?"

"We find no reason to require Mrs. Wallace to give her children money. We talked a bit, then voted, as one, in favor of Mrs. Wallace."

"Give your verdict to the clerk." He said to the jury, "Thank you for your time. You are dismissed."

The oldest son yelled out, "You haven't heard the last from us."

"Bailiff, bring that man and both lawyers to my chambers, immediately." No one else was privy to what happened, but Randy learned later, the Judge threatened to put Mr. Billy Wallace in jail, and said he would have him arrested if he approached his mother or Attorney Barnett for any reason whatsoever.

Randy and Bob took Wanda Wallace out to lunch. "Well, WW what do you think?" Randy asked. "Randy, you know I had a wonderful husband. He would be so embarrassed if he had been present today. It looks like we failed in disciplining our children. We were so much in love, but we also loved them. I have no idea how my son knows how much money I have. Do you suppose someone at the bank has revealed my position? How can I find out?"

"They may not know how much you have, but they are assuming you have a lot, but I will find out if there is a leak somewhere."

"Which one of you good looking men is going to take me home?"

"How did you get here?"

"I rode the bus. I know how scarce parking is."

"Wow, you amaze me, WW," Randy said.

"Randy, find a realtor to sell my house, I'm going to be moving."

"Where?"

"I'll tell you later."

"All right, I know a good realtor. She will be calling you tomorrow. Bob, can you drive WW home, and meet me back at the office?"

"Sure, let's go Wanda."

———

Back at the office, Randy said to Bob, "You did a good job today. I got the feeling you liked WW."

"She's a good looking woman, but I'm not interested."

"Her husband was a lot older than her, but they were one happily married couple. They may have had such a great romance, but they failed in bringing up their children. Bob, WW stirred my mind a bit. I may have an idea about the leak on her bank account. I just remember something, I know the president of the bank she uses, and I have information that he takes pride in helping WW with her investments. I believe they are sort of sweet on each other. I'm going to make some calls. Just sit here a minute. Mr. George Thompson, please. George, you may have a leak in your bank. Do you have anyone employed there who is a member of a country club, and who plays golf with Billy Wallace who is Wanda Wallace's son? You know the man I'm talking about? Okay. Okay. Will you do some sneaking around on your computers and see if he is communicating with Mr. Wallace about his mother's finances? Okay, let me know as soon as you can. Thanks."

Bob said, "Randy, you should have been a trial lawyer. You're good."

"Let's just sit here and wait. George said to give him a little time. He knows the person I'm talking about. If he can't find anything right now, he'll keep looking." Peeping out the door, he said to Ms. Bee, "Will you send someone to get sandwiches for us?"

"Wait a minute. I'm looking for someone, but I don't see anyone," she said.

"Where is Cassie?"

"She's with a client, and there is no one else here."

"I got you, (he winked at Bob). I'll just send Bob while I wait for a phone call."

"Oh, that's right, there is someone else here. Good choice," she said.

"Is she always that sassy?" Bob said, knowing she was listening.

"I heard that," she said.

The phone rang about thirty minutes later; it was George Thompson. Randy turned the speaker on. "Randy, you have a good nose. There is definitely a leak, and I can't believe it. This person, Timothy Davies has been communicating with Mr. Billy Wallace frequently, and I believe we've found a code they use to discuss his mother's finances. He has been a good employee, so I am shocked. I'll get down to business on this, and call our lawyer immediately. You have a good nose for trouble. Why aren't you a trial lawyer?"

"Bob Barnett, sitting here with me, just asked me the same thing. For both of your information I like what I do."

The following day, Randy, Bob, George, and the bank's attorney, Michael Fulton sat in the office waiting for Timothy Davies to enter. Michael Fulton began, we have some papers we want you to review for us." Laying the copied communications on the desk, he asked Mr. Davies, "Can you explain these communications between you and a Mr. Billy Wallace?"

"They are friendly notes between the two of us. I'm not sure what you mean showing them to me."

"Let's look at the notations and the numbers which are supposed to be golf scores. This is *supposedly* the amount you spent on a party, but it appears to be the amount someone else spent on a party." He slapped papers on the desk, "And this communication, and this one, all these have meanings. Now look at the notations Mr. Wallace has in his reference to your findings. What do you have to say? What I want to know is how in the hell did you get into Mrs. Wallace's business?"

"I refuse to answer any of these accusations. I believe I need to call my lawyer. You have copied my computer without my permission."

"Mr. Davies, your damn computer belongs to this bank. Every bank employee knows that. What in the hell were you thinking, Timothy? Call your lawyer. We will wait right here for him or her to come. Here use this phone."

In less than twenty-four hours the mystery unfolded. Mr. Wallace and Mr. Davies were summoned with a warrant, and it appeared some of the other children might be brought in. Bob and Randy were no longer involved. Bob wanted to be the one to tell WW what they had discovered, so he made a reservation at The City Café to give her the news. She was not at all surprised. Bob was amazed how well she took the findings. She said, "It is plain unnerving to know a child I birthed could be so sneaky and greedy, but let's put the subject away for the evening."

"I agree," said Bob, "let's just celebrate."

"What are we celebrating, Mr. Barnett?"

"Friendship and success," he said.

"I'm afraid I don't celebrate with lawyers, I pay them."

"I'm sorry, did I misuse my words?"

"You are a good lawyer, Mr. Barnett, and you tell Randy Walker I thank both of you for returning my sanity. I'll be going away for two months, so tell Randy I have hired around the clock security at my home and they are changing all the locks today. Also tell him I want it sold by the time I return. Thank you again Mr. Barnett for doing a good job at the hearing. By the way, if I were a bit younger, I would beg you to go with me. I haven't had sex in so long, I'm hungry, but I might need you again. Sleeping with one's attorney is not a good idea."

"And I might have gone if you had asked. You are a beautiful woman. I hope you find what you are looking for."

"I believe I have. He is someone who doesn't want my money, and I believe we will have a good time together, but I'll never marry again. The loss of one's lover is too painful. Thank you the good job you did in court. Send your bill to my bank. They have permission to debit the money from my account."

"Wanda, you are an amazing person. I wish you happiness on your journey. Your gentleman friend is a lucky fellow."

"I know."

CHAPTER 57

Margaret

Bob called Margaret, "Hello, Margaret, are you available this evening?"

"What? No how-are-you-doing after all this time? Or, that evening with you was unbelievable."

"I'm sorry I must learn how to court again. I seem to ask women the wrong questions. Let me start again, when will you be available to go out to dinner?"

"Women? How many have you asked?"

"Actually, there was one woman, but since I am her lawyer, she turned me down."

"When was that?"

"A few minutes ago. Damn, I said the wrong thing again."

"Call me later when I'm not second choice," Margaret said, and hung up.

"Margaret? Damn it, she hung up on me. Damn it to hell; I need a life."

He called her back. "Margaret, don't hang up again. Can we at least talk and not get our feelings hurt? For weeks I have been busy helping one of Randy's clients get her children off her back and out of her money. I'm sorry if I don't have proper courting skills right now. She jokingly said to me, if I wasn't her lawyer, whoopee. So I exaggerated, Okay?"

"Go on," she said.

"How are you and Michael?"

"Wait until you see him. He is growing faster than I can buy clothes. I was angry having to raise him by myself, but my secretary-nanny, Becky has taught me a lot about babies and children. If I didn't have her I would be in deep shit. Business has been good. Now is that enough information?"

"Margaret, I'll ask you again, when can we get together?"

"How about tomorrow evening?"

"That would be great. Can I pick you up around eight? Will you have to get a sitter for Michael?"

"No, Becky will take care of him and take my calls. She also helps me on jobs when I need her."

"So it's working out for both of you?"

"She has saved my life, and Michael loves her."

"You are lucky to have found her. See you around eight."

"Should I wear a dress or pajamas?"

"Don't be ridiculous, Margaret."

"I just need to know which kind of me you prefer."

"Good night, Margaret."

Margaret had given security permission to admit Bob. She met him at the door with Michael in her arms. "Well, here is the kid who changed my life. Hold him while I get my purse."

"Goodness, Michael you are a big boy. Margaret, what are you feeding him?"

"Ask Becky she's coming to take him to bed."

"Hello, I'm Becky, Margaret's full time nanny, secretary, confident, and errand lady. I'll take him off your hands now."

"Wait a minute. It's been so long since I held a baby in my arms, I would like
to remember the feeling."

"Looks like you are a natural," Becky said. "Margaret said you have a daughter."

"Yes, and she is beautiful. At least that's what I believe. She is in college, and wants to be a cardiologist. Okay, you can have him now." Michael began to cry. "All right I'll hold you a few more minutes. How about a kiss? Wow, you give a juicy one."

"Here is a towel to wipe your face," Becky said. "Michael, tell Mr. Barnett bye."

"I'm rescued; here comes my date."

In the car, Bob said to Margaret, "You are lucky to have Becky. I didn't know there were people like her any more. By the way, I've made a reservation at the Dining Room at the Ritz Carlton."

"I've been there before. I like the place *and* the food."

"I'm sorry I ticked you off, Margaret. I'm not sure whether I was tired or angry. Randy and I just completed the weirdest case, and both of us were exhausted. I despise greed, and the trial was full of it. I don't know why I'm talking about business. You probably find it boring. Guess I'm trying to explain something, but I don't know what."

"Well, I bared my naked body to a man, and he doesn't call. That seems to mean that he saw enough of me."

"No, no, on the contrary, Margaret. I've spent hours and hours trying to figure things out, and you were in that category. I need time to think about how my life got in such a mess, and how I can be there for Julie through the next years of her life. I haven't had much social life lately. You may not believe this, but it had been a long time since I even considered having sex, before that night with you in Savannah. After my experience with Judy, sex seemed kind of useless. The surprise experience with you really blew me away. It felt like I had an out of the body experience."

"Really, and how so?"

"I had never felt so free, so self assured, and so excited, and you were fantastic. Our sexual experience awakened me. Honestly, I couldn't figure out why it happened, but I didn't want the sensation to stop, but you left so abruptly. You said something, but I was still in shock about our experience, so I wasn't exactly listening to you. I was mesmerized watching you dress. Your quick departure make me angry, and I had that old feeling return - what did I do wrong this time?"

"It wasn't all about sex to me," Margaret said. "It was real, more real than I ever experienced, and I wanted to stay all night. I couldn't figure out whether I was just available or whether our connection had meaning."

"Margaret, that evening was truly wonderful. After your left I began wondering whether your excitement was about missing Leonard."

"Leonard! He *never, ever* did the things you did for me. *Never*. He was a prude."

"I don't know where to go from here, Margaret. I have re-lived that evening over and over, almost like I am watching a different man in the bed, and I don't know where to go from there."

"Then let's don't go there again; it's that easy. Let's have a delicious dinner, kiss each other goodnight, and go about our lives as usual and see what happens."

"That sounds almost like a contract."

"What if it is?"

The meal was delicious. They laughed, tasted each other's food, and occasionally held hands. On the way home Bob said, "I can't lay our earlier conversation to rest. I want to take you in my arms and hold you. I fear you will disappear from my life."

"Bob, drop me off at my condo. I believe both of us have a lot to think about, and there is no one else who can give us the answers we need. I have a child and a large business. You are a busy lawyer, and in a position to meet exotic women. I believe you are undecided about a commitment with me that would include Michael. Of course sex without commitment could be exciting. I might be able to handle that, if that's what you want. Goodnight." She kissed her fingers and pressed them onto Bob's lips, opened the car door and left, just like she did in the hotel. He yelled, "You are running away again." She didn't turn around to answer him. He couldn't move as he watched her disappear into the night. He was angry with her and himself. He sat in the car and cried for the first time in years, and cursed himself for letting her go. He headed home totally confused, hitting the steering wheel over and over with his hands, talking to himself: *What is wrong with me? What is damn wrong? Can I ever trust another woman? I'm not sure trust is a word I can grasp. Is the past too fresh? Maybe I need counseling. Hell no, I'm a smart man. I have to find the answers for myself.*

When he opened the door, he could hear someone leaving a message. Hoping it was Margaret he listened to the call, "Bob, this is Georgia Parker, give me a call as soon as you get in; I need a favor." He called, "What's so important, Georgia."

"I'm calling you because Randy said I couldn't have him, so he suggested I call you. He's so much in love he can't even look at other women."

"Well, that was a mouthful. Nothing like being second choice."

"Oh hell, at our age sometimes that's what we are. I need someone to take me to the Chamber Banquet, the type of event I detest. The mayor called me today and threatened to send his wife over to pick me up - dressed or undressed - and take me to the damn banquet. I told him I don't do banquets, and he said, 'my wife will be picking you up regardless, so be ready. If you don't have anything to wear, by God, wear blue jeans.' I hate threats. And blue jeans? Who in the hell would wear jeans to a banquet? Banquets make me sick having to look at all those dolled up women wearing their husband's money, or the other way around. If I'm going, I want to make them jealous. I want to be hanging on the arm of a handsome man. How about it? The banquet is this Friday evening. Do you want to think about it and call me back?"

"Wow! That was a fine speech. Sounds like you will be Cinderella and I will be the Prince. I don't need to think about it. No plans for Friday night, so I'd be thrilled to escort Cinderella to the ball, whose alias is Best Lawyer in Town, *and* most beautiful."

"Don't try flattering me; it's just a favor. Maybe you can make those women jealous, or pretend to at least."

"I won't have to pretend, Georgia. What time should I pick you up?"

"Dinner is at 8:00, but at all those kinds of events people stand around trying to make conversation, so how about 7:30, and wear a tux."

"No Levis for me, huh? Got you! See you then." *Well, that was a surprise. Could be fun.*

The evening of the banquet, Georgia was right, everything and everyone looked phony. The women wore enough jewels to buy a small country, and the men looked pleased to be escorts. Georgia had a simple gold necklace around her neck and no other jewelry except a small ring. She looked gorgeous in a black cocktail dress that was just below the knees. She didn't need jewels to impress people. He had no idea how old she was – maybe forty-five or fifty, but she was beautiful, and he was proud to be her escort. One of the women came up to them, "Bob Barnett, I haven't seen you in ages. Where are you keeping yourself?"

"Let's see, I don't get around much. Just got through a nasty trial, and I'm working on making my daughter happy for the rest of her life. And you, Georgette, what are you up to lately."

"Same old, same old. Just got back from Sweden. Marshall has relatives over there, lots of Pettersens. Rather boring country if you ask me, and the food tastes all the same."

"Georgette, you would enjoy Sweden *only* if the Pettersons were the royal family," Georgia said.

"Oh, hello Georgia, I didn't see you standing there. Bob, did you know Georgia and I are first cousins? Her mother stole the name Georgia so my mom had to name me Georgette. My mother said her sister knew all along that I was the one to be named Georgia."

"No, I had no reason to know you are cousins, and I think your name is just fine. It has sort of a swing to it. Your mom could have named you George the Second. How would you have liked that? Don't answer. Nice talking to you Georgette, and I wouldn't worry another minute about your name, or Georgia's name, but next time don't pretend to ignore my date, even if you *are* cousins."

His words went right over her head. She asked, "By the way, Georgia what do you hear from Richard?"

"Haven't seen him in ages, nice of you to ask."

"And Charlie?"

"Actually, Georgette, you don't have to bring up my exes to Bob. He could care less, and besides I'm doing quite well, considering I don't have a man around to tell me what to do, what to wear, and where I can go. Have a nice evening," and she turned and walked away.

"You really enjoyed ticking her off, didn't you?" Bob said. "The two of you must have an interesting history. I don't know whether she despises you or is envious of you, but I think jealous is the best word I can think of. I could see that right away. For the sake of safety, the two of you should never be in the same room together, but nice to run into one of your cousins. Do you have a lot of them in Atlanta?"

"Quite a few. There are several families of Lang's, my mother's maiden name and Parkers, part of Dad's people. A little Jewish blood is thrown in with the Feldmans, and then there are the Morrisons. Well, I could go on, but no need for that. Oh yes, I'm even related to Wanda Wallace. Thanks for the fine job you did for her. She called me and told me you were about as good a lawyer as I am. I love her. She is different from anyone I know."

"Forget the small talk. I think we should eat and get out of here as soon as we can," Bob said.

"Can't do that. The city council always gives some sort of honors after dinner, and anyway the mayor will shame me if I leave. Got to secure what little business I get from the city."

A lavish dinner was served, much more than a person could eat at one setting. Bob gulped his down as if he could speed up the evening. Georgia ate less than half of hers, except for the dessert. "I never leave anything chocolate on my plate," she said. "The person who discovered chocolate should be honored, definitely. By the way, I'm surprised you don't come to these banquets. Aren't you a member of the Chamber?"

"Sure, we almost have to be a member in this city, or be given the guilts."

The first award, presented by the president of the Chamber, was given to the Company or Business who had contributed the most to make Atlanta a better city. It went to some large company that had chosen to make Atlanta its home a couple of years ago. The second award, presented by the secretary of the Chamber, was to the person who had contributed their time and energy to enhance the culture and arts of Atlanta. There were several other awards for different civic organizations. The last award was the Person of the Year. The mayor stepped forward, opened a page of notes and said, "For years the person selected for this award has given her time and money to give legal help to people of this city who have no resources. This woman is known throughout Georgia for her work with women, even traveling out of state when necessary. She finds jobs and homes for women who have few choices in life, often using her own money and her home as temporary shelter. She is honorable, talented, and known for her ability to settle disputes. She is one of the finest citizens in this city, and much more should be said about her if we had another hour to do so. I am proud to present the Person of the Year, Ms. Georgia Parker, a distinguished lady and a brilliant lawyer!"

Georgia was shocked. She whispered to Bob, "Oh shit! Hide me, or help me get up there." He put his arm around her waist and helped her up the three steps, then waited on the floor. He knew Georgia was not happy, but he felt like the proudest person at the banquet, being her escort. Georgia said to the assembly, "I am totally shocked. There is no way I deserve this award, Mr. Mayor, but I am glad you didn't tell all my secrets. There are many people in Atlanta more deserving that I am, but for the sake of diplomacy I accept this honor. Thank you."

After the applause, the mayor whispered to Georgia, "Wouldn't you like to introduce your escort, Mr. Barnett, who finally came to a Chamber banquet?"

"I also thank my friend, Attorney Bob Barnett for accompanying me tonight and for pushing me up here." All the people were standing, laughing, and applauding. Bob stood aside while pictures were taken. Finally, when he took her arm to help her down the steps, he whispered in her ear, "For the sake of diplomacy? *Really*, Georgia?" A photographer took their picture just at they stepped off the podium.

———

The following morning the pictures of the honorees appeared on the front page of the Atlanta Journal Constitution, and there, for the world to see, was Bob Barnett helping Georgia down the steps, appearing to kiss her.

Becky brought in the newspaper, and read the front section while having a cup of coffee. She put the paper in a drawer just as Margaret entered the kitchen. "Don't put it in the drawer just yet, I'll read some of it before I get dressed. Becky put her cup down, and went in to get Michael. "You don't have to leave just because I came in."

"Yes I do. Enjoy your toast."

"Guess I'll read about the Chamber awards, at least it won't be about robbery and killings that corrupt our city." Margaret unfolded the paper and saw the photograph, and gasped. "Think I'll wait awhile to finish the paper," she said into the air, and went to her room.

Becky finally came and knocked on her bedroom door, "Might as well come on out, you have a client later this morning. Did you hear what I said? Forget the paper; you have to get dressed. You don't want to keep the Fletchers waiting."

"Call them and tell them I'll be late."

Across town, Bob saw the picture: "Damn, I don't even remember the photographer taking that picture. I need to get to Margaret's house now."

He called, and Becky answered. "This is Bob Barnett, don't let Margaret leave, I am in the car headed your way."

"Mr. Barnett I think she has already gone."

"You think? She'd better be there. I need to talk to her."

Becky whispered into the phone, "She saw the picture."

It took him forty minutes to get to Margaret's because of the famous morning traffic in Atlanta. Becky let him in and pointed to the bedroom door. "Margaret, this is Bob. Open the door!"

"Go away; I'm getting dressed. Remember we made no promises to each other. We are free to do what we please."

"I have a promise now. Open this door. Margaret, what you saw in the paper is not what you think. I went with Georgia to the banquet. She did not have an escort, so I agreed to do that for her. Let me in, or I'll kick this door down." Margaret peeped out the door, "I can't talk now, I have an appointment with the Fletchers," she said.

"Give me their number. I'll call them and tell them you have a crisis, and you'll be there later. Margaret, I believe I love you, did you hear me?"

"Yes, I *believe* I heard you. After only two dates, what does that mean?"

"It means I sat in the car after I left your condo the other night and cried because I thought I had lost you. And besides, it's not like we've only known each other after two dates. We've known each other for years. Georgia asked me to escort her to the banquet. It was not a romantic invitation! She had no idea she was going to be the Person of the Year. She was actually trembling when the announcement was made, and I had to drag her up to get the award. No one in the whole town would believe Georgia was actually scared. I don't think she liked being surprised. She couldn't believe the nomination had not leaked out. Are you listening to me?"

"Yes," she said, as she opened the door. "I don't know why I'm upset. You did right by escorting her. I just thought it would have been nice to know you were escorting one of the most glamorous women in Atlanta before I saw it in the papers."

"Margaret, I have known for a while that you are a very special person, but I had to be sure we could love each other. I realized it when I sat and watched you go inside the other night. It was stupid of me not to go in with you. When I saw that picture this morning, I freaked out. I wanted to get to you before you read it."

"I can hear you in there," Becky yelled. "Close the door!"

"Margaret, do you believe me?"

"I'm trying to let all this soak in. I'm confused. Why were you kissing her?"

"I wasn't kissing her I was mocking her statement about diplomacy."

"What's wrong with the word diplomacy?"

"Oh, for heaven's sake, nothing. It just sounded weird to me. Margaret, I'm not used to this dating thing. I think we are too old to date. Do you think you can love me?"

"Bob, you knocked me off my feet in Savannah. I swooned for weeks like a teenager, but I wasn't sure it was love. It seemed more like romance."

"What's the difference?"

"Forget it, I'm tired of words," she said. "If love is being hurt when you see the person, you *think* you love, kissing a beautiful, successful woman then I must be in love."

"No, that's jealousy."

"Jealousy! You idiot. You thought you lost me the other night, and I thought I lost you when I saw the scene in the morning papers. Why are we screaming?"

"Margaret, let me whisper something in your ear if it will help." He grabbed her and whispered into her ear, "I believe I am in love with you. Now that is not what I said to Georgia."

"I suppose I could say the same thing or I wouldn't be so mad. Let's just try to stay on the same page, okay?" Bob opened the door and yelled to Becky, "It's a beautiful morning, and she thinks she's in love. Get her ready for her appointment. I don't dare watch her change clothes."

Margaret went to her appointment, and Bob went into the back door of his office. There was someone waiting, but he had to shave first. He called Georgia to thank her for the evening, but it went to voice mail, "Georgia, thanks for inviting me. I'm proud of you. By the way did you see Georgette's face? I could have taken a picture of it and named it *Jealousy*." He called his secretary, "Maggie, can you come here for a minute?"

"Oh, you are here. I'll be right there."

"Who is in the office?"

"Freddie Winchester."

"Freddie? Does he have an appointment?

"No, he does not."

"Did he say why he is here?"

"Yes. He wants to see you."

"I think I know why. Ask him to come in."

CHAPTER 58
Freddie Winchester

Bob rose as Freddie Winchester entered the room, "Good to see you, Freddie. What can I do for you, son?"

"My daddy suggested I should come see you."

"What's up?"

"Sir, I'm in a fix. I guess you know by now that I married Celeste Murray."

"Yes, I know. Word travels fast among friends."

"I can't figure out if I need a lawyer or what is ethical in my position."

"Back up. I know something about your getting married and the break up of the Murray family. Tell me why you are here."

"Sir, I don't have a marriage. My life is really screwed up. Celeste has been so depressed she is unable to do her work. Her company gave her thirty days sick leave to try to pull herself together. Right now she is living with a girl friend to try to 'figure things out' as she says. Losing the connection with her mother has just about driven her insane. At this time she won't speak to me, or anyone in my family. I used to be best friends with her brother, but even that is a conflict. I've been told her father wants her to go away for a rest before she makes any decisions. My question is, do I have a say in this?"

"Whoa, that's a lot of information. Why don't you start at the beginning?"

Freddie described the quick trip to Hawaii, the marriage, the night he and Celeste returned home, the miscarriage, and the events of the few days following. It was obvious to Bob that Freddie was in great distress.

"Well, Freddie what do you want to do?"

"She wants a divorce so she can start over, but she wants money to do that, and I don't have a lot of money. I could ask my parents for money, but I need to do this by myself."

"Where are you living?"

"In the apartment she and I rented, and all I have is my paycheck, but I am about to move back home."

"Let me ask you again, what do you want to do?"

"I've thought about trying to save our marriage, but I realize there is no way that is going to happen. Seriously, I believe Celeste has a mental problem. I believe a divorce will be the best situation for me."

"First of all, let's not say Celeste has a mental problem. You could file with the court that she has left you and is living somewhere else, so she has abandoned your marriage. Then we can file for an annulment. How long has she been living with her friend?"

"Two months."

"When was the last time the two of you were intimate?"

"Not since we were in Hawaii after we married."

"Really?"

"Well, she lost our baby a few days after we returned, and she wasn't agreeable to be intimate."

"Do the two of you speak?"

"Never. She emails me several times a day that she wants a divorce and money. She says I owe her because I ruined her life and destroyed her relationship with her mother."

"Let me see what I can do. Save all the communications received from her, and do not respond to any of them. I am very serious! Let's see what she does when you don't. I'm sorry you're going through this, Freddie. You come from a great family, and I want the best for you. Make records of any calls, threats, or whatever. Okay? (Freddie nodded to confirm he would agree.) Let me remind you, no dates with other women! No intimacy with *anyone* until this is over. Do you understand? Celeste may have someone approach you to prove you are unfaithful."

"Thank you for meeting with me, Mr. Barnett, and for giving me some direction. I'm hurt, mad, intimidated, and stupid getting myself in this situation."

"You are not the first person who made this mistake. Tell your parents not to talk to Celeste. Give a picture of her to your employer. Inform the company she is not to approach you at any time. If there is an opportunity to travel with your work, take it. Turn your apartment back to the realtor, and rent a one-room efficiency apartment. Contact Celeste and tell her you are moving out, and that her things will be sent to storage. I am pushing the button a little, but I believe this is within the ethical rules."

"Thank you, sir. That is a good idea."

It was a long day at the office. Bob couldn't shake the talk with Freddie Winchester, but all he could do right now was wait for what happens next. After the last of his clients left, he spent a good bit of time updating himself on the state's laws proving abandonment in a marriage. He decided to call Frederick. "Frederick, I saw Freddie today. We had a fairly long and serious discussion. I just want you to know that I will do my best to help him."

"I know you will, Bob. Thanks for seeing him."

"I want to see Freddie at least once more before I do anything. There may be situations I don't know about his involvement. For right now I have pretty well informed him of what he has to do in the next few weeks."

"Freddie doesn't have the money to retain a lawyer, but I told him he is responsible for making payments to you. Elizabeth thinks I am too hard on him, but he needs to learn there are consequences for his actions."

"You are right, but there is another reason not to give him money. I don't want her lawyer trying to pick your pockets. Freddie may want to move back home. I suggested that you not allow that."

"Thanks, Bob for all you are doing. I want him to learn from his mistakes."

"Believe me, he is learning."

After handing up, Bob called Georgia. "Georgia, this is Bob. No time for small talk. I need a favor for a client."

"Okay, spill it," she said.

"Unless I can settle a situation before it goes to court, Dr. Louise Murray may call you to represent their daughter against Fredrick Winchester's son. As a favor I'm asking you not to accept their case. I don't want to us to go to war against each other. I believe you can find several reasons not to do it."

"Thanks for the do-me-a-favor request, but Louise Murray has already called, and I have refused to represent her daughter because of my relationship with Fredrick Winchester's daughter, but thanks for the call. You can use your 'do me a favor' another time."

"I should have known you wouldn't go there. I'm proud to be the only person who has *ever* seen you afraid, but most of all you deserved that honor. Did you hang your award on your wall?"

"You know I didn't. I'm embarrassed so many people know about it, and no, I did not see Georgette's face. Dr. Murray is such a nice person. It's a shame his wife is such a bitch. I wish they would get their daughter to agree to annul the marriage, and let all of them find some happiness. The Murray family could save themselves a lot of heartache," Georgia said.

"That's what I'm working on. This whole situation is a sad story. Nice talking to you, Georgia."

CHAPTER 59
Rick

Joan went through her mail and found a note from Frankie: *"Dear Joan and Randy,* I write this with a sad heart to inform you Rick is very ill. His doctor says he doesn't have long to live. We are beside ourselves, for we do love him so. He requests that I ship all his paintings to you, and he trusts that Pearl will know what to do with them." Sincerely, Frankie

Joan cursed herself for not looking at her mail for several days. She called Frankie. "Frankie, I don't know how fast I can get there. I will let you know in an hour or so."

No need to come, Joan. Rick died this morning. We are so despondent. He requested that his body be cremated and shipped back to the states. With your permission we will begin that process as soon as possible. One of us will bring his ashes home to you. He left us money to hire a company to pack his paintings so we can ship them to you directly. I have already called Pearl. Always remember this, he was doing what he wanted to do, where he wanted to do it, and created some beautiful works of art on his short journey. We were so proud of him."

"Oh, Frankie, I am crushed. I will get back to you soon."

She called Randy's office, "Ms. Bee, I must talk to Randy immediately."

"Ms. Walker, are you crying?"

"Yes, please hurry."

"Mr. Walker, your wife has an emergency."

"Joan, what's up? Can I call you right back; I have a client."

"Rick has died."

"Oh my God. When?"

"Randy, as soon as you can, please come home; I need you."

"I will be there shortly. Ms. Bee, cancel my appointments for today. Our son Rick has died this morning."

"Oh, Mr. Walker, I am so sorry. I will do that immediately."

After Randy arrived, Joan was upset so he made all the calls, first to Cassie, who was moving into their new home. Then he called Ana and Pearl, and said he, Joan, and Cassie would be there in an hour. Having no children, Pearl had great affection for Rick, and they had been communicating quite frequently. She had great hopes for his ability to become a well-respected artist.

Unknown to Rick, Frankie had written Pearl of the seriousness of his health. Pearl regretted not having informed Joan, but she couldn't think about that at the moment. Right now she had to console her.

Pearl staggered to the door to let them in. She appeared to have aged over night. She had been in mourning for a long time, for she knew Rick's death was imminent. She and Ana had black stoles slung around their shoulders even though it was mid morning, and neither of them had removed their nightgowns. After hugs and kisses an eerie silence filled the room. No one knew what to say. Finally Pearl opened a bottle of sparkling wine and offered a toast, "Here's to Rick, beloved son, our friend, and a great artist. " Sadness hung in the air like a fog, and everyone seemed to be studying the patterns of the carpet on the floor.

Finally Cassie broke the silence, "I am going to call Rev. Marshall. I believe we could use a spiritual adviser at a time like this." No one objected. Then she called the person on duty to let her in. That short break in the silence helped, so they talked about Rick as they drank the wine and waited for Rev. Marshall. Sarah knew the family was basically agnostic, but she was pleased Cassie had asked her to come join them. She informed her staff and left.

"Rev Marshall, please come in," Cassie said. "I'm sure you remember Randy's mother Ana and his Aunt Pearl."

"Thanks for calling me, I came as soon as I could. There's no way to predict traffic this time of day. How can I help you this morning?"

Cassie said, "We are not at all certain what kind of help we want. I suppose your being here with us is as important as any words you might have to say. Perhaps we could just sit here and talk for while and share in this small gathering to honor my brother, Rick."

Joan said, "Rev. Marshall, Rick told us he enjoyed talking with you at Cassie's wedding, and he found you to be a good listener."

"Oh yes, I had a long conversation with him," Sarah said. "He marveled at the support all of you were giving him. Pearl, he talked about your art with such enthusiasm I went to a gallery that displays your paintings and purchased the one with a group of women sitting in knitting circle. I love it. Ana without a doubt, you became his grandmother."

"Pearl said, "My goodness, I am so pleased you bought one of my paintings, but wait until you see Rick's paintings. You might like his better."

Randy said, "Sarah, how can we get through a time like this. For me, I found a son, and now I've lost him, but I am thankful for the time I had with him. Even though Joan and I are his parents, and Cassie his sister, I believe my mom and my aunt Pearl became quite attached to him in a short time. It's amazing how they bonded. Art does wonders, doesn't it? Even though I am a late arrival in this family, Rick and I shared some neat moments. He was hungry for acceptance, so we understood each other. I loved him."

Cassie said, "Growing up Rick and I always had each other, and Mom you were both mother and father to us. Thank you for coming into our family, Randy. You believed in Rick. He would have chosen another career if you had not helped him accept what he wanted to do with his life. Thank you. Rev. Marshall, you may not realize it, but you made a significant change in my life. Just the few words you said at our wedding have never left me."

Ana spoke. "What a family we have. I regret I had a husband who was so unsuited for marriage, but I always had Pearl to rescue me, and Randy you have Joan. I am so happy for both of you. Cassie, I loved Rick, and I love you. Even in such a short time, you have become the grandchildren I never had. Rev. Marshall, you are hearing too much, but thank you for being present today."

Pearl, who had expected to be a large part of Rick's career, said, "I am almost without words (she paused) to describe how I feel. This talented person has been taken from me. He had such a marvelous gift. The last note I had from him was about going to a local cathedral's Evensong. He wrote of being relieved of the burden of dying, and found peace just sitting in the pew." Joan glanced over at Randy, and he took her hand.

Sarah thought it was odd that no one spoke of the reason for Rick's death, but she did not sense the need to ask. Randy was trying to find a place to interject the words that would crush Joan, but he decided to save it for another time. "What all of you have expressed is very spiritual," Sarah began. "You speak of life, death, family, love, and thanksgiving. I believe those are gifts from a higher power. Perhaps what Rick was searching for, most of all, was peace. To find peace he went to a Cathedral, and how he found peace there would be interesting to know. Was it the music of the choir, the holiness of the interior of the Cathedral, or did he find the peace only God gives? For a long time each of you will reflect on the words spoken here, and you will eventually find peace. Thanks again for inviting me to be with you. I would like to say a short prayer if no one objects." She paused to find the right words. "Lord God, thank you for the members of this family who came together to honor and remember the one person who is missing from this gathering. Touch their minds and hearts to understand that all life has meaning, and even in death we can find intrigue, honor, and peace. Guide this family to the acceptance of these words, and help them to honor you by honoring the one to whom you gave such great talent, and who, one evening, sought peace in your Sanctuary. In your Holy Name, Amen."

Six days later Frankie arrived with Rick's ashes in her suitcase. Two days later the paintings arrived. Pearl invited a couple of art critics she trusted to view the art. Randy propped the paintings on chairs, on the floor, and the sofa in Ana and Pearl's living area, as if they were the honored guests being presented for confirmation. No one dared break the silence as the paintings spoke to them: children on swings flying in the sky on a hot summer day; a baker wrapped in flour admiring his latest creation; sightseers peeping out the windows of a bus; faded street bricks sparkling like rainbows after a hard rain; candles twinkling inside a Cathedral, and a stream of light falling upon a little girl sitting on the front pew holding her doll, probably waiting for her mother to finish singing. Those and more captured the meaning of life among the people who took the American artist into their hearts.

Joan was happy when she saw the works of her son, "Rick had eyes for the ordinary, and was able to tell stories on canvas," she said. In a low, soft voice Pearl said to Joan, "One can only imagine how long the little girl will wait for the last song without getting restless. Will she fall asleep? Will she wave to her mother? Does she know where the bathroom is? It is not the cathedral the artist is capturing, it is the child holding her doll, waiting and waiting."

Pearl was amused as she watched the critics shuffling back and forth, occasionally stepping on someone's toes. They huddled and spoke softly of the beauty, the passion, and the colors. One of the critics said, "If this were my son, I would have a hard time parting with any of these paintings, but they must go to others to be seen and not hidden away. These paintings are brilliant."

Cassie and Robert moved toward the little girl in the Cathedral. She could not imagine it going to any home but to her home, so she stood by the painting, almost daring anyone to bother it. One of the critics said, "Let's find a place to exhibit these paintings, so they can be admired by a few art collectors I know.

Cassie pulled Pearl and Joan aside, "I have fallen in love with the child on the pew in the Cathedral. Please do not allow her to go from our family."

"She shall not. She shall be yours," Joan said, "but let's exhibit it with the others."

"I know just the place," one of the critics said. "I have a friend who has occasionally offered her gallery for special events. She does this sort of thing to instill more interest in art. If there is no objection, I will call her now." There were no objections. He left the room to make the call, and upon returning said, "I have convinced her to allow the showing of these paintings and it was not hard to do. We will get together with her and your family to set a date. I hope it can be soon."

"What happens at these events?" Joan asked. "I don't wish the paintings to be priced and sold so soon."

"They shall not be. It may happen that someone makes a bid in writing, and I suppose that will happen, but the family is no obligated to accept any bids." As he was preparing to leave he said to Pearl, "Thank you for inviting us to your place. Are you working on anything at present?"

"No," she answered. "My life is on pause at the moment."

"Pearl, Pearl, you must keep painting. Artists paint in peace and sorrow, sunshine and darkness, and sometimes your best is right in front of you when your life is on pause."

"I know," she said. "I know."

A month later the Gastone Gallery, owned by Suzanne Gastone, was opened by Invitation Only to view the art of Richard Randolph Walker, a native son of Atlanta. All twenty invitees were required to show their invitations. The paintings were hung, along with a picture of Rick standing behind his easel in his makeshift studio. Several members of the family were also present to answer any questions. The primary critic and art dealer of Atlanta, gave a short introduction of the young artist, his training, and his studies in Paris (with the help of Pearl's notes, of course). She said, "I believe you will see a fine selection of art this evening, and we hope you enjoy your time with us. You have been given a slip of paper and an envelope. We are asking for your comments on the paintings. Please place your notes in the basket by the door."

Joan had expected the evening to cause the family sadness, but that did not happen. Perhaps it was the wine and the excitement watching the critics. The family mingled casually among the guests, chatting and answering questions, but the stars of the show were Pearl and her friend Frankie who were able to communicate intelligently on the subjects and the colors. The evening seemed to be a success. After everyone had departed, they opened the envelopes, one by one, and discussed the comments. There were words like classic, interesting, valuable, and indeed bids were in the basket. A few of the guests asked for opportunities to purchase after the paintings were valued. The highest bids were for the child in the cathedral, which did not surprise anyone, and the others seven bids were also generous.

Randy asked, "Mr. Rodgers, what have we accomplished here this evening?"

"The family has a decision to make, to sell or not to sell. One of the visitors here was the art critic for the newspaper, and she will have an article in the paper this week. I took notice that she talked to several of you."

"That was rather sneaky, don't you think?" Cassie asked.

"Well, yes and no. She has a pretty good idea of valuable art. It doesn't really matter what you said to her, she will write it the way she wants, and I assure you it will be well written," Mr. Rodgers said.

"How long shall we leave the paintings here?" Joan asked.

Mr. Rodgers said, "We must remove them this evening. I don't imagine they are insured yet, so we can't take the risk of leaving them." Joan said she would like to take the paintings home with her for the time being if there was no objection. "I just want to look at them and think of Rick. Frankie, how long can you stay in the states? We have enjoyed being with you and would love a few more days with you."

She said, "Perhaps another week. I tried to get Gracie to come over but she declined. She says her arthritis has flared up. That is always her excuse. Randy said, "Joan, we will stay here until the paintings are packed, and the company can follow us to our condo."

It was 2 a.m. before everyone left Joan and Randy's. Joan sat on the sofa with Rick's picture at her side, and she wept for what she had lost, and for the legacy he had given her. "I don't know if I can let the paintings go," she said to Randy. "Every one of them is so precious to me. When he was a child I remember him swinging so high it scared me. He said he wanted to see the colors of the sky a little closer. Once he painted the bricks on our sidewalk all different colors. Rick thought they were beautiful, but John was so mad he made Rick remove the paint. It took him hours. I remember taking him to New York when he was about seven. He kept looking up at the buildings as if studying them. He said to me, 'Mom, are there more of these buildings in the world?' I said, Of course. And he answered, 'let's buy one and live in it.' I said these buildings are very expensive. I don't believe we have enough money to do that. I'll never forget what he said next, 'I tell you what, Mom; you take a picture of that one over there, and when I get home I will draw it. We can put it on my wall, then we can own it.' "

"What a smart kid," Randy said. "He had some imagination."

"Do you know what I am going to miss the most, Randy?"

“What are you going to miss?” “The other paintings that won’t be.”

CHAPTER 60
A Gathering

It was Sunday morning. Joan invited their friends over for coffee and rolls, and to see Rick's work. Frederick and Elizabeth skipped church services and arrived early. They had quite a collection of art themselves. To no one's surprise Bob brought Margaret. Roger and Joanna also came. It felt good having everyone together after so long. While the others were admiring the art, Bob motioned for Frederick to meet him outside on the balcony.

"Frederick, I went by to see Dr. Murray this week, and told him of Freddie's visit in my office, and how pitiful he was. I asked him how we could settle this whole mess with Celeste so it would not bring war between the two families. He said he had already been thinking about that. At this time in his life he does not want any legal action since he will be involved with his wife in another issue. Dr. Murray was not surprised Celeste has taken the actions she has. He said she is not listening to him or her brother, and is living with some friend of hers. If it comes right down to it, he has agreed to help her get the divorce or an annulment, and get her settled somewhere. If Freddie will agree, that's what he will do."

"Thank the Lord," Frederick said. "It sounds too good to be true."

"I have his word, and I believe he will do as he says, but we have to cross our fingers that Celeste will agree," Bob said.

"Bob, it's a chilly feeling to think that Celeste has reconciled with her mother. At this moment she is probably working on finding her an acceptable man to marry."

"I believe you are right and Dr. Murray feels the same."

They went back inside to see the art. They had watched Rick grow up from the day he was born, so they were proud of his achievements. Joan said, "Last night Pearl, Cassie, Randy and I thought a long time about what to do with Rick's work. It appears the critics have their own opinions, but their opinions do not overrule ours. We would like to share something Pearl suggested. Rick's life was short, so unless we do something special in his honor he will be forgotten, not by us, of course. She would like to see us to start a Richard Randolph Walker Scholarship Fund to help students study and create art."

"What say you?" Randy asked.

Roger said, "That is a wonderful idea and a neat way to remember Rick."

After more comments, Randy said, "First, Pearl has promised the *Child in the Cathedral* to Cassie, and she has agreed to participate in the scholarship fund in Rick's name. Everyone who wishes may choose a painting, and your donation can be given later. Please don't ask Joan to set a price, just give what your heart dictates. Oh, yes, another suggestion, since Leonard is not living, if Margaret wishes, she may choose for her family, that is if you would like to do that, Margaret."

"Thank you for that privilege," Margaret answered.

Joan said, "Pearl has agreed to help Mr. Rodgers sell the other paintings, and that will increase the scholarship fund."

After everyone chose a painting, Randy said, "When you pay for the painting, Cassie will put the money in a bank account for the Scholarship Fund to be established. At the proper time you can use it on your taxes."

The rest of the morning was spent telling stories about Rick. Each person had something personal to say. It was a fun way to honor him. Elizabeth said, "I do wish Molly could have been here. We always thought she had a crush on Rick." Bob said, "I thought the same about Julia." And they all laughed.

Roger raised his glass, "Long live our friendship, and may we always care for each other and our families, and hopefully add to the scholarship fund through the years. Joan and Randy, losing Rick has been a tragedy for you. His life ended much too soon. All of us are sharing that grief with you. Having one of his paintings will help us remember him." Everyone agreed. Their newest member, Roger's daughter Joanna asked, "May I speak?" And everyone said, "yes of course." "I feel very privileged to be a part of your lives today. You have been very gracious to me. Thank you."

"Joanna," Joan said. "We are so glad to have you."

One by one they left, feeling a certain satisfaction that what they did was helpful, not only to Joan and Randy, but for their own families

---

Two weeks later on a Thursday morning, Dr. Murray, Freddie, and Celeste met in Bob's office. Dr. Murray had to threaten Celeste to get her there. She was mad because they would not allow her girl friend in the conference. "That's not going to happen," her father said. "Mr. Barnett has drawn up some papers for you and Freddie to sign. You will sign these papers, Celeste."

"I will not."

Bob said, "Celeste, you have abandoned your husband and are living elsewhere. He is filing for an annulment of your marriage. I suggest you sign since neither you, nor Freddie, have the funds to go to court. Your father and I have not asked your mother, but I am sure she will be extremely happy for you to end this marriage. You have no money, and your father is not willing to pay for a lawyer and the cost of a court hearing. Is that correct, Dr. Murray?"

"That is correct," he answered. "Celeste, you will sign these papers and get on with your life, and you will also sign this agreement to have you name changed back to Murray. You have always trusted me to do what is best for you, and I believe this is the best."

"Freddie, how could you do this to me? I thought you loved me."

"I have asked Freddie not to respond to you, Celeste."

"Do you not have a tongue, Freddie?"

"That is enough, Celeste, sign the papers!" her father yelled.

"Freddie, how am I going to live? I don't have any money."

"That is not Freddie's problem. He wishes to get his life straight, and he wants you to do the same," Dr. Murray said.

"Mom was right, I married a black coward." Freddie started to leave the room, but Bob pushed him back into his chair, "Let her say anything she wants to say. Don't let her comments bother you."

Freddie spoke. "Celeste, I hope you can find happiness; I'm going to try."

"Okay, give me the papers. I'll sign them if somebody will give me some money to live on until I find another job."

"Celeste," her father said, "I will help you do that, but I suggest you allow me to find you a place to live, until you find another job."

"I'm got going anywhere unless my girl friend Charlotte can come too."

"I am not supporting your friend."

"So, you will just throw me out on the street?"

"Yes, I will."

"Then throw me out."

"Sign the papers, and we will work something out."

"What will we work out? Put it in writing."

"Mr. Barnett, have your secretary write this letter to my daughter: *Dr. Thomas Murray has agreed to give his daughter, Celeste $5,000 to live on while she finds employment and a place to live, that and nothing more.* Now sign the annulment papers."

"Mom has already agreed to give me more than that, but I'll sign the damn papers." She signed, and left the room. Bob, Thomas, and Freddie sat for a few minutes without speaking. "I'm so sorry, Dr. Murray," Freddie said. "I'm sorry for so many things. I wish we had never gone to Hawaii. It will take me a while to get through this."

"Freddie, don't look back. You and I seem to be in the same position right now, but I believe both of us are going to be fine, just fine. Good luck, son."

"Thank you, Sir and thank you, Mr. Barnett for everything you did for me."

"Can't get off with just *a thank you*, Freddie. "You are going to owe me a little money, and that will complete our contract. My fee is $1,000, and you may pay the money $100 monthly."

"Sir, I will pay you $200 now, and the other monthly. I don't like to have debts."

"Good for you. Just keep that in mind as you grow older."

"Yes, sir."

CHAPTER 61
The Convent

Frankie was given a send-off party before she returned to Paris. She had stayed long enough to witness the surge of excitement over the paintings. She was honored in small crowds as one of the persons who guided Rick in his career and cared for him while he was ill. Everyone was in agreement that Rick's ashes should stay with Joan and Randy until they could decide where to place them. The original viewers, who viewed the paintings at Gastone Gallery, purchased the remainder of the paintings. The money was put into an interest account, waiting for the scholarship fund to be formed. Hopefully they would find a university or organization that would accept the funds. One university appeared to have interest, but said the scholarship would not fit in their program.

After contacting several colleges, whose interests were minimal, the family began considering other solutions. They decided the best solution was to start their own foundation. Cassie and Robert agreed to research the process, and then they could elect officers and find a way to discover artists who would qualify for the scholarships. Pearl agreed to be on board with them, for her contacts might prove to be helpful.

———

Joan tried to start writing again, but ideas for a new book did not happen. She was not eating well, and when she did eat, quite frequently she vomited, and there was no desire to shop or have visitors, and sound sleep was impossible.

She began to wish for a place to get away, a place to find peace and renewal. How could she tell Randy she wanted to do this by herself? He would be hurt for sure, but she felt a collapse was near. He was busier at work that he had ever been, but she had nothing to hold her interest. Her focus seemed to be searching for the meaning of Rick's death. Rick knew he was sick, but why didn't he tell her, and why didn't he want her to care for him. Then she had a flashback about his illness. How could she have missed it? She realized why he was sick. That is why he went away. *My god, my son could not tell me how sick he was. He didn't want our friends to know. Did he think I would be embarrassed? Maybe he would have been ashamed. Did he think I would desert him? I am over whelmed with sadness. I let him down. Where can I go to wash away my hurt, my anger, and my sorrow? I will talk to Randy tonight, but I must have something in mind first.*

For some reason, she decided to call Pearl. Thank goodness she answered the phone, and not Ana. "Pearl, It's hard for me to admit this to anyone, but I need help. I have reached an impasse, and realize I am deeply depressed. I need an intervention - a place or persons - to help me get through this sorrow and to learn how to live with myself. Do you know of such a place?"

"Let me think about it, and I will call you. Right now get in the shower, or have a long hot bath, or make an appointment to get a massage."

Joan hung up the phone. She could do none of those suggestions. The weight of fear, anger, and sadness was such that she could not think, so she paced back and forth, waiting for Pearl's call. How could she present this to Randy? Would he understand?

Pearl called. "There is a place near Augusta, a convent, and I know several persons who have been there. I spoke to one of the nuns, and they will be looking for you. I will take you there in the morning."

"Tomorrow? So Soon? How can I tell Randy?"

"I don't understand why you would say that. You know each other intimately, I presume. Your bodies act in harmony, so why shouldn't your minds? If you must conceal your feelings tell him you and I have planned a trip, but I don't believe that is the right solution."

"You are right. I will tell him tonight."

"Good. See you in the morning at 9:00, so we can be there by lunch. Pack light. Listen to me, Joan. I will not be staying with you. I will be taking my paints and a canvas or two to capture some of the scenery while we are there. You don't need to comment on my decision, it is firm."

"Thank you, Pearl."

After dinner Joan said to Randy, "Sit with me. I have something to tell you."

"What in heaven's name? You sound scared. Are you sick?"

"In a way. I am troubled and sad, and yes, sick. I need to find a place to relax and learn how to accept the past events."

"Both of us may need that. Let's go to Maud's Inn for awhile."

"Randy, tomorrow Pearl is taking me to Augusta to a convent. I'll be there a week. Hopefully, I can try to piece together all that has happened these past few weeks. Please don't be angry with me. I have to do this, or I will become ill."

"I'm not angry, but I do have a feeling of being left out in the decision, but if this is what you need, you should go. But don't you think you might need to see your doctor first?"

"No, I thought about that. What I need is a spiritual person to listen to me, someone to help me understand what's going on in my heart. Randy, if you need to do something like this, I will support you."

"I know you would, but you are firm that you need to do this alone?"

"I am. Randy this is a convent for women. You couldn't go if you wanted to. Oh, I love you so much, but if I don't take this chance I may become an angry person. If you need to see someone maybe you should go to one of the monks at the monastery in Conyers. Think about it."

"If I find I need help I'll make the arrangements. Joan, you are my life, and I have no doubt that I would die without you. I've known for several days you were sinking into a hole, but I thought you just needed time to get over Rick's death. Go my love, and come back to me soon."

"Thank you, Randy. It was difficult making this decision because I would not be with you. Remember this, nothing in this world will keep me from loving you. Randy, I wondered why Rick's illness came so sudden. You knew he had AIDS, didn't you?"

He couldn't speak for a while, for he had withheld this important information from Joan. It sort of broke an unspoken trust between them. Finally he was able to answer. "Yes, but he asked me not to tell you, and I kept my promise. I loved him for his courageous decision to make the best of his last days. For that, you and I should be happy. Please don't be angry with me."

"I don't know why I didn't think of it. It just came to me recently. I can't put it out of my mind. He died without me being beside him. Not knowing about his illness was cruel thing to do to me."

"No, Joan cruel is not the right word. He would have never painted so beautifully and desperately here in Georgia with people feeling sorry for him, including you. He relieved you of seeing him waste away, and that, my dear is not cruel; it is love."

"Oh, Randy your words help me understand, but they do not lift this sorrow."

Both were restless in the night. Once she cried, and he held her in his arms until she fell asleep. In the morning Randy waited for Pearl to pick her up before he went to work. He waved until their car went out of sight. It was a lonely view.

The ride to the convent seemed a long journey to Joan. She was like a blank page in one of her novels: *Where do I take the characters from here? Nowhere today. Just walk away and wait for another day. The signs of the little towns and counties along the expressway depress me. Who lives there? Are there schools and churches? Where do the residents shop? I must remember to do a search on them. Why am I worried about that? Maybe I'm thankful for the diversion.* Atlanta seemed far away.

They arrived about noon. Without looking toward her, Pearl introduced her to Sister Elizabeth, and then disappeared. That was the last time they would meet until the end of the week. She was taken to a small, almost bare room, and the nun said to her, "Here is something to read that explains what takes place while you are here. I will return to bring you a small plate of food, since we have already had our mid-day meal." Joan flipped through the papers then went back to the first page:

DAILY INSTRUCTIONS FOR YOUR VIST

Our schedule is carefully planned to teach order in one's life: sleep, sustenance, learning from others, time alone, and spiritual discipline. Place the following instructions on the table beside your bed. The hours below are strictly followed to help us function properly.

6:00 Morning. A bell will awaken you for chapel; wear your provided smock.

7:00 a light breakfast.

8:00 quiet time in your room.

9:00 first day, someone will come to take you to the meeting rooms.

12:00 lunch.

1:00 walk outside in silence; enjoy the scenery. Raincoats are in your closet.

2:00 meet with spiritual advisor assigned to you.

4:00 quiet time to read or write. Paper and pen are on the nightstand.

6:00 supper.

7:00 each day choose a different companion for an hour visit.

8:00 quiet time in your room.

9:00 lights out.

By the third day, Joan was into the routine and pleased how much better she was feeling. She was able to relax because there was routine and no pressure. She listened, she learned, and began to understand that even though she had a good life and a wonderful marriage, pain can slam one into depression. She began to realize she had never faced the consequences of her marriage to John. She had simply rationalized it. She had endured his long absences and his cruel remarks as being part of marriage. And she had never reconciled his long infidelity with one of her friends. Betrayal was a word she had not accepted. John's rejection was the same as her rejection of the disease her son suffered. Also she had never analyzed the coldness and lack of love from her mother and absent father. In Rick's death she began to see the life she had lived was almost a fairy tale adventure – the Princess went from rags to riches, and she was not worthy.

The week went by too fast. Deep inside she wanted to linger, but knew she must leave and return to the same world she left, but with more insight. One of the nuns preferred the word, wisdom. In their last session each woman was asked to talk about whatever they wished, for there was no script. The words of the other women were inspiring. When it was her time to speak she said to the group, "I will rise each morning and say, I am becoming a new person. Not there yet, but *becoming*. You have helped me understand how the death of my son brought me to lapse into depression. And you have taught me that the past can never be buried alive, it will rise up to haunt, as my spiritual leader said to me. I am humbled for what I experienced and grateful to the staff who have given me a way to begin healing. I will always cherish those of you who have been my companions on this journey."

She left the convent with the sincere feeling she had been baptized, as some of her Christian friends called it.

———

Riding back to Atlanta, she saw a road sign, SOCIAL CIRCLE. "Pearl, can we veer off to see this place with such an interesting name?"

"Sure, why not. It's a lovely place. Ana and I have stopped there many times. It is a good place to get gas, and you do not have to pump your own. If it weren't so far from Atlanta I'd drive out here. Pumping gas is a task I hate."

She was surprised Pearl knew the owner of the station and some of the town folk. They went inside one of the antique shops where Pearl bought a small gift for Ana. "She loves this place."

"How do you know these people?" Joan asked.

"I knew a woman."

"And?" Joan waited, but Pearl did not respond.

———

They arrived home in the late afternoon, and Randy was waiting for them. He had prepared a light meal, but Pearl said, "I must run along. Ana has been by herself too long, and she will be looking for me." Joan gave Pearl a kiss and a long hug, "Thanks for everything. I love you."

The afternoon was delightful. Randy listened as she poured out her experiences, hardly stopping to breathe. "More people should be informed of this convent. I was told they had allowed me and another lady to come even thought the group was filled. We were able to learn a lot from each other and about ourselves. I remember our leader saying, 'there are no wrong questions, comments, or answers, so say what is on your mind.' Those words were so liberating. Thank you, Randy for understanding my need to get away. Because you and I love each other so much, just going away together would not have helped me, the way the visit to the convent did. When we left I had the greatest joy of anticipation that you would be here waiting for me. Sadly some of the women would not have that pleasure."

"Do you think you will ever see any of those women again?"

"I doubt it. We were instructed to introduce ourselves by our first names only, and our places of departure were not to be mentioned. That and wearing the cotton smock and no makeup made us more equal and comfortable with each other."

"I'm so glad you went, even after my poor attempts to stop you. Long ago I felt forced to reconcile my past, especially with my father. He had very little influence on my life; my mother saw to that. You know my biggest regret? It was so late in my life when I had a chance to love children. I want to be sure that you know, even the short time I had with Rick, and I loved him just as I love Cassie."

"I am sure Rick realized that, as does Cassie. Thank you Randy for loving all three of us. You are my hero. By the way, have you ever ridden with Pearl?"

"No, I don't believe I have."

"Then don't. She scared the hell out of me before we got to Augusta."

"But isn't she a dear?"

"You bet."

"We stopped in Social Circle on the way home. Did you know she had known a woman who lived there?"

"Yes, I knew her."

"And…"

"I don't know what happened, and I never knew whether they were friends or lovers. Thanks for sharing your experiences with me, Joan. I'm so pleased with your enthusiasm, and happy to hear you laugh. Are you too tired to ride over and see Cassie and Robert's new home? I need to see my daughter."

"What a great idea. Of course, you've already told them we would be there."

CHAPTER 62

Planning the Chapel

In September a crowd of residents, friends, and dignitaries gathered on the site near Maud's Inn to break ground for the Chapel at Maud's Inn on land given by Charlie Fowler. One could feel the excitement in the air as they stood on the exact spot the chapel would be built. The Planning Committee, and other interested persons, had been meeting at the inn with the permission of the church governing body in Atlanta. This meeting was called to bring the final plans to the prospective members. At present they had a prospect list of eighty-five adults members, and at present twenty children.

There were two sets of plans to examine, the formal architectural drawings and the visional concept of the outside of the building drawn by one of the residents. The work showed a rustic cedar building, with a vaulted roof, and a porch, much like the designs of churches built out in the country over a hundred years ago.

One of the local leaders, Benjamin Thompson explained their plans and hopes as he drew the plans on a large easel. He began, "There will be no need for fancy pews, only padded chairs with arms, that can be moved around for dinners, meetings, and gatherings, and no stained glass windows so that the woods can be visible from inside. At the present time there are four prospective members who play musical instruments, and they have agreed to lead the music. So a piano or organ is not in the plans at this time.

"Volunteers have already built a table for the Sacraments and a Baptismal Font, and that includes a crystal bowl for the water. No nursery is planned at this time. The children will be invited to remain during the service, and crying will be permitted. Children will be allowed to bring a toy – but maybe not a slinky. (Everyone laughed.)

Here are the plans you may examine more closely later. Notice, a small kitchen is planned for here, and two rest rooms with four stalls each. One will be enlarged with a changing room for babies and two rockers already donated.

"Two generous families have donated the lumber and the heating and air systems. There was some discussion not to have air conditioning, but we remembered the hot Georgia summers. Two other families are paying for the chairs. Another is furnishing the kitchen and bathrooms. Several persons have promised to participate in the cost of other items, and of course we all know the land was donated. Today is Wednesday. On Monday morning the surveyors will be here. In a couple of weeks the lumber will be delivered." One of the Atlanta church officials interrupted, "This is amazing. I have never seen anything like it. My friends, it appears you will have a beautiful place to worship very soon."

There was discussion about a name for the Chapel. Charlie would have liked the name to be the Chapel at Maud's Inn, but the majority opinion was Chapel in the Woods, but to Randy and friends it would always be The Chapel at Maud's Inn.

Joan, Randy, Bob, Frederick, and Roger drove back to Atlanta. Joan said, "This may be the best thing we ever accomplished and without recognition. I am so proud of what we are doing for the Chapel. I hope it is permissible to boast to each other?"

Roger said, "I am sorry that Margaret and Elizabeth, were unable to be here to experience the excitement of the residents. I am certain they will come to the dedication when the chapel is finished. Joan, as long as we can express our feelings to each other, no matter what the subject is, I think we are all right with the Good Lord."

Bob said, "Amen to that. My Julie and Roy Fillmore seem to be headed down the aisle. I believe the chapel would be the perfect place for their wedding."

"How about you and Margaret?" Joan asked Bob.

"We seem to be satisfied just the way we are for the moment, but who knows what the future holds. We don't talk about marriage anymore, though we are looking for a place that has a separate suite for Becky. She and Margaret don't want to live apart. They work together like twins or best of friends, and Becky is a special person to Michael. Sometimes I wonder if he knows, or cares, which one of them is his mother."

"Both of them are lucky, and so are you. How does daughter Julia fit into this picture? Frederick asked.

"Julie is definitely a part of our lives. She and Margaret have a great relationship. They talk on the phone frequently. Julia said to me the other day, 'Dad, please don't get jealous, she is a mother to me.' "

Roger said, "I just thought of something remarkable. Bob, and Randy have something in common." They all pause to listen. "They have the ability to accept and love another person's child.

The others laughed, "We raised you well, Roger," Randy said.

"Hear, hear," Bob and Frederick chimed in."

"Roger, we have been friends so long we almost know what each one of us is thinking. Am I right?" Randy asked.

"Well," Roger said, "You did not know I lusted for Joan, did you? You always ran me away."

Randy said, "Oh, I knew, but all of us thought of you as a kid – too young for a relationship. Getting back to my statement, it's impossible for me to define our relationship, but it has been wonderful."

"Has?" Frederick asked. "Are you planning on leaving us?"

"No! Those words just came out. I love all of you, and I know you love me."

"That's true. I can't imagine life without any one of you," Bob said. "Without each of you, I would not have lived through all that mess with Judy. By the way, did I ever say thanks?"

"You did in many ways," Joan said. "But I am thinking that friends should not have to keep thanking each other. Friendship is like an extended family: when we need each other, it's natural to be available."

"Well said, sweet Joan. Merrily we roll along with each other. Let us keep on rolling," Roger said.

"I can't believe you said that. Maybe we should sing it. Something all of you don't know, "Merrily We Roll Along" is Randy's favorite song. Don't ask why."

Randy started it, "*Merrily we roll along, roll along, roll along. Merrily we roll along o'er the deep blue sea.*"

They sang it over and over until Roger stopped them. "Does anyone know what o'er the deep blue sea means? That is a long time to roll along."

Joan said, "Maybe it means whatever obstacles we have in our lives, we just keep going. All of us have done that, and you know what else?"

"What?" They all said together.

"We haven't had to roll over the deep blue sea alone."

"Amen and amen," Frederick said. "It's a beautiful day."

CHAPTER 63

Summertime in the woods

Weeks passed and summer came with a blast of pollen and hot air. Molly was home for part of the summer, and she was determined to get the younger group of her friends together. She said to her mom, “We young adults, in this weird circle of friends, never have any time together. I’m going to call Freddie, Joanna, Julia, and Cassie to try to get us a weekend together.”

“That’s a great idea. Would you like for me to find a place for you?”

“Mom, we can do that. We are adults now. I think Maud’s Inn would be a great place to meet. I’ll call Mr. Charlie Fowler, and see if we can meet at his place this weekend. What do you think about that, Mom?”

“I’m not involved in this, remember?”

“Sorry, thanks for reminding me.”

Molly made the arrangement with Charlie Fowler, and everyone agreed to meet at Maud’s Inn late Friday, spend two nights, and get back in town by late Sunday. Molly had to threaten Freddie into going. “You need to do this,” she said. “Get over whatever is holding you back. Get a life!”

It would be a lovely homecoming for Cassie and Robert. They had planned to go back to the Inn some weekend, but never got around to it. Everyone agreed to go in their own car in case they would have to leave earlier. Charlie was tickled to have them coming. Randy warned him that the kids were big eaters, so he planned the meals accordingly. I’d come out to help, but they would run me off.”

Charlie had completed some remodeling. He had modernized the inn with new appliances, and a large part of the remodeling was an entertainment room with a pool table, a jukebox, and a small dance floor. To maintain the feeling of driving into a wilderness, the room could not be seen from the entrance of the inn. When the kids saw it they were amazed. Charlie said, "I thought this might appeal to the young set. People our age have to get with change, so we can attract younger adults."

"Well done," Freddie said. "You'd better be careful not to let this get out. You don't want to ruin this hideaway."

"I had to create a new space for the meetings we are holding here in this beautiful wilderness. Sometime in the near future it looks like there is going to be a new chapel nearby to accommodate all these neighborhoods growing up around here."

"That's great," Cassie said, "And the new pastor will be…?

"Rev. Marshall is certainly a possibility," Charlie said, "but that's all in the future. Lunch is at 1:00. You will have to share rooms, settle in," he yelled to them. "When I ring the bell, get here fast so the food won't get cold."

At breakfast the next morning Charlie gave them a quick history of the Chattahoochee River. "It begins about ten miles north of the little town of Helen, Georgia, and is a fairly wide stream by then. You can even go tubing if you go there. It forms from rivulets coming down from the Tennessee Valley Divide in the Wildlife Management area, and it wiggles around for miles and miles down the west side of Georgia toward Alabama, finally becoming the border between Georgia and Alabama, then onward to the coast. The river brings water to many cities and fertilizes land for miles and miles, and it is a beautiful sight. Several creeks fall out along the way bringing inland water. One of those small creeks runs through this property. The Chattahoochee isn't the Mississippi, but it's our river and it's beautiful. Then he gave them a quick story of Maude's Inn.

———

Later, looking across the river Joanna said, "Oh, it is lovely, it looks very wide from here. My dad showed me the Mississippi River on our journey, and told me many stories about it, but your Chattahoochee River is also beautiful. I need to see this town of Helen. I have never seen the birthplace of a river."

"Maybe we can take you there sometime. What do you think, Julia?"

"Sure, why don't we?"

"I would love it. Maybe we can go on another Saturday trip and spend the night."

"Great idea," Molly said. "It's a strange little town, Joanna. All the downtown stores are modeled after the architecture of the Bavarian Alps. The town holds festivals there every year, but I would prefer to plan a time when there are not so many tourists.

Cassie and Robert followed the trail toward the swing by the little creek, the swing they sat in the day they planned their wedding. It was sweet being there. They both admitted it was almost like renewing their vows. "We need to take more time on the weekends for trips like this. All work is not good for us. What do you say, Cassie?"

"You are right! "Both of us are Georgian by birth, and there are many places we haven't seen. Let's do it."

The bell rang calling them to lunch. Charlie had a feast waiting for them, and said, "Guess who drove over here from Atlanta to see all of you? Ta dah. Sarah, enter!" They ran to her as if she were a mother hen. She said, "I'm just here to help Charlie with the dinner and cleaning up, but it's good seeing all of you without your parents. I have to get back to Atlanta, but in a few months I may be moving out here to start a new church. Charlie said he mentioned it to you."

"But not very much," Julia said. "He's a man of few words. Will this church be a connection with your church in Atlanta?"

"That church will be one of its sponsors. Hopefully it's going to be a community church that accepts all people who want to worship, and perhaps there will be a way people can drop in, during the week, for meditation. There are neighborhoods being built all around here, but I'm sorry it's going to be out of your reach to attend."

"Who says so," Freddie said. "It wasn't too far for us to come this weekend."

Charlie interrupted, "I forgot to tell all of you, there is a group of Georgia Tech students coming this afternoon to do an environmental study of the woodlands, soil, and animal habitations. I checked them out with the school. They will also be spending the night, but they won't need a bed since they are bringing their sleeping bags. Julia, your father is the person who suggested this place to them. See how connections help?"

About that time a vehicle pulled up, and the boys began taking all kinds of equipment out, then came inside, "Are you Mr. Fowler?"

"Speaking," Charlie answered.

"I'm Johnny Stephens, and these other guys are Bill Carson, Jerry Williams, and Roy Fillmore, Jr." Looking at the others at the table, Johnny said, "If you have any food left over, we would appreciate a light lunch and of course we'll pay for it."

"Sure, we can cook up some sandwiches," Charlie said. "Molly, run and tell the people in the kitchen to make some sandwiches for four hungry Rambling Wrecks from Georgia Tech." Molly's crew and the Tech crew spent about an hour talking. Charlie said to Sarah, "It's amazing now quickly young people get to know each other."

Freddie asked the Tech boys, "Are you spending the night?" All three of them said, "Yep." But Johnny reminded them, "First, we have a job to do, let's get with it, boys. Mr. Fowler, what time is supper?"

"The dinner bell rings at 8:00, so just in case you get too far out, watch the time."

Molly said to the Tech boys, "Is there a possibility you could use another participant?"

"Watch out boys, she's a senior at the Naval Academy," Freddie said, "She might try to take over your project."

"Oh come on," the three of them said, motioning to her.

Turning to the group, Freddie said, "Sometimes Molly forgets she is a female."

Freddie, Joanna, and Julia spent the afternoon walking the trails Charlie had made through the years. Julia was the first to notice a cabin among the trees. Freddie took pictures of the girls standing on the steps. That was before they looked in the window and saw a table and two chairs, a cot over in a corner, and gross unmentionables hanging from the ceiling. Freddie yelled, "Hello," but there was no answer. Since it wasn't locked, they sat on the steps wondering whether to go inside. "What is going on here?" said a voice. All three of them jumped. "Sir, is this your house?" Julia asked.

"Well, I reckon it is mine for a spell. I am a biologist, and there are a lot of things to study around here. Name is Horace W. F. Smithson. The scuttlebutt is, I got fired from my job, and so Mr. Fowler lent me this little cabin for a while. Getting away from those people might be the best thing ever happened to me. You best be running along now.

"Yes sir, we didn't mean to intrude. We're sorry if we interrupted you."

They started out. "You might think about turning yourself around. You are heading in the wrong direction."

After walking about fifteen minutes they realized they were in unfamiliar territory. "Horace W. F. Smithson must have a sense of cruelty. I believe we are lost," Freddie said. About that time Julia stepped in a deep hole, and it took both of them to pull her out. Finally they came out of the woods onto a dirt road, and saw the back road that led to the Inn. They followed the sound of the dinner bell.

Where have you been?" Asked Molly. "We've been wondering what happened to you all."

"Some old feller sent us in the wrong direction on purpose. He seemed to be mad that we found his hideout."

"Is Smithson still out here?" Charlie asked.

"Yep, that's his name. He looked more like a bear than a human."

"He was supposed to be gone by now. He claims to be a biologist, but I think he's hiding out. I called the police before I let him stay, but they couldn't find anything bad about him."

Julia said, "By the way, being a biologist; I wonder if he'd be of help to the boys from Georgia Tech."

At dinner Freddie mentioned their encounter with a weird guy named Horace W. F. Smithson. Bill Carson said, "That name sounds familiar. Boys, does it sound familiar to any of you?"

"Wait a minute," Roy said, "Didn't he used to be a college professor somewhere up the coast."

"You're right. He's the one who lost his position for supposedly faking some of his work. My dad said he thought he was framed. The school just found a way to get rid of him because he was getting old and cranky."

Bill said, "I want to meet this guy. We're going out there in the morning."

"If you want me to show the way, I can go with you," Freddie said.

"Too bad you didn't know the way back," Molly said. "Since you've already been there, I'd like to see the place. Just tell me how to get there."

The evening was spent in the new room. They didn't have to put money in the jukebox, just punch the number for the song. Some of them played pool, but Johnny Stevens wanted to dance. He invited Molly, and she accepted. Freddie asked Joanna to dance, and Roy Fillmore, Jr. asked Julia. Cassie and Robert stayed for about thirty minutes, then excused themselves. Freddie winked and said, "Guess they'll dance in their room."

Freddie thought Joanna was beautiful and smart, and he was impressed that she knew another country, for he had never been out of the States. "I would like to go to Israel one day and a lot of other places."

"Israel is lovely, but so is your country. I had no idea how different each state is. Several years ago, my uncle took me to New York to see my mother. It was awkward, but at least I got to be with her for a short time. They said she was looking for my father. About all I remember is crowds of people and bridges across the waterways. It was a confusing place to me. My mother left Israel when I was very young, but I was in a loving home and had many friends. When I was in New York I remember thinking, "Is she going to take me away from my home? Isn't that strange, Freddie?"

"Nope. What that means to me is you were happy where you were."

"Recently I asked Molly about you. She told me about your marriage and the outcome. Be strong, and you will be all right. I knew a lot of young men in Israel, but all they wanted was to marry and have lots of kids. It seemed they are taught to expand the population of Israel. I have always believed there is someone out there for me, and I am willing to wait for that special person. Since the time I was in New York, with my mom, I wondered about my father and why his name was never mentioned in our household. I'm sorry, am I boring you?"

"Of course not. I like hearing you talk. Joanna, would you be agreeable to go out with me sometime?"

"Actually, I talked to my dad about dating, and he looked alarmed. I reminded him that I am past the asking age. He wants what is best for me, but he is so protective."

"Your dad is smart man, his advice was good. When the time comes, perhaps you will consider going to dinner with me?"

"Yes, when it is time."

CHAPTER 64

Horace W. F. Smithson

The next morning, Johnny said, "So who is going with us to seek out Mr. Smithson?" Molly agreed to go with them. "Be careful," Freddie said.

After awhile they found the cabin. "Dr. Smithson," Johnny yelled. No answer. "Dr. Horace W. F. Smithson, are you there?"

A voice yelled, "Who in the hell wants to know?"

"Georgia Tech Students; they want to talk to you." They waited.

"Come on out, Dr. Smithson, I'm Molly Winchester. These boys want to talk to you. By the way, you sent our friends the wrong way back to the inn. That wasn't nice of you. If fact, they are mad at you."

He stepped out of the door. "They found their way back, so no harm done."

"Dr. Smithson, I'm Johnny, and these are my friends, Bill, Jerry, and Roy. You just met Molly. Can we come inside?"

"Nope. What do you want with me?"

"We want to know what you are studying. We came to do some studies ourselves, maybe you could help us."

"What kind of studying?"

"The environment out here: animals, plants, etcetera.

"Etcetera is a pretty wide field of study."

"Well, help them narrow it down," Molly said.

"Little gal, see what you got me into calling me out here."

"Sir, I am *not* a little gal. I am a Midshipman at the Naval Academy, so have some respect for me, or I'll holler *attention*!"

"I bet you would. Come on in. Might as well get this over with. How did you know it was me, boys?"

Roy said, "My father is a professor at Duke. He told me about you. I'm glad we found you. He thought you were treated poorly."

"Damn idiots. They did not fire me! I quit."

Looking around the room, they saw all kinds of pots with plants in them, and there were species of flowers and animal skins hanging from the ceiling. Pieces of paper were plastered on the walls, and piles of animal skins were spread out on a table. "How long have you been out here?" Molly asked.

"Where did you boys find this good looking Cadet?"

"Are you trying to be Henry David Thoreau?" She asked.

"What if I am? This is not Walden Woods; it is more interesting."

"Dr. Smithson, what if these Tech students could study with you this summer? Looks like you need some help."

"I do *not* need help, and I am not looking for respect either. You can forget the Doctor shit. Why do you want to study out here?"

"Because we're interested, but she has to return to the Academy. She wants to be a JAG lawyer."

"She is a bit better looking than the four of you. Too bad she cannot stay."

"These are good boys," Molly said, "Why don't you make this summer interesting for them?"

"I think you are going to be an admiral. You have spunk."

"Thank you, sir," and she saluted.

"Stop that. I am not in the Navy."

"Well, what do you say, sir?" Johnny asked.

"All right, but I do not like people knowing where I am. You have to tell your parents, but that is all. You can stay with me for two weeks, if you behave yourselves. Bring your own bedding and food, unless you want to eat squirrel, and plan to work."

"Yes, Sir, thank you Sir," all of them said.

"It is not going to be easy. I am not used to company."

They went back to the inn, and spent the afternoon down at the river. Molly didn't care to go with them. She wanted to spend time with Joanna and Julia.

"Joanna, what are your plans?"

"Right now I am getting used to America and my father. I fear he enjoys treating me like a child. I keep reminding him I am of age. He seems to be trying to make up for times he missed. You asked about my plans? I cannot walk into a school and apply for a teaching job, but right now my father and I are thinking and planning. He is trying to find an investment project for us. Maybe we could start a business, or create something. We are doing a lot of searching."

Julia said, "I am certain you will find the right career. Take it easy. Your dad is a smart man, and he will guide you in the right direction. Speaking of direction, I enjoyed talking to those boys last night, but who would ever want to spend the summer with a man named Horace W. F. Smithson? It's not often you hear of someone our age giving up their summer to wallow in the mud. I could fall for a guy who has that kind of spunk."

"You know absolutely nothing about them, except talking to them this weekend," Molly said.

"Oh, can't I think out loud?" Julia asked. "This is a fun weekend, except for hurting my foot. Guess I'll have to let my doctor look at it. I want the two of you to know that I am enjoying being with you. Thanks for planning everything, Molly. The last few years have been havoc for me, and I never thought I would be able to say these words, but I am finally learning how to relax."

"Julia, you have been very brave. Both you and my brother Freddie deserve to have good years from now on," Molly said. "Good luck in medical school. Joanna, you have a big dream. You can do anything your heart desires."

"I do not know how to find work here, but listening to your plans, I am beginning to think I need to do some planning on my own."

"Hey, you're becoming an American fast. Go girl!"

"The two of you have inspired me."

Molly interrupted her, "Anything you would like to do, besides teaching?"

"Well, in Israel I designed some clothes, and had a company produce them. It was more or less a fancy of mine. How does *Designs by Joanna* sound to you?"

"Wow! Who would ever guess, a designer in our midst? That would be wonderful," Julia said. "I'll be your first customer. I'll need something other than scrubs when I'm off duty. You know, I believe your dad would go for a designing career. Drop it to him when you get home, and let us know what he says."

"I will *drop it* to him." They all laughed at her expression.

Before they left the inn, everyone congratulated Charlie on his expansion and his hospitality. "We'll be back soon," Johnny Stephens said, "and we might have to come over here when we get tired of eating squirrel."

CHAPTER 65
Joanna

Returning to their Condo was a bit of a let down for Joanna. She realized she needed company other than her father, but he would be hurt if she told him. So she said to him, "What a super nice weekend we had, and such interesting personalities. I am becoming friends with Julia and Molly, and both of them are poised for interesting careers. Father, in Israel, I designed some clothes and they sold rather easily. I believe I have a yen for that kind of art. How would I start such a career in the states?"

"Wow, I am surprised you never told me. *A yen*, where did you pick that up?"

"From the girls this weekend. I like the expression. Father, there are a lot of things we have not talked about. I have decided, I do not wish to be a teacher. I talked to Molly and Julia about designing, and they were most enthusiastic."

"All right let us look into it. You might need to study with someone to understand the process and the business?"

"That is a possibility, but that was not necessary in Israel. Of course business may be more complicated here."

"Look, if you would like to try it, we have money to take the adventure. We can search for someone to help you get started, probably in New York. Do you still have copies of the designs you made in Israel?"

"Not here, but I can get my family to send them to me. I kept them rolled up in my room. I will call my Bubbe right now.

"Bubbe, this is Joanna. Yes.... Yes.... Of course...me too. I need a favor. I need you to mail to me the drawings of the designs I made a few years ago. Yes... Could be... Doing fine... Miss you. Thank you, Bubbe. I am sorry I awoke you. I will be more conscious about the time change from now on."

"Well, that was easy. Was she excited to hear from you?"

"Oh, yes. Perhaps we can bring her to the States one day, though I would have to convince her she is not too old to travel."

"We could go over and fly back with her," Roger said. "So she knows where the drawings are?"

"Yes. She has looked at them many times, and would always shake her head and say, 'Impossible, Impossible.'

While waiting for the copies, Joanna bought the necessary supplies to begin to draw. The clothes had an old fashioned Asian hint about them, and were unlike the clothes hanging on the racks in the local stores. There were wrapped skirts, lots of scarves, and some of the pants were pleated and banded at the ankles. Shirts were longer in the back, and were cut on the bias. And with her coloring pens she used wild, vivid colors. Though he did not say it to Joanna, Roger was a little worried whether her designs would sell in the States.

———

In a few days he package from Bubbe arrived, still in neat rolls as she had left them. Opening them, one at a time, was like watching a parade of women on the runway at a show. Even Roger was impressed. For once he was excited and felt the fear of failure flow from him. "These are pleasing. Indeed, they are excellent. Joanna, we must move with caution. We have to find out if they have been copied in Israel. So we must get a patent, or register the designs, or whatever ones does, to protect them."

"I am so proud you like the designs."

"There is much we have to do. I need to get the advice of lawyer, and then we will have to find you a business location and a staff?"

"You mean this soon? Father, first I need to think about finding a pattern maker, a seamstress, and the materials. I believe I can get the same company in Israel to make them, but we need to slow down while I work on more designs."

"You have your mother's looks and talents. We will make this happen, but you are right, we have a lot to do."

For the next few weeks, Joanna worked in creating new designs. Roger had to remind her to eat. She said, "I must create one very different design that will be made first, and I do not have it yet, so I am becoming a little disappointed. Maybe I need to think, see a movie, walk the streets, or go out to dinner with someone. What do you think dad?"

"What! A date? Am I old fashioned to think the male makes that call?"

"Sure you are. I am going to call Freddie Winchester and ask him out to dinner. No, you cannot go with us, and no, this will not be a sexual arrangement. It will be an evening out to clear my head."

"There is a lot of good ideas up there in that head of yours, and I want you to be focused on ideas right now."

"I have a good idea," she said. "Do you have someone you would like to take to dinner so you will quit worrying about me?"

"Let me think about it. My first choice would be Margaret, but she is already involved with Bob Barnett. Seems as if I always lose to another man, but I miss little Michael. There is *one* lady I admire from a distance. Maybe I will call her sometime."

"A lady, give me a name? Why not call her now? "

"Not yet, to both. Call Freddie and see if he is available, then call the guard to let him in."

"I am calling Freddie now. Freddie, how would you like to go out to dinner tonight? Okay. Good. Father, he knows the routine to get in. He said he would be here in thirty or forty minutes. How do you like being a Father? I have been meaning to ask you a question? Do you mind if I start calling you Dad? All my new friends use that expression. It seems more American."

"I love it! Dad it is. I love every minute I have with you, but if anything happens to you that would be the end of me.

"Oh, that is so sweet. I need to get dressed. Now I do not want you to be anxious."

"I used to tell my dad the same thing and it got me you."

"I want to hear that story one day."

"Never! It hurts to remember it, besides I missed all those years with you."

"Fa…Dad, we are together now. It all worked out, except you still miss my mother. From what you have told me, she would want you to have fun."

"Yes, she actually said that to me."

Freddie called from the lobby, and Roger invited him up. "Hello Mr. Waddell, is Joanna ready?"

"Not yet. This is Joanna's first evening out with an American guy, better make it a safe one."

"Yes sir, I understand. We men are terrible, aren't we?"

"Do not mock me, son, just have a good time." He whispered low, "Ask her what she's planning on doing."

Freddie asked, "She isn't leaving to go back to Israel is she?"

"Not right now. Here is my beautiful daughter." He watched as Freddie's eyes nearly popped out of his head when he saw Joanna.

I have to let her do this. Nothing is going to be easy any more. How well I remember. The day I left for the States, I literally bawled all the way. Leaving Roberta hurt so bad my throat was sore for weeks. I could still feel her kisses and the glorious entering of her body. I believed there would never be anyone else. I wanted to run away, but I had never hurt my parents, so I obeyed them and left for the states. Why did I not write to Roberta? I must have believed she would get on with her life, a life without me.

As Joanna and Freddie left, Roger said, "Just have a good time. Freddie, you are welcome to come in for a while when you get back, if you have time."

"Yes, sir. Thank you, sir."

CHAPTER 66

Georgia Parker

An eerie silence filled the room. He picked up a book, but put it down. He knew he would have to start again, somehow.

I have lost touch with young people today, but from what I read they are much bolder than when I was young, yet I am frightened for Joanna. I cannot lose her again. Well, I might as well call someone to go out with. Only woman I know who is not presently committed is Georgia Parker.

He picked up the phone, put it down, and picked it up again, "Georgia Parker, this is Roger Waddell. I believe we met a good while back. I am wondering if you are available for dinner this evening."

"Roger Waddell, most eligible bachelor in Atlanta. What inspired you to call?"

"Well, I just saw my daughter go out to dinner with a man, and I am lonesome and tense. She has hardly left my side for months. I am sure it was about time for her to do this, but it worries me."

"Isn't she old enough to make her own decisions?"

"Does that matter? Back to the dinner, you did not say yes. Is that a no?"

"Do you always make dates at the last minute?"

"Cannot say that I do, since I have not made a date in so long."

"Poor little rich guy. Well, I'm interested. Where do you want to meet?"

"Meet? Is that the way it is done now?"

"You really are lost. Okay, I will come to your place since I know you want to be there when your daughter gets back. I'll pick up dinner along the way. Okay?"

"That would be fine. Let me tell you how to get here."

"Roger, I know where you live, my favorite guy lives there."

"I am not going to ask who that is."

"Give me thirty or forty minutes." By that time, Roger was sweating. He thought about calling her back and cancelling, but he knew he had to wait.

———

The evening was exciting for Freddie and Joanna. Freddie felt he had been given a new chance, and Joanna felt free to be herself. They ate at a little café not too far from the condo, and were nearly the last ones to leave. Joanna said, "Food tastes better when you are sharing it with someone else. Do you agree?"

"I agree. Though this is our first time alone with each other, we've been together with family and friends, and there was the weekend at the inn. Joanna, I need to go slow with my personal life right now, but I would like to get to know you."

"Well, slow will be good, especially for my dad." They both laughed. "Freddie, I am about to go on a great adventure. In Israel, I designed some clothes that sold very well, and I am hoping to enter the designing business full time."

"Whew, I thought you were going to say you were going back to Israel."

"I will be going back for a while to reconnect with the company who sold my first designs. I may have the clothes made and sold there, and but also sell them here. Dad will back me, so there are no financial worries. I will have to publicize my product, which means I have to be visible over there for a while. If they sell in Israel I am certain there will be a market here."

"Joanna, that's wonderful. I'm proud to know a designer. I hope you don't think I am too forward, but I have dreams of loving again one day. I feel honored that you shared your plans with me. I wish you success in your renewed adventure, but don't forget the people here who have learned to love you." He rose from the table and gave her a hug. She did not know what to say, but relaxed in his arms. Somehow it felt good to be caressed by a man other than her Dad.

Driving back to the condo their talk was light and awkward. Both of them had a lot of thinking and planning to do. He went up with her to their condo to say goodnight to Mr. Waddell, for Freddie knew he would be waiting. They both got a surprise to find a woman with him. "Joanna, Freddie, this is Georgia Parker. I asked her to come over tonight to keep me company."

"He's serious," Georgia said. "I had to hold his hand while the two of you were out. Now that you are back maybe I should go."

"Please stay longer," Roger said, "I have enjoyed your company."

"Well, that's old fashioned enough." She sat down, "I'd love to stay longer."

Freddie said good night to them, and Joanna walked him to the lobby. When she returned she sat a few minutes to learn about Georgia, and then made an excuse to leave the room, "Maybe I need to get back to the drawing board."

Georgia said, "Your dad told me about your designs. I would like to take a peek at them, if I may." When Joanna laid them in front of her, Georgia was speechless, but not for long. "I've never met a designer, but I buy their clothes, so I can tell you these are marvelous. I wish to be the first to wear this outfit," pointing to her latest design.

"*That*, Ms. Parker may be my signature, and even Dad has not seen it yet. I wanted him to be surprised."

"Wait a minute," Roger said, "now I have to see it." She placed it on the table in front of him, and he was totally stunned. "This is it, Joanna, this is it! The banker will pay for this one."

"Can I be a partner? Please, please, Joanna," Georgia begged.

"I don't know, talk to my banker-dad."

"Well, Joanna if I can be of any help just let me know."

"Joanna, you will need a lawyer, right?" Roger asked. Ms. Parker will you consider being her attorney?"

"What an opportunity! If that is the only way I can get inside this company, I'm ready. Yes, I will consent to be your attorney."

"Thank you, Ms. Parker, I might need you. Oh, yes, thanks for Dad-sitting. I have some designs to work on. Good night to both of you."

"What a beautiful daughter, actually she is absolutely stunning. You're going to have to turn her loose one day."

"I will get her started in business first," Roger said. Georgia stayed late, and both of them enjoyed talking. When she rose to go, she put her arms around his neck, and kissed him on the cheek. For a minute he felt awkward, but he enjoyed her touch. "You still have it in you, Roger. I enjoyed this evening with you. Maybe we can arrange another last minute meeting."

"We will," he said. "I feel I should drive you home."

"Why not? I'll leave my car here, and you can pick me up in the morning for breakfast. I don't work on Saturdays."

"I will need to tell Joanna."

"She'll hear the door close, don't you think?"

Roger didn't talk much along the way, but Georgia filled the silence. Finally they arrived at her home. "Georgia, this is a beautiful place."

"Why don't you come inside and see the rest of it?" It was indeed beautiful outside and in. "You have exquisite taste," Roger said, "Maybe I should have hired you to decorate my condo."

"What are you talking about? Can't you see Margaret's signature? She is the best in town. Your place is great. I'm just glad she didn't allow you to make it into a man-cave." He frowned. "You don't know what a man-cave is, do you?"

"No, the term is not familiar, but I get it. How do you always know the right words to say, Georgia? I have enjoyed this evening, and I am *quite* surprised by admitting that. Maybe getting out of the nest for an evening helped."

"Come here, Roger. When we hugged earlier tonight, you were a bit stiff. I think you can do better than that." He did not feel awkward kissing her. It was the first time in a long time he felt the urge to go further, if only a fleeting moment. He was a bit embarrassed, for he was sure she felt his erection. "Roger, one of these days you are going to have to tell me about the wonderful woman who captured your heart so completely, but perhaps there is someone else who can make you surrender again."

"I am sure there is, Georgia. Tonight has been great. Can I pick you up about 10:00 for breakfast?" She winked at him and said, "I'll be waiting."

Both Roger and Joanna awoke early. "Last night was a lovely evening, Dad, and you have nothing to worry about. I told Freddie my new adventure would require me to spend time in Israel, and he talked about starting over. But this I must say to you, he is not the one for me. I will let you know when I find that person."

"I am somewhat relieved," Roger said. "Freddie needs time to distance himself from his recent experiences, and he needs to mature. Joanna, I believe you and I are going to spend some sweet time in Israel. I am actually looking forward to seeing your sassy grandmother again."

"You can help me get started, but you will not need to stay long."

"I am the banker, and bankers watch their money."

"Then shall we leave in a few days, and get everything started? I am hoping to employ the same people, so I need to make phone calls tonight, but I have to watch the time zones. Dad, did you enjoy being with Ms. Parker? I liked her. She has quality, and I bet she is an exciting woman."

"I know," he answered her, "I am surprised to admit I felt an attraction to her. To be honest with you, I am a bit excited. We are going out to breakfast this morning, and then we will come back here to get her car. See you later."

Georgia was waiting for him. She opened the door and said, "It's been a long time since last night. I missed you. We are eating in. I don't have the desire to be in the crowd of people who eat out on Saturday mornings." She recognized how nervous he was, "Sit down and try my coffee, if that doesn't wake you, I might have to pinch you. I am impressed with your daughter. You are lucky to have a child. A child was not in my horoscope, but neither of my husbands would have made a good father, lucky for me. Well, I haven't given you a minute to say anything. Your time to talk."

"Joanna is a perfect jewel. These past few months I have dreamed of re-writing my life story just to hold her in my arms when she was a baby. That is why I give her a lot of hugs. Georgia, I loved my wife Roberta. She had her reasons for not revealing that I was a father. She must have realized I would not be able to take care of a child, since I was only a teenager at the time Joanna was conceived. And she was right. By the time Roberta and I met in New York, Joanna was happy in her surroundings in Israel. Most likely Roberta did not want to interrupt her life. Those are the best possibilities I can imagine. To describe Roberta I would have to say she was both beautiful and exotic. We had some great years together." He paused. She died of breast cancer as I held her in my arms. I do not know if telling you all that was a good idea, but for some reason I wanted you to know. Georgia, you are beautiful, smart, and interesting, and Joanna called you exciting." He paused, "I cannot believe I told you that."

"Thanks for trusting me with your story. I'll accept beautiful, smart and interesting, but if you had added *exotic*, I would have known you were lying."

"I am rather anxious right now. Being so near you is - well it is unnerving. You are the kind of person any man would be happy to take you to bed, and I am one of those men, but this does not seem the right time. I will be leaving for Israel shortly, and we would not be able to follow up."

"Follow up? How unromantic is that? But I can wait. Just don't follow up with some gal in Israel while I wait here."

"If Joanna and I should need your help, would you be able to fly over? You may not know this, I was an attorney for a very brief time, but I do not care to discuss those boring months. Would you have the time to brush up on the laws of Israel concerning marketing of goods?"

"Yes, I will come. In the meantime, I will research and see what I can find. I have no urgent clients right now, but if anything comes up, I'll turn it over to Bob Barnett."

"He was a classmate of mine."

"I know that."

'Will you come to Israel even if *I* am the one who needs you and not Joanna?"

"In that case, I will come quicker."

"You are amazing," Roger said. "How could I be so lucky? May I kiss you?"

"Usually the guy doesn't ask, he just grabs the gal, pulls her toward him, and lays one on her."

"I am not up to date on all this. Can I start over? He moved toward her, took her hand and gently raised it to his lips. Without a word he opened two buttons on her blouse to be able to kiss her neck and shoulder. From there he moved slowly to her lips. He was totally lost in the majesty of the kiss. He stood back, took her by the shoulders and said, "That was not rehearsed; it was for real. Is this where the guy sweeps the lady off her feet and carries her into the bedroom?"

"Not unless the guy completely loses his mind."

"Georgia, I do not want to start something just when I am about to leave. I desire you, and that is an understatement. I am looking for something more than a sexual relationship, a partner who is successful in her own right, but who might enjoy cooking breakfast for me some Saturday mornings, and maybe sit up late with me. At this moment I believe you are that person."

"No man has ever said those un-romantic words to me, but I like them. Oh, that was a silly remark, but I meant what I said. Okay, go to Israel, and in two weeks send for me. By that time I'll have my schedule in order."

"Wonderful idea. Have you ever been to Israel?"

"No, but knowing you and Joanna will be there, I'm looking forward to being there. Two weeks is a long time. Give me a kiss that will hold me 'til then." It was settled; they would meet soon. It was as if one of them was going off to war, and the other would remain faithful.

Joanna contacted her former pattern cutter and her seamstress, and they were excited about renewing business with her. The next day she called Paula Bergman, the owner of the company who produced her designs before, and she also sounded eager, "Joanna, you must come as soon as possible. We have to be ready for the marketing season." That evening Joanna arranged the designs in her attaché case, and started packing.

CHAPTER 67
Israel

Business had taken longer than expected. Roger thought there was red tape in the United States, but he discovered Israel has its own ways of delaying business. He called Georgia every day to let her know their progress. Finally, after twenty-one days there wasn't anything left for her to do, but he wanted her there.

He was on edge waiting for the plane to land, and waiting was never his best attribute. He paced back and forth for an hour – from desk to gate, inquiring why the plane was delayed. Finally, an employee motioned him to the desk, "Sir, the plane is landing. She must be a special person." He stood at the incoming passenger's gate and waited, folding and unfolding his arms. Georgia ran to him, and they kissed right in front of everyone. Some people applauded. Georgia said, "We were on the ground in Atlanta for such a long time. The man sitting beside me, on the window side, said officers were removing some luggage from the plane. Then two officers came aboard and removed two men off the plane. I did *not* have a good feeling, but here I am."

"Georgia, there are no words to explain how excited I am to see you. Since that last night, I have kicked myself for going home so early. I know you must be thinking how soon this is, but I am in love. I have waited a long time for someone like you."

"Roger, Roger, not now; people are listening."

"Listen everybody, I am in love. I am in love with this beautiful lady. It is all right if you applaud." And they did.

"I don't imagine this happens too often here," Georgia said.

"It happens all the time," a stranger answered. "It must be the air."

The wait for transportation wasn't long, and soon they arrived at the hotel where he and Joanna were staying. "I see you have two bedrooms."

"Naturally, may I introduce you to one of them?"

"So soon?"

"What do you mean, 'so soon?' It has been a lifetime. Let me help you with your luggage." He placed the luggage on the floor and approached her. "If you need to wash up, I can wait."

"You don't know how to say 'pee?' "

"It is not a word I use."

"Don't we need to shut the door?"

"I will, but Joanna will not arrive until evening. Georgia, it has been a long time since I have been in bed with a woman, but I do not want you to believe that sex is all I want. Here is my proclamation: I want to watch you walk across the room, sneak a peek as you lie asleep - nude or covered head to toe in a flannel gown. I want to catch you from behind as you attempt to make an omelet. One day soon, I want to see you in action in the courtroom. It will be a thrill to observe the person known as one of the meanest and best lawyers in Atlanta."

"If you do decide to come to the courthouse let me know first. I don't want to be upended by your presence. Now moving on, it's been a long time for me also, Roger, but I suspect we will remember how to proceed with a ritual as old as time, but new for us this time."

They lay on the bed face to face, searching for clues in each other's faces. *He thought of Roberta, on the riverbank so many years ago, and again in their quaint little Inn in Maine. As if a page of his life turned without his permission, the beautiful image he had carried in his heart for so very long, but could not touch, seemed to drift away. He knew the person lying beside him was a gift for a new life, one that would be different, but just as exciting.*

She looked at the man who was about to devour her life. She knew he would love her like no other man had ever loved her. He would be faithful and never ask her to give up the things she loved and the people she served. She would be happy with this man who asked nothing of her but to love him.

Their laughter broke the silence. "It is nice lying here together in another country with only ourselves to think of. Georgia, what is your pleasure? I will do anything for you."

"Though that's a crazy question, I can be receptive to it. I want you to make me forget there is a courtroom out there, or former husbands. I want your undivided attention. Turn me away from anything that takes our minds from this room. I want you to search my body, so there are no secrets. It's an old body, but it's mine to give."

"Old body? Are you kidding? I have said the words *I love you* to three other women in my life, my mother, Roberta, and Joanna, and my heart says I should say it now, so I will. Georgia, I have been looking for you. I knew you were out there somewhere; I just had to wait. How can I be in love with you so suddenly? I do not know, but I know in my heart those are the words I must say. I love you. I want you to be a part of my life. The day you can say those words to me, I will search no more."

"Roger, why would a woman go half way around the world just to shake hands with a man she hasn't been intimate with? Why were those weeks apart like two years? I don't want an affair - here today and gone tomorrow. I want to hear a man say *I love you* and know that he is sincere. I'm certain you could have any woman in Atlanta, but I'm thrilled to be the one you love. If all those words made sense, I meant them to say I love you. I admire you for the pride you have for Joanna. I like the way you and your long-life friends share your lives. I respect your reticence in Atlanta to throw me in the bed. I cherish your parting question in Atlanta, 'If *I* am the one who needs you, will you come?' You know, I believe we both hit the jackpot."

He did exactly what she wanted. He saw every part of her body, the slightly limp breasts with brown nipples, a tiny roll of fat around her waist, one crooked toe, smooth skin, a faded appendectomy scar, the most perfectly shaped lips, flashing auburn hair, and beautiful brown eyes. His hands floated across her body, until finally she rose up, put his face into her hands, and brought his mouth to hers. Frantic with passion, their bodies exploded. After a short silence he said, "I'm sorry, but it has been so long for me, and I have been imagining the thrill since we last met."

"That body search may have lasted too long. Roger, we have these days here and many more years to enjoy each other." That afternoon both of them reveled in celebrating new love. There were not enough words to explain it.

Joanna came home about dusk, and was thrilled to see Georgia and her dad preparing dinner. She ran to Georgia, hugged her, then stepped back and said, "If he did not ask you, I will. Will you be my mom?"

"He did, and I will. How's that?"

"This calls for a celebration. I brought the perfect wine." That evening the three of them told stories and reveled in the discovery of each other. Roger sat watching the two women he loved. He realized that Joanna would be on her own one day, and suddenly the fear of that happening disappeared. Finding Joanna had made him the happiest man in the world, he was sure of it, now he saw these two strong women changing his life. Happy was not the best word for him now. He wallowed in anticipation.

That evening Joanna suggested they return to the states in about a week. By that time she would have completed all the necessary preparations to make her debut successful, and she was pleased with her product. Now she wanted to get away from the stress, and let the women finish their work.

It was a week Georgia would never forget. As a child, she had sat in church pews trying to imagine those distant, holy places, Jerusalem, the Wailing Wall, and Bethlehem. She and Roger rented a car and visited those and other notable places for three days. They went to see the Jordan River, and she put her foot into the water. She said to Roger, "It's like seeing the stories of the Bible come alive. My grandmother used to say, 'if only I could see Bethlehem before I die,' but it didn't happen."

"Perhaps you are seeing it for her. So you know the Scriptures?"

"Not very well, but I have memories. I haven't been to worship in years, but this makes me want to go when I return to Atlanta. I know seeing is not believing, but it is *very* close."

"We can do that. My mother would be proud if I went with you."

They would have stayed longer in Israel, but the Sabbath was the next day, and they wanted to leave before the restrictions began. There was plenty to see as they drove to Tel Aviv. Georgia called their trip the pre-honeymoon.

On the flight Georgia whispered to Roger, "Was this week too good to be true?"

"No," he answered. "Every minute with you was perfect, and we will remember it, always."

The flight was long and tedious. When they landed Roger wanted to kiss the ground as he had read in a book somewhere. They strolled to the baggage section, the threesome – a proud man with a beautiful lady on each arm. He said, "What a lucky man I am. Look! People are admiring us." Georgia said, "If you say so." Roger wondered what would happen when they arrived home. Would Georgia have to go to her home? "Georgia, is your car at the airport?" She answered, "No I took a cab. I assumed you would be taking me home, I mean to my house, but perhaps home is where you are."

Roger said, "Home? You have raised a subject I was afraid to ask. I am sure you have things that must be done."

"And you don't?"

"I can think of a few things." After dropping Joanna off, they drove to her place. On the way he asked, "Georgia, what do you see as our immediate plans?"

She responded, "I thought about that during the flight. I need a couple of days to catch up at the office. How about picking me up Thursday morning so we can go to the courthouse to get our marriage license?"

"That sound like a good plan. I will spend Wednesday night with you, so you do not back out."

"Don't joke about this, Roger; there is no turning back. I meant what I just said about home being where you are. Don't you think we should call your friends? I want them to be a part of this."

"They are your friends now. I will call them tomorrow. I hate leaving you, even for one evening."

"Then call Joanna and tell her you won't be home tonight."

"Good idea."

Waiting for them at the courthouse, on Thursday, were Joan, Randy, Frederick, Elizabeth, Bob, Margaret, and Joanna. "What in the world?" Roger asked.

"Well you did call and tell me, 'we are getting our license Thursday at11:00 at the courthouse.' That directness appeared to be clear to me," Randy said.

"This is not the ceremony, you know. Maybe I should ask for a vote on the marriage date," Roger said.

The clerk looked surprised when the whole group came to her desk, "You know witnesses are not required to get a marriage license."

"Really, we must have been misinformed." Randy said, and they all laughed.

After the documents were signed, Joan asked, "Does anyone have to get back to the office today?" They all said they did not. "How about riding out to Maud's Inn for lunch. Actually, I've already called Charlie."

"Sneaky, sneaky, Joan. Are we getting rooms?" Roger asked.

"No, it's just a celebration. Come on, I have hired a limousine. Charlie will be waiting for us."

"Limousine? Joan, you are amazing," Roger said.

Indeed, Charlie was waiting. He and his caretaker had thrown strips of red papers all over the lobby, candles were everywhere, and the jukebox was booming from the back room. When Sarah came out of the kitchen with a cake, Georgia said, "What the hell!"

Sarah said, "Georgia, you may not know this, but Roger is special to me and Charlie. The three of us sort of bonded when we took a long trip together. He'll have to tell you about it one day. We put our lives in the hands of this fellow, but never ever thought he would get married, so it's time to celebrate. You must be some lady."

Georgia turned to Roger, "Are your friends going to be everywhere after we are married?" Roger said, "Perhaps. It may be hard for you to get used to them, but we have shared our lives so long we do not function well without each other."

"Welcome to the family, Georgia," Elizabeth said, "When is the wedding date?"

Roger looked at Georgia, "Well?" She said, "As soon as possible. Is next week too soon?" Elizabeth said, "Perfect. Is this a good place?"

Roger said, "A perfect place. Ole Charlie knows how to plan a wedding and Sarah knows how to do the ceremony. When are you available, Sarah?"

"How about Thursday evening next week?" Everyone raised their glasses, and said, "a toast to Thursday." Georgia was speechless. She laughed and shook her head in disbelief. "Don't worry, my dear Georgia," Bob said. "You are now a member of our family, so you can call your cousin, Georgette, and tell her to get lost."

"What's that story?" Joan asked.

"You might want Margaret to tell you that one," Bob said. Right Margaret?"

"Pay no attention to him, Georgia."

Randy said, "Since we are not privy to that information, let's move on."

The trip back to Atlanta was a let down. Randy said, "Every time I go to Maud's Inn I wonder why all of us don't build houses out there. No, I'm just kidding; it's more fun to visit. Georgia, we are glad to have you with us. I hope you can stand the thrill of it all, but it's not like you are a stranger. You have worked with Bob, Frederick, and me, and now you can work with Roger. It's going to be a good marriage. Ole Roger is an easy touch."

"Georgia," Roger said, "I have known these guys and gal since I was a teenager, and they have never changed, and never will. You already know too much about us, so I believe you will fit right in." They all said, "Hear, hear."

CHAPTER 68

Roger and Georgia

There were no invitations to the wedding, just a few personal calls. All their friends were there plus Joanna, and four of Georgia's colleagues and her office staff. Roger's friend Justin and his wife Sasha traveled from Cyprus on quick notice. Roger suggested that Charlie not decorate the Inn, but asked him to hire a string quartet to play from the balcony. Rev. Sarah Marshall used her special litany for the event. She asked Roger and Georgia's friends to tell one story each about them. Justin's comments received the most laughter with his tales of two poor little rich boys learning about life all over the world. Charlie told the story of three strangers planning a trip, and Frederick painted the picture of the skinny young man who came out of nowhere, and dropped into their college lives. Georgia's friends gave some interesting stories about her. Bob Barnett interrupted, "Oh my gosh! Georgia, you forgot to invite your jealous cousin, Georgette."

"Bob, you will never forget, will you?" Georgia said.

When Sarah asked the usual "do you take" questions, all the friends, including Justin, responded with him, "We do." Georgia asked again, "So this what I have to live with the rest of my life?"

"Yes," they answered. She could tell their responses pleased Roger so she said, "Well if that's the way it is, so let be it."

After the ceremony Roger walked over to Bob Barnett, "When is your wedding, Bob? Is it any time soon?"

"Conditions are complicated, Roger, too damned complicated."

"Complicated, hell! Everything worthwhile is complicated. Do not mess up your relationship with Margaret, she is a special woman."

"You ought to know."

"What does that mean? If you are insinuating that I had a relationship with her, you are wrong. I helped Margaret out in her worst times, and she will always be my friend. Get that? Always."

"All right, all right, so I'm an idiot. It's the child, not Margaret."

"If you love someone, the child comes with it."

"Just get off my back, will you? I'm too old to raise another child."

Roger said, "All right, you need to tell Margaret that, and move on." He walked away. When Bob went outside Roger went over to Margaret, "What is this 'complicated' noise Bob talked about when I asked him about marriage? Are you and Bob on track?"

"This is not the time to talk about it."

"When is a good time? You two are perfect for each other."

"I do love him, and I know he loves me, so maybe he'll change now that you've married. I believe he has always been jealous of you, and he doesn't seem to be comfortable with Michael."

"You are a fantastic woman, Margaret, and I enjoyed being with you and Michael. I will always have a special relationship with Michael, and I hope you are my friend forever. Bob will just have to figure that out."

"I've told him that, but with one disaster behind him, he over analyzes everything on earth."

"Then perhaps you need to move on, since he is afraid to commit?"

"I've thought about that, but I don't want to lose him."

"Is he good in bed, Margaret?"

"That's a little forward, don't you think? But the answer is *yes*."

"At least that works, but it is not enough, is it?"

"No, but it helps."

"Margaret, move on. Sex is a wee part of marriage."

"Yep, very wee with Leonard - only enough to get Michael. So I didn't have sex, and now I do. I doubt I'll ever find both in one man. Thanks, Roger for letting me get these words out in the open. Move on, here comes my dilemma and my lover."

After the wedding, Roger and Georgia spent the night at Maud's Inn, then decided to stay at Georgia's house a couple of days until they decided where they wanted to go and how to rearrange their lives. Their picture appeared in the society section of the Atlanta paper with the headline, ATTORNEY GEORGIA PARKER WEDS WEALTHY ENTREPRENEUR ROGER WADDELL. Roger was embarrassed, but Georgia said to him, "Dude, in Atlanta that's a compliment."

"You guess they will be flashing their cameras everywhere we go?"

"Get over it. The truth is, society news fades fast in Atlanta."

"This is going to be fun. I have hit the jackpot and proud of it. Georgia thanks for coming into my life, and I love your humor. First I found Joanna then you. How could a man be so lucky? Making love with you is unbelievable. You send me into some sort of space I have been longing to find for years, and sex is not the proper word for I what I feel."

"I don't know about your finding me. I noticed you a long time ago. That night you called me I was waiting by the phone saying, *call me, Roger Waddell, call me, damn it, call me.*"

"How often do you lie? I need to know now."

"Not very often, only when it's appropriate." Their decision was not to go out of town until later, and of course a lot depended on Georgia's schedule, so Roger reserved a suite in the Ritz Carlton for a week, calling it a neutral residence until they could decide where they wanted to live. Georgia had a good offer on her house, and Joanna left for Israel immediately after the wedding, so two situations out of the way for the time being. Roger liked where he lived, and Georgia was ready for condo living. He was hoping a small unit would open up for Joanna in his building, if she would be agreeable. He wanted her near, but not in the condo with them.

The Ritz Carlton proved to be the perfect neutral place to reside. They slept and ate whenever they wanted, and depended a lot on room service. One morning Roger said, "Georgia, I want to buy you a present, something our grandchildren will say, 'This jewelry was given to our grandmother by our grandfather to celebrate their wedding.' What would you like?"

"I need nothing and want nothing. That is my answer."

"So you *need* nothing, but I *need* to buy you something. I want you to have a gift, and it must be unique and special, so do not try to stop me."

"I'm taller than you and meaner," she said, "but I yield to your wishes. So let's go out and about, as my mother used to say."

They walked across the street to Saks, a good place to start. It was interesting seeing all the designs in the jewelry cases, but nothing impressed Georgia. A salesman approached them, "I'm Richard Feldman, if I can be of help let me know." Georgia was not interested, so she walked away to look at something else. The salesman was not pushy at all, just a nod and a look that meant, *I will be near if you should have any questions*. Roger liked that about him. He wandered over to a glass-enclosed cabinet, and tried to open it. It is embarrassing to pull on a door of a display cabinet and find it locked; makes one feel like a criminal. Locked cases always mean the items inside are pricey. But Roger was excited. The case held the most beautiful pieces of jewelry he had ever seen. He motioned for Mr. Feldman, held out his hand and said, "Roger Waddell. I am looking for a gift for my new bride, Georgia Parker. There is a long rope of diamonds and pearls wrapped around the mannequin's neck, may I see that?"

"I recognized both of you. I read the Atlanta paper. Let me get the key and I'll be right back." He returned quickly. "We have to keep this case locked, and there is also an alarm on the back side within the case." Holding up the rope with both hands, he called the name of the designer, which meant nothing to Roger. "This is a one-of-a-kind piece. Feel how heavy it is? It is made to put one loop around the neck, like this, he put it on his own neck. See the two large emeralds on each end? When this is wrapped around the neck, with one loop in the front, these two emeralds need to lie on the chest - one about two inches above the other. It is a classic piece with pearls, emeralds, and diamonds entwined with gold. Are you interested, sir?"

"I am, but I need an alternate. How about that bracelet?"

"You have a good eye for jewelry, sir. You can see it has alternating diamonds and rubies, and there is a double clasp for safety."

"I believe she would prefer the bracelet. She is a very modest person when it comes to wearing jewelry, but she is a hell of a lawyer. No modesty there. I believe the bracelet will be excellent."

"If it needs to be adjusted to her wrist, we can do that right away."

He went looking for her, and found her in the shoe department. "Can you leave the shoes alone and come to the back of the jewelry department."

"I like shoes. A girl can never have enough."

"Okay, we will look at shoes later. Come on."

"Georgia, hold you arm out for Mr. Feldman and close your eyes."

"Don't be silly, Roger; I'm not a child."

"No, you are my wife and the most beautiful person in this store. Behave."

Mr. Feldman placed the bracelet on her arm and fastened both safety catches. She was blind and silent for a few seconds. Opening her eyes she said, "Roger, it's lovely and perfect. I don't even own a bracelet. Did you know that?"

"No, I did not. Let Mr. Feldman check and see if it needs adjusting."

"Don't you move, Mr. Feldman you shall not take it off my arm. It is perfect."

"I enjoy meeting a lady who knows her jewelry."

"You like it better than that rope necklace?" Roger pointed to it.

"Good gracious, Roger that's monstrous. It's lovely, but not for me. Mr. Feldman, does this bracelet come with one of those satin-lined boxes? I want it to have a comfortable bed when I'm not wearing it."

"Yes, Madam it does, and with an appraisal to put inside the box for insurance purposes."

"Roger, we need an appraisal!" He said, "I am afraid so."

"Then it's too expensive. I don't want to break you."

"Mr. Feldman, please package the box and the appraisal, and here is my credit card." He returned with the box, the appraisal, and a receipt. "It has been nice working with both of you. You are very much in love. I can always tell. Ms. Parker, the bracelet is lovely on your wrist. If I ever have need for a lawyer I will remember you."

"Just stay out of trouble," she said.

As they left the store she said to Roger, "What did you pay for this bracelet?"

"You do not want to know. Do not lose it."

"So we are not to nose around in each other's business?"

"You got that!"

After the failure of Georgia's two marriages, and the tragedy of Roberta's death, the two of them had found peace and healing. He kissed her when they returned to the room and said, "Let me tell you how I feel at this moment. My mother used to talk about going to revivals when she was growing up in West Virginia, and how she would feel so perfect for a couple of weeks afterward. My father did not understand since revivals are not a Jewish event, but often he goaded her into explaining her feelings. In his life anything that could not be explained was not worth mentioning. She would say something like this, 'we sang until we were exhausted, and we heard what are called testimonies, where people reveal their gift of salvation, or secrets that should best be left at home. Then we walked down the aisle to re-dedicate our lives, supposedly. The preacher would lay his hands on our heads, and pronounce, *you are clean; go and live likewise*. I loved the word likewise, through I did not know exactly what it meant, maybe the same as the word salvation. But the devil could not touch me for a while.'

"My mother would tell that story over and over. It pleased my father to listen to her. He did not believe that was the way to salvation, but if it helped her he was okay with it. My mother said if I wanted to grow up Jewish, she guessed salvation was about the same. The truth is, I never remember them going to a worship service. Sometimes my dad would disappear for a few days to have a conference 'with fellow Jews,' as he would say. I thought he might be going to a revival, but my mom said it was about money. They never encouraged me to attend a church or the synagogue. I am sorry, my dear Georgia, I did not mean to bore you. You are my salvation from years of wandering. Thank you. If Sarah's denomination builds that chapel, I might visit it."

"Roger, I love your mom's story. I'm afraid I can't compete with that. My family has always been Methodist, and I was christened, water sprinkled on our heads, when I was a baby. Being a Methodist seemed like a practical way to salvation. Mostly we went to church on religious holidays, Lent, Palm Sunday, Easter, Pentecost, Advent, Christmas, and a few other Sundays. That's the short history of my religious experience. I agree with you, I could attend a church that welcomes all people. But can we not discuss religion right now? I would like to be your total focus. You have given me hope. Just yesterday I realized I could drop my fear of growing old alone."

"Wow, are we getting old already?"

"Are you making fun of me? I'm serious. Haven't you ever thought of that?"

"No, that is probably a woman thing."

"Don't be silly. What I'm trying to say is I have fallen in love, and suddenly I'm not thinking about aging. I want to live in the now with you. I don't want to think about the past two marriages ever again, and pay off, to get out. I don't care anymore. I have a new life and a lovely daughter. Wherever we live will not matter, as long as you wait up for me when I come home late. Thank you, Roger, for everything. I love you."

"Come close to me. I am proud that you enjoy a profession I detested, and I promise not to fall asleep in the evenings until you come home. I want to be your lover in every way, not just in the bed. But right now, you have excited me, and I must take advantage of it." He kissed her brow and her cheeks, and with his finger played with the suprasternal notch of her throat, then kissed the spot. He caressed her small breasts and slid closer to her. There were no surprises since he had totally discovered her body when they were in Israel. Enchanting was the best word he had for her.

The following day Georgia introduced Roger to things people do in malls, everyone but him. They walked the full length of Lenox Mall, both upstairs and down, sampled candy from a Kiosk, and tried on a dozen pair of sunglasses at another Kiosk. Georgia said, "I feel free, a freedom I can share with the man who is the surprise of my life. My office and courtrooms are far away today. How about you?"

"Well, I have not had an office lately, but I understand what you mean. Though I abandoned the courtroom years ago, I want you to continue your work. I am delighted to be married to the Atlanta Person of the Year. And I am totally surprised I do not worry about Joanna any more. You are the reason for that. It is time to encourage her to do as she wishes. I will support her until she finds success. I hope that does not bother you."

"What's the matter with you? Why don't you re-phrase that sentence, *we* will support Joanna? After all she did ask me if I would be her Mom."

"You are correct; I sincerely apologize. I must remember to talk in the plural from now on. That mistake will not happen again." Later that afternoon they went to a movie at the Tara Theater, shared a giant bag of popcorn, drank a large coke, using two straws, and munched on M&Ms. "Where has all this kind of activity been? I missed out," Roger said.

"Another thing," Georgia said, "You are not supposed to talk during a movie."

"I have been to movies before; I just do not remember when. Such frivolity was not encouraged when I grew up, but being with you is never a waste of time."

That evening, at Georgia's request, they sat in the hotel lounge holding hands while they listened to the pianist. He thought of the hotel his parents had owned, and wondered if they might go there one day. "One day I want us to make a trip to New York. There is something I want to show you."

"What? Tell me, I don't like secrets." He said, "The hotel my parents owned."

"Hotel? You are not kidding, are you?"

"No, but sometimes I am sorry I sold my share to the partners."

CHAPTER 69

Time flies

The next years were proof that time really does fly. Molly, the little girl her Dad's friends had watched grow up, was in her final year at the Naval Academy. She had applied for law school and was accepted at several universities for future entry. Hopefully she could start after she finished her first tour of duty. She was a determined person and had the perfect personality and endurance to be a lawyer. Her brother Freddie still didn't seem to have his life in order, nor did he seem to be working on it. Two children, coming from same uterus, were so different.

Bob was seeing Margaret frequently. He asked Randy's advice about moving in with her, with Becky living there. Randy said, "Bob, I don't see the problem. I believe the two of you can work it out. I am pleased you are considering it."

Julia, the survivor of chaos, was a second-year student at Medical School of Georgia, and she was in love with Roy Fillmore, Jr. who she met at Maud's Inn one summer.

Cassie enjoyed her job at the office with Randy and Ms. Bee. She and Robert were still working on establishing the art scholarship fund. It was not as easy as they expected, but Cassie was determined.

Joanna traveled back and forth to Israel. He clothes were selling well in Israel. She had about decided not to have an office in the States, but her clothes could be bought from their magazine.

Life is good!

Out at the Inn, Horace W. F. Smithson was still on the property. It appears that he had made himself a permanent residence, and it was fine with Charlie, since he didn't bother anyone. His four students from Georgia Tech returned to visit him several times while in College. Smithson had worked them hard, and they formed a strange bond. At times "the professor" came out of him as he taught them. He was proud his work showed promise, and believed he had found the old bed of the Chattahoochee River. By luck one of the students dug up a strange creature that appeared to be some sort of fish. Smithson would search for its identity. Their biggest find happened one weekend when Roy stepped into a hole up to his knees. It appeared someone else had already stepped in it and loosened the soil. Out of curiosity, they dug further to find what appeared to be human bones. Smithson regretted he had to inform Charlie who called the police. They were certain it required legal attention.

Being diverted from his projects irritated Smithson, but he watched as the bones were taken away. The officers agreed to leave Smithson out of the report, since he was not the person who discovered the body. One of the officers said, "No telling how many bodies are out here. Call us if you find any more." Smithson said, "That is not going to happen." He had most of the material he needed for his book, and he did not like being disrupted.

Weeks later he received a note from Johnny about a paper they wrote after that first summer. The letter was sent to Maud's Inn, and Charlie delivered it. They left his name out of the report, as he requested. Down on the bottom of the last page Johnny wrote, "I hope it is all right with you if we tell people about the grumpy old man who allows us the privilege of studying with him in the summers. Don't worry we will not use your name. Anytime you get lonesome out there, you can contact us through Charlie. Have him write us if he hears information about the bones the police dug up. Roy Fillmore believes Julie fell into the same hole. Hope to see you again in the future."

Finally, spring arrived in Atlanta. Oh, if only winter came and went as fast as it does on paper. The preceding winter was the worse in years. Three inches of show fell in north Georgia, not once but twice, and in February a ferocious ice storm blocked Atlanta traffic for two days. A frantic father-to-be trudged up and down the highway searching for help to deliver his baby. Word passed from car to car hoping to find a doctor. Thank goodness a doctor, whose car was also stuck in the snow and ice, came to their rescue. He delivered the Ice Storm Baby, as she was called, and wrapped her in his coat. Those who had crowded on the side of the road gave a loud cheer. At least it was a diversion. Some people walked to the nearest exit. A few people were injured, but no one died. Many stories came out of the confusion, some written in the local paper, and others told at bars and parties. One transplanted Yankee ridiculed the southerner's inability to survive a little snow and ice storm. She wrote to the Atlanta paper that she was planning to write a book, "Survivors of the Great Southern Storm." She was blasted in the next edition with statements such as, "The reason Yankees like snow is they are cold-hearted," and of course, "If you like show so much, why don't you go back to New Jersey?" In the next paper a Yankee answered the writers, "Don't be so territorial. Remember you are a conquered territory."

CHAPTER 70
Graduation

September to April passed without catastrophes for the Winchesters. They were preparing to attend Molly's graduation at the Naval Academy. The family was proud she was finishing near the top of the class and was commissioned to attend law school in the fall, but she would still have summer commitments with the Navy. Elizabeth had tried several times to find Freddie, but his employer told them he was out of contact for three to six months. Elizabeth and Frederick were shocked Freddie didn't notify them. Frederick contacted the company for information, but was told Freddie had asked for privacy from everyone, including his family. He threatened to get an investigator to find Freddie's location. They remembered that Freddie seemed distant and restrained the last time the saw him, so they began to worry. Frederick decided to get inside information through the company's emails, so he contacted a person known for being able to trace communications. They discovered he was in Nashville, Tennessee in an anxiety-depression clinic on the recommendation of his company.

With that information the Winchesters decided not to interfere for the time being. Frederick called Freddie's company and asked to speak to the President. "Mr. Roberts, this is Frederick Winchester, Freddie Winchester's father. I have discovered our son is in a clinic in Nashville on his superior's recommendation, and that we were not to contact him."

"That is correct. He is a fine employee, but we feel he needs some help at this time in his life, Mr. Winchester."

"Mr. Roberts, will you let us know when we may see him or talk to him? We are a very close family, and if he needs us we want to be there."

"I understand, and I will let you know."

"Thank you, sir that's all we ask of you."

The graduation ceremony at the Naval Academy was impressive. Elizabeth and Frederick were proud of Molly. She had fulfilled a dream, and was ready to get on with the next step. After the ceremony there was a large reception. Molly introduced her parents to many of her instructors, and celebrated with friends. Susan brought her parents over to meet the Winchesters. Mr. Matthews said to Frederick, "We thank you for being there for Susan. We are proud of the way Susan and Molly handled themselves." About that time Molly brought John Wilson Stoddard over to the group, and introduced him. Having finished a year before, he came to see some of his friends graduate. "May I say something to all of you, for this is probably the only chance we will have this encounter?" Frederick extended his hand, and said, "Sure, son go ahead; we are listening."

"One afternoon, as a foolish young man, I made a ridiculous blunder I will regret for the rest of my life. After that situation Molly and Susan literally saved my career, and I am forever grateful for their generosity. You have two fine daughters." As he turned to leave Mr. Matthews extended his hand, "It took courage coming over to us this afternoon. My wife and I have no animosity towards you, for we understand you took your punishment as directed." Mrs. Matthews said, "We are proud our daughters did not seek revenge. We hope you have a good career in the Navy."

"Thank you. Susan, I hope you enjoy flight school, and Molly, you are going to make a great attorney one day. If I ever need a lawyer, I will look you up."

"Same to you," both of them replied. Frederick put his arm on John's shoulder and walked away with him. He did not reveal their conversation. After a couple of hours, Elizabeth helped Molly pack, and they decided to drive part of the way home.

Arriving home about noon the next day, there was a message on the phone, "Hi, this is Freddie, I want you to know I am getting better here in Nashville, but not quite ready to return to Atlanta. I will call you again in a few days. Tell Molly I regret missing her graduation. Love all of you."

"I want to go see him," Molly said, "It isn't right that we aren't allowed to have a visit with him. When he calls back, I'm going to ask him if I can come see him."

"Not yet, Molly. He needs to do this on his own," Elizabeth said. "He's trying to straighten out his life, and this time he has to make peace with himself, without interference from any of us."

"Mom, I'm not talking about interfering. I'm talking about letting him know I admire what he is doing."

"He knows that," Frederick said.

"But you came to me when I was in that situation at the Academy."

"You were in trouble; Freddie is sick. Understand the difference?"

"Yes Sir, I do."

"What are your plans for the summer?" Elizabeth asked.

"Later on, I have a Navy commitment. But right now, I want to sleep a week, then I am going to call Julia and get with her. Too bad Joanna is in Israel. Hey, maybe Julia and I can go to Israel to see her."

"Not a bad idea. Have you saved money for the trip?" Frederick asked

"Are you are kidding? Why can't that be my graduation present?"

"That's a pretty big present," Elizabeth said. "Mom, that was the answer you always gave me when I was growing up? It always meant *no*."

"Pretty good answer, isn't it, Frederick?

Frederick said, "I believe a trip would be a fine idea. A little traveling would do you and Julia good."

"Dad, you are so great!"

"Frederick, you always spoil her."

"I know, Elizabeth but this time she deserves it. First, I have to investigate the situation over there."

Elizabeth left a message for Roger. He returned her call that afternoon. "I am happy the girls want to visit Joanna, but now is not a good time; there is too much unrest. She is lucky to have dual citizenship, but since I do not, I have not been there lately, yet the Jewish side of my inheritance has a yearning to go more often. Joanna will be having a large showing in a few weeks, and she will be home after that. If the girls can wait, Joanna said she would love to spend some time with them."

"The girls will be glad to hear that."

CHAPTER 71

Randy, Joan, Cassie

Randy came in from the office whistling. Joan asked, "Aren't you home a little early tonight. Nothing to do at the office?"

"I have more time than I used to have since Cassie came. She is doing a great job with the clients. Some of them are even requesting her, and I'm not a bit perturbed about it. She is good and easygoing, and she has Ms. Bee captivated. They even drink coffee together! That has never happened with Ms. Bee and me."

"Have you ever asked?"

"Are you kidding? She would never consider socializing with her boss. As far as she is concerned it's against her principles."

"How do you know that?"

"She would think I'd lost my mind if I invited her for coffee. I don't know what she and Cassie talk about, but I hope it helps Cassie, she's a little 'down in the mouth' as my mom used to say."

"What do you mean by that?"

"I don't know, but my mom used that remark when I was upset about something, but Ms. Bee seems to get Cassie going in the mornings. I wouldn't dare ask them what they talk about. I'm out-ranked on women talk."

"I'll invite Cassie to lunch. Mothers can sense when something is wrong."

"Didn't I just tell you I could sense something?"

"Yes, *down in the mouth*. You might as well have said she's having her period."

"Okay, you beat me on that one. Let's change the subject. I bought you something. It's an odd gift, but when I saw it I couldn't resist it. I hope you like it."

"What a beautiful box. Oh, Randy it's a Celtic cross. This is a wonderful gift."

"How do you know it's a Celtic cross?"

"Wouldn't you like to know?"

"Well, after your visit to the convent I thought it would be the perfect gift. You can keep it in your drawer, wear it around your neck, or hang it somewhere. I want it to be a reminder of your week at the monastery, and it relieves me of guilt for not wanting you to go."

"It's perfect. I can't wait to show it to Cassie. I'll try to have lunch with her tomorrow, that is if you will allow her a longer lunch break."

"Now Ms. Bee will want a longer lunch break."

"She brings her lunch, remember?"

Joan and Cassie met for lunch at the Café in Neiman Marcus. It had several tables where diners can hear themselves talk, unlike a lot of restaurants. While they were waiting for their order Joan said, "Cassie, Randy said you appear to be "down in the mouth" a bit lately."

"Good Lord, I haven't heard that expression, but if it means I am a little out of sorts, then it's true. I guess you invited me to lunch to find out why I'm *down in the mouth*."

"If you want to talk about it, I'm ready and willing to listen."

"All right, here goes. Robert is pressuring me to have a baby, but I'm not ready for that. In fact, he isn't ready either. The truth is we haven't been using any protection lately, but it hasn't happened. His mother is the problem. She keeps telling Robert, 'I want a grandbaby before I get too old to enjoy it. It's not going to happen with your brother, so make me happy.' She has visions of keeping the child while I work, God forbid, or coming over and playing with him or her. I told Robert to tell her it is none of her business, but of course he won't." They hesitated while the server was putting their food on the table. "The fact is, Mom I hate to say this, but here it is: Robert and I don't have sex *that* often. For some reason it doesn't seem easy for him. I'm the one who instigates the procedure, and that is just what it is, a *procedure*. Mom, can a marriage like this survive?"

"I don't know how to answer that. With your dad it was always when he wanted it, never when I did. I would say it runs in the family, but John and Robert are not related."

"Mom, what am I going to do?"

"You and Robert need an honest session with each other. Maybe he isn't having sex to spite his mom, or maybe he needs to see a doctor since he might be slightly impotent. Does any of that make sense?"

"Yes, but he talked about children right after we married, so I don't understand his reluctance. Thank goodness I have a job I like. I love my work with Dad and Ms. Bee. Mom, the other day I went to the courtroom to watch Robert defend a man, and his abilities are unbelievable. He is stunning in the courtroom. It's like he knows the law better than anyone I know except, maybe, Georgia Parker. By the way if I were interested in courtroom action, I would beg her to hire me. Mom, but if you have any advice, I'll listen."

"I'm not certain what advice I have, but whatever you do, do not let Robert's mother decide when you have a baby. If, and that is a strong *if,* Robert or both of you would consider going to a counselor, I would suggest it. If not, you have some decisions to make. What I'm going to say next is conjecture. Could Robert be interested in someone else? If so, who could it be? Or Robert may think he's gay like his brother. Or maybe he has a medical condition? That's all I have to say."

"Mom, you have always gone right to the point. First, if I ask him to go to therapy, I know what he will say, 'You go if you think it will help you.' Another person on the side; how could I find out? Medical condition? That's a possibility."

"Cassie, do you want to save your marriage? That is the first decision you have to make. If you do, perhaps you need to do some investigating."

"What kind of investigating?"

"Hire an investigator. That's what I should have done."

"Mom, why does marriage have to be so complicated? I fell hard for Robert. Maybe it was because he was so smart and handsome. He literally sent my heart spinning, but after a few months, he seemed to lose some of his passion. Do you suppose someone like Robert gives all his passion to helping other people, and since I don't need any help, I'm second on his list?"

"That is a possibility. Cassie, we've about talked this through. You are going to have to work this out, and soon. Something is definitely not right, and until you find the answer it is going to control your energy. Have you thought about talking to Randy?"

"If I weren't in business with him, I would.

"Well, talk to him in off hours, when he's your dad, not your business partner. Give him an opportunity. I know he will give you sound advice. I still remember how amazing he was with Rick."

"I ruined our lunch didn't I, Mom? I'm so sorry, but today our usual 'small talk' would have been impossible."

"No, you didn't ruin our lunch. This was my opportunity to find out what is wrong with you. Actually your dad brought it up. Remember *down in the mouth*? He loves you, Cassie, so give him a chance."

"Thanks, Mom, I will. I am so lucky to have good parents. There is something else I need to talk about. I haven't had my period for a long time, but maybe that's because I've been under so much stress. The one time we had sex was over eight weeks ago. Do you suppose I could be pregnant?"

"Oh, my god, Cassie, go to the drug store, get a test kit, and call me right away."

"Mom, changing the subject before I forget, Robert and I finally set up Rick's scholarship fund, and it looks good. Robert was amazing; he knew exactly who to contact and how to write it. We listed it on line with several other scholarship possibilities, and we also built a web site. If an artist wants funds, our scholarship will not be hard to find. Robert has asked several large companies to donate, and we have agreed to be conservative with the principle until the interest builds up. On the web page we are featuring a few of Rick's paintings."

"That sounds great. It makes me both sad and happy. I'm sure that took a lot of your time. Thank you, and Robert for doing that."

Joan could not get Cassie off her mind as she rode home. For some reason she felt a chill and sensed danger. She spoke aloud, "Oh, Lord, I've lost one child; please don't let me lose Cassie." She repeated it over and over like a mantra, and felt relief that she could actually pray. At that very moment her mind floated back to the convent, and it was a relief: *When I get home, I am going to put my new cross around my neck. I know it isn't a religious relic, but I need to find some comfort.*

CHAPTER 72

The Courthouse

When Cassie returned to the office Ms. Bee was waiting for her, "My dear, you have had several calls, but when I picked up the phone, whoever was on the phone would not answer. A few minutes ago you had a call from your husband. There was something strange about it, like he was whispering. I had a difficult time understanding him." Cassie called, but couldn't reach him. She tried his office and his parent's house. She went into Randy's office, and asked him, "Can we talk?"

"Certainly, close the door."

"I am concerned about Robert. Lately he is distant. Our sex life is about nil, and now I can't reach him on his phone or his office. Mom suggested you might have some insight into our problem."

"Whoa, too much information at once! What could he be worried about? Is his practice doing well?"

"Worried? I can't imagine why, and yes his business in good, but we never seem to have serious talks. Cassie's phone rang. "Hold on Dad, it's Robert."

"Cassie, listen carefully. I'm in the courthouse behind a table…a guy has a gun…I've been shot in the leg."

"Who's that talking over there? Give me that phone," a voice yelled, "I told you not to move." They heard a shuffle and a voice, "Talk again, and I'll shoot you where you won't be able to talk."

"Oh, my God, my God. Dad I can't breathe. Robert's been shot."

"Ms. Bee, bring Cassie some water!" She rushed into the room and saw Cassie sitting on the floor, crying. "What happened? Should I call an ambulance?" She bent over her, "Cassie, my dear, what is wrong?"

"No, we don't need an ambulance," Randy said. "Let's get her on the sofa. Be careful, don't hurt yourself."

"Do not keep me in the dark; what has caused this child to faint?"

"A call from Robert," Randy said. "There appears to be a man in the court room with a gun, and Robert's been shot. Hand me the phone, I need to call 911. Hello, this is Attorney Randy Walker. Are you aware there is a gunman in the courthouse?"

"Yes, Sir, we are aware."

"My son in law just got a call through to us, and he's been shot."

"We have it covered, Mr. Walker. Who did you say called?"

"My son in law, Robert Sanders."

"How do you know he's been shot?"

"He called us on his cell phone, then we heard a man take his phone from him, and threaten him."

"Hold, on Mr. Walker." She came back, "We are not aware that anyone had been shot. The police are on the way, and they will try to get an emergency team inside."

"Whoever you are, you are not listening! This is Randy Walker, an attorney. I tell you my son in law just called us. He has been shot! Get someone in there!"

"Yes Sir, Mr. Walker. A car in on the way."

"Ms. Bee, get Bob Sanders, Sr. on the phone for me. Bob, are you aware there is a gunman in the courtroom?"

"No! Hold on, let me get to a television."

"Robert made a short call to us. He has been shot in the leg."

"Oh, my goodness. I need to get over there. I can walk from here."

"Bob, Cassie and I are going to try to get there if the streets are not blocked."

"Both of you stay where your are. You won't make it downtown. Stay off your phone. I'll keep you informed."

Randy called Joan, "Joan, go over and pick up Grace Sanders, and bring her to the office. Robert has been shot in the leg, and a gunman is holding him and others hostage in the courthouse."

"Oh no! I'm on my way." She called Grace on her cell phone, "Grace, this is Joan Walker, where are you?"

"What an odd thing to ask. I am shopping at the grocery store."

"Stop shopping. Leave your groceries and go home now! Drive carefully. I'm on my way to pick you up. Don't ask why, just go."

"My goodness, wait a minute. Oh, someone is talking about a shooting. Joan. It's about a shooting at the courthouse. Is Robert hurt?"

"He's been shot. I'll be at your house by the time you get there."

They huddled around the television at the office, but most of the information was from reports outside the building. Bob Barnett came down from his office to sit with them. Suddenly, people began running out of the building, and the EMTs began going in with stretchers. They saw Bob Sanders walking down the steps. When they saw him get in an ambulance they knew he would be with Robert. Two more stretchers came out. Reporters gathered around the officers on duty trying to get information. Bob Sanders called from inside the ambulance, "I'm with Robert. He has been shot in the thigh and hit in the head. He's in a bit of pain, so the technicians have sedated him. I learned that an officer was able to get inside, and when the shooter got clear of everyone, the officer shot him. I believe he is dead. One of the officers said the other person injured did not have a life threatening injury. Stay where you are; I will keep you up to date." While he was talking they saw several reporters rushing toward the ambulances to get the name of the hospital where they were taking the injured. Others advanced on those who were witnesses, trying to get the details. The whole place was in the condition of madness.

About an hour later, Bob Sanders called, "Robert has been taken to surgery. I will stay close until I learn more. The nurses are trying to bring some kind of sanity to the emergency room waiting area, so I'm going to the cafeteria to get out of the way. I know John Bergman, the surgeon operating on Robert. He will call me after the surgery. I believe the confusion will slow down soon, so if any of you want to come, you know where to find me." Grace suggested Randy and Cassie go, and she would stay with Joan and Ms. Bee.

Parking was scarce, so Randy and Cassie had to walk about two blocks to get to the hospital. Finally, they located Bob in the cafeteria. “Thanks for coming to sit with me.” He embraced Cassie and said, “I’m so sorry, my dear, but Robert is lucky to be alive. Let’s be grateful for that.” Cassie was out of breath from walking so fast, but she whispered, “I am grateful, so grateful.” Several persons who knew Bob and Randy came by to greet them. The discussion was light, so they had no idea Robert had been shot. It seemed forever before Dr. Bergman called Bob, “The wound was terrible. It seemed like it took forever to clean and repair the wound, but we finally closed it. It must have been one of those weapons meant to kill, and there is a wide gash over his right eye that needed several stiches. The police said the gunman hit him with his pistol.”

“John, my daughter in law is here with me. Is there any chance she can see Robert for a few minutes?”

“Let’s not do that today. He is so sedated he wouldn’t recognize her, and there is plenty for the nurses to do right now. Give me her number, and I will call her as soon as she can see him. I suspect he will spend at least two nights in critical care. I’m so sorry this happened to Robert. I think a few prayers would be appropriate right now.”

“Thanks a million for taking care of him, John. Keep us informed.”

On the way home Randy had to pull off the road for Cassie to vomit. “I’m sorry you are having to go through this. You’re going to have to lie down when we get home. Go ahead get everything out of your stomach. I’m calling Joan to see where she is. Hi, where are you and Gracie? Okay see you soon.”

Between heaves, Cassie said, “Just stop talking.” Finally they arrived at the condo just in time for Cassie to rush into the bathroom. Joan put her on the couch and gave her a Coke to sip on, to settle her stomach.

Grace said, “You look so pale, Cassie. Have you eaten anything today?”

“Yes, Mom and I had lunch, but it all came back up. Mom, do you have any crackers?” There was not much to talk about, so Grace and Joan went to sleep in their chairs, and Randy called Ms.

Bee, "Were you able to cancel the two appointments?" She answered, "Yes, I believe that is what you told me to do. How is Cassie?"

"Vomiting and scared," Randy said.

"Poor Cassie, tell her I am thinking about her. Now I remember why I am never married."

"Like I said before, you would have had beautiful babies."

"Shame on you. Will I see you tomorrow?"

"Yes, you will, but Cassie won't be there. Joan is going to take her to the hospital when they allow her to visit."

The next day, about 6 PM Dr. Bergman called Cassie, "Robert is asking for you. You can come for a very short visit. I'll call the unit and tell them to let you in, but only for a few minutes. Okay?"

"Great, I'll be there."

As she started toward Robert's room, she was tense and still nauseated: *will he be awake? Can we have a conversation?*

The nurse took her inside the room and said, "Mr. Sanders, your wife is here. Can you open your eyes to see this beautiful lady?"

"Cassie, I love you. They say I am pretty well shot up, but they are taking good care of me. I think my head hurts the worst; it feels like a baseball bat hit me. See the trouble you can get into being a lawyer."

"Robert, I love you. You realize you got that hit on the head for calling me? I hope it was worth it. Everybody is thinking of you. Your mom spent yesterday with us, and you may not remember it, but your dad rode in the ambulance with you." Robert fell asleep while holding her hand. The nurse came in and suggested she leave. "Where is the bathroom," she whispered to the nurse, "I have to vomit." The nurse pointed toward a door and went with her. She wet a towel and held it on her head. "He's going to be fine, dear. Now you go home and don't come back tomorrow. He will be sleeping most of the day, anyway."

CHAPTER 73

Cassie

Joan spent the night with Cassie, since she was so ill. The next morning Cassie was too sick to leave the bed. Joan brought her some coffee and dry toast, and sat on the side of the bed. She said, "Cassie, if you can keep this toast down, I am going to take you to see my gynecologist, Dr. Rose Lambert. From what I remember you saying, you could be pregnant. This reminds me. I nearly vomited my head off when I was pregnant with you."

"Mom, you can't be serious; I'm just upset. Besides, I don't believe I can ride in a car today, and I don't want to know if I'm pregnant."

"I have already talked to Dr. Lambert, and she called in a prescription for nausea. I just picked it up, so here it is, take it." In a little while Cassie was able to eat the toast and get dressed.

They made the trip to the doctor without any problem. After the examination, Dr. Lambert did a sonar gram. "Congratulations, Cassie you are pregnant."

"I can't be. I mean I don't want to be pregnant. The timing is wrong."

"There is a human being growing inside of you, Cassie. Think of this child as a special gift."

"This is not the gift I want at this time, especially without Robert. If you are absolutely certain, can you do something to change the situation?"

"No, not even if I could. You carry this child, nurture it, and you will love this little person as you have never loved anyone."

Joan followed Dr. Lambert out while a nurse helped Cassie get dressed. "Rose, thank you for seeing Cassie on such a short notice."

Dr. Lambert whispered to Joan, there is a possibility two babies are in that uterus. It's too early to be certain, but don't mention it until I see her again."

"Great! One for me and one for Grace."

"Grace?"

"Cassie's mother-in-law."

Joan went back to get Cassie. "Cassie, this may be the only grandchild I will ever have, so if I have to put you in my home and watch you every moment, I will. So let's move on and make our next appointment."

"It's not *our* appointment."

"Sure it is." Cassie wanted to call her mother in law to give her the news, but she wanted to tell Robert first.

The next day Joan took Cassie to the hospital to see Robert. He was sitting up in the bed eating a cracker and drinking Ginger Ale. "Robert, I can't believe you're eating! Besides the black eye, you look good to me. Can I kiss the other side of your face?"

"I've missed you so much. Feels like I have been trapped here for weeks. When this is over, you and I are going away for a long time. And I don't wish to see the inside of a courtroom for quite a while. Hello Joan. Nice to see you also."

Joan said, "I am going to leave you two alone for awhile. You need some time together."

Cassie sat on the bed beside him. "Robert, you had a close call. You could have gotten killed. It scared the hell out of everybody. You know what I was thinking yesterday."

"I hope it's a good thought, for I need one."

"I was thinking if that bullet had hit your heart you would never get to see your first child born."

"I'm glad for that. Wait! Is there a covert message in that remark, or did I just fall asleep?"

"Robert, we are going to have a baby. I am eight weeks, or so, pregnant."

"Mama will be happy."

"Mama! What about you?"

"Cassie, I'm just kidding. It's been so long since we had sex, I can't remember."

"Well, I do, about eight or nine weeks ago after Bill and Suzanne's party."

"Now I remember. That was some night. Cassie, forgive me, but it is true my mother will be the happiest person in the entire world."

"In the world, Robert?"

"In the whole world."

"Can you be the second most happy?"

"Cassie, this is great news. This will force me to hurry up and get out of here.
Are you feeling okay?"

"I could be if I could stop vomiting every hour. You can come in now, Mom. I know you are listening at the door. Robert, rest and get back in shape. We have a lot to look forward to."

"Joan, please take care of her until I get home. I will be forever grateful."

"I'll hold you to that."

On the way home, Cassie called Grace to see if they could drop by. When they arrived Grace said, "Come in, come in, you're just in time for a cup of hot tea."

"Cassie said, "That might be good for Mom, but I get sick every time I think of coffee or tea."

" I didn't know that, Cassie, "I am so sorry. Anything else I can offer you?"

"Don't think so, but I have something to offer you. Please sit down."

"Is something wrong with Robert?"

"Not exactly. When I left, he acted sort of stunned. You see, Grace you are about to become a grandmother."

"Cassie, you mean we are going to have a baby?"

"Yes, *we* are."

"Oh my! Oh my! What a wonderful gift. I have to call Bob right now. You just sit put. Bob, Cassie and Joan are here, just wanted you to know."

"Why is that unusual?" he asked.

"Cassie wants to talk to you." She handed the phone to her.

"Bob, are you sitting down?" Cassie asked. "If not, you had better. You are about to become a grandfather."

"Wonderful! Wonderful! Did Grace jump and yell hallelujah?"

"Well, not quite, but close."

"I guess you have already told Robert. We'll have a party when he gets well. May I speak to Grace?" She handed the phone to Grace. "Grace you and I will be going to visit Robert after work and then go out to celebration. I'll pick you up about five."

She turned to Cassie, "Bob just said we are going to celebrate tonight after we visit Robert. Thank you Cassie, thank you. Joan, I know you are as excited as I am."

Robert came home the sixth day after the shooting. Cassie hired a nurse to be with him after she went back to work. He had begun walking at the hospital, but the wound was still painful. It was several days before he could walk without help, and he was not a good patient. He spent a lot of time on the computer and the telephone. He called the judge and suggested they have better screening at the courthouse, and was told the plans were already in process. *It is not going to happen again*, were the words of the Judge. Robert was impatient and angry that his pain would not go away. On the tenth day, he asked the nurse to help him dress, "I want to go to the office for a little while."

"You are not well enough to do that. I'll have to call your doctor."

"If you won't do it, I'll call a cab. This is important. I want to drop by Cassie's office on the way." She called Dr. Bergman's office and talked to his nurse, "Hold on, I'll go ask him… he said take him wherever he wants to go, just don't stay out too long."

When they came into the office, Ms. Bee said, "Good Lord, what are you doing out? Go home and get well."

"Hello to you too, Ms. Bee. Is Cassie busy?"

"She is on the phone right now. I will use our secret buzzer."

Cassie came out and saw Robert, "What is this? Does your doctor know you are out of the house?"

"I love you, too. Yes, he agreed I could be out for a short time. Ask my nurse, she talked to him." The nurse nodded it was true. He tried to sit down, but almost fell. It took the three of them to get him to Cassie's office.

"We are going to take a run by my office, but I wanted to stop by here first to see you and Randy – well, also Ms. Bee."

"Randy is not here. He went out to lunch. I'm glad to see you, just don't overdo this little outing. I'm sure your office is taking care of your work."

"Have you been vomiting today?"

"Only twice, but it's getting better."

"I'm sorry both of us are sick right now, but we'll get better." She stood in front of him, and he said, "I'll be damned, Cassie I believe you're getting a stomach. I didn't know it would happen this fast."

"It's supposed to happen sooner than later, Daddy."

"Daddy! That sounds so weird. I think of my father. I'd better get used to it. Got to be going before my nurse gets angry with me. Tell Randy I'm sorry I missed him, maybe he can stop by and visit me."

"I'll tell him."

"Randy came in the door as they were leaving, and almost knocked him down. Ms. Bee popped out of her chair expecting to catch him, but the nurse steadied him. They chatted for a few minutes before he and his nurse left.

"Ms. Bee said, "Marriage and babies. All this baby stuff scares me."

"Ms. Bee, maybe it isn't too late for you, "Cassie said.

"Do not be nasty, I have enough to do taking care of you and Mr. Walker."

"And you do a good job. Hey, maybe you can baby sit."

"Go back to work. I cannot take things like this very well. I am used to a civil office. Set your husband straight, he needs to stay home and get well. Tell him you will come home the next time he needs to see you."

"Please, Ms. Bee, I can't take your being angry with me, I might vomit on the floor. This is a tense time for us – the shooting, now the baby. I wish I had waited until he got well to tell him."

"My dear, he would not have taken it any better, so quit second-guessing."

"Will you be an Auntie to my baby?"

"My oh my, a new title. Sure, Cassie just for you."

Robert dropped by his office for a few minutes. He could tell his father was not pleased he was out. Before he could speak, Robert said, "The doctor said it was fine – just for a little while."

"Well, see if you can still sit at your desk. It's been lonesome."

"Dad, I miss being here, thanks for taking care of my business. Give me two more weeks."

"How's Cassie?"

"She's still sick a lot. I went by her office before coming here. Are you really excited to be a granddaddy?"

"You bet I am. That baby is going to be spoiled. We can hardly wait. Go home, son, you look gray. I'll walk to the door with you."

"I told Cassie that Mom would be the happiest person in the whole world."

"Did you forget about me?"

"Dad, there is so much going on right now, I'm frightened. I need to get back to work. Got a child to think of now."

"That's not why you need to get back. You are damn good at what you do, and you miss it. Right?"

"You are correct, but I'm sick in my stomach right now. Maybe I'd better get on home."

"I'll drop by on my way home."

"Thanks, Dad."

CHAPTER 74

Rev. Sarah Marshall and Charlie

Joan opened a hand-written note from Rev. Sarah Marshall, and started laughing. "Randy, let me read you something? *Dear Joan and Randy, Charlie and I invite you to our wedding, September the 10th at 5:00 in the evening at the Southside Presbyterian Church. Your presence is the only gift expected. Charlie is excited we are saying our vows in the company of the people I served all these years, and also with our friends who have meant so much to us. Randy will you sing a solo*?"

"It does not say that."

She was laughing so hard she could barely talk. Finally, "Yes it does, look."

"It's not funny to mock a tone-deaf person. She's going to be sorry she asked me to sing. I just might surprise her."

"Which song do you plan to use? How about an Elvis song?"

"I hate cruelty, and you are making fun of me."

"I know dear, and I am enjoying it."

The ladies of the church had been told about the wedding, and they expressed their love for Sarah by decorating the sanctuary with roses. Roses everywhere, on every pew, on stands made for candles, on the communion table, and on every table at the reception. Sarah was lovely, wearing a beige evening dress with a lace jacket, and Charlie looked every bit the groom in his afternoon tuxedo. Roger was thrilled being asked to give a brief story how Sarah and Charlie met and fell in love. He wasn't brief, but everyone enjoyed his talk, especially the members of the congregation. A contralto from the choir sang an oldie, *Ah Sweet Mystery of Life*. Charlie had chosen the song because it was his mom's favorite American song. Sarah had asked the Elders to stand down front as witnesses to the occasion. When the Interim pastor, Reverend Carol Lofton asked, "Who gives this woman to this man?" The Elders stood and answered, "We do." Not knowing Charlie, and having known Sarah only a short time, there were no stories to tell, so she presented the sacred vows, and blessed the event. It was a beautiful service.

At the reception Sarah thanked the members for planning such a wonderful banquet, and for allowing her to be their minister, and they accepted her thanks with a long applause. Then she said, "I have asked Attorney and good friend Randy Walker to sing for us, but since he claims to have no musical abilities, he wrote a poem. Come forward, Mr. Walker."

"If I were to sing today, most of you would stop up your ears, but I can read a poem I wrote."

Strangers: Sarah, Charlie, and Roger
sat in the dense forest
near the Chattahoochee River
pondering their future.
On the spur of the moment
the odd couple of three
planned a voyage
to tour the world together.
Somewhere, over there
Cassie and Charlie fell in love.
And this day he sweeps her away
back to Maud's Inn in that dense forest.
Once Sarah held your hands
blessed your marriages
healed your wounds
and baptized your babies.
Who knows how long it will be
'til they find their own child
among those woods
under a bush in the forest.
One day these words their child will hear:
"You were the dream for our *family*
conceived right here, named
for your loving uncle……Randy. Amen!

There was a pause until the people realized the punch line. They laughed, and those who didn't get it had to be told. Then quickly Roger stood, "I would like to offer toast."

May your love last forever,
but forget me not, for
I am the one who brought you together.
So, the second babe who comes to your lodge
whether be it girl or boy,
shall be named for good ole Roger. Amen!

The people burst in laughter at the poor attempt of poetry. The reception was a lovely event, good food, lots of laughter, and some of the people even cried.

A few days earlier Roger had offered them a trip to Maine, but Charlie refused his generous gift, "Thanks Buddy, but there is a lot to do right away, mainly getting Sarah's house ready to sell. And we will enjoy relaxing by not having to jump around from Atlanta to the inn all the time."

Roger said, "How thoughtless of me to offer you a trip to an inn when you are living in the best little inn in the state of Georgia. I can still see the look on your faces, sitting in Maud's Inn, when I suggested our trip, and my surprise when you agreed. It was a trip of a lifetime, not only for you, but also for me. All three of our lives were changed forever."

Georgia sensed he was emotional and hugged him, "Everything is working out just fine, Roger, just fine."

"I know, I know. As long as you are near me everything will be fine."

When Charlie and Sarah arrived at the Inn the caretakers, Robert and Mary, surprised them with an intimate meal, including candles and flowers. They were dressed in their finest for the occasion. Mary said, "We figured you wouldn't be able to eat at the reception, so we prepared your wedding meal right here." Robert pulled out Charlie's mother's old record player. The first record he played was *Only You*, by the Platters. Of course it was as much for them as it was for Charlie and Sarah. Robert said, "We'll go now and clean up later. Congratulations to both of you." Charlie said, "Many thanks for the dinner, my friends. Good night."

Charlie scanned the room and said to Sarah, "It was in this room we met, thanks to Roger Waddell. How could life be so sweet? It has been a long wait from that trip to this day, but now we can move forward together." Sarah kissed him and said, "Charlie, we've had some good times and bad times waiting for this day to come. What I'm going to say may strike you as jumping too far ahead, but here it is: I want a child, and I don't want to wait much longer. I have to know how you feel about it."

"Sarah, I'm ready to be a father. Our child will be a gift and he or she will enrich our lives. I believe we are both on the same page."

"Thank you, Charlie. My mother believed the day of conception decides whether you have a boy or girl. I wonder if this day will produce a boy or a girl." She laughed.

"Well, I have never heard that expression. Anyway, I'm kind of hoping for twins, one of each."

"No! No! Not two at once, please. There's one more thing. I don't want every time we are intimate to become a planning session for a baby. Let's remember how lucky we are and how much we love each other. That is enough."

The night was beautiful and peaceful. She didn't have to rush off to the church, and he didn't have to take care of visitors. Lying close to Charlie, Sarah thought: *all those nights we were apart I longed for this day, and it is as beautiful as I imagined. Tonight I don't have to worry if it is improper for a minister to be intimate and not married, and I don't have to rush off to be some other place. No one is waiting for me to return a call. How can I frame this moment? Freedom. Yes, freedom is the right word.*

Charlie broke the silence, "Though we are quite familiar with each other, I believe we should make love as if it were the first time. You remember how hungry we were for so long until we gave in to each other?"

"I remember. I was reluctant at first, but it was indeed wonderful. No, let's don't go back, let's start a new tradition. I'm free to be me." Charlie was a great lover, slow and gentle, but that night he was wild with a passion that surprised Sarah. Finally she relaxed and gave her entire mind and body to him. Afterward, he put on his robe, wrapped her in a blanket and led her out onto the balcony. There they sat holding hands without saying a word. Around midnight they wandered down stairs, and had a glass of wine. He went to the old record player, and from his collection of records, he chose the smooth voice of James Taylor. They danced and danced, stopping only to sip their wine. Robert found them the next morning cuddled on the sofa, "Mr. Fowler and Rev. Marshall, what can I fix you for breakfast."

Startled, Charlie answered, "Is it time to eat?"

"I suppose so, if you plan to eat with all those people who are driving up outside."

"Good lord, are you kidding me? Guard the door, Sarah is not dressed."

"Good morning," Roger yelled as he burst in the door with Joan, Randy, and Georgia.

Charlie said, "You didn't have the decency to call?"

"No, not a one of us is decent. What's for breakfast?"

"Georgia said to Charlie, "Your friends are the strangest people I've ever met. No one else in the world would crash a honeymoon. These idiots made me come, but I wouldn't have missed it."

"All right, settle down everyone. Robert, plug in the waffle iron." Sarah pretended she was trying to wake up. Roger sat down beside her. "Randy and Joan, this is the couch where it all started. I was sitting here with Sarah, and Charlie sat over there. All three of our lives were changed. Give me a hug, Sarah and quit pretending you are sleepy."

"Oh, Roger I am glad to see all of you. It was getting quiet around here. We haven't slept much (they all laugh). No, I mean we came down and danced awhile, then being exhausted we fell asleep. But I would have combed my hair if I'd known all of you were coming. Charlie, bring me a robe."

"Well, Georgia, Randy, and Joan have not seen you uncombed, but Charlie and I have. You look great. What next?"

"Roger, right now I'm hungry. Georgia, what have you done to this man? I believe you have revived him. Both of you look great."

"Thanks. I'm getting used to these strange, on–a-moment's-notice outings, but I love it. Roger and I are having a wonderful time. I'm trying to understand this weird circle of friends, or clan, or whatever it is. Recently I took Roger to a movie. I had to teach him how to crunch on popcorn and slurp through a straw. Can you believe it? *And* he had never eaten M&Ms."

"Roger, a southern lady is going to teach you how to live."

"She can teach me anything she wants to. You know, I have heard she is mean in the courtroom. Is that so, Randy?"

"All I can say is you don't want her to be against you. Get Frederick to tell you

about the Naval Academy. By the way Frederick and Elizabeth are overseas, and Bob? Well, he's going through whoever-knows-what."

Mary yelled, "Who wants the first waffle?"

"Give it to the newlyweds. We'll watch them eat."

"No, all of you eat. I'm going to dress. It isn't nice to be wrapped up in a blanket when all of you look so neat. Charlie, put on another record. Roger probably hasn't ever seen a record player."

"Are you serious? That is all I ever had."

"Poor Roger," Randy said.

Charlie said, "Let's toast with orange juice; this is the best honeymoon ever."

CHAPTER 75

Cassie and Robert

At the breakfast table Cassie punched Robert on the shoulder with her finger, ''Remember? Today is our appointment with Dr. Rose. Meet me at her office about 1:00."

"Sure, but if she can't find a way to stop your vomiting, we may have to search for another doctor."

"Don't be negative now. Remember: I carry the baby and you carry me. Anyway, I'm almost sixteen weeks, so she said my vomiting should go away pretty soon."

———

After the examination Cassie lay on the table, and Dr. Rose had the nurse ask Robert to come in. "Well," Robert said to Cassie, "Is everything all right?" She started crying. He said, "Wait a minute! If there is something wrong, I need to know it, now!"

"Robert, we are going to have twins."

"Twins! Are you sure?"

"Yes," Dr. Rose said, "As positive as I can be, but let me show you the proof on the ultrasound. There they are."

"Where? I'm new at this."

Dr. Rose drew him a picture with her finger. "Oh my God, my mom must have prayed too hard." And they all laughed. "Does your mom know about this, Cassie?"

"No, we just found out. Robert what are we going to do?"

"What do you mean, what are we going to do? We are going to have twins, one for my mom and one for your mom, and maybe we will get to see them occasionally. Cassie, this is great news. What this means – we will have both our children at the same time." He looked at a puzzled Dr. Rose, "We sort of have an agreement to have two children. Right, Cassie?"

"But not at the same time," she yelled.

"Dr. Rose, is this the moment the wife blames the husband?" Robert asked.

"Yes, sometimes, but you not going to do that, are you, Cassie?"

"It wouldn't help if I did."

"Come on now, Cassie. Calm down, get dressed, and we'll have a dinner party tonight. I can't wait to see the reactions of our parents. This is going to be fun, and it's going to be *interesting.*"

"Why are you thinking of a dinner party when I can't eat?"

"It's not for me and you, it's for our parents. Dr. Rose does she, or shall I say we, have to do anything different during the rest of this pregnancy?"

"No, I wouldn't think so. Cassie, there is a possibility you might get fairly large, but not for long, because twins tend to come a little early, so you might think about arranging your clients so your dad can take charge of them for you."

"Robert, one thing *is* going to be fun, Ms. Bee reaction. I can't wait to tell her; she might faint." The two of them laughed so hard, Dr. Rose asked, "Ms. Bee?"

"Oh, you will have to meet her one day. She is the president, director, and ruler of our office. I'm serious. We don't cross Ms. Bee. She's both fearsome and funny. She said to me one day, 'you need to make arrangements for this baby, bringing it to the office would not be a good idea.' So two of them! I'm going to torture her."

On the way home Cassie called their parents and asked them to come for dinner, and "no" was not an option. Stopping at one of their favorite places to eat, they ordered food for dinner, including dessert, because they didn't have anything available at home.

Robert met both sets of parents at the door with a glass of red wine, and gave everyone time to catch up on their events before dinner. Grace wondered why Robert was bringing in the food while Cassie sat, so she asked, "May I help you, Robert?"

"Nope it's my treat." The dinner went fine, but Joan saw that Cassie was not eating, so she asked her, "Are you still nauseated," Cassie. Before she could answer Robert jumped in, "Cassie and I have some news to tell you, but I'll wait until we are through eating."

"You're not moving, I hope," his mother said.

"No, we are not moving, so go ahead, Robert. I know you are bursting."

"Robert said, "Everyone, raise your glasses, all except Cassie, to good news. This has been a tough year for us, and we want to thank the four of you for supporting us when we needed it. And for that we have a present for you."

"No need to do that," Joan said, "We loved helping you."

"Yes," said Grace, "We truly did."

"Well, just the same, I think you will enjoy this gift. Listen carefully, and please do not fall out of your chairs. You lucky Grandmothers and Grandfathers, we are going to have twins in this family."

At first there was silence. Then Grace asked, "Are you certain?"

"As sure as we can be. I even saw their pictures with this machine the doctor used, like an x-ray." Cassie corrected him, "ultrasound." Everyone began talking at once until Robert held up his hand, "Do not get alarmed, we are quite happy and Cassie has stopped crying."

"Why were you crying, dear?" Grace asked.

"I'm not used to double surprises. First, I find out I'm pregnant while Robert is in the hospital, and now it's twins. I'm just scared. Dad, can we hire a sitter at our office?"

"Oh my God," Randy said, "I can't wait to tell Ms. Bee. She is going to flat-out faint. She already expressed concern about one child interfering in her office space, now there will be two. Cassie and Robert, I am so happy for you and for all of us. This is going to be some adventure. I never thought I would have children, and now two grandchildren are going to be a bonus. This is going to be interesting."

"Grace, you know what Robert said at Dr. Rose's office? He said you had prayed too hard. Then he said one baby is for you and one for my mom."

"Why did you leave out the grandfathers?" Bob asked.

"Oh Bob, they're going to be ours too. What a night!" Randy said. "Let's name the babies. Of course, we'll have to choose names that would fit a girl or a boy."

"Too early, Dad. After they are born, I suppose we can all camp out and come up with something," Cassie said. "It's been a busy day, and I'm quite exhausted, so I'm going to bed. Robert, you tell them when to leave."

"I think we all need to go," Joan said. "It has been a wonderful evening, and there are more to come."

After all the hugs, kisses, and goodbyes Robert said, "Well, that went well. I believe we made four people very happy. I think I'll call my brother while you get ready for bed."

He tried, but there was no answer, so he left a message. In a few minutes, he decided to try again. "Buddy, I've got good news, Cassie and I are having twins. Just wanted to let you know. Give me a call." The phone rang about midnight. The message started before Robert could get to the phone, "Hey, brother thanks for giving me the good news. It's late, so I will get back to you." Then he was gone. Robert thought, *I would call him back, but if he couldn't wait long enough for me to get to the phone, he probably wouldn't answer...again.*

At the office the next morning, Cassie was bursting to tell Ms. Bee. She was determined to make a production out of it, but first, she had two appointments. Randy was out to lunch with Bob Barnett, a visit he sort of dreaded. After Cassie was finished, she and Ms. Bee had the office by themselves. Cassie said to Ms. Bee, "Do you have time to talk with me. Maybe we can eat our sandwiches together."

"I have never thought about sharing lunch in the office, but if you insist."

"Oh, come on. I'm not your employer, Dad is. I'm your friend, formerly your trainee."

"If you say so, but it will seem odd."

"What kind of sandwich did you bring?" Ms. Bee.

"Today I brought soup. I have enough for two if you would like some."

"Thanks, but I have a banana sandwich and some fruit. That will stay down as good as anything."

"I would hope so, but that does not sound very nutritious to me. I have heard of the saying, you are eating for two.

Good, she opened the opportunity, “No, Ms. Bee, I’m eating for three.”

“I beg your pardon. Why are you eating for three?” That is not a saying I am familiar with.”

“Ms. Bee, hold on to your seat, I have a surprise for you. Robert and I are having twins!”

“Oh, my Lord, when did that happen?”

“Several months ago.”

“I mean, when did you discover you are having twins?”

“Yesterday at the doctor’s office. Are you happy for me, Ms. Bee?”

“I am not sure. That is complicated, very complicated. Oh my, Cassie, you will have to quit work.”

“Only for a little while. I can bring them to work. When I have a client, I can put one of the babies in here with you and the other with Dad. It’s going to work out fine.”

“Cassie, I am not equipped to take care of a baby.”

“What do you mean *equipped*? You won’t be nursing the baby, just holding him or her if one of them cries.”

“We need another employee, that is for sure. I have been telling Mr. Walker that for months. You know I am proud of you, but I am a little unsettled right now.”’

“Don’t be. I’m kidding about babysitting, though you might like it if you try.”

“Oh, my, I have been so comfortable working for Mr. Walker, then you came, which was just fine as it turned out, but this is beyond me.”

“Just wait. When you see those babies, I bet they will change your mind. I want to tell you something. I didn’t think it was a good time to be pregnant, with Robert being in the hospital, so I asked Dr. Rose to do something about the pregnancy. You know what I mean. (Ms. Bee raised her eyebrows.) I couldn’t look that far ahead, but she refused. On the way home Mom shamed me, and I’m glad she did. I think she would have locked me up if I had not changed my attitude. So don’t worry about the change, besides you’ll have a few more months to think about it.” She leaned over and kissed her on the check and said, “You know I love you, don’t you? Can I hug you?”

“Oh, my, I have not been hugged since that man…”

"A man! Ms. Bee, you've been keeping secrets."

"I am sorry, I spoke out of frustration. Do not ever remind me about it."

"It's our secret. Dad would have to torture me."

"Thank you dear, now go back to work. I must put myself together before that new couple comes in. Go away. Get busy."

"Yes Ma'am."

CHAPTER 76

Fredrick and Elizabeth

As Frederick and Elizabeth prepared to land in Atlanta, the last city they visited was only a memory. Their European and Asian trip had been the experience of a lifetime. For Elizabeth, the excitement of visiting the places she lived when her dad served in the army, and for Frederick an understanding of how the early years made Elizabeth who she is. The cities they visited were not the same as she had pictured in her mind, but it was a successful trip. What they gained in intimacy was even better than focusing on her childhood. Being together, with no one else to be concerned about, they were closer than they had been in years. They rarely mentioned Frederick's work, the children, or their church. They tumbled in bed as if they were twenty years old. Both were surprised at the passion they still had for each other, and in bed they did things they had never heard of when they were in their twenties. "Elizabeth, you are beautiful," Frederick kept saying while holding her hand. "You were pretty when we married, but now you are beautiful. I love you so much." Telling Frederick he was more handsome than ever seemed like an echo so she said, "Frederick, let's never forget what we are to each other. Having finally turned our children loose, we are beginning to experience a freedom we haven't had for years. We always seemed to be more focused on our children than each other. This trip has given us a second chance, our own Epiphany."

"We did a pretty good job raising out children, but the next years of our lives shall be for us. I plan to enjoy them; that is a promise."

———

When they arrived home from the airport there was a message on the phone from Freddie. "Mom, Dad, I feel like a new man with a mission. One day, I will repay what I cost you in energy and worry; I promise. I am enjoying my work in Louisville. Looking forward to hearing from you."

"Shall I call him back?" Frederick asked.

"Even though it sounds like good news, I don't want to break the magic we have experienced."

Freddie still had that stinging fear of running into Celeste, so he was always on alert. Frederick and Elizabeth were pleased when the president of his company asked if he would be interested in going to their Louisville, Kentucky office for a couple of months to see if they could increase their presence there. Freddy jumped at the opportunity. Years ago, that would have meant taking piles of paperwork, but now all he needed was his mission, a temporary residence, and clothes. There would not be as much paper work either, for the changes they made with their software had made the communications between offices more practical.

Frederick and Elizabeth watched those months in Louisville change Freddie's life. It was the freedom he needed, and two months turned into four. He told them about meeting a young woman at a diner. She was a graduate from Brown University and was working for an accounting firm nearby. She was divorced and had a young son. They could tell Freddie was fascinated with her, so they were worried. During one of their conversations he described her as energetic, poised, attractive, but best of all she was smart, and could hold his attention. She was past skinny and wore loafers without hose or socks, and he liked the way she would flip her hair out of her eyes and laugh. He told them he was taking the situation slowly, for he was not ready for a commitment. He was also concerned about having the responsibility of a child. His primary mission was to focus on his work and continue sessions with a counselor. It appeared he had learned a lot in therapy. They had noticed a drastic change in him, and knew he was in the right place.

After five months, seeing how Freddie had improved their company, the President asked him to make Louisville his home. The first year they would pay for his residence until he decided to buy a place. It was very good news for Frederick and Elizabeth.

There was also a voice message from Molly, "Hooray! I've turned the corner. I see the road ahead of me, and I can hardly wait to get there. Mom and Dad, I know I will be good at this, and I'm looking forward to traveling all over the world." They were not surprised at the next comment; "I have become friendly with a man, but nothing serious at the moment. He's a good tennis player. You would like him; he's intelligent and rather handsome. His home is in Denver, and he promises to take me there to see what it's like living a mile high. Hope you had a good time on your trip. Remember I love you."

Frederick reminded Elizabeth he had made reservations for dinner. They could answer their children's calls later. He requested a table in one of the more secluded areas of the restaurant. Before their trip he always preferred to sit in the middle of the restaurant so he could speak to friends and clients as they left or arrived. At the table he took Elizabeth's hand to ask the blessing, and immediately felt desire for her. *God forgive me. How can her hand remind me of intimacy?* "I have to go back to work on Monday, but I am not eager. All next week will be catch-up and finding out what they saved for me. It's going to be a tense week, but I will have you to come home to."

"You will get back in the swing of things quickly, and I will be waiting to help get your mind off work."

"Yes, yes," he said. "The problem will be remembering why I'm working," He raised her hand and kissed it.

CHAPTER 77

Cassie and Robert

Cassie woke in the middle of the night with cramps and pain in her stomach. "Robert, Robert, wake up! I believe I am in labor, or either experiencing the worse cramps of my life."

"Does it always have to happen in the middle of the night?"

"I haven't researched that. Remember? Dr. Rose said I might deliver early since we're having twins. Everything ready?"

"Yes, but shouldn't we call her?"

"The hospital will do that after we get there." Robert grabbed the bag they had packed earlier and went to the car. When he realized Cassie was not there he ran back into the house. "What are you doing?"

"Putting on my makeup."

"Why are you doing that? Nobody will care."

"I will." *Patience, I need to be more patient*, he thought. So he stood beside the sink and waited for her to finish. "Aren't you afraid the babies will come while you are putting on makeup?" Very calmly she said, "Nope. Okay, I'm finished; let's go."

At the emergency room an aide put Cassie in a wheel chair, and Robert gave the keys to an attendant to park the car, a courtesy for fathers. At the check-in desk the woman asked for his wife's name and looked it up on a sheet. "Having a baby tonight?"

"Nope, two babies," Robert answered. He looked around and a nurse was wheeling Cassie down the hall. He called their parents and told them they were at the hospital, and it was the real thing. "No need to coming right away; we just got here." Even though Robert and Cassie had attended a couple of birthing classes, he couldn't remember where he was supposed to go or what he was supposed to do. He wandered down the hall peeping into room after room. A nurse saw him, "Can I help you?"

"Someone took my wife while I was checking in, and I have totally forgotten where I'm supposed to go."

"Follow me," she said. Are you the father who is expecting twins?

"My wife is, but I believe I'm more frightened than she is." The nurse smiled, and said, "Come with me, she said." He found Cassie, and she was looking quite comfortable propped up on the bed. "So is this the real thing?" He asked.

"Yes it is. Doctor Rose is on the way. Robert, remember you said you would be in labor with me. Have you backed out?"

"No, but I would like to. I called our parents and told them it is the real thing. I'm positive they will be here shortly."

"Real Thing? That is so funny. Robert, don't you dare leave me, not even to go out and check on our parents. I want you to be the first person to hold our babies. Well, except the doctor or nurses. Remember they will come one at a time, so it might be a long delivery."

"Good Lord, Cassie I didn't believe they would both come at once. Give me a little credit. This is one time I am glad I'm not a woman."

"We're in this together, daddy, so suck it up. And don't let me die. You would have to raise two children by yourself."

"Why would you say such a thing? I've never heard of a woman dying from having a baby."

The nurse entered the conversation, "Wait just a minute we're talking about life, not death."

"Yes ma'am, you're right, Robert said.

Cassie went into hard labor around six o'clock a.m. Robert, dressed in a scrub gown and a paper cap to cover his hair, stood on one side of the bed, holding her hand. Once his knees starting shaking so hard, he thought he would have to find a chair, but he looked around and there were no chairs. At 7:00 a.m. Cassie made a terrific scream and their baby daughter came quietly. She was so tiny it frightened Robert, but he dared not comment, and shortly afterward, at 7:15 their son arrived screaming and shaking his arms and legs. Robert said to the nurse, "I just watched two human beings enter the world. I never thought I would see that." She said, "Amazing, isn't it?"

After wrapping the babies the nurse put both of them in his arms so he could show them to Cassie. She was too tired to say much, but she touched the blanket and smiled. He was reluctant to hand the babies back to the nurse, but she said, "Time to take them to an incubator."

He moved over to Cassie, and said, "You did great. You were so brave, but I have to tell you, there was a time I almost fainted, but I couldn't. A nurse kept wiping my head saying, 'Just hold on, it's almost over.' "

"Listen to me, Robert Sanders, if there is another baby in this family you are having it, or we will order one from a catalogue."

"Does she know what she is saying?" He asked the nurse.

"You bet. Mr. Sanders, can you step out now. We need to take care of your wife? Someone will come and get you later."

"How do you know where I will be? I don't."

"Just turn right when you leave, and the waiting room is down the hall.

"Get some rest, Cassie. I'm going out to check on the grandparents."

The grandparents rose to hear the news. "Well, the four of you should be very proud, we have a proper little girl and rambunctious boy. She just floated out like a angel, but he came out screaming."

"Oh, that's wonderful, Robert. Wonderful. When can we see them?"

"I have no idea. They are taking care of Cassie right now. She is literally rung out. Oops that sounds too graphic. She was so exhausted, but not so much that she said to me, 'Robert, if we have another baby in this family, you are having it, or we'll order it from a catalogue.'" They all laughed. "I can't believe how brave she was, so I hope they let her sleep for awhile."

Later they were led into the nursery viewing area to see their babies who were in an incubator.

"Why are they in an incubator?" Grace asked.

Robert said, "According to the nurse, it's a precautionary method since they are so small. They are not quite four pounds each." He talked about the delivery and felt smart having participated in something he never dreamed of doing. Randy was quiet. He had a sinking realization of being the only person present having no experience in what just happened. Realizing why he was quiet, Joan snuggled up to him and whispered, "It's never the same. Every birth is both frightening and exciting. Just enjoy being present at this special event."

I was just thinking... Never mind I'm going to love those kids. They may not have my blood, but since they have yours, they are also mine."

Bob said to Randy, "While these grandmothers bathe in exhilaration, why don't you and I go for a cup of coffee and a roll."

"I think that would be a good idea. I'm afraid my knees are beginning to shake." At that time of day all they could find was a coffee machine, but it didn't matter.

"Randy, stop me if I get too personal. Those babies may not have your blood, but they will have your love, and love beats blood any time. You and I may get lucky enough to hold them every now and then, only after the grandmothers have their turns. I'm happy to be a grandfather with you."

"Thanks for your words, Bob. I suppose it was obvious I was mooning back there. I was thinking how lucky you are, but you have helped me feel lucky too."

When the babies were four days old Randy called Bob, "Don't you think it's time we have a naming session?"

"Yes, I will arrange it." He made the calls, and just like that, they agreed to a meeting at the hospital so they could look at the babies.

All six of them stood at the nursery window waving at the twins. Cassie asked, "What is your middle name, Grace?"

"It's Elizabeth."

Robert asked Randy, "What is you middle name?"

"Phillip."

"Good," Robert said. "We just gave our twins their first names. How does this sound to everyone Elizabeth and Phillip."

"Oh, how sweet," Grace said. "Are you pleased Randy?"

"Very pleased."

Cassie said, "Robert, when they get older, I can't wait to tell the twins that we announced their first names while the six of us stood looking into the nursery like they were monkeys in a cage. Elizabeth and Phillip are beautiful names, but if you grandparents don't mind, Robert and I have reserved the rights to choose their middle names."

"Of course we don't mind," the grandparents said together.

"Cassie said, "Well here are the middle names. Last night we picked Alicia in honor of you, Mom, and Andrew in honor of you, Bob. So, it's done: Elizabeth Alicia and Phillip Andrew. Everyone happy?" It was sort of silly, but they applauded right there at the window of the nursery.

The babies came home in three weeks. They were kept a few days longer than usual so they could gain some weight, and also because Phillip was a little anemic. Cassie and Robert went to the nursery once a day to hold them and feed them. They had decided using the bottle would be easier for Cassie to return to work earlier, and besides Robert could help. "Just imagine," he said, "if we had only one baby, we would have to share." Cassie was amazed how affectionate he was with the babies. He even came home for lunch to help her. Also Grace and Joan took turns helping during the day for a couple of weeks.

Finally, Cassie realized they needed to find a full-time nanny. She and Robert interviewed several ladies, but checked the references of only one of them, Helen Jenkins, and they hired her. She was another Ms. Bee, a bit fussy and in control all the time, but she became a gift to their family. She was tall and thin to the bone. She never had children, and one of her references said she was widowed when she was in her mid-forties. Her family emigrated from Ireland when she was eight years old, and she still had that sweet Irish lilt to her voice that ended every sentence with a question mark. Knowing the babies would be in capable hands, Cassie returned to work three days a week. On the days Cassie worked, Robert came home for lunch. Miss Helen was not happy he woke the babies, but she saw how much he loved them, so she tucked them down after he left.

CHAPTER 78
Bob

Bob woke in the middle of the night in a cold sweat. He had decisions to make, but couldn't focus. He had no doubt that Margaret was special in his life and good for him. He did love her, and knew he would never find another person like her. *So what is wrong with me? Randy suggested I see a counselor. I need a miracle to happen for me to accept Michael, and then there is live-in Becky. Margaret needs her, but what position would she have in our lives? Right now Julia thinks she is in love, and I need to get to know him. Julia likes Margaret, but it's not a simple decision for me. Then there are my Mom and Dad. They love Michael. I can see it in their eyes. Randy is right, there's something wrong with me. Judy was always in love with another man, and Margaret has a baby, and I'm not his father. I'm screwed up, and I don't want to ruin Margaret's life. I know she loves me, but she could find someone else. I need to get away.* The next morning, he called Randy, "I need help. Can you talk now?"

"Sure. What's up?"

"Do you know of a place I can go that is both therapeutic and with a tad bit of spirituality? You know I'm not very spiritual, but I believe that will help."

"I've heard about a place. Go back to sleep and let me work it out."

"Are you sure?"

"Yes, go back to bed. I'll call you before eleven."

Randy called The Monastery of the Holy Spirit in Conyers just outside Atlanta. He spoke to one of the monks about his friend. The monk said, "Let me call you back within the hour." Randy waited. Father Raymond called, "We have made a place for your friend, but be certain he understands he is to bring only the clothes he is wearing. Take all his belongings, including his wallet, from him before you leave. Tell him to expect to stay at least six days. Bring him tomorrow morning."

"I will take care of those things; see you tomorrow."

He called Bob. "Tomorrow, I am taking you to a place of retreat. Don't ask me where. Cancel all appointments for seven days. Let Julia know you can't be reached for those days. I will pick you up at 7 A.M., so be ready. No suitcase, only the clothes you are wearing. Everything else will be furnished. No! Don't interrupt me. See you in the morning, and by the way, it would be a courtesy to let Margaret know you will be gone for a few days."

"I will be ready. Thanks Randy."

Randy told Ms. Bee, "Rearrange my appointments for tomorrow, or let Cassie handle them. One of my friends has emergency, so I will be gone for the day, and don't ask who, where, or what."

"Have I ever done that before?"

"No, I just wanted to made it sounded important."

"Well do not ever insult me again or I will quit."

"No you won't. I wouldn't be able to do my job without you." He left the room before she could answer.

That evening Randy said to Joan, "Bob is in a crisis. Of course you already knew that. I'm taking him to a Monastery tomorrow. I will not be staying, but will go back and pick him up when I get the call."

"Did he fight you about going?"

"He did not, and I was surprised. He finally recognizes he needs help. He doesn't even know where I'm taking him. I will wait to tell him on the way. Thanks to you and Pearl for giving me the idea. I believe your time at the convent was a great help. I'm hoping Bob will find some answers or peace."

"You are a sweet man, and I love you for helping him."

"Bob and I are like brothers. We would die for each other. I feel the same about you, Frederick, and Roger."

Joan said, "Not many people can say they are part of a group that would die for each other, except maybe soldiers in combat. I'm proud to be included in it. There is something unique about being in a group. Working, thinking, or even praying together can make things happen. There is a theory for that, but I can't remember what it is."

"I believe the word is the quantum theory," Randy said. "Look it up when you have time. There appears to be some sort of energy that a bonded group of people have in peace or crisis. The six of us always seemed to get things accomplished because we trust each other. Of course there are five of us now- a circle of friends equal in value to each other. Together we can do many things we can't do alone. What we have in common is rare these days. Individualism is changing our world. I am a weary man tonight. If I can sleep it will be a blessing. Read something you have written to me, until I can go to sleep. Wait a minute. I almost forgot to tell you. Bob and I helped one person recently, Wanda Wallace. We froze all her accounts this month until she can get resettled in Barbados. Her former broker, George Reese will be joining her. She and her husband had known him off and on for years. He turned all her accounts over to another broker, and she changed bankers after that idiot at the bank messed around in her business. He was fired and is facing fraud charges. Bob takes care of all her investments, etc., and I have the details of her will. I must say it would be fun to see her children's faces when they discover she is gone, her properties sold, and investments frozen. I am so happy she has found contentment."

"Those sorry kids can't touch anything she has. Isn't that wonderful?"

"You're a good man, and so is Bob. I do hope he can find peace."

When Randy picked up Bob he explained, "Bob, I am taking you to a Monastery. There is a monk there who will be spending time with you. You will have sessions with him, and hopefully you will worship with him. I'm guessing they will have something for you to wear, and there may be other men there for group discussions. I have no idea of the set-up. You will stay at least six or seven days. Do you understand?" There was silence for several miles. Randy reopened the conversation, "When you are ready to leave, have one of the monks call me. This is an opportunity to talk about some of the issues you have been unable to conquer by yourself. You are not to worry about taking care of anything but yourself."

"Thank you, Randy. That's all I can say right now." There was very little conversation the rest of the trip.

"Here we are. They told me where to take you. Father Raymond will meet you in his study."

"Wow, this is a beautiful place."

"Yes it is, and I understand it is a great sanctuary."

"Father Raymond, this is Bob Barnett. I leave him with you."

"Have a safe trip back, Mr. Walker. Mr. Barnett, give Mr. Walker your wallet, Jewelry, telephone, and any other personal items you have with you. You won't need them here."

CHAPTER 79

Joanna

The telephone rang as Roger was reading the morning paper, "Dad, this is Joanna, I am coming home. The political situation here is not good at present, so it is time to leave."

"Great, come on. Who will be taking care of your business?"

"I am leaving my manager in charge."

"Manager? When did we get a Manager?"

"Do not worry, my profits are paying for her, and she knows the business. Remember, I have some authority over my business."

"I am sorry, of course you do. Looking forward to seeing you."

"Dad, I am bringing someone with me. His name is David."

"David? Who is David?"

"Someone special. I will tell you about him later. We should arrive in Atlanta around noon tomorrow."

"Do we need a room for David?"

"Dad, just trust me."

"Okay, guess I will have to wait until tomorrow to find out."

"Yes, Dad. I love you."

He called Georgia, "Guess what, Joanna is coming in tomorrow and is bringing someone named David. Georgia, I do not know who David is."

"So? Don't you trust Joanna?"

"Certainly, I do."

"Then what is your problem?"

"Who said I have a problem?"

"You might as well have said it. Why don't you wait until they get here to decide if you have a problem?"

"You should have had kids."

"I do. Remember? By her own words, I am her mother."

"Come home early tonight, I need you."

The plane landed at noon. "There they are," Joanna whispered to David, as they came off the ramp. "Look over there and wave. Now put your arm around me as we approach them, and give me a good-to-be-on-ground kiss. I want to see my dad's face."

"You want to torture your parents?"

"Just my dad. Let us try it."

"Dad and Mom, it is so good to be home. How I have missed you! Let me introduce you to David Benson. You can turn me loose now David. I am safe at home." She winked at him.

David said, "We need to go for our luggage. Each one of us has two suitcases."

"Traveling heavy?" Roger asked.

"Mom, I brought you one of my new outfit. Just wait till you see it. Sorry, Dad you can't wear the clothes I design. Mom, I am glad you sold your house. You will make Dad's condo more lovely than ever."

"Am I a bad housekeeper or something?" Roger asked.

"No, Dad, it was just a compliment."

"I need to learn to understand women."

David said, "You and I may *never* learn."

"Well spoken. Georgia has food at home, so we will not be eating out."

"I like that better," Joanna said.

During dinner, Georgia Inquired about the business, and listened as her daughter gave the most interesting information about her success. Where Roger used to see dollar signs, now he saw happiness in his daughter's eyes. She said, "My grandmother is well, and can you believe it, she accepted a couple of outfits I made for her. She wouldn't admit it, but she was pleased. I insisted she try one of the outfits, and she agreed. She said, 'Where can I wear this?' And I said to her, "You can wear it when you shop so your friends can envy you," and she smiled. I do wish she would come to America to visit, but that is not going to happen.

After dinner they moved to more comfortable seating. Roger said, "I am waiting to hear about you, David. Which one of you is going to start that conversation?"

"Go ahead, Dad. You may ask David why he came with me."

"David, Georgia and I would like to know something about you."

Georgia said, "I'm okay, David. It's Roger who needs to know."

"Mr. Waddell, I was born in Savannah. My parents are Marsha and David Benson, Sr. I graduated from the University of North Carolina with a degree in art and music. That did not get me a lot of job opportunities, so after bouncing around a couple of years two of my friends and I decided to go to Israel to teach. It was something like *Jews return to your homeland.* I've been over there three years."

"So you are Jewish?"

"Yes, but not particularly, if that makes sense."

"Well it does. My father was Jewish. I have never understood which part of me is Jewish." There was a short pause as David looked toward Joanna.

"I met Joanna at a social I had no intention of attending, but a friend insisted I needed to get out and meet people. I think he was worried I was growing old without an attachment." Roger was shaking his head. "Really. I wasn't looking for anyone, but I went. I saw Joanna who looked like she wanted to get away as badly as I did. After we talked awhile, we left and realized we had a lot in common. She didn't know it, but she had me hooked that evening. I am in love with your daughter, Mr. Waddell, and I believe she loves me, but she said she would not say those words to me until I met you and her mother."

"You are a good daughter, Joanna."

"Dad and Mom, I cannot wait for you to see his art. He is very talented. He is an eclectic artist: scenery, people, and oh yes, he is painting abstracts at the moment."

"Were you able to bring any of them home?" Georgia asked

"Yes, I shipped them, but Joanna put a couple in her suitcase."

"Shipped them where?" Roger asked.

"To this address. It was Joanna's idea."

"Have you left Israel for good?" Georgia asked.

"Yes, ma'am, I believe so. My mom and dad had begun to worry about me, so I decided it was time to leave."

"Are you two…uh?" Roger stuttered.

"Roger, can't you wait a while to ask that question?" Georgia asked.

"Dad, let me say this to you, I love David." Turning to David she said, "I have loved you from almost the moment I met you. To answer your question, Dad, we were living together in Israel. After we visit David's parents, we will decide what to do next. It is an exciting time in our lives, so we want to include the two of you and his parents in our decisions."

Georgia said, "This is good. I believe we need to have a toast to your homecoming and your good news for our family. Roger, go get our best wine and show our kids how happy you are."

"Before we toast," David said, "We need to toast another event. You might want to sit down for this one." There was a long pause. "I don't know how to say this, but I am guilty. Joanna and I are expecting a baby."

"What! Georgia and I are going to be grandparents? That is wonderful, but I had better sit down to see if I am dreaming. Joanna, thank you, and thank you, David. When? We need to put the date on our calendars, Georgia."

"Dad, I was so scared to tell you. I thought you might be unhappy with me."

"Joanna, I can see that your dad is too emotional, so I'll talk for him. This is the greatest news ever. I never thought I would become a grandmother. You have made both of us very happy."

Finally Roger said, "We need a marriage. This baby has to come from married parents. I want both names on that birth certificate."

"Mr. Waddell, when we get back from North Carolina, that will happen. I'm certain my parents will want to be here. How about four weeks from now? There is a lot to do, like getting a license, and a place to live. Do either of you know a Rabbi in town?"

Georgia said, "I have a good friend who is a Reformed Rabbi, I'm certain he would be thrilled to marry you. He owes me a favor."

"You need to know this," Roger said. "Almost everyone in Atlanta owes Georgia a favor. David, Georgia was "Person of the Year" in Atlanta. She is a famous lady."

"Kids, let that remark pass," Georgia said.

"That's wonderful!" David said, "^know a celebrity!"

"Dad, we need to rent a car. Where can we do that?"

"I will have one for you by tomorrow morning."

"I have a question. Can we use my bedroom tonight?"

"You do not have to ask to use your bedroom, but David does."

"He's kidding. Of course you both can use your bedroom. Welcome to our home, David." Georgia said.

Roger said, "I was just about to say that. Welcome, David."

Later that evening, Georgia said to Roger, "Give you car keys to Joanna and David. Tomorrow I will drive you to the Cadillac place so you can get another car."

"That is a great idea. You are taking this Mom deal seriously."

"Yes, I am. There is *no way* my daughter and her baby will ride around in a rented car. Got it?"

Joanna accepted the use of Roger's car without question. The two of them communicated well. Watching them drive out of the condo parking lot Roger said, "I just learned again why I love you so much. You are the greatest! Damn I forgot to ask them if they needed any money."

"You wouldn't. You didn't pay for their flight home did you? They have money." What Roger didn't know was, Georgia asked Joanna about money earlier.

The next morning Georgia dropped him off at the dealership and said, "Get a roomy one that will hold four people and a baby!"

"Yes, ma'am."

Roger met the salesman who had sold him his present car. He selected the first car he saw. The salesman said, "Mr. Waddell, there are other cars to look at."

"This one looks fine to me. I will take it."

"I need to do the paper work and get it serviced."

"I will wait." He called Georgia and invited her to lunch.

"Pick up several sandwiches and drinks and bring them here," She said. "Too much going on for me to leave, but it would be nice to have a sandwich with you. Come on, maybe I'll get a peek at the car."

"I am in one of their rental cars while mine is being serviced. Is it all right for me to drive around in a rental?"

"You're bullet proof."

At her office he had to wait awhile for her to get free. He could not believe this was the first time he had been there. It was far fancier than the office he was stuck in years ago. Also he met her associate Alice Vickers. He didn't even know she had an associate. He thought to himself, *I need to get around a little more. Maybe I need a job.* Georgia sent her secretary out to get him, "Ms. Parker said for you to come on in, and wants to know if you brought extra sandwiches."

"Yes, in fact I did. I have five roast beef and five salads. Would that help?"

"Great! We've been so busy we haven't been out." He felt like a delivery boy creeping down the hall, not knowing which door to enter. "Roger, you've already been past my door once. Here I am."

"Well, you should not hide from me. Your office is large."

"It's about time you saw where I am when we're not together. Roger, I am in the middle of a tough case. I'll tell you about it tonight. It is consuming me right now, but I'm glad you came."

While they were eating, Roger said, "I need a job, Georgia. Everybody I know has a job, but me."

"Who is everybody?"

'That is just an expression."

"Then find one. Why don't you look into public service? I know some organizations that are crying for help. Since you don't need to earn any money, give some of it away."

"Let me think about it. I am going to leave now, and I am going to do something I never had an opportunity to do as a teenager. I am going to pick up my new car and ride around for everyone to see me."

"Don't pick up any women. I'll put them in jail."

"I have two women in my life, and that is all I need. One of them I love so much I have a difficult time being away from her, and the other has become the love of someone else, but that is the way life is supposed to be."

"Don't get too sentimental, but you are right. I have a suggestion. The mayor and I are good friends, why don't you pay him a visit. I bet he can put you to work."

"I do not know the Mayor. It would be awkward walking in and saying, "I am Roger Waddell, married to the Person of the Year, and I need a job."

"I didn't know you were so dramatic."

Georgia was exhausted when she came home. "I'm sorry we didn't get to spend much time together when you came by, but I had a lot of things going."

"Are you allowed to talk about your *things*?"

"Sure, I can with you. I am defending a young girl who was raped, and I've asked Bob Barnett to work with me. He is a smart lawyer. But the strange thing is, I'm unable to get in touch with him. His absence is delaying a few decisions. His office said he was away on urgent business. I even called Randy and he said the same thing. Interesting."

"Should I ask who is supposed to have raped the girl?"

"You have a law degree, would you tell me?"

"Yes, because we know the law and we trust each other."

"She is accusing Lamar Whitten, a partner of my cousin's husband."

"Oops! This is going to be interesting."

"You bet." She walked over to her closet and found the package Joanna left, and opened it. "Roger, just look at this outfit. Isn't it wonderful? Look at the brilliant colors. It's the picture I saw before she left for Israel. Our daughter is something else. Thank you for sharing her with me. I *have* to try this on. Look, both the skirt and top hang to fit almost anyone. I love it, and the length is right at my ankle. Perfect. Whoa! There is a necklace in the bottom of the package. Here, help me fasten it. How do I look?"

"Well, I have not been able to get a word it, but the outfit is beautiful on you, but you would look better naked."

"Don't be crude."

"I am joshing, Margaret. It is a beautiful outfit and perfect for you. Look in there and see if she brought me a shirt."

"No, but you can wear my top anytime you like."

"Pull off those clothes. It has been a long day, and I have not had you to myself."

"Aren't you hungry?"

"Yes, but not for food." He watched her as she undressed. When she put the outfit on the hanger she hand-ironed the material, put it to her nose, and took a deep breath. He saw tears falling from her eyes. "Georgia, she loves you."

"I know. It's such a generous gift and made especially for me." She went over to the bed, took off her bra and kissed him. "You gave me the world when you gave me a daughter, so again, I thank you. Never have I experienced such joy." He stood and took her breasts in his hands, gently caressing them, then kissed her nipples. His hands wandered down her body, and she trembled. "Are you cold?"

"No. Being cold is not on my mind. When you touch me, I have no words to describe how I feel." He put his hands on her hips and pulled her to the bed. Cupping his hands around her face he kissed her, starting at the brow, then the cheeks, then moved to her mouth. The pressure to enter her was so great he could not wait. She opened her legs to receive the gift that lifted her far from the events of the day. The rocking was like waves lapping on a beach, too intense and too savage for the mind to grasp, and the heat was stifling. Then like magic a cold fell upon them and every bone in their bodies relaxed. There were no words, only the sensation of gratification and peace. They lay beside each other. At that moment their love for each other was all that mattered in the world. He reached for her hand, and they both fell asleep.

CHAPTER 80

Bob, Margaret, Michael

"A Father Raymond is on the phone," Mr. Walker. "Thank you Ms. Bee."

"Mr. Walker, you can come for Mr. Barnett. He seems more focused than when you brought him. We worked together one on one, and we also dropped him into a group of four other men who have been meeting once a month. It is amazing he has been functioning at all, but I believe he has the ability to work out most of his problems. He is not entirely focused, but it is impossible to solve everything in such a short time, so encourage him to continue meeting with our monthly group."

"How about work?" Randy asked.

"Working will be good for him. His major decision, seems to be about a relationship he has. That will have to be handled eventually, and I believe he will make the right decision."

"Thank you, Father for seeing him. We go back a long way, and I will encourage him to participate in your group."

Bob looked relaxed when he and Randy met in the parlor. "I could live here," he said. "It's so pleasant and not like any place I've ever been. I intend to come back at least once a month. Just being here and walking around in silence might be enough. You ought to try it, Randy."

"That's what Joan said."

Driving back to Atlanta, Randy kept the conversation light until Bob asked, "Anything going on I need to know about?"

"A little business perhaps. Georgia has been trying to get in touch with you, something about a rape case involving a partner in the firm of her cousin's husband."

"Yep, I figured Georgia would want me on that. Lamar Whitten! He's an idiot and arrogant as hell. I am going to love it."

"It will be good for you. I know you have a lot of decisions to make. Maybe you'll have a clearer mind after this trip. When you get back to your office, mark off those group days on your calendar."

"I will, don't worry, I will. Thanks for taking your time to help me out. I'm surprised I didn't know about the Monastery. I need to focus more outside the range of my daily life and take advantage of places that are right under my nose. Here I am middle aged and always focusing on helping other people. I have learned I can't take care of them unless I take care of myself."

Roger said, "We all need to learn that lesson."

It was a much better ride back to Atlanta than away. Bob talked and Randy listened. It appeared he had come away more relaxed that he had been in a long time. "Randy," he said, "I believe you could benefit from a week at the monastery.

"I'll consider it."

"Well, here you are back home," Randy said as he stopped in Bob's drive way. "Thanks for trusting me with your life." Bob was shaking his head. "Seriously, I mean it, Bob. Getting back to work will be good for you. Remember to call Georgia as soon as you can. By the way Joanna is back in town. She brought her boyfriend, and they are expecting a baby. Ole Roger is taking it well. He said to me, 'but they are getting married. I told them I want two names on that birth certificate.' That's the story's short version."

'That sounds like him."

"He has called all of us except you, so when he calls don't mention that I told you. Cassie and Robert's twins are doing well. You will not believe this, that mean courtroom lawyer has become a doting father."

"That's good news. I'm surprised Georgia didn't call Robert Sanders to help her out, but that's beside the point, isn't it?"

"Yep. What are your plans for the afternoon?"

"I plan to call Margaret, and give her some idea of why I didn't let her know I would be out of town. She's going to be mad again. God, I love her. Randy, how did you get so attached to Joan's children, and so fast?"

"Because I loved Joan, and anything, or any person, that came with her was a bonus for me."

"Wow! Do you think I can do that?"

"Only if you want to."

"And there is Becky, her employee."

"Well you could create an apartment for her. Just imagine, anytime you and Margaret want to go out, she'll be there, and remember Margaret has trained her in the business. That's a plus. Why am I talking about all this? Sorry. I am not your therapist. I have enough decisions of my own."

"You are, and always have been, a great friend. Thanks for the ride. I won't need your transportation again. I can find my way back."

"You are a smart man and an excellent lawyer. It's time you put some of the past behind and live in the present. Well, I could say that about all of us. Losing Rick was one of the hardest things I ever had to deal with. No, that's not true. Watching Joan with John Randolph was harder than that, but that's another story. Good Luck, brother."

"Thanks again, Randy."

"Hi, Margaret, I'm back in town give me a call." That was as simple as he could make it. He waited, but there was no return. So he listened to his messages: *Bob, where are you? This is Georgia. I need you to call me as soon as you can.* Another call: *Bob, I need you on a case. Call me right away.* The third call was from Margaret: *Bob, where are you? I am at the hospital. Something's wrong with Michael. Call me.* He tried to call her, but no answer. He made a call to Randy, "Margaret left a message on my machine that Michael is in the hospital. Ask Joan if she knows anything about it?"

"She's not here. She left a note that she was going to Piedmont Hospital to be with Margaret."

"Piedmont. Thanks. I'm on my way. Georgia can wait."

Bob rushed to Piedmont, and got the room number from the receptionist in the pediatric ward. He went in the wrong direction. *I hate hospitals. There needs to be a better configuration.* Finally he saw the pediatric sign. Joan was in the hallway. "Joan!" he called out.

"Bob, thank goodness. The doctor is in the room with them now. Now that you are here, I'm going back home. Keep me informed."

"I'm going in. They may kick me out, but I'm going to try it." He slipped in and saw Margaret watching as the doctor examined Michael. He went to her and put his arm around her, and she didn't resist. "When did you get back?" She whispered.

"About an hour ago. What's wrong with Michael?"

"This is Dr. John Gilbert. He believes Michael has whooping cough."

"Bob-bob," Michael said when he opened his eyes.

"Hi, I'm here, buddy."

Michael held out his hand. "Not yet, Michael," the doctor said. "So you are Bob-bob, he has been calling for you." Michael has a good case of whooping cough, pertussis to some people. We are giving him medicine to make the coughing less severe and some antibiotics. It will just take time now."

"Where in the world would he get that?" Margaret said, "He's had all the vaccinations."

"And that is the reason he is not worse than he is. Do not enter or leave this room without washing your hands thoroughly with this special soap. Take every precaution, and I would prefer no other visitors."

"Thanks, John," Margaret said. "This is Bob Barnett."

"Nice to see you in person. You defended one of my associates, Dr. Janet

Mears, and this talented lady decorated my office. She came up with all the safe toys for children to play with. Michael calls you Bob-bob? Are you and Margaret…he twisted his hand back and forth?"

"Yes, I remember Dr. Mears and yes, Margaret and I are more than friends. I've been away for a week; just got back in."

"I'll be going now, see you tomorrow, Margaret. If Michael has a good night he can go home tomorrow."

"Margaret, I'm so sorry I wasn't here. Seems I have a habit of being in the right place at the wrong time. I'll have to tell you about my visit when Michael gets better. How long have you been here?"

"Wait a minute, we're more than friends? When did that happen? Are you dying?"

"Yes, to the first question if you accept, and no, I am *not* dying."

She smiled and said, "I'll have to think about it. Anyhow, a couple of days ago I realized Michael had more that a cough, so I called John's office, gave the staff his symptoms, and they sent us here immediately."

"Is Becky taking care of business?"

"Yes, I'm lucky to have her as my assistant."

"Would you like for me to stay with Michael tonight?"

"No, I want to be here. Look he's awake."

"Bob-bob."

"Hey, Michael, I'm sorry you don't feel good. You get well, I have to teach you how to play baseball." Michael smiled.

"Margaret, can I bring you anything?"

"No, I threw some things in a bag just in case."

"Margaret, I love you. There are a lot of things I need to do to make our relationship better and permanent. It will take time to work things out, but we will get there if you still love me."

"Better and permanent?"

"Better is why I went off for a week, and permanent is when I heard Michael was in the hospital. You don't have to say anything right now, just take care of Michael. I've got to contact Georgia. She's been trying to get me to help her on a rape case."

"You go, I can handle tonight and Becky will be here tomorrow. You could take part of tomorrow night if Michael is still here."

"Will do." He kissed her. "Bye, Michael, see you tomorrow."

CHAPTER 81
The Whitten Case

Bob contacted Georgia early the next day. "Georgia, is this a good time to talk?"

"What happened to you? Did you drop off the side of the earth?"

"Just about, but don't ask; it was private."

"I need to see you as soon as possible. When can you be here?"

"Give me a couple of hours."

When Bob arrived at Georgia's office, she gave him some papers to read until she could get the other items together. "Lamar Whitten, son of a bitch, at his daughter's spend-the-night party at his own house. Good God, I can smell evil. Let's see, she's fifteen and her name is Beth Jefferson. Are any of the other girls willing to corroborate?"

"Don't know yet, haven't met with any of them."

"Rape test?

"Yes, her mother took her straight to the hospital, and it was positive."

"And Whitten says…"

"Haven't spoken to him, but he will deny it."

"Of course he will. We've got to get our brains together on this. He's a powerful man in Atlanta, and one of the most unscrupulous men I know. Have you decided on a starting place?"

"We can require him to have a sperm test, but most likely he has a prominent attorney, so they will definitely stall that procedure. The Jefferson's called me, and I have talked to their daughter, and she was pretty damn factual. I asked her parents, Forest and Lillian, if they would allow me to tape a conversation with Beth, and they signed the consent, and I also had Beth sign. Let me play some of it for you. I'll go straight to the recorded conversation."

The recording

"Beth Jefferson, I am Georgia Parker, an attorney in Atlanta. Did you agree to allow me to record this conversation about an incident that occurred at the Whitten's home?"

"Yes Ma'am, I did."

"I am not here to blame you, Beth I am here to help you. Are you ready, now?

"Yes, Ma'am, but I am ashamed. Mom, Dad, I am so sorry."

"Beth, who is in the room with us today?"

"Both of my parents are here."

"Beth, have your parents agreed to have this conversation recorded?"

"Yes Ma'am, they have."

"Why were you at the Whitten's home on the night in question?"

"Their daughter invited me to a spend-the-night party."

"Had you been there before?"

"Yes, several times."

"Why were you outside the house at the pool?"

"One of the girls came up to me and whispered, "There is someone at the pool who wants to talk to you."

"Beth, who was that girl?"

"Her name is Sandra, Sandra Carver."

"Did anyone else hear her?"

"I don't think so. She sort of whispered to me."

"What happened next?"

"When I went out to the pool the only person I saw was Mr. Whitten. He said he wanted to show me something interesting. He always seemed like a nice man when I visited his daughter before, so I trusted him. He told me that he has been noticing me for a long time, and that I was pretty, and there was something he wanted me to see. Then everything happened so fast. He pushed me into the pool house suite, and began touching me all over. I panicked, and tried to escape, because it was evident what was going to happen. I said stop it, let me go, and I tried to scream, but he covered my mouth and told me that he knew I wanted him, and that a lot of my friends had already had sex with him. Then he threw me on the bed." She began crying. "Beth, do you want a break?"

"No, Ma'am, but I don't like to talk about this in front of my parents. I am embarrassed."

"Mrs. Jefferson, you wish to speak?"

"Yes, I do. Beth, you need to do this. If he has raped you, he will rape other girls."

"I am so sorry, Mommy and Daddy. I just didn't think fast enough."

"Honey, this is important, and we are not blaming you."

"Mr. Whitten put his fingers into me first. Oh God, Mom." She stopped and tried to breathe. "Then he held me down and raped me. His body was so heavy; he almost smothered me. Then I heard Victoria calling my name and beating on the door. He got off of me and tried to wipe himself off with the sheet, and he left in a hurry, out a door on the backside of the room. All he said was, 'God dammit.' I finally let Victoria inside from the poolside, because she said, 'if you don't let me in I'm going to call the police.' She asked me if I was all right and that she had been looking for me. Victoria was mad at me. She said, 'oh my God, Beth. Did he rape you? Why did you go out here with him? Didn't you know what kind of man he is? Why didn't you run? He tried to get me one time when I was here. Get up, and let me take that sheet. I read some where to do that.' I don't remember exactly what I said to her, but I felt ashamed, because she seemed to be blaming me. She's always been my take-charge friend, so she called my mom to come get me." Georgia stopped the tape.

"Great," Bob said, "She took the sheet. What a smart girl. Where is it now?"

"Her mom took Beth straight to the emergency room. She had a laceration that needed repair, so the doctor asked her, 'who did this to you?' And Beth told her. 'were you a virgin?' Beth said, 'Yes Ma'am,' the doctor said, 'the son of a bitch.' They left the sheet with the emergency room doctor. She said she would make certain it didn't get lost until she could give it to the police. That's all on the tape. You can listen to that part later."

"Did the doctor give any indication that she knew Lamar?"

"I didn't ask that question," Georgia said, "But her anger sounded rather personal. All during the recording Forest Jefferson kept pacing the room. He never once looked up or sat, and Beth's mom cried the whole time. I'm surprised Beth was able to talk. I can tell you, sweat and anger filled that room, because the devil had entered it. It was a critical situation. I begged Mr. Jefferson not to take the law into his own hands, but allow me do what is right. I told him, do not even *think about* confronting Lamar Whitten or calling his office, you could be put in jail. Beth needs both of you right now, and I want her to see a counselor beginning this week. Here is the name of the person I suggest, but you may know someone else. Tell her that I said that it is important that she sees Beth right away.

"Mr. Jefferson finally spoke, 'there was a time in the South when we took care of matters like this. Even today, it would take only a few minutes for me to call the right persons. He deserves to be beaten with a whip.'

"I said to him, you may be right Mr. Jefferson, but your being arrested would not help your family right now. He said, 'I want him in prison for a long time, and I hope he gets raped every day by inmates.' Beth said, 'daddy, I am so sorry this happened,' and he answered, 'it was not your fault, Sugar. We will get through this. Yes, we will.'"

"Will Victoria help us out?" Bob asked.

"Who knows? But the girl I want to have a conversation with is Sandra Carver, the one who set her up, and I want to know why. We need to find out what kind of favors she gets for setting girls up? There is a lot of work to do."

"I just got in and went straight to the hospital to see Michael. He's been diagnosed with whooping cough, and he'll be there at least another twelve hours. If he's still in the hospital, I'll be staying with him tomorrow night. Let me take your paper work and the tape with me. I want to go through it several times. We can't afford to make a mistake on this. Georgia, you must have something up your sleeve."

"I'm betting on those other incidents Victoria hinted at. The individuals are not going to be easy to find, but I know they are out there. I have a feeling his wife knows all about Lamar preying on young girls. She couldn't be that blind. Yep, we're starting with his wife."

"Okay," Bob said, "I'll talk with you tomorrow. By the way Georgia, how's Roger doing?"

"Our daughter Joanna, I love that word *our,* is back in town with her boyfriend, David. Roger's beside himself; he's going to be a granddaddy."

"Wow, all that at once! I'd better check on Julia. Don't want to get that kind of surprise with this guy named Roy."

"Roger and I are beyond happy, if there is such a condition. You have known him for years, was he always this contented?" Georgia said.

"Roger is a unique individual," Bob said. "He was the one and only special child of parents who thought giving him an education by introducing him to different world cultures was better than money. We had no idea how wealthy his parents were when he came to school, but it was obvious he had great social skills. Yep, we got the impression he was dirt poor. If he ate off campus with us, one of us always bought his dinner. I forgot about that; he owes me a lot of money. He's not a pretentious person, and he's one of the most brilliant persons I have ever known. A lot of the material we studied in college, his father had already taught him."

"I guess I shouldn't be talking about my private life, but I've never been loved like this before. Bob, do I look like a grandmother?"

"You'd better dye your hair white, or quit dying it red."

"I didn't ask you to be a smart aleck."

"You're beautiful, Georgia, and you know it. You will be beautiful when you are eighty. I had the time of my life escorting you to that annual awards party."

"Gee, I'm glad you came by; thanks for the compliments. I know you have to help with Michael right now, but study all this information as soon as possible. Any ideas, give me a call."

"Will do."

The drive home was lonely and much too introspective: *There are a lot of decisions hanging over my head.* Stopping at a traffic light he put both hands over his face. He heard the horn on the car behind. Okay, I'm moving. Okay, Okay. *Idiot. I must quit worrying about the worst that can happen and focus on the positive. I'm tired of that pitiful look in my friends' eyes knowing they feel sorry for me. Margaret is the best thing that has happened to me in a long, long, time, and I know she loves me. I need to thank Randy for giving me a kick in the ass, or was it an ultimatum? Maybe he was tired of me leaning on him for support. God knows I could use a bit of luck, but if I'm taking on the responsibility of Margaret and Michael, I need to get my life straight. Hell, what am I thinking? Margaret doesn't need me to take her on. I learned something about prayer at the Monastery. Now may be the time to use the language.* When he got home, Margaret called. She and Michael were home.

CHAPTER 82

Louise Whitten

The following morning, Georgia decided to take a chance and call Louise Whitten. Finally, after two hours she reached her. "Mrs. Whitten, this is Attorney, Georgia Parker. You may not remember me, but we have met before. You and I need talk."

"Yes, I know who you are. What does this concern, Ms. Parker?"

"Can we talk in private and not on the phone? I can come by and pick you up in about an hour."

"I don't know." There was a long pause. "Actually, I am quite busy at the moment."

"Mrs. Whitten, I can have you subpoenaed, but I would rather not do that. Would you be willing to come to my office?"

After another long pause, she said, "No, Ms. Parker. I would rather we meet somewhere more private. How about my church, the large Methodist Church on Ponce de Leon? I'll meet you in the parking lot. If I cannot get in touch with my pastor, I will call you back."

"Mrs. Whitten, though this meeting will be private, my co-attorney will also meet with us. I am sure you know Bob Barnett. Also, I suggest you ask your own attorney to be present."

"Yes, I know Bob. I do not have an attorney, but if I need one, I am sure there is someone out there. I'll meet you in a couple of hours."

That was too easy, Georgia thought.

Georgia and Louise arrived about the same time, and they waited for Bob in the parking lot. Georgia stood on the steps, but Louise waited in her car till Bob arrived.

Louise said, "My pastor is waiting inside for us." Bob studied Louise. He had known her for quite awhile. *She was the kind of woman who stopped conversation upon entering a room: beautiful, elegant, a graduate of Agnes Scott, and from an old Atlanta family. She could pass for a twenty-five in any crowd. According to what he had heard, Louise was known for working in her church and supporting a couple of charities, one of them the Methodist Children's home. What man would risk losing her?*

After being introduced to the Reverend Paul Lee, they were seated. Georgia couldn't help noticing the picture of Jesus on the cross above Pastor Lee's head. She thought to herself, *an unsettling image for this meeting.* "Georgia asked, "Louise, do you have an idea why I asked you to meet with us?"

"Yes, Ms. Parker I have an idea."

"Have you contacted an attorney?"

"No, I have not had time to find one who is not my husband's friend."

"We should get started. I need to tape this meeting, because, in reality, we have nothing without the tape."

"I thought you might. What do you think, Pastor?"

"You have to make that decision, Louise. You have asked me to be an observer, but according to what you have already told me, this is a serious situation. Ms. Parker, I will not testify of this meeting under any circumstance, unless my Bishop allows it."

"I understand, Reverend. Mrs. Whitten, if you agree, after you read this introduction of time and place, sign your first and last name on this line, but read it first, especially where you agree for us to record this meeting, and check on the last line that you do not have an attorney present."

"Now that done, so let's begin. Mrs. Whitten, were you aware that on the night of August 8th your husband took a young girl out to the pool house at your daughter's spend-the-night party?" There was a long pause. "Should I repeat the question?"

"You do not have to. Yes, I was looking out from an upstairs window."

"Did you even consider going down to intervene?"

"Maybe I should have, for the girl's sake. I was just hoping she would run. I have known for some time my husband likes young girls, and I am ashamed I have not done anything about it. This may sound selfish, but my first priority is to protect my children and my parents."

Mrs. Whitten, why have you agreed to this meeting?"

"That particular girl was Beth Jefferson, the daughter of one of my best friends. She is a beautiful child. I am embarrassed that he would do that. He may have chosen her on purpose to spite me." There was a long pause. "Is there some way we can keep this from going to court? This will destroy my family." Suddenly Georgia noticed a picture on the wall of Jesus surrounded by little children. *Damn walls. What are these walls trying to say to me*? Both Bob and Rev. Lee noticed her staring at the picture.

"Are you saying that you want to stay married to this man?"

"No, but I want my children to hear this from me, not the newspapers."

"That is not going to be possible unless your husband comes forward and admits to his crimes. Are you aware that he raped other young girls? And we know of one who successfully got away from him, a very close friend of your daughter."

"Yes, she did run from him. That would be Victoria Morrison."

"Oh, my God, were you *actually* watching her?" *Oh, Jesus, get out of this room.* "Do not judge me so harshly, Ms. Parker. I would do anything to save my reputation and protect my children." She looked toward her pastor, "Reverend Lee, was I so wrong not to intervene. Please help me out here?"

He appeared to be uneasy, but finally spoke, "Louise, I am trying to word my comments to not harm the ministry of this congregation. Help me understand your position. Are you saying that you sacrificed young girls to protect your own children? If that is true there is a possibility your children are going to lose both of their parents."

"Pastor, this is not a trial. Please do not interject any more remarks. We don't want to put you in a compromising position with your church. You and Mrs. Whitten will have opportunity to talk after we leave."

"Thank you, Ms. Parker, I understand."

"To protect others, we must see that Mr. Lamar Whitten is arrested as soon as possible. First, are there other girls you have watched from your window?"

"I would rather not say at this time.

Oh Jesus, protect those others.

"But you knew this had to come to a head sooner than later, didn't you?"

They waited for her answer. "How shall I say this? There is no good way. For a while now, I have begun to realize, by keeping this secret, I was being a part of his disgraceful conduct. I am deeply ashamed. Very soon I am going to be without friends, and my children are going to hate both of us - me for not reporting my husband's disgraceful behavior, and him for what he did to the young girls, friends of my own daughter."

Bob Barnett said, "I have no pity for you, but I am deeply sorry for your children. You need to put them with a counselor right away, but not with your pastor. Am I correct, Reverend Lee?" He asked looking toward Rev. Lee.

"Sadly, you are correct," he responded. Georgia dismissed the meeting. Pastor Lee said he would like to end the meeting with a prayer. Bob said, "I don't believe this has been a religious meeting, Reverend, so I would rather you not do that. You can pray with Mrs. Whitten after we leave."

On the way out Georgia said, "I was distracted by Jesus and the children."

"I saw you looking. The wrong children were in that picture."

Three days later the magistrate issued an arrest order for Lamar Whitten, and he was arrested and taken to jail. Georgia asked that bond be denied because of the seriousness of the crimes, and the fact he might try to contact the girls he abused. Bond was denied. His lawyer asked that information not be leaked to the public. The judge said, "Now how are we going to do that? Not possible. Bailiff, take Mr. Whitten away. At this time he is not allowed to have a phone."

Gossip circulated around town about the arrest, and of course Whitten's lawyer issued a statement that he was innocent of the charges – just a group of people who wanted to hurt him.

Two days later Georgia's Paralegal said, "Ms. Parker, there is a phone call on line one. The lady says she is Sandra Carver's mother, Jeanette Carver."

"Ms. Parker speaking."

"This is Jeanette Carver. I understand you want to talk to me."

"Who told you that?"

"I had a call from a woman who did not identify herself."

"Yes, I do need to talk to you. When can we meet?"

"I have already talked to my daughter, Sandra. You may come to our house."

"Give me the directions and a time to come?"

"I was hoping you could come right away."

CHAPTER 83

Sandra Carver

It was obvious Jeanette Carver had been crying when she opened the door. She was very attractive, though a bit over weight. She had the aura of being well bred. Georgia was stunned at the lavish furnishings of the home. The social area of the house was decorated with cool colors of blues and grays, accented with gold, and absolutely nothing was out of place. Mrs. Carver invited Georgia in and led her to a small suite where Sandra was sitting at her desk. "This whole situation is terribly embarrassing, but I am not mad at my daughter, Mrs. Parker, disappointed, but not mad. Lamar Whitten has put her through hell these past few months. I have called her father, and asked him to be here. We are divorced, so he may decided not to come since he and Lamar are good friends."

"Mrs. Carver, I need you to be present while I talk to you daughter, and if the two of you agree I would like to record our conversation."

"I do not know about that. Sandra, what do you think?"

"Mom, what does it matter now?"

"I guess not. You have our permission."

"Please sign this permission form, Mrs. Carver. Sign on the top line, and Sandra, put your signature on the next line."

"Sandra, I'm going to get right to the reason why I am here. Were you giving the names of your friends to Mr. Lamar Whitten so he could approach them, lure them, or force them into having sex with him?" She looked toward her mother, "I am so sorry, Mom. Yes, he gave me a hundred dollars each time I helped him out."

"So you realized he was using you to have sex with your friends."

"Yes, I knew what he was doing."

"Why would you do that?" Mrs. Carver asked.

"He was going to tell my father that I was having sex with him, and that *I* was the one who approached *him*. Mom, he is a very bad man. I was afraid of him. If my friends find out about this I will have no friends."

"Sweetheart, an evil man brought you into this hell. Now we have to find out what we can do about it. That's the doorbell; let me get it. Come in, Richard. We are in Sandra's room." He threw his coat on a chair, and moved into the room, "What is so important that I have to leave my office in mid-day?"

"Mr. Carver, I am attorney Georgia Parker. Let me bring you up to date on why I am here."

"I've met you before Ms. Parker. Why are you here?" As quickly as she could, she explained the reason for her presence. "For Christ's sake, Sandra do you also have to ruin *my* life?" He turned as if to be headed toward the door.

"Mr. Carver, your daughter was raped by Mr. Whitten, and he used her to get other girls to have sex with him, by threatening her."

"I don't believe it. He would not hurt my daughter."

"Yes, Daddy, he did. He has ruined my life."

"What do you want me to do about it?"

Mrs. Carver said, "She wants you to care about her, that's what?"

"Damn it, Jeanette! Couldn't you have handled this situation yourself?"

Georgia said, "No, Mr. Carver she should not have to. This is more than *a situation*. If this goes to trial I may put you on the witness stand. (He shook his head.) Yes I can. So I suggest you get a lawyer, and it can't be your friend Bob Barnett, because he's working with me on this. I want the court to ask you what you know about your friend. You are a pitiful man and worse father that you do not care that you daughter has been raped. Your friend's latest victim was Beth Jefferson, and her parents have the evidence to prove it. Wake up, Mr. Carver; you are best friends with a rapist! Try to care about the many girls Lamar Whitten has raped, that is, unless you approve of what he has done."

"God damn it! Don't accuse me of that. Will I never have any peace? God knows I have tried."

"It's up to you, Mr. Carver. Can you put your nasty divorce behind you, and help your daughter get through this?"

"Oh, my God, Sandra what happened?"

Sandra began with the rape, the threat to expose her unless she helped him with other girls, and her embarrassment for what she did. "I am an idiot. I have ruined my life and the lives of my friends. Daddy, I am a traitor. I don't want to live. Beth Jefferson was one of my best friends, but Mr. Whitten specifically asked me to get her to go out to the pool, or else."

"Or else what?"

"He would tell you I was the one who asked him to have sex with me. You and Mom have to believe me, I did *not* do that. One day he was waiting for me at school. He told me that you asked him to pick me up. After he raped me, he said it would be his word against mine unless I helped him. He said he had influence in the city, so no one would believe me. Daddy, he is gross."

"Oh, my God."

"Do you have anything to say other than *Oh my God?*" Jeanette asked. "We need to work together on this for our daughter's sake."

"All three of you have been privileged to this matter," he said. "Right now I feel jumped upon. I am just trying to get my feet on the ground. What kind of proof do you have, Ms. Parker?"

"Right now two girls have definite proof, but I believe there are many more. How many did you contact, Sandra?"

"I don't want to tell that. Do I have to?"

"No, you don't have to, but it might help convict Lamar Whitten." Sandra paused as if she were counting. Besides Beth there are five, but there are others he bragged about. "Give me a pen and I will write their names." She read their names and handed the list to Georgia. "Five more!" Lamar said. "The son of a bitch! Sandra, are you certain? This is serious business."

"Yes, Daddy I am the one responsible for them." The air in the room grew thin, and the persons in it froze. The chimes from the hall clock struck 3:00, and seemed to say*, it's too late*; *it's too late*. After what seemed an eternity, Sandra jumped up and raced to the bathroom with her hand over her mouth and her mother followed. Georgia and Mr. Carver could hear her retching. Georgia said to Mr.

Carver, "Would you stay with them for a short period? I believe they need you. I am going to leave now. Please be a father today, even if it takes everything in you to do that. This is your only child and she needs you."

"I will stay until she settles down. If she wishes I will take her home with me tonight. It seems I don't know my daughter, and this might be the best time to try to change that. Ms. Parker, I have been through hell these past few months. I thought I had a perfect marriage. Now *this*. I am definitely in shock."

"Just remember this is not about you right now."

"I am not sure about that."

After Sandra washed up, he took her home with him, even though she was reluctant to go. They did not talk to each other during the drive. After getting her settled he said to her, "I need to return to the office for a little while, but I won't be gone for more than a couple of hours. We will make some plans for dinner when I get back. You just relax on the sofa. There are some cokes in the refrigerator and some interesting magazines on the coffee table."

"I wish you wouldn't go. I'm not familiar with your place."

"Then maybe the best thing you can do for yourself right now is rest. It sounds like you have been through a lot these past few weeks, so don't worry you will be safe here. Then he left.

When Sandra heard him drive away she walked though the rooms of the condo, she had seen only once, to find her father's bathroom. She opened the medicine cabinet and found what she wanted, three bottles of pills. She didn't even bother to read the labels. *I remember in some movie just how the actress did it; didn't look hard to me.* She turned on the water and dropped all the bath salts in and waited for the water to get warm. The salts bubbled and made her nose sting like they did when she was a little girl, but a nice aroma filled the bathroom. She was fascinated watching the event. She swallowed all the pills, waited until the bathtub was full of water, and without removing her clothes entered the water and began to relax. The water was warm and inviting. She closed her eyes and slowly drifted into sleep and peace.

A couple of hours later her father entered the house through the kitchen and yelled, "I'm home Sandra. Ready to go get something to eat?" No response. "Sandra, where are you? Are you in the bathroom?" He went through the house calling her. He knocked on the bathroom door, but there was no response. The only sound was a little dripping of water, so he opened the door. "Sandra! Oh, dear God, Sandra what have you done? Come on let's get you out of the tub. Oh my God, oh my God, not this! No, not this." He sat on the floor and rocked her in his arms. Speaking out loud to nothing but the bathtub, he shouted, "I am an idiot. What I need to do is get my gun and kill myself." He sat on the floor rocking his beautiful limp daughter in his arms, and became nauseated with the stink of the bath salts that filled the room. He cursed and wished there was a way to drown himself. Finally, he straitened her body, covered her with a towel, and lay down beside her. He reached for his phone and called 911. Then he called Jeanette, "She's dead, Jeanette. She did it in the bathtub. I lifted her out, but she was gone. I'm so sorry. I'm so very sorry."

"Were you there?"

"I stepped out for a little while. It's my fault. I'm so sorry. Did I say I called 911?"

"You are an idiot. You have killed our daughter! Do not let them take her until I get there. Can you do that?"

"Yes, I'll wait for you. I'm so sorry."

The police entered through the open garage door. They followed the sound of a man crying. When they walked into the bathroom, the aroma of the salts hit them in the face, and they saw a lifeless young girl in the arms of a weeping man. No one talked. Even the police were sobbing. One of them said, "What a beautiful girl, even wet and dead. Why little girl? What could be so bad you had to do this?" One of the EMT's lifted her body and placed her on the bed. He examined her, and pronounced her dead. "We have to take her? I need you to sign some papers."

"Please wait, her mother is on the way."

Jeanette entered the condo. She had called a friend to bring her, for she was certain she would be unable to drive. There are no words to describe the lamenting of a mother when she entered the bedroom. Her screams and words pierced the hearts of those in the house, and caused extreme distress to the officers. Two of them left the room. They could hear one of them retching over the railings of the deck. "Jeanette, I am so sorry; it's my fault. I want to die with her."

"Don't talk to me, Richard. I don't want to hear your voice. Now that she is dead you are going to claim you have feelings for her. I know you; something else was more important than staying with her. I hope you go to hell." He backed away.

"Mrs. Carver, we have to remove her now. Here is where we are taking her.
Someone will take you home. Do you have anyone to stay with you?"

"No, there is no one in this town who would dare. Richard, do you believe her story now?"

"Yes. Jeanette, let me take you home."

"Why would you do that? Besides I have a ride."

"I need to be with you. I want to call your Rabbi. It's important to me. I need help. Maybe there is something he can say."

An officer intervened, "Wait a minute. Both of you need to stay here until we finish. I have some questions and more papers to sign."

After everyone left Richard was left in an empty house. He fell to the floor on his knees, and knocked his head over and over, and cried out for God to strike him for his sin. Finally, he rose, and called Rabbi Levine. It was hard to tell him the reason for the call, but he explained what had been happening in his daughter's life, and now her death. Actually, he did not remember what he said, but the Rabbi agreed to meet with them at Jeanette's house the next morning.

The Rabbi sat in the den for ten uncomfortable minutes before there was any conversation. The only sound was the clock on the mantle striking ten times. Finally he spoke, "Let's talk about what happened. But first let me remind you, I am not a psychologist. What I have to say should be followed by seeing a counselor - both of you. For the time being, stop blaming each other for this tragedy. This is a shared tragedy. I hate to make this statement, but something like this happens all over our culture more than you could ever imagine. According to our conversation on the phone, Richard, I understand that an evil man turned your daughter into a traitor in her own eyes. She was smart. She knew all her friends and their families would condemn her, and she would be an outcast. What does a child do when that happens? Obviously, she did not choose either of you to confide in, until it was too late. The most important words I have for is this: You have to find a way to heal, not today or tomorrow. Do not think you can do this yourself. To get through this tragedy you are going to need help, a lot of it. There are decisions you have to make in the next few days. Your child was harmed beyond her, or your, imagination. It is hard to believe neither of you knew what was happening, but that is not unusual. Adults put too much trust in their teenagers, trust not warranted. We can't seem to fathom how much evil is out there, even in people we tend to trust. Tonight I want to hear you talk to each other, not in blame, but what happens next."

Slowly Richard began, "I feel responsible, and I do blame myself. I should have spent the evening with her. But since I saw her so rarely, I figured we wouldn't have much to say to each other. Our divorce hit me by surprise and sent me reeling. I have kept busy trying to get my own life in order, but sadly I abandoned my child. I should have ended my life when I saw her. The pain of my failure is too horrible to live with."

"Pity won't help at this moment," Rabbi Levine said. "What you do after this tragedy is the most important decision in your lives. You need to see that this man who assaulted your daughter is punished, not by your own hands, but legally. When you discover the names of the other girls who were assaulted, you need to meet with their fathers. Maybe you can save other fathers from this horror."

"I am devastated beyond belief," Jeanette said. "Maybe I spent more time on my own pain and anger than hers. I want to die, really I do. I cannot live with this."

"That cannot be all you have to say," The Rabbi said. "You know there is more to this whole event, but you can't change anything from the past. You have to move forward."

"How? Richard, I needed you to be a part of her life, if not mine. She was not at fault for our separation. I was the one who broke our marriage vows, not her. You had a right to hate me, but not her. I've ruined our lives."

"Now that you have sufficiently blamed yourselves, what are you going to do?" There was another long pause.

Painfully Richard began, "Jeanette, I will agree to go to counseling, and would like for you to go with me."

"I don't know. It is too early for me to commit."

"Then I have nothing more to say," Richard said.

"Don't give up so quickly, Richard. Why did you just refuse his offer, Jeanette?" The Rabbi asked.

"I need time to grieve; maybe in a few weeks I will go."

"I didn't mean tomorrow." Richard said.

Jeannette said, "Okay, maybe later, but first we have to take care of our daughter. I don't even know how or where. I'm so confused. I don't want a funeral. I can't handle that. All those people out there; they will know everything."

"I will take care of that," Richard said. Rabbi, will you help me?"

"We'll work together on it. At least we have accomplished that today, but nothing else. You realize you will not recover from this for a long time. You both need help, for what happened yesterday will stay with you for a lifetime. If you do not seek counseling together, then find a counselor for your own sanity."

Jeanette and Richard agreed to have their daughter cremated, against the wishes of the Rabbi. Her ashes were placed in an elaborate urn and Jeanette kept the urn. Both parents were consumed with anger and guilt. Within six months, Mrs. Carver put her house on the market, and moved to Jacksonville, Florida. Mr. Carver took a position with a firm in Memphis. Removing themselves from the area is how they decided to take care of their pain.

Since Sandra had given them names, Georgia and Bob contacted the five girls' parents. Three of the victims, who had been raped by Lamar Whitten, agreed to come before the judge in a closed session, and Beth Jefferson's lawyer appeared with her and her parents. He had obtained the document concerning the evidence of the sheet. The recording of the interview with Sandra Carver was also played. Two other girls asked not to appear, but sent statements by their lawyers. Lamar Whitten attempted to leave the session, but was forced back into his chair by two policemen. He remained silent as he listened to the proceedings. When his lawyer burst out in disagreement during the proceedings, Lamar ordered him not to speak again in his defense.

Faced with the evidence and possibility of a trial, Lamar Whitten pleaded guilty to the rape of each girl as their names was called. The Judge said to him, "If it were not for the hard work of two good lawyers, you might have continued your sorry behavior." He pointed to a policeman, "Take him to jail and put a twenty-four hour watch on him. I don't want him to do anything to himself that will keep him from going to prison." He was taken back to jail to await sentencing.

After Lamar was removed the Judge addressed Louise Whitten who was brought to the meeting by two officers of the court. The judge chastised her for failing to report the actions of her husband, and ordered her to be arrested immediately. He said to her, "I want you to remember the rest of your life that you were very much a part of the actions of your husband. You knew what he was doing, so your failure to report your husband's rape of young girls is beyond comprehension. You must pay for that omission. You owe that to these parents. Whatever will become of you, I have no idea, but you and your children will have to live with your silence for the rest of your lives. I want you to stand trial, so arrange a placement for you son and daughter. You realize they will suffer because of your neglect. Take her away."

———

At the end of the day Georgia and Bob were exhausted. They needed time to get away. Georgia mentioned to Bob that she felt dirty. He responded, "I have been trying to decide how I feel, but "dirty" is not a strong enough expression for me. I feel totally discussed with the human race. It frightens me to wonder how many people are taking part in such evil. I have the strangest urge to get my daughter and take her away to some less evil place, if there were such a place. Of course there isn't."

Georgia said, "Come home with me, Bob. At least come for a while. I feel the human race has let us down. Let's try to find some closure tonight. Roger has a way of listening that empowers me. He almost always has some expression that gives me relief, and you and I need that."

They drove in silence to the condo, and entered without speaking. Roger brought each of them a glass of red wine, and listened as they poured out what they had witnessed. Tears began to fall down his face. When they stopped and began to stare at the floor he said, "I am so sorry you had to deal with this situation, but it was given to you, and I am certain you did what you were called to do, much more than many lawyers would have done. You should get thank-you notes from the girl's parents, but I doubt that will happen. I would hope something like this horrible incident would awaken parents to the activities of their children. When I grew up my parents were my role models, but that does not seem to be the standard today." He paused. "Have you eaten anything today?"

They looked at each other, "No, I don't think we have." They sat silently as Roger went to the kitchen and brought out some fruit, cheese straws, and more wine. Roger said, "The two of you have the agony of knowing too much about people and coming face to face with evil. There will be better days, but none will be more important than what you have done these past few weeks. There must be some salvation in realizing you did your best." The weight of the tension began to fall from them, and the three of them sipped their wine and cried together.

Finally, Bob rose to go, "It's over. I'm glad it's over. I have an awful feeling I'm dirty because I know too much. I'm going home to wash the filth off my body. Goodnight to both of you. I need a hug." They embraced.

The next morning Bob called Margaret to check on Michael. "Do you need me today?" He had never asked such a question to Margaret, so she was surprised. "No, we are fine. I've let my work schedule get tight, so I'll be busy. You do what you have to do." Bob said, "Margaret, I love you, but I don't want to burden you with the case Georgia and I just finished. Someday I will tell you about it, but it is too fresh right now. I need to go to the Monastery in Conyers for a couple of days. Somehow, I need Father Raymond to help me wash the filth out of my system. It's only about forty minutes from here. I'll call you as soon as I get back."

"Thanks for saying you love me; I need to hear that more often."

"You will from now on. That is a promise."

CHAPTER 84
Joanna and David

In a few days Joanna and David returned from North Carolina. It was apparent that Joanna was pregnant. Roger whispered to Georgia, "I want to listen to Joanna stomach." She said, "No way unless the privilege is offered."

Roger said, "How was your trip, David? Were your parents excited? Tell me everything."

"They were glad to see us, and were excited about the baby. But just like you, Dad said, 'your mother and I want two names on that birth certificate."

"We must get started on that," Joanna said. "We need a marriage license and a Synagogue, so we need to contact the Rabbi."

Georgia has already managed that. He is free to marry you. I called Charlie about using the Inn for the reception, and he said to give him a week's notice. Tomorrow we will take you to get a license. Does that cover it all?"

"Thanks, Dad. Do we have the condo?"

"The condo is yours." Roger said. "You do not have to sign any papers, just promise to be good residents." They both hugged him. David said, "I hope you don't mind; my family is a hugging bunch."

Roger said, "I can live with that. I cannot remember *ever* being hugged by my parents. Do not look so sad, I knew they loved me. Now that hugging is settled, let us go see your new home. I have the keys right here."

The four of them stood looking in the condo waiting for someone to speak. Georgia said, "You will need to get a decorator soon, Joanna. Do you remember Margaret?"

"Yes, I do. Is she going to do the work?"

"Recently her little son, Michael was in the hospital with the whooping cough. That has put her a little behind, but her assistant,

Becky has agreed to meet with you. Here is Becky's number. She will be waiting for you call."

After getting off the phone with Becky, Joanna said, "Dad this place is perfect."

David said, "Mr. Waddell, maybe we can pay you back one day."

"David, I believe this is a gift. My daughter loves you, and that is enough for me and for Georgia. For so many years I did not know Joanna existed, so I can never do enough for her. Since she loves you, the gift includes you; that is, if you are always nice and sweet to her."

"Yes, sir, I understand. She is making me the happiest man alive."

"Well, I doubt that; *I am* the happiest man alive."

Georgia said, "Joanna this is a perfect place for you and David, but let's get something settled, Roger and I want you and David to be free to have your own lives. I may have to hog-tie your dad at times, but you don't have to include us in everything. Just wanted to get that out in the open. I would like to meet with you and Becky, if you don't mind?"

"Can I also meet with you?" Roger asked."

"What do you know about decorating?"

"I can watch and listen?"

"Oh, well, you can watch and listen."

"Thanks to both of you, we can get settled, and David is going to start looking for a teaching job," Joanna said.

"I'm afraid I can't help you there," Georgia said, "but there are a lot of schools around Atlanta, but what about your art?"

"If I can find an academy, I'm almost certain they will have an art department. I like the freedom of a private school."

"Roger, even though you were taught by your parents, maybe you can help him. Don't you have some connections?"

"I met a lot of professors and teachers when I was the janitor at a local church. Maybe I could start there." Joanna and David looked puzzled. "Oops. That is a story for another day."

"Maybe they don't want to wait another day," Joanna said. So he told them the story of his redemption at the Presbyterian Church.

After his explanation Georgia said to Joanna, “Your dad wants to listen to your stomach and see if he can hear a heartbeat.”

“I thought you said I was not to ask.”

“You didn’t ask; I asked.”

The four of them went back to their condo. Joanna sat in a chair and Roger knelt on the floor and put his ear to her stomach. “I am not certain whether it is your heart that I hear or the baby’s, but I hear a beating.”

“Dad, we’ll try in again in a month. It should be obvious by then.”

“Well, I can wait, but I want to hear that part of my genes in your womb, and one day hold the baby the two of you have created – of course, the two of you and God.”

“Roger, you do believe!” Georgia yelled.

“Who said I didn’t.”

Georgia arranged an appointment with the Rabbi, and he agreed to explain the ceremony to the non-Jewish members of the family. A date was set so David’s parents, sisters, and grandparents could make plans. Georgia asked Joanna, “Would you prefer no guests other than family, or can we invite some of our friends?”

“Of course; friends would be great. I do not want to leave out Dad’s clan and my friends, Cassie, Julia, and Molly, but remember we do not have the funds for a very big reception, so we need to keep it simple.”

“I am of the opinion,” Georgia said, “That parents are supposed to pay for the expenses of their child’s wedding, including the reception. Isn’t that right, Roger?

“She is right, and she is the only one around here who knows protocol.”

“Maud’s Inn will be wonderful. I can hardly wait for David to see it.”

“By the way, Georgia and I realize you need a car. Here is the title on our car that you are driving and the insurance card is in the folder.”

David said, “I’m almost speechless, and still don’t know what to say.”

"Do not get speechless. Georgia made me buy a new car so you could have mine. Now it belongs to you. Here are the keys."

"David, just say thanks," Joanna said. "I lost my dad for so many years, so I am not ready to be far from him and my new Mom. Their offers are generous, but they mean well. Right, Dad?"

"Joanna, for you and Georgia I would do anything. Anything! Let us go see how Becky plans to do in your condo."

———

"Oh, David the place is perfect. I can see us living here and the baby will have a room also. Thanks, Dad and thanks, Mom. We are so lucky."

"No, Georgia and I are the lucky ones. To have you near us is the most important thing in our lives. Georgia, I might not need a job after all. They are going to need some help with the baby. I had a lot of experience with Margaret's little boy, Michael. I even changed his diapers."

"What you will need is permission. Joanna, you're going to need a doctor. Call Cassie and see if she would recommend her doctor. By the way, about when is *our* baby due?"

"We are not exactly certain, but perhaps four months at the most."

"We need to get moving!" Georgia said.

———

The Wedding

The weather was perfect for the wedding, as Roger assured them it would be, and Charlie and Sarah put up a few decorations. It was the first Jewish ceremony many of them had attended, so it was a learning experience. Joanna and David had given them an idea of the ceremony, and brought yarmulkes for the men to wear. Of course the women could choose to wear one. The Rabbi used English in the ceremony, but sang one song in Hebrew. Georgia whispered to Roger, "I'm going to start reading about Jewish traditions. After all, we are about to have a Jewish grandchild."

"I can teach you a little, but remember I am half Calvinist and half Jewish, and do not know how to be either one."

"Maybe you don't have to choose which one. You can learn from both."

"You are a good lawyer, Georgia. Thanks for interpreting that for me."

"Joanna is beautiful. Does she look like her mom?"

"Maybe, but soon she will look like you, because you love her." Georgia pressed his hand for he could not have said more beautiful words to her.

Having been told to expect a crowd, Charlie and Sarah prepared a feast. As always the group had a great time together, but they were careful to include the Benson family. They were impressed with the Inn, and Mr. Benson asked Charlie, "I am wondering, who was Maud?" After a short explanation he captured the feeling. Even the old picture on the wall fascinated him, and he made a note to research the artist. He asked to speak to the crowd. "This has been a great day for our family. We are proud of our son, David who has chosen another daughter to be in our family. Joanna is beautiful, graceful, talented, and loves our son. We would have picked her for David out of a catalogue. (Everyone one laughed.) Marsha and I are excited about this first grandchild coming into our family. May we always be friends, and may God pour many blessings upon our families."

Roger spoke, "Thank you, Dave. This is indeed an exciting time. I will always remember the day our daughter landed in Atlanta on the arm of your son. I said to Georgia, look at that! Who is that guy kissing our daughter? (Everyone laughed) Later, I discovered Joanna was provoking me. And when we returned home we learned they brought us a special gift inside Joanna. Thank you for your blessing. And thank everyone who came today. May God shower all of us with love and peace." Everyone applauded. Aside, Georgia whispered to Roger, "Wow! Your Jewish blood came right out of you. Great blessing."

Baby Rachel was born in July. When she was four weeks old, Georgia and Roger's condo was filled with friends and family admiring the newest member of their fellowship. "Rachel is just the first," Joanna said, "I want a big family."

"Whoa, let's slow down," David said, "I've just stared teaching. One baby on teacher's salary is enough for now."

Frederick said, "Give the boy a little time, Joanna. I'm not sure Roger can handle more than one grandchild." Frederick asked, "Roger can you give her up for a minute, and let me hold her?"

"Sure; here. Now hold your hand under her head." The words sounded so funny coming from Roger. Looking into her face Frederick wondered if he would ever be looking into the face of his own granddaughter.

When she was returned to Roger, he carried her around for all his friends to kiss and make predictions. He promised her everything. "Little Rachel, you have given me great joy. Your grandmother and I will cherish you forever."

"Of course we will, but remember she has parents. We are her *grand* parents. We have to get permission to spoil her."

"Georgia, don't burst his bubble," Randy said. "Roger is a miracle himself because we practically raised him. Right, Joan, Bob and Frederick? How much money do you think he owes us?"

"Plenty," Bob said, "but I've forgiven my debt. He needs all his money to keep Georgia happy. Do you ever take that bracelet off, Georgia?"

"Well, I don't sleep in it, if you must know? If I ever get to sleep." And they all laughed.

Bob was very moved when he held Rachel. He had no words, only thoughts. It had been a long time since Julia was so tiny. He remembered holding her in his hands and wondering if he was her father. Only Randy noticed his tears, and was sad to see the past still haunted him.

CHAPTER 85
Ana and Pearl

Randy's mother, Ana was not well. Pearl was beside herself trying to keep her from dying. Finally, she relented for Randy to hire a live-in aide to assist them. "To take care of them," was not an expression he was allowed to use. In the long process of interviewing, the only person Pearl liked was Bertha Morris, a middle-aged lady who could move in with them immediately. Pearl said, "She is a no nonsense person, attractive, and can cook. We hit the jackpot." On her first day, Pearl took Bertha aside and said, "Your job is to keep Ana alive. I can take care of myself. I don't want her to die first. The thought of living alone scares the hell out of me."

Bertha said, "You won't be alone, I will stay with you." (Randy had already arranged for her to stay as long as Pearl was alive.)

"You are not Ana, but thanks for your offer," Pearl said.

Ana died on her birthday. A few weeks prior to her death she talked to Randy about her wishes. "If I should die I want no ceremony or rituals. Cremate me and give my ashes to Pearl, but first tie a purple ribbon around the box. She is the only person I have ever known who likes the color purple. She creates something purple in every painting, or haven't you noticed? I've had a good life and a wonderful family; no one should ask for more. Take care of Pearl, for she is not well. You can have a party when I die. That will make Pearl happy."

Ana was cremated and her ashes were given to Pearl, as she had requested. Two days later, Joan had lunch delivered to the condo for the family, including Bertha. Randy asked Pearl to tell stories about her and Ana's shenanigans, and it pleased her.

She started slowly, but they could tell she was pleased that everyone was focused on her. One of her stories was the most amusing. "Ana and I were at a showing of my art at one of the galleries in midtown. A man, believing Ana was the artist, knelt on the floor in front of everyone, and proposed to her, saying 'my dear, I cannot resist a lady of so much talent. You would be doing me the greatest of honors by agreeing to marry me.' I heard her say, 'you are so kind, but I must refuse your offer. A nice-looking gentleman, like you, might interfere with my work.' I was standing nearby, and the fool passed me without speaking. I was terribly insulted, and Ana never let me forget it." Everyone laughed and applauded. "She and I had some mighty good times. I must tell you about a mystery. I did a portrait of her. It was so like her, but she hated it. She said to me, 'don't you dare hang that painting. I do not want to be looking into a mirror all day.' I must say, even though I was the artist, it was beautiful. But it disappeared, and I never saw it again, and she never mentioned it in all those years. I don't believe she would destroy it, but you must find it."

Telling her stories seemed to relax everyone. Pearl spent the rest of the day showing her art, and encouraging Cassie to continue her painting.

Randy was concerned about Pearl, so he was glad Bertha would remain as her companion. For some reason Pearl did not resist Bertha's staying. She said to Randy, "Bertha is a good person. She doesn't go around quoting scripture or talking about heaven." Of course, she intended for Bertha to hear her.

The wait wasn't long, six weeks later Pearl died. She said to Bertha, "Life is not worth living without Ana. I'm ready to go. If there is a place for an after life, I'm going to be raving mad if Ana is not there waiting for me."

Bertha told Randy, "Pearl willed herself to die. She puttered around for days without eating, and finally went into her bedroom. She gave me explicit orders not to disturb her, and shut the door." Her ashes were placed in the urn with Ana's, and Randy took *them* home. Randy paid Bertha to stay until the condo was sold, and gave her a choice of one of the ten paintings found in the closets and under the beds. They kept the portrait of Ana, which was found between her mattress and box springs. Sure enough, hanging it on the wall would be like having Ana in the house.

CHAPTER 86

Randy, Joan

One morning Randy said to Joan, "I've never imagined there would be so much going on in our lives. It seems that you and I are invited to dabble into everything with our family and friends. Are we considered the pillar of this group, or whatever you call it? Lately I've been getting dizzy and am tired most of the time. Cassie is in and out of the office, but she keeps her appointments. Ms. Bee is threatening to retire. Whatever, she is not over-loaded. She's remembering when the two of us ran the office, as she said 'most efficiently.' Bob called this morning to tell me that he has finally bonded with Michael, and he admitted that his monthly monastery visits have been most helpful. And Roger is happy with his grandchild, but still wishes he had some sort of voluntary work. I don't believe he really wants to volunteer. Maybe Georgia needs to use him as a gofer. Wouldn't that be hilarious?"

"Wow that was a long list, but go back to dizzy and tired. Are you serious or was that just an expression? If 'dizzy and tired' needs to see a doctor, get going. This is not the time to ignore symptoms."

"I meant it to show frustration, but it's true, I haven't had a physical in years. I don't know what happened to all that energy. Well I might as well see about it."

"Good, make the appointment in the morning."

"By the way, Cassie and Robert enrolled Kip in an Atlanta Arts Center program, using money from Rick's foundation. Seems the boy has immense possibilities."

"Oh, that's wonderful, Randy. Just think, if he hadn't shot Bob, he might still be raking leaves for Fred Mills."

"That is an interesting remark. There is something else going on. Kip's mom is dying. Fred Mills called me the other day and wanted to know how he could start the process of adopting Kip. How about that?"

"Is he serious?"

"Yep, very. Mrs. Jones gave her consent. I also believe it's a wonderful thing for Kip and for Fred. He has no children, and he's crazy about Kip. He bought him a new car recently, and he moved Mrs. Jones from the garage apartment into his house and hired caretakers to tend to her full time. While we were talking about the will, Kip said he had never had a proper name, and asked if he could be Fred K. Mills Jr., and still be called Kip. Mr. Mills actually cried. You are right, that shooting changed a lot of lives. I think Kip has an angel named Fate looking out for him. Have I told you that Cassie has one of Kip's paintings in her office? Rick would be proud of him. I can't forget the little girl in the cathedral. That painting could even inspire me to paint."

"I never thought of Fate being an angel. Good Example, Randy."

Kip's mother died after being in Fred's house only a short time. With Kip's approval Fred had her cremated, and gave her urn to Kip.

On Thursday Randy went to his 10:00 appointment with his internist and friend, Dr. Paul Richards. "What's up, Randy?"

"Well, lately I've been tired all the time, and dizzy sometimes. I believe I have too much going on. All our friends seem to be leaning on me right now, but I'd probably be pissed if they didn't. I must have the *let me help you* look, if you know what I mean."

"I know. First, I need to give you a good physical, which will include, among other things, urine and blood samples."

"Are you going to hit my knee with that rubber hatchet?"

"I might. Here, pee in this cup. I want to see that result first, and then I will send the nurse in to get your blood. She'll need about five samples. Wait here."

"Five samples?"

"You can afford it."

After a few minutes Paul came back into his room, "Everything looks good, and we will know about your blood by noon tomorrow. I don't feel a growth anywhere; throat looks good; heart beat is a little irregular; feet and legs are a little swollen. You are a pretty healthy man. Do you have any trouble performing intercourse?

"Since when did you start calling sex a performance? No, I'm not having trouble desiring or having sex, none at all, but I waited so long to be with Joan, I may be over-doing it at times."

"All right. I don't hear that very often from men our age. I want to see you in a week. You and I have known each other a long time. We both should be taking more time off to play or sit in a rocker and read. How is Joan?"

"She is on her fourth book. She amazes me. I told her to keep going as long as I am not one of her characters."

"And Cassie?"

"She's a good lawyer, even balancing twins and work, and the clients love her. She and Robert hired a nanny when the kids came home from the hospital, and she has become a part of their family. How are you and Tracie doing? We used to get together once in a while."

Paul paused for a few seconds as if deciding what to say, or how to say it. "Randy, Tracie had a positive mammogram recently. She's devastated and so am I. She had another one to confirm the first one. A couple of surgeons are looking at the pictures to decide what to do."

"I'm so sorry. Allow me to be the doctor right now. How are you dealing with all that and working too?"

"Not very well. I have a need to hug and kiss her more. She is my life. We haven't told the kids yet. That is going to be painful."

"I am so sorry. Paul, if you need me, I'll be there for you. Tracie and Joan use to be tennis partners. Do you mind if I tell Joan?"

"Tell you what, I'll have Tracie call her. First hand information is always best. I do need you to do something for me. Look at our wills and see if anything needs to be updated. But it's not a good time to tell Tracie that I asked."

"I'll take care of that, Paul.

A week later, Randy returned for his follow-up visit. Paul said, "Your blood work was fine, but you still have swelling in your feet and legs. I'll give you a prescription for that and one for your heart. Put your feet up when you can. In six month call me for another appointment."

Randy said, "About your wills. The only thing we didn't do was name an executor in case both of you died at once, but that is not your concern at this time. You are the executor of Tracy's will, but if she dies you will need to appoint an executor for you. Enough about wills. I have a suggestion. You and Tracy need to get away before the operation. Here is a number for Maud's Inn on the Chattahoochee River. I believe it would be good for both of you."

"Before you ask, Tracie has decided to have both breasts removed and have reconstruction surgery. That seems to be her best chance of survival. The surgery is scheduled for next week. I'm pleased she made that decision. You know, Randy our culture puts far too much emphasis on women's breasts, even though that is where most cancer begins in women. Strange, isn't it. I do think going away for a few days would be good for both of us. I'll call the Inn after you leave."

"Paul, you know my friend Roger Waddell. After his first wife, Roberta died of breast cancer he said to me, 'When Roberta had both of her breasts removed I said to her, 'I love every part of you, even the missing parts.' I believe those words are the loveliest words I have ever heard."

"Wow! They are, and I'm going to remember them."

A week later Paul Richards called. "Randy, it was too late for Tracie. They removed both breasts, but no need for her to go through reconstruction surgery. Just wanted you to know. I'm going to take some time off to spend every minute I can with her. Thanks for telling me about Roger's words to his wife. They mean more to me now that ever, and we enjoyed the Inn."

"Paul, what can I do for you? There must be something, anything."'

"When she gets to feeling better, maybe the four of us can dine out."

"Looking forward to it. Take care of yourself."

"This latest information is *in house* for a while, but I don't mind if you tell Joan.""Got you. Give me a call."

Tracie died in two months. A tremendous crowd filled Dunwoody Methodist Church in Roswell. Randy and Joan were there. He said to Joan, "I can't imagine how Paul is coping. If that happened to you, I would not want to live."

Joan said, “But you would still love me.”

CHAPTER 87

Anniversary of The Chapel

Randy shook his head while reading the invitation. "I can't believe this."

"What is the matter?" Joan asked.

"We are invited to the 10th anniversary of the Chapel on the 20th of April. Ten years! What happened? I would have said five at the most. I can't believe it."

"Let me see that. You're right!" Joan said. "Look at it this way, wasn't it about the greatest ten years ever? But I still can't believe they didn't name it Maud's Chapel."

"Can I call it that in private"

"If you must."

"Back to the anniversary, do you think I should go to the nursery and have them put some large azaleas in pots all around the area?"

"I don't think that would be necessary. The azaleas that the nursery planted years ago should be in bloom."

On the 20th the air still had that cool late April nip, enough to require light coats. What perfect timing! The dogwood trees were in full bloom, both the white and the pink, and sure enough, the pink azaleas were in abundance. The elders, standing at the door greeting the people, seemed to have the enthusiasm of welcoming visitors to the Atlanta Alliance Theater.

Joan and Randy, Bob and Margaret, Frederick and Elizabeth, Roger and Georgia, a part of the founding/funding group of the Chapel, rented a limo for the day. They were excited to be celebrating the one thing they did together that made them proud, something that would be there long after they were *dead and gone*, as Frederick put it.

Getting out of the limo they watched Charlie, Sarah, and their two children on the porch. Land grantor, Charlie rubbed his hands across the board and batten planks he insisted the architect put into the plans. He wanted the chapel to look as if it had been built years ago, and it did. The boards had weathered well. They knew what he was thinking: *yes, these boards feel as good as the day the chapel was built.* Inside, Sarah would study the ceiling, remembering the placement of every beam.

Roger took a deep breath when he entered, and saw the early pencil drawing by the architect still hanging on the entrance wall to remind the people of their vision. Glancing around, he thought, *the wood that Randy, Joan, and I bought is holding up. It was the best lumber that could be found. Other than red cushion on the chairs, everything looks the same. The Steinway piano looks new, but it has been there about three years. It was best Piano I could find in Atlanta. I believe Jonathan LaSalle, a well-known Atlanta musician, comes over every Sunday to play it, and quite often, a soloist comes with him. The congregation believes they are offering their time, but they aren't. The oak communion table, pulpit, and font have aged well.*

There is still no nursery. During the service, Joan noticed two little boys playing with toys on the window side aisle. Nobody but her seemed to notice.

The basic beliefs of the Chapel have always been those of the Presbyterian Church, which gives the people a foundation, and keeps the church from being just another place to meet and greet.

The first part of the Celebration Service was a liturgy that celebrated the miracle of cooperation for the many people who participated in the building and furnishing of the Chapel. After that, an elder spoke, "This Chapel is a place where residents of this area can come for spiritual nourishment and friendship, and it has become the main location for those who want to be a part of worship. There has never been any drive to bring in new people, for we are well known in the area. Some of us come and welcome obligations, and others of us come because we need to find peace. Both of those reasons, and many more, are acceptable."

Looking around at a full house, Roger knew very few people in the crowd. He whispered to Georgia, "This is great. If I were a Christian, I might think about standing up and shouting hallelujah!"

"You would never do that."

"Did you know hallelujah is a fine Jewish expression? I wish I had the guts to say it. Anyway, there is bound to be a good offering today."

"I'm about to pinch you."

"Well every congregation needs money, right?" She pinched him.

The pastor of the Chapel, The Reverend Juanita Rowlings led the service and a professor from Columbia Theological Seminary preached.

Before the service ended Sarah was asked to say a few words and give the benediction. She said, "What I remember most was the enthusiasm of the founders of this Chapel. No one pushed to be in the leadership position. There was unbelievable cooperation. Any plan or idea was laid out before the people, so a consensus could be reached. The meetings were calm and there was an air of dedication akin to holiness. Those meeting gave the chapel the reputation it has: all are welcomed and no one is criticized for their differences of belief. Go in peace, be grateful for life, and carry in your heart that which you saw and learned today."

After the service the people enjoyed a feast prepared by a caterer. As the old saying goes, "a good time was had by all."

During the trip back to Atlanta they were in high spirits being together and having witnessed the success of the Chapel. "Well that was a good day," Roger said. "But does it seem odd that a person, who had never been there before, was chosen to preach for such a special day? Not once did he refer to Maud's Chapel. Besides, who reads a book called Habakkuk? I hate it when preachers make me feel dumb."

"Reading the book of Habakkuk can be your task tonight. Maybe then you will know what he was talking about," Georgia answered.

"How about you?"

"I don't analyze sermons. I thought he did a fairly good job."

"Fairly good means almost good."

"Whatever. Let's change the subject."

Joan said, "You know what? That chapel is definitely the best creative effort this group has ever been a part of. I don't think it mattered to me if the sermon or food was bad or good. I just wanted to be a part of a near-miracle."

Frederick said, "I believe you are right. It's nice to do something and not take credit for it, yet I was pleased when I went into the bathroom to see Elizabeth's and my toilets and sinks. They are as good as new. And I loved that changing table." Everyone laughed.

Roger said, "Did you enjoy listening to my Steinway?" And they said.

"To tell the truth," Bob said, "those pads they put on my chairs fit my tail bone better, didn't yours?" All of them agreed. "I never dreamed of them being red, but it works. It is kind of fun, just between us, to talk about our gifts to the Chapel. It's similar to venting among friends, isn't it?" In chorus, they all said hallelujah!

"Is this a good time to talk about our kids and grandkids, and get that out of the way?" Joan said.

"Sure, why not?" Margaret said, "I'll begin. We are moving into a new house and Bob and I are getting married. I think it's about our wills, property, etc. It may not sound so romantic, but I can handle that."

Bob stepped in quickly, "It was both Julia and Roy who talked to us about it. I guess it's good to have a lawyer and doctor in the family so we can do things the right way. Their kids call Margaret Grandmother and Michael calls me Dad." Margaret's eyes filled with tears. Bob put his arm around her and said, "It's going to happen this summer, in Savannah. That's a special place for us." Joan looked at Randy. It was unusual for Bob to show affection. "Julia has used her inheritance well from her uncle and from John Randolph. Sorry to mention that, Joan. She loves Cardiology, but she was too late to save her high school friend. Most Sundays Michael and I attend the church his father pastored. I think he likes the attention from the older members who remember his dad and his baptism. That's about it from our side."

"Thanks Bob. I know you must be proud of Julia and Michael," Randy said. "Here's to Bob and Margaret." *Here! Here!* They all said.

"You two of you are lucky," Elizabeth said. "I am not certain we will ever have grandchildren, but Molly and Freddie are doing what they enjoy, and seem to be happy. We believe Molly is in love, but her career means everything to her. By this time they would probably have to adopt a child, but that would be all right with us."

Roger said, "Elizabeth, I can sympathize with you and Frederick. It took a long time for me to find Joanna. Your time will come, just wait. Back to you Bob, let me give you some words of wisdom. Julia and Joanna have something in common. Joanna has come to depend on the wisdom of Georgia more than mine, but I love watching them together. So Bob, get used to it. When it comes down to making decisions Julia will go to Margaret, not you. Why is that good? You and I get all the kisses, not the problems."

Bob, Frederick, and Randy laughed, "We raised you well, Roger," Randy said.

"Hear, hear," Bob said. "We forgive all your debts."

Frederick said, "Damn, I was counting on your money to pay for a bracelet for Elizabeth. Roger, you started it. Georgia, I believe the highlight of my career are the two days you and I spent at the Naval Academy."

"Yes," Georgia said. "I have always wondered what would have happened if we had not been there. We did a good thing, Frederick. Did you ever tell Elizabeth we roomed together?"

"Sure did. Don't use any imagination on that; we had work to do."

"We've been friends so long, we almost know what each one of us is thinking. Am I right?" Randy asked. Georgia said, "That's kind of spooky."

Randy said, "It's impossible for me to define our relationship. I'll just say life has been good to all of us."

"Has?" Frederick asked. "Are you planning on leaving us?"

"No! Those words were meant to show appreciation, I guess. I love all of you, and I know you love me."

"How true. I can't imagine life without any of you." Bob said.

CHAPTER 88
Time Flies

Randy said to Joan, "Time seems to be our enemy. We like to be in charge of the time we have, but it moves too fast and astounds me. The first six years we are the cream of the crop and the smartest child on earth to our parents. The next six years we are brats, and our parents wonder what they did wrong. The next six years our parents pray every time we take the car out, or attend parties without supervision. They hope we would pass college entrance exams and get out of the house. Finally, they pack our suitcases, check their bank account to see if they have enough money, and send us off to school. Then they are so proud when we finally finish college and learn how to live our own lives, but we are still their children. That's life. We all want to get somewhere, but are never quite certain when we arrive. Suddenly we are thirty with children, and forty is around the corner, and fifty is not far away. There is some truth that we wish our lives away, and when we are old we wake up and want the years back. Time is irreverent; it mocks us."

Joan said, "Well, t*ime passes fast* is an old adage, but it is the truth. The loss of time has been expressed in many ways as you just mentioned. So now we have finally hit the age of wisdom, but let's don't count on that to be true."

"There is no way to remember all that has happened to our friends: weddings, births, deaths, travels and so on," Randy said, "And how about the number of grandchildren all of us have. We couldn't get everyone is the same room any more."

Randy, Bob, Frederick, Roger, and Joan seemed to get even closer as they aged; more like family than friends. They spent time together telling stories and remembering, than making new plan, a sure omen of aging.

CHAPTER 89

They knew Randy was very ill. He had not been well for a while. Recently he said to Joan, "Drive me out to Maud's Inn. I want to see the place you and I love." They made the trip, but he went to bed when they returned home, and didn't rise again. Joan sat beside his bed for days holding his hand hoping for a word, a nod, a sigh, or a sign that he recognized her, like squeezing her hand that would mean *I love you*, but it never happened.

"Where did all those years go?" She asked him. "Did we do everything we planned? What happens without you? How will I survive? It's the first day of September, and the leaves have begun to color. You used to love this time of the year. Cassie and Robert and their children are here. Bob and Roger have been in and out the last few days. You are the brother neither of him had. They talked to you. Did you hear their words?" He never opened his eyes, but they were certain he smiled every now and then.

The heart attack hit Randy in early May, which put him in the hospital for several days. He grieved over the death of Frederick, and knew Roger was not doing well. "How did we all get so old?" He said over and over. When Frederick died, he was devastated. Leonard's death was so long ago, but he had begun to think about it. One day he said to Joan, "I believe a countdown is happening."

Cassie and Robert came in and out, and the twins, Elizabeth and Phillip, dropped in occasionally. Robert lost both of his parents, Grace and Bob, several years ago. Ms. Bee was eighty when she retired, and didn't live long afterward. She didn't want a retirement party, but got one anyway. Randy told her she had been retired for the last ten years; he just let her come to work. She said, "I am not too old to spank you." He loved her repartee, but would never have told her.

Kip dropped by earlier. He had grown into a handsome fellow and had managed his adopted father's estate very well. He married Jill Rosser, a professor at a local college, and they chose not to have children. He had concerns a child might inherit the traits of his father. Kip was known as a successful artist and teacher, and had several promising students. One student was Cassie and Robert's daughter, Elizabeth. Elizabeth and Phillip stayed with Kip and Jill while Cassie and Robert went to Ireland. He started teaching them how to paint. Elizabeth took it seriously while Phillip painted for fun, but both had talent. Elizabeth had a genuine knack for mixing colors. She loved painting abstracts, even though her father tried to get her to paint something he could appreciate. Cassie continued to paint in her spare time. She said it helped her remember her brother, Rick. His cathedral painting was her inspiration.

Randy died on the 18th of September 2001. It was not the way Joan wanted it to be. They didn't get to say goodbye. She always imagined his last words to be: *It's been a wonderful life, Joan; I love you. Let's be thankful for the years we had together.* Perhaps that is the way love stories end in books and movies, but it did not happen. She longed to hear one last "I love you." She stayed beside him, waiting for him to open his eyes one more time. As she waited, she studied the room and its furnishings. She remembered where they bought every picture, the furniture, the antique rug, lamps, and his slipper chair, and how Randy entered everything in a notebook he kept in his desk. On the bed was a quilt purchased in the North Georgia Mountains years ago, and she thought about the two bedside tables that were crafted by an old craftsman they met at an art show. She wondered how she could manage sleeping in such memories after he was gone.

Roger came into the room. He had inherited his mother's ailment, rheumatoid arthritis. He was unable to drive that day, so he rode with Bob. At Randy's last breath Roger put his head on the sheet and cried. When Bob helped him out of the room, he turned and said, "I love you, my brother. Many thanks for all the good years we had together."

Cassie looked at Phillip and said, "It's hard to believe there is no blood between you and your granddaddy. You look just like him the first time I met him. He was so handsome and so in love with mom that he was lit up all the time. He has always been proud of you and Elizabeth."

"I'm proud for you to say that, Mom," Phillip said. "He used to say to me, 'when you love someone they begin to look like you, like you and me.' " They left his bedside so Joan could have some time alone with him. She held Randy's hand as it was slowly cooling. "Was it so long ago that I looked in the mirror and saw your face behind me? Why, in a flash, did I know you and I would spend the rest of our lives together? I can see your eyes looking into my face when you lifted my chin to kiss my lips. Even now I can feel the touch of your hands roaming over my body in Maud's Inn, searching to enjoy what you had missed." She paused to wipe her tears. "Here, let me put your hand on my breast before they take you away. Your lips, I touch, are still a delight even in death. How I long for all those moments we shared. Holding your hand makes me cold, but I can still feel the warmth of your body close to mine. Goodbye, my love. There has to be a heaven; a sweet place to meet again. Wait for me. Until then: Merrily we long along, roll along, oe'r the deep blue sea. You and I had a great roll."

———

The Celebration for Randy's life was held in the lobby of Maud's Inn two days later. As Joan scanned the room she thought of their first night in the Inn, and chills ran through her body. *This was always the place we came to get away from the city to rediscover nature, and to have uninterrupted time together. Perhaps our room in the Inn was really our chapel.*

Rev. Sarah Marshall Fowler spoke at the gathering for Randy. She had been retired for years, but was glad they asked her to be a part of the service. She began,

Let Us Talk of Memory

"In the transition from life to death
a little part of the person remains with us.
And we, the survivor's, lose a part of ourselves
in their transition.
That is the reason we grieve.

So it is reassuring to believe that
when we die
we will not be forgotten.
Our image and deeds are like
the butterfly that is transformed
into something it was not.
It teases us and darts away in an instant.
I wonder if memory has ever been the subject
of someone's thesis.
If not, there should be such a document
to capture the mystery of it."

Walking outside, after the gathering, Roger paused to catch the wonder of the land, and said to Georgia, "My dear, look at the trees; they are already beginning to color. That seems to be a little early for September. And the sky is so blue, with not a cloud anywhere. But I wish it would be raining with tears for our friend." He leaned on his cane, put his free arm around Georgia and said, "I will always love you, Georgia be you alive or be you dead. Though you may dart away one day your image is pasted in my heart."

The End

Epilogue

The main characters in this book, Jane, Randy, Leonard, Frederick, Bob, and Roger, shared an unusual relationship akin to marriage. Not one of them decided to belong, nor asked to be invited into their fellowship. They were in no ways alike or related, and their backgrounds were not similar. Religion, wealth, talent, heritage played no role in their connection. I am envious of such unbelievable bonding, and questioned myself as I was writing. How can this be? Is it too perfect? Is it a longing for what I did not have? Yet, I believed in these people, and somewhere in the world there are such relationships. Why and how does that happen?

Relationships are built on love, trust, respect, and forgiveness.

If we love each other, we will stand by each other in good times and bad.

If we trust each other, we can have confidence secrets will not be shared.

If we respect each other, we will never dishonor each other.

If we forgive each other, we will have hope for our own failures.

People who have such relationships often develop an attachment akin to dependency. It is natural for that to happen. Relationships that endure for a lifetime are similar to a constant encounter, not the dreaded kind of encounter, but the predictable. Almost, but not really, they become a part of each other. Six friends found a place of refuge and an opportunity to make a difference in each other's lives and the lives of people in the community at Maud's Inn, on the Chattahoochee River in the state of Georgia, U. S. A.

There are so few people who make a significant difference in our lives, and even fewer who are life-long friends. Not many of us are a part of a group of six best friends who have the freedom to call upon each other in any circumstance and for any reason. Good friends, like the six friends in this story, do not have to declare their relationships or prove their love. Their being available is all that matters.

Special friendships also bring outsiders into our lives, enriching us even more. I haven't counted all the people in this story who were in and out of the circle of six friends, but there are more than a few, in goodwill and in tragedy. People outside our close friendships can teach us, bring us new discovery, or dump sorrow upon us, but their traipsing through our lives keeps us from being closeted. Invited and uninvited guests are part of our fate whether we want them to be or not.

———

Acknowledgement

I am indebted to my two Editors without whom I would have been at a loss to correct myself. Jean Westmacott corrected my manuscript after the first draft and inspired me to do better. In the final draft Patsy Vedder held me accountable to even the slightest mistakes. Hopefully they will forgive me for the mistakes I made after their editing.

About the Author

Jan Blissit lives in Stockbridge, Georgia with her Cavalier King Charles Spaniel, Georgia Belle. She is a retired Minister and has a blended family of seven children and many grandchildren. Besides being a writer, she is a collector of the works of artists who painted in the1920s to present times.

Her first book was "Under My Robe, Holy and Irreverent Stories."

www.ingramcontent.com/pod-product-compliance
Lightning Source LLC
Chambersburg PA
CBHW020602310726
48979CB00008B/1318/J

* 9 7 8 1 9 4 5 1 9 0 5 9 9 *